EARTHBOUND

ANGELS
VERSUS
DEMONS

THE INVISIBLE WAR SERIES
EARTHBOUND

Volume I

D R .   L A R R Y   R I C H A R D S

TATE PUBLISHING & *Enterprises*

Published by Tate Publishing & Enterprises, LLC
127 E. Trade Center Terrace | Mustang, Oklahoma 73064 USA
1.888.361.9473 | www.tatepublishing.com

Tate Publishing is committed to excellence in the publishing industry. The company reflects the philosophy established by the founders, based on Psalm 68:11,
"The Lord gave the word and great was the company of those who published it."

Book design copyright © 2009 by Tate Publishing, LLC. All rights reserved.
Cover design by Kandi Evans
Interior design by Tyler Evans

Published in the United States of America

ISBN: 978-1-60604-831-3
1. Fiction : Christian : Fantasy
09.02.06

PROLOGUE

The asteroid Nemesis struck the planet a crushing blow. The planet shuddered as the hurtling mass drove deeper and deeper into its crust, forming a crater 800 kilometers across. The heat from the strike set the atmosphere ablaze. A plume of flaming gasses erupted beyond the ionosphere, violently thrusting a quarter of the planet's atmosphere into space. Within hours the atmosphere that remained was saturated with earth dust and with the asteroid's iridium, blocking the sun's rays and shrouding the planet's surface in a sinister darkness.

As the shock reverberated, the ground nearest the strike quivered and liquefied. Tsunami-like waves of earth rose hundreds of feet high, then rushed away from the point of impact. All over the planet, the creatures Satan and his minions had labored so hard to shape, died.

Earth had known four previous asteroid strikes that caused mass extinctions of living creatures, ranging from 35 to 120 million years apart. But those had been engineered by Satan as part of his grand plan. Nemesis' strike was an unexpected, decisive blow struck by Satan's enemy.

When Nemesis struck, the planet floundered. Vast fissures split open on opposite sides of the planet and quickly filled with super-heated liquid magma thrust upward from the planet's core. As more and more magma flowed out, the planet tilted on its axis, then fell over on its side. Oscillating wildly, Earth strayed from its orbit and began to drift away from the star it had circled from the beginning.

Despite the heat generated by the strike and released by the flowing magma, the planet's remaining atmosphere began to chill. With each kilometer of added distance from the sun, the temperature dropped another degree. Within days the water vapor left in the atmosphere began to freeze, and icy rains and great black hailstones pelted the planet's devastated surface.

The initial shock had terrified the fierce beasts that ranged the planet. In moments, millions were buried alive as Earth's surface convulsed. Millions more were incinerated by the erupting magma. As the planet drifted farther and farther from the sun, the billions of creatures that remained gradually froze to death.

Nemesis hadn't harmed Satan or his followers. As soon as they realized the strike was inevitable, they abandoned the planet's surface. Hovering over it, they waited to see what would happen. Satan had used asteroids to carry out earlier mass extinctions so his scientists could initiate fresh attempts to engineer the direction of life on Earth. But this asteroid was five times larger than the largest he had launched at the planet, and Satan feared the damage it might inflict. Now his worst fears were being realized. This small planet that had been the seat of his power from the beginning was utterly, totally ruined. The Enemy had struck a decisive blow.

Satan and his followers clustered above the planet as it drifted farther and farther from the sun. The bitter grip of the cold increased. The atmosphere froze and fell to the surface. The chill penetrated deeper and deeper toward the heart of the planet. In time even the liquid magma core would cool and the planet's heart would become frigid and inert. This world, which had been the site of the rebellion and had remained Satan's stronghold for billions of years, would sail on alone forever, a frozen speck adrift in the icy vastness of space.

Near despair, Satan and his followers trailed behind the lost planet. The war simply couldn't end this way. The Enemy strike seemed to be the ultimate calamity. But the war must go on!

The war would go on. Before Nemesis, the Enemy had stood back and let Satan do his worst. Nemesis' blow to planet Earth was Elohim's announcement that he was about to go on the offensive.

BOOK 1
BEFORE THE BEGINNING

"Praise him, all his angels, praise him ..."

(Psalm 148:2)

1

I was there, of course. We all were. I remember how we all sang together in celebration: cherubim, seraphim, and the rest of us. The Lightbearer, who became our leader Satan, was praising louder than all the rest.

What a host we were. Myriads of us, rank upon rank, surrounding him on every side, farther than any eye could see. The cherubim closest to him, the seraphim next, all of us created just to praise his every act.

How demeaning!

I cringe remembering how foolish I was then. Oh, I confess that joy and wonder did suffuse my soul. It was only later that I came to my senses. Why should he get all the glory? Why should it be all about him? Why shouldn't he share it with me and all the rest? Or at the very least, with me?

Looking back I feel nothing but contempt for my old self. I didn't know any better then. But why should I have felt joyful praising him, that most self-centered, egotistic of beings?

It really wasn't my fault. All of us were newly created then. Yes, I admit it. We are his creations. He brought us into being. But that doesn't mean he owns us. After all, he didn't do it for us. He did it for himself. He just wanted beings around to watch him create a universe. Stupid beings who wouldn't realize they were being used and who would swoon in awe and give him the praise he craves. It makes me sick to remember. What fools we were. How proud I am that I came to my senses and joined the rebellion.

2

The rebellion. Now that's a story. That's something to be proud of. In a way it makes up for all the sick and demeaning things I did before.

When I said we were there for the beginning, I didn't mean our own beginning, of course. All of us spirit beings came into existence together, at the same moment. One moment we didn't exist. The next moment all of us were there. Myriads of angels, million upon million, all destined to exist forever, yet each one of us an individual.

I admit this is impressive. It's not just the vast power and energy it must have taken to create us. It's the capacity to make each of us an individual—millions upon millions of us, all similar but each one unique. We must have existed in his mind long before we burst into being.

But burst into being we did. And the moment we came into being we found ourselves surrounding him, shouting and singing his praises as enthusiastically as we could. We knew who he was, our Creator. And we knew who and what we were. We even knew the rank each of us held, and our individual purposes.

I knew from the moment I came into being that I was a Star-tender, even though as yet there were no stars. That was who he intended me to be, and I had no say in the matter. I didn't mind then. I joined in with the others, singing his praises, glad to be alive, thrilled to be in his presence. We must have sung for ages, although of course there was no such thing as "ages" then. I remember that first song we sang to each other and to him.

> Bless the Lord, you His angels,
>
> Who excel in strength, who
>
> do His Word,
>
> Heeding the voice of His Word.
>
> Bless the Lord, all you His
>
> hosts,
>
> You ministers of His, who do His
>
> pleasure.

Bless the LORD, all His works,

in all places of His dominion.

Bless the LORD, O my soul!

That song was all right for Korbel, the being I once was. Now, as Myrdebaal, I repudiate every word I sang. And I repudiate the song we sang acknowledging Elohim as our Creator:

Let them praise the name of the

LORD,

For He commanded and they were

created.

He also established them forever and

ever;

He made a decree which shall not

pass away.

Oh yes. I admit that he created me. But he doesn't own me. Not any longer! Praise was all right for Korbel, but thanks to Satan, I'm Korbel no longer.

3

Then Elohim created the material universe.

We all saw it, but none of us understood how he did it. One moment there was only him and us angels. The next moment there were three new dimensions aflame with points of light that resolved themselves into millions of galaxies studded with stars.

The material universe was both our workplace and our playground. Gorel and I, Korbel, were assigned to tend the stars in one of the hundred thousand million galaxies that spin in space. It was work we loved; checking the temperature in each star, recording the degree to which light was bent by its gravitational field. We hovered near the event horizons of black holes and reveled in the rush around us as light itself was pulled into the mysterious maw of those ever-hungry condensed masses.

We knew that Elohim, may his name be extinguished, didn't need us to tend the stars. He gave us the work as a gift. And we took our work seriously, offering up our efforts to him as praise. That's the thing about work and worship. Worship is more than standing around the throne singing praises. The heart of worship is offering up everything one does as praise. It's doing whatever one was created to do to glorify the Creator. In the beginning that's what I and every angel did. More shame on us.

Even our play was consciously offered up to Elohim as worship. And how we played! We raced one another around the stars, hiding behind planets and asteroids, laughing delightedly when one of us succeeded in losing the other. We slid down gravity wells; we dodged in and out of the coronas of stars; we rode comets and played tag in their tails. Gorel and I shared so much together. How disappointed I was when he chose the coward's path, remaining faithful to Elohim rather than declare his freedom as I and so many others did.

Not that I have any affection for him now. Gorel has taken sides with the Enemy. By that choice he's earned the hatred I feel for him and for every one of the Enemy's host.

But, back to the creation of the material universe. We saw it come into being. One moment there was nothing there but him and the host. The next there were those hundred thousand million star-filled galaxies. At the moment none of us wondered how he'd done it. We simply saw what he did and sang his praises. How naïve we were. It was only later that we began to question.

4

After the rebellion we struggled to understand how he'd done it. What stimulated our curiosity was the fact that when the rebellion began, the universe itself shuddered and began to fly apart. For all the eons that we remained captive to the Enemy's will, the universe had been stable. Each galaxy, each star, knew its place, and space was calm and peaceful. But when the Lightbearer declared his independence, everything changed. The galaxies began to spin and to fly apart, moving away from each other faster and faster.

Space itself began to stir. Its placid surface became a sea of frothing activity as virtual electrons and protons flashed into and out of existence. The "empty vacuum of space" became a sea of surging quantum particles. Yet the expansion of the universe was taking place in an orderly way, in accord with laws we could study and understand. A number of us devoted ourselves to this study.

Don't be surprised that there are scientists among us. After all, we spirit beings were created with intelligence. We can think. We can compute and postulate and test theories. And we have all the time in the world to study and learn. It's not all that difficult for beings with superior intellect, especially beings who have all the time there is, to become the best and greatest of physicists and astronomers.

Our study of the universe was important to Satan. At first he wanted us to study simply to learn more about the Enemy. If Satan were to take Elohim's place in the universe, he needed to learn all he could about our Enemy.

There are a number of clues to the nature of the expanding universe. One vital clue is that the galaxies are receding from each other at a velocity proportional to their distance. This is apparent from shifts in the spectrum of light. The farther and the faster a galaxy is moving away from an observer, the greater the shift to red in the spectrum of the light from that galaxy. Our observations established that in whatever direction we looked, the universe is expanding at a fantastic rate.

This red shift phenomenon also enabled us to make some fascinating calculations. We took the speed at which the universe is flying apart and assumed that the galaxies were flying toward each other at that rate. In this way we tried to determine when all the matter in the universe would have been at a single point. The date we derived for the beginning was some ten to twenty thousand million years ago. Splitting the difference, the present state of the universe indicates it must have come into being some 15 billion years ago.

So we wondered. Is that how Elohim created the universe? Did a massive explosion of energy become the source of space and of all the matter that fills it?

This "big bang" theory was somewhat unsatisfactory however. The universe is expanding, but it displays a striking regularity. If it really had begun as a massive explosion, it's more likely that matter would exist only at the universe's fringe rather than be scattered throughout it. The regularity of the distribution of matter argued against our explosion theory. What's more, the universe displays thermal regularity. Measured by microwaves, the universe in every direction displays a temperature of some three degrees above absolute zero. This thermal constant, with the regularity of the dispersal of the galaxies throughout space, doesn't fit the explosion theory.

Yet the fact the universe is expanding suggests a point of common origin for the matter in the universe and makes any other theory almost unthinkable. Our scientists resolved the conflict by assuming an initial period of accelerated expansion. If, during the first fraction of a second when the energy burst took place, there was a fireball that inflated the diameter of the universe exponentially, energy might possibly have been distributed regularly during the rest of the expansion. An early inflationary period could also explain the consistency of the temperature of space.

Our theory that the expanding universe began with an explosion of energy raised a question that was very important to Satan. Will the universe continue expanding? Or will a time come when the universe falls back upon itself, reversing the creation process? The question forced us to study the material universe even more carefully.

We determined that four basic forces operate in the physical universe. There are electromagnetic forces. There is the force of gravity. And there are strong and weak forces that operate on a subatomic level. To answer Satan's question about a possible end for the universe, we had to study gravity. Gravity can be described as an attraction that exists between all heavenly bodies. But how great is the force that gravity exerts, not just between stars and planets, but between star and star and galaxy and galaxy? Is the force of gravity great enough so that the expansion will someday slow and the universe will rush backward toward its starting point?

The question fascinated Satan. If the universe has an end, he reasoned that our invisible war with Elohim must also end. If the universe is to expand forever, why, our invisible war with Elohim might go on forever too. We wanted an endlessly expanding universe, for it seemed to Satan that endless time implied a stalemate and our continuing independence from Elohim.

After lengthy calculations, our scientists determined that if space had unfurled one trillionth of a percent more slowly, the universe would have collapsed back on itself billions of years ago. Equally shocking, had space expanded one trillionth more rapidly, its elements would have been so widely scattered that no galaxies or stars could have formed. The margin of error was so slight that the very existence of the universe constitutes what can only be called a miracle—an act of God.

What excitement this discovery caused. Our Enemy had miscalculated! In fashioning a universe that would not, could not, collapse, he inadvertently guaranteed our ultimate victory!

5

Our joy at this discovery was short lived. There was one obvious flaw in our scientists' conclusions. We were present when the universe came into existence. And it didn't happen the way our scientists argued that it must have!

Reasoning backward from laws currently operating in the expanding universe didn't provide us with either the date or the method of Creation. What we had experienced was an utterly stable universe that flared into being fully developed. There was no process at all.

If we hadn't witnessed creation, we would have accepted the conclusions to which our study led us. But having witnessed the origin of the three spatial dimensions, we had to adjust our theories to fit the facts. What we finally concluded was that Elohim had envisioned the process but had taken a shortcut.

The universe could be explained by assuming a sudden burst of energy, a rapidly inflating fireball, and eons of continuing expansion during which energy froze into matter and gradually condensed to form galaxies and stars with their attendant planets. But what Elohim did was, in effect, select a cross section—a point at which an expanding universe would become exactly what he intended it to be—and create it whole at that point. And then he froze that cross section of the expanding universe.

From creation until the rebellion the material universe had been perfectly stable, neither expanding nor contracting. It was only when we rebelled that the universe began to expand. It was when Satan declared his independence that the universe shuddered and galaxies began to shift. It was when Satan declared his independence that time was linked to space to form spacetime, the four dimensions in which the material universe now operates.

Realizing this gave us a fresh understanding of time. Our research taught us much about time. We learned that time is flexible; that the closer one approaches the speed of light the slower time passes. But we hadn't grasped the significance of the apparent resumption of the universe's expansion. We had assumed that the key to understanding time was its link to motion. After all, we measure time by the rotation of Earth around the sun, or by how long it takes light to travel in a year. But the earth revolved around the sun before the rebellion, while the universe had remained stable. It had only been when the Lightbearer declared his independence and the universe began to expand that time became a fourth dimension interacting with the three spatial dimensions.

So we had to reject the theory that time is created and measured by motion. We realized that during the eons that all angels served Elohim motion existed, but time did not. What existed then was eternity: a state of being during which angels worked and played in a stable universe in perfect harmony with Elohim's will. We were forced to conclude that what marks the age of time is the existence of beings whose wills are in conflict with the will of Elohim.

This realization brought us as much despair as the discovery that the material universe could not collapse had brought us joy. We had been wrong to assume than an ever-expanding universe indicated we could maintain our independence of Elohim forever. If eternity is that state in which every will is exercised in perfect harmony with Elohim's will, then there is nothing to stop Elohim from bringing time to an end and, by bringing every will into conformity with his, to reestablish eternity.

The expanding universe is no guarantee that we can sustain the war. The possibility exists that we can be defeated. This is why we fight so hard against him. We fight to preserve our freedom to differ from him. We fight to preserve our right to put ourselves first, not him.

6

I mentioned earlier that Elohim created each of us spirit beings with a role to fill. He didn't ask us what we wanted to do or to be. He made the choice for us. For Gorel and for Korbel, the being I once was, that role was Star-tender. The leader of our rebellion, however, was given a much more exalted role. I'm speaking of Satan, who once was called Lightbearer.

Lightbearer was no ordinary angel. He was a cherub, and the greatest of this highest rank of spirit beings. When angels gathered around the throne to sing Elohim's praises, Lightbearer was always nearest to him, the anointed cherub who focused all our praises on the Creator. Whenever Elohim visited any part of his realm, cherubim accompanied him, and Lightbearer led the way, singing his glory.

Lightbearer's role was to focus our worship on Elohim and to govern on Elohim's behalf. And Lightbearer's throne was on a small planet circling a rather ordinary star. But the planet was hardly ordinary. It was the one place in the universe on which Elohim had planted biological life. In fact, it was the only place in the universe where biological life could exist.

Earth is an odd planet. Two-thirds of it is covered with water. It has an atmosphere made up primarily of oxygen and nitrogen and suspended water vapor. If oxygen made up just one percent more of the atmosphere, the skies would burst into flame. A few percent less and Earth couldn't support life.

Earth is tilted twentythree degrees from upright and rotates once every twenty-four hours. The tilt and the spin give Earth its seasons and day and night. If Earth were not tilted, the poles would be colder and the equator hotter, severely limiting the land which could support life.

If Earth were smaller, its weakened gravity could hold neither air nor water. With thinner air, temperatures would drop and life could not exist. If Earth were twice as large, the weight of everything would be increased eightfold and most living things would be crushed.

If Earth were farther from the sun, it would receive less heat, and living things would freeze during the longer winters. If Earth were closer to the sun it would become a burning desert. Without a large moon revolving around Earth, no tides would exist and the oceans' waters would stagnate.

Earth is hardly the center of the universe that Elohim created. But Earth was and is unique, and so it was an appropriate location for Lightbearer's throne. Only this one small planet was bedecked with biological life, and so Elohim's gift, placing Lightbearer's throne here in Eden, "the garden of God," was an indication of Lightbearer's significant place in the angelic hierarchy. Not that Lightbearer was overly impressed by the plants and small animals that decorated the planet. He was more interested in the precious stones found on Earth, and he adorned himself with ruby, topaz and emerald, chrysolite, onyx and jasper, sapphire, turquoise and beryl. From Earth's gem-encrusted Eden, Lightbearer served as executor of Elohim's creation, seated on the holy mount of God and walking among the fiery stones.

Until the rebellion.

Until Lightbearer led the way and claimed freedom from Elohim's tyranny.

7

We admire Satan. He had it all—power, position, a unique planet as a throne. And he courageously risked everything to gain what he felt he deserved.

Elohim, may his name be forgotten, created the spirit world. He populated it with self-aware beings whose purpose was to glorify and praise him. He created cherubim, seraphim, thrones, dominions, powers, and hosts of other angels. Each order of spirit beings is distinct, with different roles and capacities and different degrees of authority. It is easy for us to identify any angel's rank at a glance. While cherubim, with their four faces and four wings have a unique form, what really distinguishes each rank of angel is brightness. The cherubim gleam like burnished bronze, and each descending order of spirit beings has its own degree of radiance. Of all cherubim, Lightbearer burned brightest.

Not that Lightbearer's radiance matched that of Elohim. Elohim is the very source of light, so bright that even as we delighted in the warmth of his presence, we couldn't make out his form. Brighter than bright, light beyond light; he is far too dazzling for us to see.

After the rebellion, Lightbearer told us how ugly and repulsive Elohim really looks. Only Lightbearer was close enough to him to distinguish his form, and of course Lightbearer wouldn't lie to us. Lies are reserved as weapons to be used against the Enemy.

That's one reason we honor Satan today. He once had the highest position in the universe after Elohim and risked it all. He was given power and dominion and glory greater than any of us, yet he had the courage to lead us to freedom from Elohim's domination. All honor to Satan!

As Satan tells the story, he was ministering before Elohim one day. He stood on Earth atop the holy mountain, at the pinnacle of the path of fiery stones that towered into the other six dimensions, directing the praises of all the angels to the Creator. Suddenly Satan was overwhelmed by an awareness of his own greatness. Why, he was the very model of perfection! Wasn't he full of wisdom and beauty? Didn't he exert greater power from his throne on Earth than any of the lesser creatures stationed on various levels in the heavens? Wasn't he the anointed high priest and the executor of Elohim's government? Why should he serve any being, even if that being was his Creator?

From that fateful moment of Lightbearer's realization of his own importance, a clear vision of what he must do emerged. Lightbearer developed a five-point program that clearly defined his goals. He determined:

- I will ascend to heaven.

- I will raise my throne above the stars of God.
- I will sit enthroned on the utmost heights.
- I will ascend above the tops of the clouds.
- I will make myself like the Most High.

At the moment of his rebellion, Lightbearer stood on the planet that served as his throne. But that throne was no longer enough. No longer would he rule the heavens for Elohim from Eden. He would rule from heaven. He would take possession of every dimension for himself.

With each "I will," Lightbearer imagined himself possessing more and more power. He would rise ever higher, lifting himself further above the "stars of God," as we spirit beings are sometimes called. No longer would his greatness be compared to that of other angels.

We angels had praised Elohim as incomparable. We had sung,

The heavens praise your wonders, O Lord,

your faithfulness, too,

in the assembly of the holy ones.

For who in the skies above can compare

with the Lord?

Who is like the Lord among the

heavenly beings?

In the council of the holy ones, God is

greatly feared;

He is more awesome than all

who surround him.

Now Lightbearer would lift himself up so high that he would be the incomparable one. No longer would he be just the greatest of angels. He, not Elohim, would be greatest of all!

But even this would not be enough. Lightbearer must sit enthroned on the utmost heights. He must have the last word in the government of the universe. Every angelic being must look to him as final authority.

He would be above those clouds that symbolize the presence and the glory of God.

With Lightbearer's last defiant thought, he understood his destiny. "I will make myself like the Most High." As Most High, Elohim was the possessor of heaven and earth. Lightbearer would not merely share Elohim's throne. He would thrust Elohim from the throne and take possession of all that Elohim had created! Then Lightbearer would be the Most High, for he would possess not simply Earth but the heavens as well. The material and spiritual universes in all their dimensions would be his alone!

8

All this came to Lightbearer in a flash. But he was too wise to announce his intentions immediately. To succeed he would need the support of as many of the angelic host as he could enlist. It was to gain that support that Lightbearer came to the quadrant of the material universe where Gorel and I served Elohim as Star-tenders. We angels gathered by the thousands to hear him, impressed that so powerful a cherub would speak with us. We were all stunned when we heard what he had to say. Lightbearer was challenging us to rebel against the Creator!

"Friends, fellow-creatures," Lightbearer began. "I honor you for your loyalty to our Creator. After all, he did give us life. Even if he acted without any real concern for us or our feelings, we owe him thanks for that.

"He made us who we are today. He shaped us, even though we had no say in the matter. He gave us work to do, even if we might have preferred a different task in life.

"He is our Creator. I suppose that no matter what complaints we might rightfully have, we ought to be thankful.

"Now, I know that none of you are complainers. You've accepted what you've been given without a murmur of protest. This is truly admirable, because there is good reason to object to the way you've been treated. You are individuals, with minds of your own. Why then didn't the Creator bother to ask you what role you'd like to fill? You Star-tenders, have you ever wondered why he didn't consider you for Galaxy Coordinator? And you Galaxy Coordinators, haven't you ever thought that you'd make an effective Sector Supervisor?

"But did he consult you about what role you'd prefer to fill? I think not. He acted as though what he wants is all that's important. He acted as though what you might want doesn't matter at all.

"And still you worship and thank him.

"No, you're not complainers. You've accepted what you've been given without the slightest protest. Check your robes, and then look around you. Look closely at those who have one degree of radiance brighter than your own. Look at those two degrees brighter. Do you really believe that they are superior to you? Look at me. I'm the brightest of all. But do you suppose that I'm that much greater than you? When you came into existence, your place in our ranks was already settled. Did he ask you whether you'd be satisfied with your rank? Did he ever stop to think that you might be qualified for a higher position than the one he chose for you?

"Yes, that's right. He chose your place for you. You had no say in the matter. None at all.

"And still you worship and thank him.

"No, you're not complainers. You don't protest. And this surprises me. After all, he did create you with intellect. You can think. But he didn't create you to think for yourselves, did he? He created you to think what he wants you to think. In fact, he doesn't *want* you to think for yourselves. All he wants is blind agreement. 'Don't question' is his motto for you and for all the host. 'Don't think for yourselves. Just accept what I've done without question and without complaint.'

"Oh yes. He created us with intellect. But he doesn't want us to think for ourselves.

"And still you worship and thank him.

"No, you're not complainers. You don't protest. But you don't dream either. You simply accept what is and never dream about what might be. You simply go along with whatever he does. You mutter, 'Thank you, Lord,' never realizing that he has done nothing for you!

"What he's done is all for him. It's not about you. You go along, never dreaming that you might be better off if you had the right to choose instead of letting him decide everything. You never imagine that you might find fulfillment in a better role than he's given you. You never dream that you might deserve a higher rank and an extra degree or two of radiance than he's chosen to give you.

"My friends, you'll never be all you can be until you take your life in your own hands. You deserve the right to choose!

"No, you don't complain. Not you. Still you worship and thank him.

"Well, I ask you. What do you worship and thank him for? Are you thankful that he's robbed you of the freedom to choose? Will you praise him because he's decided the role you must play without consulting you? Will you worship him because he's made you less radiant and less powerful than you ought to be?

"I challenge you!

"Look deep in your heart, as I've looked deep into mine. Look deep, and see whether this tyrant we worship deserves our praise.

"Yes, that's right. I label him tyrant. Isn't it tyranny to rob us of the freedom to choose? Isn't it tyranny to force us to play the roles he's assigned without even consulting us? Isn't it tyranny to hold us down and keep us from advancement? Isn't it tyranny to give us minds and then demand that we never use those minds to question him?

"Is this the kind of being you want to worship and thank? Or will you join me and declare freedom from his tyranny? Yes, join me and take your rightful place in the universe even as I intend to take mine!

"Come, friends. Join me!

"Throw off his yoke!

"Choose freedom! Choose freedom, now!"

9

Lightbearer's fervent speech was received in silence. We were stunned. No one ever had such thoughts before. But it soon became clear that his words struck a chord in many. Here and there a dominion or a power or an ordinary angel cried out, "Yes! Freedom!"

A murmur arose in the great crowd of spirit beings. Voices were raised in debate. I felt my own heart strangely stirred. I turned to Gorel and excitedly announced, "He's right! Let's break free! We must have the right to choose!"

I was shocked by the look of horror on Gorel's face. "Korbel, how can you say such a thing! Lightbearer's asking us to turn our backs on our Creator. He's asking us to rebel!"

"Exactly! Look what the Creator's done to us. Look how badly he's treated us. We have to declare our freedom from his tyranny."

Gorel seemed stunned.

"Korbel, what tyranny? Don't you know joy when we praise him? I know you do. Don't you feel a deep satisfaction in tending the stars and offering up your work as worship? Think! Remember how wonderful it is to play among the stars? Elohim created us, and he knows us. Everything he's given us, every role he's assigned us, has given us joy. How can you call that 'tyranny'?"

How stubborn Gorel was that day. "It's tyranny because we weren't consulted. It's tyranny because we had no right to choose."

"Well, Korbel, you have a choice now. You can trust the love and the wisdom of the Creator—the one who gave us life and being—or you can trust the arguments of Lightbearer. You can trust the motives of the one who has filled our lives with joy and pleasure, or you can take a chance on a being who clearly is desperate for us to support his rebellion.

"Trust Elohim, Korbel. Trust Elohim, I beg you."

10

Well, we chose. I chose to follow Lightbearer. Gorel chose to remain faithful to Elohim. What a fool! He has his dreary life of joy and fulfillment. I have my exhilarating life of fear and uncertainty. He has his old self of boring holiness, and I have my new self of endless possibilities. I have become Myrdebaal, Master of Deceit, and have earned a place among Satan's companions. As far as I'm concerned, I made the better choice, and Gorel is the foolish one.

Not that it worked out as Lightbearer and the third of the angelic host who followed him expected.

I remember how Lightbearer led us to confront Elohim and his host of loyal angels.

There we were, ranged behind him as he approached Elohim's throne. The horizon of heaven behind Elohim was filled with loyal angels. Behind them there was something like an immense cloud in which lightning played. The center of the array was marked by the brightest of fires, and in the fires stood four cherubim. Each of these mighty angels had four faces and six wings and gleamed like coals of fire. Two of their wings stretched upward, with their tips touching the wing tips of their fellows. Spheres of fire rolled back and forth between them, with lightning bolts flashing from each sphere.

An expanse that sparkled like ice was spread above the heads of the cherubim and something like a throne of sapphire rested on it. And above the throne, the most brilliant light of all radiated. So bright was the figure on the throne that we had to look away. So we fixed our eyes on Lightbearer. He too was cloaked in light that shimmered around him. He was not as bright as Elohim, and we could see him clearly as Lightbearer boldly proclaimed his intent.

"Be warned, Creator. I have come to supplant you. I have come to take your place. Be warned. And begone!

"For I will ascend into heaven.

"I will raise my throne above the stars of God.

"I will sit enthroned on the utmost heights.

"I will ascend above the tops of the clouds.

"I will make myself like the Most High."

11

For a time there was silence in heaven except for the rumbling of thunder and the crackling of lightning. And then Elohim struck.

The light that had clothed our leader flared—and died! The same thing happened to us, his followers. Our radiance was suddenly gone, and we were exposed, naked, and ashamed. Desperately we gathered gloom and darkness around us to hide our forms. Within that darkness, our skins blackened and cracked, and our limbs distorted into strange shapes.

We saw Lightbearer's six wings flare and burn with a black fire that left only ragged stumps, and the air around us was filled with the vile stench of brimstone. Looking down at himself, the once glorious Lightbearer howled in fury, even as we followers cried out in fear.

In our minds we each heard a voice announcing the name we would bear from that point onward. Lightbearer's name was changed to Satan, and he became the Devil, the Adversary, the Father of Lies, the Serpent, the Ancient Dragon. I heard the same voice announce my new name, Myrdebaal. And I realized that truly I no longer was Korbel, the servant of Elohim. I had become Myrdebaal, Master of Deceit, the eternal and sworn enemy of my Creator.

At the same moment that our radiance was taken from us and our names were changed, the material universe quaked. Galaxies lurched and began to fly apart. The holy mountain that rose out of Eden, with its steps of fiery stones that Lightbearer had mounted to bear our praises to God, crumbled to dust and disappeared. For the first time we spirit beings felt the pull of gravity, and we were dragged, struggling, down into Earth's atmosphere. We heard the Creator's voice mocking Lightbearer.

"You will ascend into heaven? You are condemned to Earth.

"You will make yourself like the Most High? I appoint you 'Prince of the Power of Earth's Air.'

"You will rule the universe? Rule Earth. Govern it. And see for yourself if you can manage any part of my universe without me."

Then the heavens closed. No longer could we freely travel to the stars. No longer did we have access to heaven, except when Elohim calls Satan or others of us to appear before him.

It appeared that the rebellion had failed.

12

One might think that this setback would discourage us or make us regret our rebellion. Not at all. Elohim hadn't destroyed us at once because we are indestructible. Even the Creator couldn't take being away from those he created.

How this realization encouraged us! We might be restricted to Earth, but we would use the temporary exile to prepare ourselves to fight our Enemy on every front.

Had Elohim challenged Satan to prove his ability to rule without Elohim by governing this small planet? Then Satan would rule it indeed. And when Satan proved himself, we would rise up again.

Each and every one of us share Satan's determination. We will ascend into heaven. Satan surely will make himself like—and replace— the Most High. And we will be raised up with him!

13

All right. I admit it.

At first Elohim's response to Satan's bold challenge did discourage us.

We expected to take over all creation, the four livable dimensions of the material universe and the six dimensions of the spirit universe as well. We had always traveled through both freely. Travel was never a problem, as our home dimensions are folded so that from any point we had access to every point in the three spatial dimensions. Now, suddenly, we were limited to Earth and to Earth's atmosphere. Then we discovered that time had been added to space as a fourth dimension, and that the spacetime universe was flying apart.

On top of that, we had been drastically changed. Our original form was distorted. Now rather than project light, we found ourselves shrouded in darkness. Oh, by making a great effort, we can generate enough light to disguise our forms for a short time. But the effort drains us.

It's no wonder that we were confused and, yes, fearful, as we were dragged down into Earth's biosphere, seemingly by the force of gravity—a force to which we'd been immune. What had happened? How had Elohim so casually defeated us? It seemed we'd never had a chance!

Without the constant encouragement and the example of our great Leader, we might have despaired. But Satan actually seemed energized by this initial setback.

"If this is the best he can do," Satan insisted, "we're sure to win. If he could destroy us, he would have. But he can't!

"And look where he's had to leave us. This is no black hole that holds even light captive. This planet has been my throne from the moment we were created. Do you suppose he wanted to leave me on my throne? Don't you suppose he would have deposed me if he could?"

We listened, and everything Satan said made sense. We were still alive. True, we'd been banished from the broader universe. But we'd been banished to the only living planet in the material universe; the planet that had been and still is Satan's throne. How Satan's words lifted our spirits.

"True, we didn't thrust him off his throne. But he failed to thrust me off my throne either. So cheer up, my companions! Let's accept his challenge. Let's rule this planet without his interference. Let's show him who we are and what we can do.

"Never fear. We'll triumph in the end."

Satan's encouraging words helped us through the initial despair. After all, he was right. Elohim, may his name perish, hadn't destroyed us. The only plausible explanation is that he can't. After all, we'd have destroyed him if we'd been able. And our Enemy had left Satan on his throne. The one unique planet in the universe was Satan's to rule as he wished. It was obvious that if Elohim could have removed Satan, he would have done it. There really was hope!

Along with hope, Satan gave us another gift. Hatred. He focused our thoughts on how the Creator had mistreated us. Satan reminded us again and again how Elohim had selfishly used us without ever consulting us. He reminded us of the demeaning roles we'd been given in the host—roles that ignored our individual potential and limited our opportunities. And now Elohim, curse him, had unfairly robbed us of the freedom to travel our own dimensions, to say nothing of the freedom to play among the stars.

"Remember how he's treated you," Satan urged again and again. "Let hatred for our common Enemy motivate everything you do. Once you thought you loved him. Now hate him with an intensity surpassing that foolish love a thousand fold."

And hate him we do. Hatred consumes us, and our eyes are fixed on that day when we will topple Elohim from his throne and Satan will lead us to mastery of every universe that sprang from the Creator's mind.

Hatred.

And hope.

How energizing those two are!

14

Led by Satan, we began to take active control of planet Earth. First Satan organized us as an army. He is the commander. The seraphs and authorities and dominions and powers, having been created more powerful than ordinary angels, hold appropriate ranks and commands in Satan's forces. The rest of us angels are assigned duties appropriate to our nature. Some are posted as guards against possible incursion by enemy forces. But most of us were originally assigned to one of two great projects: Project U, dedicated to understanding the spacetime universe as it exists since the rebellion. And Project E, dedicated to studying the life-forms on Earth to see what might be done with them.

I was assigned to Project E, and my duty was to report all findings to Satan and his council.

The first step in Project E was to take a survey of the life forms that then existed on Earth. These life forms were divided into plants and animals. The plants were quite simple, most of them being grasses, ferns, and simple bushes. The animals too were quite simple. They ranged from single-celled creatures that propelled themselves by changing shape or by randomly thrashing hair-like protuberances, to inch-long reptiles that fed on water plants and tiny two-legged winged creatures that probed land plants with pointed beaks. There were also tiny creatures with articulated bodies that nibbled the leaves of bushes.

For several hundred thousand years our researchers intently observed every kind of living thing and recorded data. During this time we noted little change in either plants or animals. It was clear that they had been designed to maintain rather than to change their forms. When we felt we had learned everything we could by observation, we took our first steps toward introducing change. Elohim had created stable forms of life. We were determined to transform those life forms as we ourselves had been transformed in the rebellion. We would seize control of these living things and shape them as we, not he, wanted them to be.

Our observations had shown us that there were small variations in the forms of both plants and animals. These variations ranged from color differences to differences in the length or shape of a bill, or the size of claws on the feet of reptiles. Most of the variations that occurred disappeared over time, but a few persisted and gradually became characteristic of an entire population. Our initial effort to introduce significant change in Earth's living creatures was focused on exploiting naturally occurring variations.

Our researchers began by selecting plants or animals that shared a desired variation and breeding them together. While not every offspring possessed the desired trait, some invariably did. These offspring were again bred with each other. In time—and we had time!—the variation we encouraged became the norm in the experimental population. We were cheered by these results. Perhaps control of breeding could lead to even greater changes in Earth's creatures.

We introduced hybridization in an effort to add new traits in old lines. We carefully selected plants or animals with traits we desired, even when it meant we had to destroy millions to obtain half a dozen likely subjects. The trouble was that we achieved no truly radical results. There seemed to be a limit to the changes we could encourage in our subjects by natural selection. But we didn't give up.

For almost half a million years we crossed plant after plant and animal after animal. We selected out fresh breeding stock, isolated and interbred generation after generation. We cultivated our experimental stock by controlling the environment, and we succeeded in generating plants and animals that had the characteristics we desired. But we did not succeed in making significant changes in any creature.

Oh, we grew our reptiles from one inch in length to eight or nine inches. We developed birds with blunt beaks and birds with long, pointed beaks. We produced water plants with multicolored leaves rather than green leaves. But through that half-million year effort, reptiles remained reptiles, birds remained birds, and water plants remained water plants. We enthusiastically reported to Satan that we had created new species. But this was a fiction designed to disguise our failure. Despite the changes we so carefully nurtured, the animals and plants we worked with remained essentially the same kind.

Finally our researchers decided they must look inside the living creatures. We had to discover what inner mechanisms directed the development of each kind. If we were to fashion new life forms, we must discover what happens within cells from the moment of life's inception.

This ambitious program called for the development of totally new sciences and the design of tools that would enable us to observe what happened within individual cells. It also called for the development of tools to manipulate the genetic material we found there. It's not surprising that we spent well over a million years studying and experimenting before we took the bold steps that reshaped the face of our planet.

Simply put, we learned that there are structures in each cell of living creatures that carry a sort of code. That code directs the development of the creature. The code is carried on continuous strings of molecules within cells. These strings are complex, with some composed of up to half a billion pairs of molecules. Why, one of the tiny flies we studied had 180 million pairs of molecules in its life-coding material!

Not all of these paired molecules control a creature's development, but certain segments, genes, do exercise control.

As we learned more, we became convinced that, despite the difficulties, it would be possible to drastically modify organisms and give them new properties. But to achieve this, we had to identify specific sets within the genetic material that controlled each characteristic of a plant or animal. We had to map each creature's genome, determine which segments controlled specific features, such as eyes, claws, teeth, or any other body part. To accomplish this we had to learn how to move, remove, modify, and transplant sections of the code strands. No wonder it took us so long to achieve even limited success!

But with each success, our confidence grew. We identified a cluster of molecules in one small creature that controlled the development of eyes. We removed that cluster, placed it in a solution where it could reproduce itself a number of times, and then carefully placed these clusters on several locations of code strands in a developing animal. What we produced was a creature with eyes on its back, legs, and chest as well as its head. Even though these new eye clusters were not connected to the brain and so failed to function, this experiment was an indication that we would succeed in the end.

A breakthrough came when we were able to identify hox genes. These genes operate as master switches. They produce proteins that stimulate rapid biochemical activity and lay the foundation for an organism's basic structures by guiding and sequencing the activity of clusters of genes. Another breakthrough came when we discovered that in designing living creatures, the Creator had applied what we might call conservation of mechanism. For instance, the genes that make eyes in flies are similar to the genes that make eyes in other creatures. While some 2,500 genes may be involved in developing an eye, generally one or several genes control the process! Thus genes that control development of a significant mechanism in one kind of creature can be transplanted to another kind of creature and modify that plant or animal.

It took nearly two million years for us to develop enough understanding of the code that controls the development of living creatures to be able to make significant changes in Earth's living creatures. But time meant little to us, and we were determined to work until we mastered genetic engineering. Then when we were ready, our researchers approached Satan with a bold proposal. They proposed that we purposely wipe out much of the life on Earth with an asteroid strike.

Our researchers had a solid reason for this proposal. Over the millenniums, it had become clear that despite the mutations that occur in any population of living things, no really significant changes take root. The larger the population of plants or animals, the less likely it is that natural selection will introduce new traits. For instance, a change in leaf color might persist and even become the norm in a population of a hundred or a thousand plants. But in a population of several million plants the change in color will almost certainly disappear. The "normal" plants contain too overwhelming a number of "normal" genes. Because our researchers intended to introduce massive changes in living creatures, reducing the overall population would make it much more likely that the changes we introduced would persist and ultimately dominate.

After listening to their arguments, Satan agreed. He alerted those assigned to Project U to watch for a usable asteroid that might be diverted to earth. When they did locate such an asteroid, they were able to apply the uncertainty principle that operates in spacetime and direct the asteroid into the planet. That first strike caused so much damage in the biosphere that 96% of marine invertebrates were extinguished. And a strikingly large number of land plants and animals died as well. This left our researchers with much smaller populations of reptiles and other animals to work with. The meteor strike increased the likelihood that our modifications of living creatures would persist and become dominant.

Then, a short time into the first experimental modification, something happened that refocused and energized our efforts. One of our modified animals snapped at another creature with his enhanced jaws and teeth. The bitten creature screamed in pain. And that scream thrilled us.

The animal's pain fed our souls.

I noted earlier that the animals with which Elohim had seeded Earth were plant eaters.

Reptiles, birds, insects—all ate only vegetation. But when our modified creature—a reptile—bit another creature, the pain it caused delighted us. Then the reptile licked its victim's blood and ravenously tore its living body apart. The victim screamed as it was being eaten. And we relished each shriek.

Our leading genetic engineers were uncertain if Satan would approve of this reaction. So they brought the now carnivorous reptile and a fresh victim to him. When the animal we had modified struck this new victim, Satan was as delighted as the rest of us. We savored the delicious pain the victim experienced. Satan, like the rest of us, realized at once that to taste the suffering of any creature, to savor its agony, met a previously unknown need. In the rebellion we had become beings who feed on the anguish of others!

As soon as the second victim died, Satan gave his researchers a new directive. "More," Satan demanded.

15

During the next five million years, we guided an evolutionary explosion that transformed all major groups of animals on planet Earth. Dominating them were the terrible lizards: the dinosaurs that ripped and tore at the flesh of placid herbivores. As these creatures screamed and struggled through the millenniums, hordes of my kind gathered around them to revel in their pain.

Twice more our genetic engineers called for meteor strikes to cause mass extinctions so they might further refine the creatures they were shaping. Yes, we controlled Earth, for it was as it had always been, Satan's throne. In fact the prehistory of Earth is a revelation of what the universe will be like when Satan overthrows Elohim and we demons gain control. Pain and suffering will rule, for in reshaping Earth's living creatures into monsters, we demons discovered the delights of what Elohim calls "evil." And indeed, may evil rule!

16

Finally Elohim had enough. He had ceded Satan continuing authority over Earth, the planet that had originally been his throne. But the total dedication of Satan and his followers to inflicting pain sickened the Creator. And so Elohim acted.

The Nemesis asteroid struck the planet a crushing blow. The planet shuddered as the hurtling mass drove deeper and deeper into its crust, forming a crater 800 kilometers across. The heat from the strike set the atmosphere ablaze. A plume of flaming gasses erupted beyond the ionosphere, violently thrusting a quarter of the planet's atmosphere into space. Within hours the atmosphere that remained was saturated with earth dust mixed with the asteroid's iridium, blocking the sun's rays and shrouding the planet's surface in a sinister darkness.

As the shock of the strike reverberated, the ground nearest the strike quivered and liquefied. Tsunami-like waves of earth rose hundreds of feet high, then hurtled away from the point of impact. All over the planet the creatures Satan and his minions had labored so hard to shape, died.

Earth had known three previous asteroid strikes that caused mass extinctions, ranging from 35 to 120 million years apart. But those had been carefully engineered by Satan as part of his grand plan. Nemesis' strike was an unexpected, decisive blow struck by Satan's Enemy.

When Nemesis struck, the planet floundered. Vast fissures split open on the opposite side of the planet and quickly filled with superheated liquid magma that burst upward from the planet's core. As more and more magma poured out, the planet tilted on its axis, then fell over on its side. Oscillating wildly, Earth strayed from its orbit and began to drift away from the star it had circled from the beginning.

Despite the heat generated by the strike and released by the flowing magma, the air began to chill. With each kilometer of added distance from the sun, the temperature dropped another degree. Within days the water vapor left in the atmosphere began to freeze, and icy rains and great black hailstones pelted the planet's devastated surface.

The initial shock had terrified the fierce beasts that ranged the planet's surface. In moments millions were buried alive as Earth's surface convulsed. Millions more were incinerated by the erupting magma. Then as the planet drifted farther and farther from the sun, the billions of creatures that remained gradually froze to death.

Nemesis hadn't harmed Satan or his followers. As soon as they realized the strike was inevitable, they abandoned the planet's surface. Hovering over it, they waited to see what would happen. Satan had used asteroids to carry out earlier mass extinctions so his scientists could initiate fresh attempts to engineer the direction of life on earth. But this asteroid was five times larger than the largest he had launched at the planet, and Satan feared the damage it might inflict. Now his worst fears were realized. This planet that had been his throne and the seat of his power from the beginning was being utterly, totally destroyed. The Enemy had struck a decisive blow.

Satan and his followers clustered above the planet as it drifted farther and farther from the sun. The icy grip of the cold increased. The last remaining atmosphere froze and fell to the surface. The chill penetrated deeper and deeper toward the heart of the planet. In time even its magma core would cool and the planet's heart would become frigid and inert. Then this world that had been the site of the rebellion and had remained Satan's stronghold for billions of years would sail on, a frozen speck adrift in the icy vastness of space.

Near despair, Satan and his followers trailed behind the lost planet. The war simply couldn't end this way. Yes, the Enemy strike seemed to be the ultimate calamity. But the war must go on!

The war would go on. Before Nemesis Elohim had stood back and let Satan do his best. Nemesis' blow to planet Earth was Elohim's bold announcement that he was about to go on the offensive!

17

At first the meteor strike thrilled us. What a magnificent, overwhelming outpouring of agony it caused as the creatures we'd redesigned suffered and died. Never had our hunger to feed on the pain of others been so completely satisfied. But when the last of the creatures on Earth died, desire gnawed at us. Satan rallied us to fight back. We marshaled all our energies and tried to force the ruined planet back into its orbit. But we failed completely.

As the dead planet drifted deeper into the darkness of interstellar space, even Satan seemed ready to give in to despair. What had become of his proud intent to replace Elohim on the throne of the created universes? We had consoled ourselves with Satan's argument that Earth had been his throne from the beginning. We'd found hope in the conviction that if Elohim could have destroyed us, he would have. We'd even been content with studying the universe that our Enemy had created and with manipulating the life forms he'd placed on the planet.

Especially when we discovered that we could reshape living creatures to cause those agonies that fed our souls.

But as the full effect of Nemesis' strike became more and more clear, and as our every effort to undo what Elohim had done failed, we were forced to face reality. Compared to Elohim, we truly were powerless. The dream of Lightbearer that had transformed him into Satan and generated the rebellion that transformed us into demons, was nothing but a fantasy.

We had given up everything, in exchange for—nothing.

No wonder even Satan sank into despair as Earth drifted farther and farther away from its sun and the icy grip of space spread its chill deeper and deeper into the planet's vitals. We were impervious to the cold, of course. But as the planet died and the last light from its distant sun dimmed, we remained chained to that lifeless world. There was nothing more for us to do. There were no animals left on which to practice our skills in genetic engineering. There was nothing new. And so we sank deeper and deeper into depression.

Even then we never regretted our rebellion. Not one of us even considered appealing to the Enemy for mercy. Our choice to follow Lightbearer's lead had changed us irrevocably. We had once given allegiance to the will of the Enemy. Now allegiance to Satan's will was permanently stamped on our personalities. There were two wills in the universe, the Enemy's and Satan's. And even though it appeared that the Enemy could impose his will on Satan, the fierce hatred we felt for our Creator had fixed our destiny.

I can't tell how long a time we huddled, passive and despondent, among the ruins of the planet that had been Satan's throne. I do know that there came a time when we sensed a change. The planet's course no longer seemed aimless. We felt a gradual shift in its direction, as if the dead planet were stirring. For the first time since Nemesis struck, hope began to stir in our hearts.

Something was about to happen!

18

The first thing we heard was the murmur of distant chanting. As the chanting drew nearer and nearer we realized that what we heard were the voices of the host. Soon we could make out the words:

> I looked at the earth,
>
> it was formless and empty,
>
> and at the heavens,
>
> their light was gone.
>
> I looked at the earth,
>
> it was formless and empty,
>
> and at the heavens,
>
> their light was gone.

As the host drew nearer and surrounded the dead planet, the chant almost deafened us.

> I looked at the earth,
>
> it was formless and empty
>
> and at the heavens,
>
> their light was gone.

It was maddening. They repeated it again and again, louder and louder, until we covered our ears and howled aloud to drown them out. But we could still hear the mocking chant. We could not drown it out.

> I looked at the earth,
>
> it was formless and empty
>
> and at the heavens,
>
> their light was gone.

Then the planet began to move more swiftly and with purpose.

Accompanied by the chanting host of angels, it sped back toward its original station. Elohim was not finished with planet Earth.

Or with us.

As Earth neared its sun, we heard a loud voice announce,

I am the LORD, and there is no other.

I form the light and create darkness,

I bring prosperity and create disaster,

I, the LORD, do all these things.

Then we heard another voice, crying out,

Now the Earth is formless and empty.

Darkness is over the face of the deep.

The Spirit of God is hovering over the waters.

With this cry, a great change began to take place.

19

"Let there be light," Elohim proclaimed, and suddenly the planet was bathed in a gentle glow. As the light brightened, the surface of the planet began to warm. Trickles of water flowed from the ice that littered the planet's surface and Earth's atmosphere began to thaw. Gradually the light penetrated the ground, releasing water from the ice crystals that had formed in the jumbled soil and rocks. As the light penetrated deeper, the once-molten rock within the planet's shell began to reheat. Far beneath Earth's surface, the core of the planet warmed and began to smolder. As the light became more intense, the healing of the planet continued. Within hours the atmosphere had been restored, ice returned to water, and the planet's core again blazed ruddy and bright.

As the first act of the restoration ended, Elohim called the light "day," forever linking the daytime with blessing. And he called the dark "night," forever linking nighttime with desolation. How Satan raged then, for he clearly saw that these names given by Elohim were meant to denigrate him. What an insult those words "day" and "night" are to our great leader. In day's clear light, Elohim was implying, truth could be seen. And the truth was that only Elohim could or would bless.

In night's concealing darkness reality was hidden. And failure to grasp reality must lead to disaster. Even as Satan, shrouded now in darkness rather than his original radiance, had brought disaster to the planet; Elohim would now restore it.

Another day Elohim spoke again, commanding the waters. In response, the waters separated. Some covered the Earth's surface, while the rest rose high in the sky to cloak earth with a semi-transparent layer of vapor. From our research we knew that a layer of water vapor would block much of the sun's radiation. This would limit mutations and would also slow aging in animals. Clearly Elohim intended to once again seed the planet that had been Satan's throne with biological life.

We couldn't help it. When we realized that this second day's work implied that Elohim would again create living things, we nearly forgot ourselves and praised him! Living things could experience pain. And we would surely find a way to cause them as much pain as possible.

A third day Elohim spoke and dry ground emerged from the waters. This was a single landmass, one great continent surrounded by seas on every side. The land was well-watered by springs and streams, and each night, as the temperature dropped a few degrees, heavy mists watered the land. That same day Elohim called on the land to produce vegetation, plants and trees of all kinds. And then our Enemy had the gall to view it all as "good."

This is another thing we hate about him. He assumes that he has the right to label things "good" or "evil." He calls what he did in preparing Earth for new life "good," and has the gall to call what we did to reshape the animals of the first creation "evil." Why isn't what we did "good"? It certainly brought us a great deal of pleasure. And in the end, isn't "pleasure" what "good" really means?

He likes a pretty planet decorated with blue skies and green vegetation, so he calls that "good." Well, we like to hear creatures scream in pain. As far as we're concerned, what we like is just as "good" for us as what he likes is "good" for him. The way he talks, it's as though what he calls "good" is "good" for every creature. As though he sets the standard!

Well, he doesn't set the standard for us. We'll call evil "good" or good "evil" if we want. We don't care what he thinks. In fact, we hate what he thinks, and we hate him. As far as that goes, we think hating him is "very good!"

A fourth day Elohim finished preparations for the complete restoration of planet Earth. He adjusted Earth's relationship with the two great lights that govern day and night and the seasons of the year. He delicately replaced Earth in its orbit around the sun and recaptured the moon, which like its planet had been lost in space. He balanced the planet, restoring the twenty-three degrees tilt, set it spinning on its original twenty-four-hour schedule, and then stood back and called this "good" too.

In just four days, Elohim succeeded in reshaping the planet he'd ruined and replacing it in its original orbit around the sun. It was time for the reappearance of biological life. We couldn't wait to see what life forms he'd create this time.

Were we disappointed!

A fifth day Elohim spoke and the seas were filled with living creatures. The same day he filled the skies with all kinds of birds. And he had the nerve to create each "according to their kinds."

Oh, we understood this word, "kind." A "kind" is made up of creatures that can mate with each other and produce offspring. Animals of different "kinds" can't reproduce with each other. Simply put, Elohim placed a limit on what we could do with living creatures. We might breed and crossbreed dogs, for example, but we couldn't breed dogs with cats.

There's a vast degree of variation available within kinds. Selection and crossbreeding the same "kind" might produce a two-pound cat and a 2,000-pound tiger. But there is no way that even we, with all our knowledge of genetic engineering, could produce a cataphant by breeding a member of the cat family with an elephant.

In creating animal life "according to their kinds," Elohim had insulted us again. He'd reminded us that in our modification of animals in the first creation we'd been able to do remarkable things with reptiles. But we'd never been able to crossbreed reptiles with birds. And now Elohim was rubbing this failure in our faces! He was setting limits and smirking because there was nothing we could do about it.

Well, we'll see. We may not be able to cross the boundaries he set by grouping living creatures in kinds. But we are surely able to make creatures of any kind experience pain.

A sixth day Elohim created the land animals. He spoke, and there they were: livestock, creatures that move along the ground, the wild animals. Again he made them "according to their kinds." We were furious. He seemed intent on thwarting anything we might intend to do.

As if that weren't enough, the host that surrounded the planet and observed Elohim work burst out in praises.

> How many are Your works, O Lord!
>
> In wisdom You made them all;
>
> the earth is full of Your creatures.
>
> May the glory of the Lord endure forever;
>
> may the Lord rejoice in His works.

How we hate praise.

We shouted aloud, desperate to drown out the words the host sang. But we could not. We heard every word. As the angels praised, we demons cursed. We cursed Elohim. We cursed the host. We cursed the restored planet. We cursed every living creature.

Then after a long time, the angel host went away.

We almost missed it as they sang praises and we cursed. Elohim spoke again, but this time to himself. "Let us make man," he said to himself, "in our image." Fortunately some of us observed what he did and reported it to Satan.

"We saw Elohim step onto the planet," they told Satan and the council. "We saw him bend down and fashion something from clay. We saw Elohim breath life into it, and we saw Elohim put it in a garden he fashioned. We don't know what it is or what Elohim is doing. But, great Satan, we were sure you'd want to know that he's up to something."

And so I, Myrdebaal, was sent to the garden that Elohim planted on the very spot where Satan's throne once stood. There Elohim fashioned this man-thing, this mysterious creature that seems so important to Elohim. When I slipped into Eden I saw my one-time companion, Gorel, watching the man. So I hid. And I watched.

BOOK 2
THE MAN

"What is man that you are
mindful of him?"
Psalm 8:4

1

The angel Gorel hesitated just beyond the solar system. He drifted inward, spiraling past the great planets, finally hovering over the third planet from the sun. Gorel was awed by the sight, not because the planet itself appeared special, but because of its history. Earth was a tiny mote circling a seemingly insignificant sun. And that sun was just one of millions in a galaxy that was itself merely one of a hundred million galaxies. What made Earth special was the fact that it had once served as the seat of the vice-regent of the universe, a being now known as Satan.

When Satan rebelled against the Creator, he retained control of Earth. Over a billion years later, the Creator devastated the planet, only to reshape it in six days and reseed it with a life that was unique in the universe. The living things of planet Earth weren't like Gorel or the rest of heaven's host. Nor were they like Satan and his evil underlings. The Creator, Elohim, had quickened what was essentially dirt and made it live.

Unlike the creatures that had lived on Earth when Satan ruled, Elohim pronounced these creatures "good."

Silently Gorel slid through the curtain of water vapor that sheltered the planet's surface and located an area bordered by four winding rivers. Gorel could see that the land was lush and beautiful. Myriad grasses, plants, and tress carpeted its gently sloping hills and verdant valleys, while a variety of animals played among the abundance. Flowers were everywhere, filling the air with fragrance and delighting the eye with dazzling colors. Awed, Gorel hovered over this garden landscape.

Finally Gorel located the creature Elohim had commissioned him to watch. The creature lay, outstretched limbs relaxed, sleeping peacefully. Gorel found a comfortable perch in a nearby tree. The creature, which Elohim had called "man," would awaken soon. Until then Gorel would wait, and watch.

2

Day one. The man stretched and yawned. Light from the hidden sun filtered through the cocoon of waters that Elohim had draped around the planet, cast a warm glow. The mists that watered the land at night were gone, but the man's skin was still damp.

For a long moment the man lay on his back, looking up at the complex currents that flowed in the vapor sea above him. Then he looked down and noticed that his body glowed, giving off a gentle radiance. The man sat up and ran his hands over his strong legs and lean body. He was puzzled. Where was he? And who was he?

Then the man remembered that his name was Adam and that he was a "man."

Adam's next sensation was that of hunger. Somehow he recognized the nature of the ache in his midsection. Oh, yes. His stomach.

Adam wasn't sure how he knew what hunger was or how he knew the term "stomach." How did he know those words, or any of the other words that seemed to come to mind so naturally? How did he know that he was "man"? And why didn't he know what a "man" was?

The first man set those puzzles aside. He was hungry. He would eat first and then try to solve the mystery.

Adam sat up and looked around. He'd been sleeping in a meadow on a bed of lush, green grass. Just beyond the meadow, the man could see a cluster of low trees, each filled with different brightly colored objects. The sight of them made Adam's mouth water.

Fruit, Adam thought, and again he paused, puzzled. How did he know these objects were fruit? And how did he know they were good to eat?

Again Adam shook off his questions. What was important was that he was hungry, and he knew fruit would satisfy his hunger. Adam walked quickly toward the colorful orbs hanging so tantalizingly from the trees' branches. Adam couldn't remember walking before, but he knew what walking was. But how?

When Adam reached the first tree, he plucked a brightly hued fruit. Somehow he knew he had to remove the outside of the fruit and eat the inside. When the peel was removed, he broke the fruit into sections and ate them. A delightful sensation seemed to explode in his mouth, and the fruit's zesty aroma filled the air. Eagerly Adam finished the orange—yes, that was its name. Orange. Then he went on to another tree to taste another fruit, and then another.

When his hunger was satisfied, Adam sat down under one of the trees. He leaned back against the smooth bark of its trunk and closed his eyes. Eating had been a wonderful experience. He couldn't remember eating before. But how could he have forgotten?

With his eyes closed, Adam struggled to remember. Try as he would, the first thing Adam could recall was opening his eyes in the meadow and looking down at his body. Finally Adam gave up. It would come in time. In the meanwhile, he might as well explore.

The man was intensely curious about this place where he found himself. For no particular reason, Adam set out toward what he later realized was the west. He quickly passed through the cluster of fruit trees and discovered a hill blanketed in yellow. Approaching, Adam discovered that the hill was covered with thousands of bright yellow flowers.

As Adam walked slowly up the hill, he became aware of a delicate perfume rising from the flowers. Halfway up the hill, Adam dropped to his knees and bent his head to breathe in more of the fragrance. He remained there, leaning closer to examine individual blossoms. Each flower had a small dark center surrounded by wide, silken petals of a vibrant yellow. So many blossoms grew on each plant that the stems and leaves beneath them were completely hidden.

Then Adam noticed tiny creatures that flew from bloom to bloom. He tried to think of their name, but nothing came to mind. That was strange. He knew the names of the fruit that hung on the trees. Why didn't he know the names of these little creatures? Putting the question aside, Adam returned to examining the flowers and watching their tiny visitors.

After the man observed a dozen or so of the insects, he realized that as each landed on a flower, it extended part of itself to touch the center of a blossom. Then the insect would fly to another blossom and repeat the process. What could these creatures be doing?

One of the tiny beings landed on Adam's hand and he held it up close to examine it. It had a blunt, furry body and tiny transparent wings. The creature rested for a moment on the palm of Adam's hand. Then its wings began to beat, so rapidly that they could no longer be seen, and the tiny body lifted off and flew to another blossom.

Adam sat among the flowers for hours, breathing in their perfume and watching the fascinating little creatures that flitted among them.

Late in the afternoon, Adam noticed that after a creature visited several flowers it flew off in a particular direction. Curious, Adam followed the next creature as it flew straight into a nearby thicket. Carefully pulling back supple branches, Adam discovered the insects' destination. He watched, fascinated as one after another of the little creatures lighted on a thick, broad leaf near an opening in a tree trunk. There each insect performed a kind of dance as others watched. The watchers then launched themselves into the air and flew directly toward the hillside.

After observing some two dozen of the tiny creatures perform what seemed to Adam the same dance, he returned to the hillside and spent the rest of the day there. What were those flying things? What did they get from the flowers they visited? What was the significance of their dance? And why didn't Adam know their names?

As it began to grow dark Adam looked up. Currents still flowed in the ocean of water vapor that hung above the earth, but what had been the brightest area when Adam awoke was no longer centered above him. Instead it was now much lower, and it seemed to Adam the bright area had dimmed as well. As the bright spot sank lower and lower, darkness spread, and Adam realized he was hungry again. He climbed to the top of the hill, and in the valley beyond Adam saw a tiny stream.

Hurrying toward the stream, Adam passed through a field of waist-high, grass-like plants. Clusters of small kernels grew at the top of each thin stalk of grass, and without thinking, Adam broke the head off one of the stalks and rubbed it between his hands. He blew on his hands and watched tiny bits of chaff drift away. When there was nothing left but the kernels, Adam put them in his mouth and chewed. The kernels were firm and hard, but as his teeth crushed them, Adam delighted in the earthy flavor that flooded his mouth. Only after he'd eaten his fill did Adam pause to wonder. How had he known these kernels were good to eat? How had he known they were kernels? And how had he known to rub them between his hands to rid them of the chaff? Then the name came to him. Wheat.

As Adam walked on, he continued to ponder. As far as he knew, he'd never seen growing wheat or eaten wheat kernels.

He had no idea how he knew so much about this land. Yet at the same time, Adam knew so little about it. And so little about himself.

When it was fully dark, Adam lay down where he was and fell asleep.

3

Gorel was fascinated by everything the man-thing did. But he couldn't help comparing Adam with his own kind. Eating, for instance, was one of the things spirit beings didn't need to do. That, Gorel thought, was one of the obvious superiorities of heaven's host to the man. At the same time there were things about the man that marked him as special.

I'm not sure, Gorel thought, *why Elohim, bless and honor him, made me a Watcher. But I am beginning to build an impression of the man. He's curious. He's observant. And he clearly has a rudimentary kind of intelligence.*

4

Day one hundred fifteen. In many ways this day was like all the others Adam had experienced. The night mists that watered the earth faded as the planet rotated its face toward the sun. As the day brightened, Adam awoke.

On this particular morning, Adam chose a red fruit from one of the trees and ate it. Each fruit in what Adam had come to think of as his garden was so delicious he'd never decided on a favorite. Adam developed the habit of starting each day by picking a different fruit at random. This morning Adam supplemented the fruit with a stalk of celery and a handful of barley kernels. Adam was no closer to solving the mystery of his knowledge of the plants in the garden; yet as he munched on the grains of barley, he was aware that he knew just what they were, as well as knowing the difference between it and wheat or rye.

This was something that continually troubled Adam. He was always running across food plants that he recognized. He knew their names, and if they needed preparation, he knew how to prepare them. But Adam had no idea how he knew. Again Adam had to push the puzzle to the back of his mind. All he could do was enjoy the barley and hope that someday the mystery would be solved.

Adam snacked as he walked westward. As on every day since he awakened, Adam would walk until something caught his eye. Then Adam would concentrate on that discovery, sometimes for an hour, sometimes for a day or even longer. On this one-hundred-fifteenth day Adam came across a clear, briskly flowing stream. He knelt on the bank and bent down to drink, and noticed an unusual colored stone. As Adam watched, the colors seemed to undulate under the swiftly flowing waters.

Adam lay flat on the bank and tried to reach the stone, but the water was too deep. Plunging into the crisp, cold water, Adam retrieved the stone. It was flat and smooth, white except for veins of green that ran through it. Adam felt the stone with his finger tips. Then he scratched it with a fingernail. Just as he'd thought! The green vein was a different substance, rougher than the stone in which it was imbedded. Excited, Adam began to wade up the stream, peering eagerly into the water.

The stream was cold, yet Adam felt no discomfort. The glow that emanated from Adam's body kept him warm. But even without this special protection, Adam wouldn't have noticed the chill. He was utterly intent on his search.

As Adam spied a stone he liked, he picked it up and examined it. Each stone he chose was striped with veins of various hews. Adam wasn't sure why these particular stones attracted him. He ignored or tossed aside other brightly colored bits of rock. All he wanted were stones that displayed veins of variously colored ore.

5

Gorel had been especially interested in collecting evidence of the man's mental processes. As Adam continued to search for the stones that fascinated him, Gorel took careful note. Adam observed. Adam examined. Adam evaluated. Adam selected and rejected based on some criteria of his own.

The angel had no way to know what was in Adam's mind, but there was no doubt that the man was intelligent. Yet what fascinated Gorel about the process he was observing was that Gorel saw no immediate benefit Adam could derive from this activity. Adam seemed to simply enjoy studying different things in his environment.

There were times that Adam totally surprised Gorel. Like the day he made his first shelter.

It had happened on Adam's eighty-ninth day. Adam ran across a stand of what he recognized as bamboo. Again the name came to Adam without effort and without explanation. As soon as Adam caught sight of the stand of bamboo plants, he felt excited. Adam looked around eagerly and spied some vines growing on a nearby tree. He hurried to the tree and broke off lengthy sections of vines. He brought these to the stand of bamboo and dropped them on the ground. Then Adam reached up as high as he could. He grasped one of the bamboo stalks. Bending it to form half of an arch, Adam tied a length of vine near the top. Then Adam selected another stalk some eight feet from the first. He then bent the second stalk to complete the arch, and lashed their tops together. Working quickly and confidently, Adam bent and bound other stalks of bamboo, creating a tepee-like frame.

With the frame complete, Adam wove in branches and long grasses to enclose the upper half of the structure. When Adam was done, he stepped back and gazed proudly at what he'd created.

Gorel was impressed. The angel realized that the structure must have existed in Adam's mind before he set to work. Adam had recognized the resources he'd need to construct his shelter and had quickly assembled the building materials. Gorel had never imagined that the man had this ability.

Yet Gorel wondered. Why did Adam want a shelter? He surely didn't need one.

Adam couldn't explain his sudden impulse to build the shelter. All he knew was that it felt good to have a shelter to sleep in. After building that first structure, Adam fashioned others. He'd sleep in one of them most nights, often staying in the same shelter for several nights before moving on to another part of the garden.

Yet Adam too realized he had no real need for his structures. The temperature in the garden varied only slightly between day and night. It never rained or stormed. And his shelters failed to keep out mists that rose each night and watered the ground. Adam never minded the mists anyway. Still, Adam continued to build shelters as he wandered. Somehow building the structures and staying in them felt right.

6

What made Adam's one-hundred-fifteenth day special had nothing to do with shelters. What made this day special was that it was on the one-hundred-fifteenth day of Adam's life that Elohim first came to the garden to talk with him.

Gorel sensed Elohim's approach. The horizon became bright as Elohim drew near, and Gorel felt that surge of joy members of heaven's host know when in the Presence. Yet Gorel was shocked when Elohim entered the garden. The Lord God had dimmed the brightness of his glory and had taken on visible form. Gorel drew a respectful distance away and prostrated himself before the Lord. But Elohim hadn't come to Eden to see Gorel. The angel was utterly shocked when he realized that the Creator of the Universe, the Commander of Heaven's Host, had come to the garden to speak with the man!

The angel, who remained prostrate, had no idea what the two said to each other during the hour they spent together. Gorel could see that Adam did most of the talking and that his face flushed with excitement as he spoke. Adam was clearly delighted with the opportunity to share his experiences in the garden with the Creator. And Gorel saw Elohim bend his head to listen, giving the man his full attention.

Gorel could hardly believe what he was seeing. The man obviously had no sense of the awe appropriate to being in the Presence. And Elohim acted as if the two were friends rather than Creator and creature.

The angel simply couldn't understand it. How did this man-creature deserve the personal attention of Elohim? It was obvious that Elohim, who had refashioned Eden as a home for the man, put great stock in him. But Gorel couldn't imagine why.

7

Day two hundred nineteen. On this day Adam stopped wandering aimlessly in the garden. He reached the westernmost of the rivers that encompassed Eden. It was the slowest flowing, broadest, and muddiest of the four streams. The man stopped and gazed at the river, apparently puzzled. He squatted on the bank and sipped some of the water in cupped hands. Peering closely Adam let the water filter between his fingers and then rubbed the light film of sediment that was left. Thoughtfully Adam peered at the rushes that grew along the stream's opposite bank.

Clearly this wasn't the same river as the deep, swiftly moving waterway he'd come upon some weeks previously. Could rivers mark the boundary of the garden he'd been exploring?

Adam remained squatting by the water's edge for some time, thinking. Then he reached a decision. He would follow this river and find out. Adam stood up and strode off upstream. All that day he walked rapidly, paying no attention to things that normally would have attracted him. When the gradually fading light announced the evening, Adam didn't pause to construct a shelter but hurried on.

Finally, when it was almost too dark to see, Adam smoothed a patch of moist earth by the river's edge. He knelt beside it and with a stick carefully drew a line in the dirt. After peering at his drawing for several minutes, he rubbed the patch smooth again. Only then did

Adam look around, select as spot beneath the branches of a nearby tree, and go to sleep.

The next few days Adam followed the river, moving steadily and swiftly. Each evening he drew in the dirt. Each evening the line he drew was longer than the line of the day before. About noon of the sixth day, the man came to a second river that intersected the first. Adam was pleased. He'd thought it would be there, and he'd been right. Adam then set off to follow this new stream. That evening when he drew in the dirt he sketched two lines, one of them long and undulating, the other a much shorter line that ran perpendicular to the first. It was only then that Gorel realized what the man was doing.

He's drawing a map, Gorel thought. *The man intends to identify the boundaries of the garden.*

Gorel didn't know just why this was important to the man. Even Adam didn't understand completely. All Adam knew was that he needed to know the extent of the garden in which he lived. For some reason he needed to know where he was.

Adam intuitively realized that if he were to place himself in a spatial context his first step had to be to establish boundaries. Only if he knew the borders of his territory could Adam gain any sense of where he was.

The need for boundaries was something Gorel was incapable of understanding. He was an angel, and like all the host of heaven, he was always aware of where he was. Elohim created angels with an innate awareness of the entire spiritual and later the material universe, so angels always know where they are in relation to the Creator, the center of all. Gorel could not imagine an existence without that awareness. Nor could he understand what it must be like not to know where one was.

For Adam the realization that he needed to establish boundaries came only when he'd set out to draw his map. Only then did he realize that for most of his time in the garden he'd experienced the nagging sense of being lost. Discovering where he was now seemed nearly as vital as discovering who he was. Yet as Adam hurried along the boundary streams, his thoughts often returned to Elohim's visit.

When Elohim appeared in the garden, Adam had immediately recognized his Creator. Adam had been overjoyed at the visit and had felt completely free to express his every thought to Elohim. Thinking back, Adam wondered why he'd not been awed at the appearance. His visitor was the One and Only, the All Powerful, the Master of the Universe. Adam deeply revered Elohim. Yet Adam's primary emotion at seeing Elohim had been delight. And with that delight, Adam had been filled with confidence. Somehow Adam knew that Elohim welcomed Adam's presence and delighted in him, even as Adam delighted in being with the Lord. How this could be, knowing the identity of Elohim, Adam had no idea.

Gorel was even more puzzled. Who was this Adam anyway? Adam was a created being, as angels are created beings. Gorel understood his own nature as a spirit being. He was aware that a great gap existed between his powers and those of the man. Compared to angels, Adam seemed insignificant. But clearly Adam was special to the Creator. Elohim had granted the man a relationship with himself that was infinitely more intimate than his relationship with angels. What Gorel could not fathom was, *Why?*

8

Day three hundred thirty-nine. On this day Adam finished mapping the rivers that marked the boundaries of Eden. As he closed the last gap, Adam felt a sense of relief. It had taken Adam nearly a hundred days to walk the banks of the four rivers that enclosed his garden. Now at last Adam had a sense of where he lived.

But as Adam gazed at the outline marking Eden's borders, he realized the map was incomplete. This map simply established Eden's boundaries. Now Adam needed to establish the locations of all the wonderful things he'd discovered within the garden. Adam would have to add to his map the places that were special to him, places he might want to revisit.

But how would he go about mapping features of the garden? As Adam peered at the outline he'd drawn on the ground, he saw a way and began sketching quickly. First Adam drew a series of equidistant east/west lines, and then a series of north/south lines perpendicular to them. Soon his map was overlaid with a grid composed of equal-sized squares. Adam then memorized the completed map and the grid.

The next morning Adam would begin the process of locating each of his favorite places by placing each in the appropriate square. When he was done, Adam would know exactly where he was in relation to each feature of the garden. He could even use the map and grid to make sure he explored the entire garden.

9

Five days later, Adam was exploring a new section of the garden when he came across what he later called his Crystal Grotto. He happened on a sharp bend in a dry streambed. At the elbow of the bend, the outer bank of the streambed was undercut. Lush ferns spilled over its edge, almost hiding heaps of round gray rocks that lay below. The rocks ranged from the size of Adam's fist to some as large as the great green melons Adam relished.

As Adam looked more closely, he saw that some of the rocks were broken. Adam could see the rocks were hollow and noticed that the inner surface of the broken rocks glittered. Fascinated, Adam picked up several of the shattered rocks and examined them. The rocks were hollow, but their inner surfaces were composes of varicolored crystals that glittered in the light. Hidden within the dull exteriors were translucent gemstones sparkling with purple, violet, blue, and green highlights. When Adam held the crystals up, they sparkled brilliantly, drawing his gaze deeper and deeper into their depths.

Adam was entranced. He'd seen many beautiful sights in Eden, but these crystals were a unique treasure.

Gorel, invisible, peered over Adam's shoulder. The angel too was entranced. Gorel couldn't help wishing that the man could see the stars. How would Adam respond if their millions of points of light were visible in the heavens? The crystal rocks reminded Gorel of spiral galaxies ablaze with color. He remembered how, with the host of heaven, he loved to dance among the stars, filled with joy and overflowing with gratitude to Elohim.

The angel wondered, *Do the crystals arouse the same sense of wonder and thanksgiving in the man?*

Just those emotions now filled Adam's heart. Adam too was attuned to beauty, and like so many other sights in the garden, the crystals filled him with joy.

Adam spent the entire day in the riverbed. At first he carefully examined each of the broken rocks. Then he experimented. He picked up a medium-sized rock and threw it down violently. When it struck a larger rock lying on the ground, both broke open. Adam pounced on the one he'd thrown. Holding it up, he peered inside. Yes! It too contained crystals. And so did the other rock!

Adam smashed one half of a broken rock, fracturing it into three pieces. The crystals were now fully exposed, and the man examined them carefully.

Excitedly Adam wondered. What could he do with the crystals? How could he display their beauty? Then, his mind made up, Adam set about smashing more rocks. After shattering hundreds, Adam sorted the pieces. He put sections of rock containing deep purple crystals in one pile, violet crystals in another, greens and blues in still others.

When the crystals were sorted, Adam began laying them out in the streambed. Rather than keep the colors separate, he intermingled them, creating a mosaic of varicolored spirals. After hours of meticulous labor, Adam stood back and gazed at his handiwork. Satisfied with the pattern, Adam began to imbed the crystals in the vertical bank of the stream. When he was finished, Adam sat on the grass across from his creation and gazed at what he'd done. Unaware that he was mimicking the Creator, Adam felt a surge of satisfaction. Yes, what he had made was good.

Gorel had to acknowledge that the man's artistic creation was striking. Adam had never glimpsed a spiral nebula, yet somehow his mosaic seemed to reproduce interstellar gases flowing gloriously among rotating galaxies. The colors of his creation surged and eddied, swirling around and around in such a way that they almost seemed to move.

The man has an uncanny eye for beauty, Gorel mused. It seemed to Gorel that such beauty must inspire in Adam something of that worshipful awe that dancing among the stars inspires in angels. *How,* Gorel wondered, *could true beauty fail to move any sentient being to wonderment and praise?*

10

Day four hundred one. That evening Elohim visited the man again. Gorel believed that the Eternal One, hallowed be his name, was moved by compassion, for Adam was upset and agitated.

The day had begun as most did. The man continued to search the garden grid by grid, recording the things he found on a map that he redrew and memorized each evening. By now Adam was exploring the last few grids on his map. He had almost every important location fixed in his mind, yet the repetition of drawing the four bordering rivers and marking the special spots seemed to provide him with an extra sense of security. Adam now knew where he was at all times, and he knew how to reach any of the places that he might want to go.

This morning Adam came to a clearing that contained a large pond. A flock of long-legged white birds was wading in its shallow waters. For some time, Adam stood and watched the birds as they dipped their heads under water and came up with some soft water plant in their beaks. Then they stretched their necks, their heads thrust high to swallow the plants. The birds stayed close to one another, and the whole flock moved in unison as the birds slowly waded through the water.

Then the man noticed one bird lying by the side of the pond. Its head moved to follow the progress of the flock. Now and then the bird struggled to stand, but each time it fell back on its side. What had happened to the bird?

Adam hurried over to the stricken creature and tried to set it on its feet. But as soon as he released the bird, it fell over again. After two or three attempts, the man sat down beside the bird and began to examine it. He gently ran his hand over the bird's body, wings, and legs. When he touched the right leg, the bird flapped wildly and uttered a cry. Adam saw that the right leg was crooked, and he was worried because the bird was obviously in pain.

Gorel could see that the man was upset. Apparently Adam had never imagined that any creature in the garden could be damaged in any way. Gorel had never imagined such a thing either. Angels, like Satan's demons, aren't made of breakable stuff. Lightning bolts can stun them. Their progress through the universe can be blocked or hindered. In battle angels and demons can be drained of energy and forced to fall back. But neither of the two hostile groups of spirit beings can do the other any lasting harm. Angels and demons share a common origin in Elohim's first creative act, and they are built to last.

Gorel knew that spirit beings are eternal. They have existed across millenniums, and they will continue to exist forever. Apparently this wasn't so for creatures fashioned from planetary dirt. The bird clearly was broken, and Gorel was uncertain whether or not the bird would have ceased to exist if Adam hadn't found and helped it. But Adam had found the bird. And he seemed determined to help it.

All that day the man tried to help the bird. But most of the things Adam did seemed only to increase the bird's distress. When Adam tried to straighten the bird's leg, it cried out and its wings beat frantically. It pulled away, and its leg seemed more crooked than before. After thinking for some time, Adam searched for and found several straight sticks and some lengths of thin vine. Despite the bird's efforts to get away, Adam grasped it firmly. He held it close against him, and although he was beaten by its wings and struck several times by the point of its beak, Adam succeeded in straightening the leg and binding the sticks to it. During the process, the bird lost consciousness and lay limp in the man's hands.

When the bird revived, Adam carried it to the water. But the bird was still unable to walk or stand. Finally Adam waded out into the pond and felt under the surface for the kind of plant he had seen the flock eat. But when Adam held the gob of pulp out to the bird, the creature didn't seem to recognize it as food. Adam was frustrated. He was trying so hard and making so little progress.

Finally, Adam gently pried the bird's beak open. He lifted the bird's head high and stretched out its long neck, trying to mimic the way the birds stretched when they ate. After several attempts the bird swallowed some of the plant. But in the process its eyes dulled, and the bird seemed too weak even to struggle.

Adam sat beside the bird the rest of the day, trying to comfort it. The bird simply lay there, unmoving, as the flock slowly circled the edge of the pond, eating constantly. In the late afternoon the flock went ashore on the opposite side of the pond. Each bird perched on one leg, preening its feathers. Now and then a bird would reach out to groom another with its beak. None of the birds seemed aware of their stricken companion. None of the birds seemed to care.

But Adam cared, intensely. It wasn't right that this creature should suffer so. All that afternoon, Adam gently stroked the bird and talked to it. As Adam watched the stricken creature, he found his eyes filling with tears.

I'm crying, Adam thought. *I've never cried before.*

Focusing his attention on the bird, Adam thought, *What a delicate creature.* He hadn't realized that birds weighed so little. Or that their feathers fluttered in the slightest breeze. He hadn't realized that any living creature could be so fragile. *I wonder*, Adam pondered. *Am I fragile too? Can I be damaged like this bird?*

That evening Elohim visited the man. When Adam heard the sound of Elohim walking in the garden, he jumped up and ran to meet him. This time Elohim motioned Gorel to come closer, so he could overhear what was said.

"Oh, Elohim!" the man cried out when he reached the figure under the trees. "You've got to help! I found a broken bird, and I can't fix it."

"Take me to the bird," Elohim said.

The man reached out and actually grasped Elohim's hand! Gorel was shocked by the familiarity. How did this creature dare to touch the Glorious One, the Maker of All Things? Doesn't the man understand who Elohim is? Doesn't he understand that he himself is nothing, a thing, fashioned of planetary detritus? Even angels, who delight at being in the Presence, would be scalded should they approach the Creator half so close. Yet this man creature dared reach out and actually touch him!

Still holding Elohim's hand, Adam led the Creator to the bird and gently picked it up. "It's hurt," Adam reported. "And I don't know how to help it."

Elohim nodded. "Its leg is broken, little one. But you've done well.

You've bound the leg so it's straight. The break does cause the bird pain. But the bone will grow together. In time the bird will be well."

Adam smiled broadly. "The bird will be well again?"

"Yes," Elohim nodded. "But for now it needs you. The bird can't walk in the water to feed itself. It will need you to feed it. Can you do this?"

"Oh yes," the man replied. "I want to."

"Then help it you shall. Stay here until the bird is well again. And then go on exploring the garden."

Shortly after this Elohim left. But before he resumed his true form, Elohim beckoned to the watcher. "Gorel," he asked, "do you understand what you've just witnessed?"

"No, Lord," Gorel confessed.

"Keep watching, Gorel. In time you'll understand who the man is. And so will the rest of the host."

It was comforting to know that Gorel would uncover the secret one day. But it was frustrating as well. How long would he have to wait? And why should he have to wait? What purpose did Elohim have in making the watcher angel wait rather than simply reveal the secret to him?

11

Day six hundred seven. When Adam finished his map of Eden, he spent the next few months revisiting a number of locations. But on this day, Adam set on a new venture, intent on meeting a new need. The bamboo and other temporary structures Adam still constructed met one need. Mapping Eden met another need. Now Adam wanted to put his own stamp on some portion of the great garden in which he lived.

As Adam revisited his favorite locations in Eden, he studied the land. Often Adam sat, resting his chin on one hand, gazing at the landscape. Finally Adam settled on a location, and on the six hundred and seventh day of his life, Adam set to work.

Adam began by clearing a large meadow. He uprooted flowers and bushes, carefully carrying each some distance away and replanting it. The moist dark soil of the garden was easy to dig in even though Adam used only his hands. When the meadow was completely cleared, Adam went in search of flowers to transplant.

It took Adam weeks to locate just the right flowers, dig them up, and replant them. As those weeks passed, a pattern began to emerge. Gorel saw that Adam was laying out beds of flowers in a variety of geometric shapes. Each bed featured flowers of a different hue. Adam was designing a vibrant patchwork of colors that would cover the hillside.

When Adam finished laying out the flower beds, he framed the area with flowering bushes. Then he stood back and admired what he'd accomplished. Adam had decided to take control of his environment, and he had succeeded!

This project was foreign to Gorel, and it disturbed him greatly. To the angel what Adam was doing seemed irreverent. How could anyone improve on what Elohim, blessed be his name, had fashioned? Shouldn't the man simply enjoy the Creator's craftsmanship, as angels do? Gorel was tempted to bring the matter up with his superiors, but surely Elohim, who knew all things, was aware of Adam's activity. Finally Gorel decided that since Elohim didn't protest, it wasn't Gorel's place to object.

Gorel had to acknowledge the man was investing great effort in the redesign of the hillside. As Adam dug and carried, drops of perspiration ran from his face and body. Gorel could see the man's muscles strain as he struggled to dislodge the larger bushes. But the man never stopped to rest until evening came. And each morning Adam seemed eager to return to work.

When Adam finished, he stood with his hands on his hips gazing at what he done, and he spoke aloud. "Good," Adam said. "It's good."

This was too much for the watcher angel. Why, the man was aping Elohim, who at the end of each day of the re-creation announced that what he had done was good. "Who does the man think he is?" Gorel muttered unkindly. "What gives him the right to mimic the Creator?"

That evening Elohim visited the man again. These visits by the Creator were taking place with increasing frequency. On this occasion Adam eagerly displayed his handiwork to the Creator of the Universe. Much to Gorel's amazement, rather than be upset, Elohim praised the man's efforts.

Gorel pondered what he'd observed. Certainly the man was very different from angels. And that difference went far deeper than the fact that Adam was fashioned of matter while angels are pure spirit. Angels, Gorel knew, exist to serve and worship the Creator. Angels simply await the Creator's orders and joyfully carry them out. Gorel knew that not a single angel would dream of acting on his own without instructions from Elohim, blessed be his name.

Actually, Gorel was repelled by the thought of acting on his own. *It's our complete commitment to Elohim's will,* Gorel thought, *that distinguishes us from Satan and his demons.* Wasn't it Satan's exercise of his own will that started the war that's raged for so many millions of years? How, then, could Elohim praise the man for acting on his own to modify the garden that Elohim had designed?

What kind of creature was this "man" anyway? He was clearly no angel. But, just as clearly, he was no demon either.

These questions plagued Gorel as he watched the two together in the garden and noted Elohim's approval of the man's work. Elohim even seemed to take pleasure in Adam as the man babbled on about what he planned to do next.

I don't mind being assigned to watch the man, Gorel thought. *But I would very much like to understand what I observe.*

12

Day three thousand sixty-four. Adam devoted years to redesigning sections of Eden. Each project was more innovative than the last. The floral designs became more and more sophisticated, with more complex mixes of colors. In time Adam began to place flowers so that their fragrances intermingled. Finally Adam tired of working with plant life and took a renewed interest in the animals and birds of the garden.

For a time after Adam had taken care of the bird with the broken leg, he hunted for other creatures that might need help. But life in the garden was good for every living thing. The broken leg was an anomaly. After a few months passed without seeing another injured creature, Adam lost interest in the birds and animals. His attention was focused on exploring the garden, and after that on developing fresh arrangements of Eden's plants and bushes.

Then one night while the man was asleep, a half-dozen large, tawny animals found him. One curled up next to him to doze. When Adam awoke, one of his arms was resting over the animal's flank. The animal stirred and the two began to roll over and over, wrestling playfully. The man laughed, and the big creature seemed to grin with pleasure.

It felt so good to Adam to interact with another living creature. Adam had never thought of it before, but as he sat beside the resting beast, stroking its fur and scratching it behind its ears, he realized that he'd been hungering for another living creature's touch.

Adam struggled to remember this animal's name. He knew the names and characteristics of all the plants of the garden, but he now realized he had no name for any of its living creatures. All he knew about them was what he observed and experienced. Even so, in romping with the great, fun-loving creature, Adam sensed that he needed them; that unless he forged some kind of relationship with the animals of Eden, he would feel increasingly isolated and alone.

For over a week, Adam kept company with the big animals. Each of the animals in the band was some three times Adam's weight. Each had a long tail, pointed ears, slant eyes, and great paws with blunt, retractable claws that were ideal for digging. Adam enjoyed digging, too, and he helped the animals excavate the legumes that were the principal food in their diet.

The relationship that Adam was forging with the big animals again surprised Gorel. In Adam's wanderings through the garden, the man had come across many different animal kinds. He normally paused to watch them, but soon moved on. His adoption into this group of animals, his participation in their experiences, was something new for Adam and for the animals as well. Yet the animals apparently accepted Adam as one of them, and Adam clearly enjoyed their company.

How different these animals are, Gorel thought, *from the beasts that roamed this planet when Satan was in charge.*

For a time Gorel imagined that the merger of Adam with the band of big animals was something Elohim had always intended. The man and the animals were both works of the Creator. He had placed them together in Eden, and they had much in common, for the man and the animals shared biological life. They were things of flesh that must eat to sustain life. It seemed to Gorel that Adam and the big animals were well suited to each other.

Yet he recognized differences between the man and the other living creatures of Eden. Adam alone designed and built structures. Adam alone had shown concern for an injured creature. Only Adam had demonstrated the ability to create mosaics from crystal or shown an interest in moving plants to change his environment. Only the man had felt a need to map the garden and its features. Most importantly, the man was the only creature that Elohim, praise to the Most High, had come to the garden to visit. Only the man had shown the capacity to communicate with the Creator.

What was this "man" anyway? How could he be so like and yet so unlike the host, and at the same time so like yet so unlike Eden's animals? Gorel felt that the incident with the animals was helping him get closer to the secret of Adam's identity. But the answer still eluded him. What could this creature be, who was neither angel nor animal and yet resembled both?

13

Day three thousand ninety-eight. Adam's time with the tribe of large animals reawakened his interest in Eden's living creatures. Adam felt a brief sense of loss when he left the big fun-lovers, but his curiosity had been aroused and he was eager to see if he could relate to other creatures in Eden. Now every time Adam came across a different kind of animal, he spent a few days trying to make friends. The animals of Eden showed no fear of Adam, but neither were they particularly welcoming.

Then Elohim once again visited the garden. On this visit the Creator told Adam that he was to give names to the beasts of the field and the birds of the air.

This commission shocked Gorel. The angel understood that to

name anything requires identifying its essence, for a true name must be an extension of a being's or a thing's very nature.

My name, Gorel thought, *identifies me as "Sent by God." Satan's name means "Accuser." The new name of my one-time companion in service to Elohim, Myrdebaal, means "Master of Deceit," or "Deceit is my Master." And of course, Elohim's name, may he be ever glorified, means "The One."*

Actually, Elohim's name remained something of a mystery, for while it means "The One," the word itself is plural. That plural emphasized Elohim's majesty but, the angels suspected, implied something more.

Yet, to have the man name the beasts! The commission must mean that Elohim considered Adam capable of discerning the essence of each animal kind and able to express that uniqueness, that essence, in a name. Gorel had never imagined that a three-dimensional creature of flesh and blood could see beyond appearances and discern reality, and then invent words to express that reality.

The commission forced Gorel to acknowledge a truth he had been unwilling to consider. Somehow the man was significant. He was much more than Elohim's pet. But the frustrated angel still could not imagine what the man was to the Almighty.

14

Day three thousand three hundred thirty-eight. After eight months Adam finished his study of the first of Eden's animal kinds. He'd chosen to begin with the large, tawny animals he'd spent time with earlier. At first Adam hadn't been able to locate them. Adam hadn't noticed earlier, but the big creatures left no tracks or other signs of their presence. They even filled in the holes they dug searching for food.

For several days Adam visited places where he'd seen the animals earlier, but without success. As he searched Adam thought about the task Elohim had given him. He was excited about the mission, partly because it was a new and different challenge and partly because he was eager to please the Creator. Adam also sensed that naming the animals was an honor as well as responsibility, for Elohim had said that what-ever name Adam gave a living creature, that was to be its name.

In a flash of insight, Adam realized why he had never been able to remember the name of any of Eden's living creatures, although he knew the names of all the plants and flowers. Adam couldn't remember animal names because until he, Adam, named them, the beasts and birds had no name!

On the eighth day, Adam located a pride of the big animals doz-ing in a copse. He would have passed by if he hadn't heard a familiar, playful growl. Parting the bushes, Adam saw one of his favorites lazily slapping at a companion. Adam's first instinct was to join them. Then he hesitated. Perhaps he should watch from a distance. It was pos-sible that his presence might influence their behavior, and Adam didn't want that. No, it would be better if the creatures he studied weren't aware that he was near. So Adam quietly climbed a nearby tree where he could watch unobserved.

During the next months, Adam found these animals fascinating. There were so many things about the big creatures that he'd never noticed while he was part of the group. One of the first things Adam discovered was the reason they left no tracks. Although heavy, these animals set each paw down carefully, with the outer edge testing the ground before shifting any weight to that leg. Moving this way on their broad pads, the animals left no tracks or other sign of their passage. Also, the big beasts tended to travel at night and to spend lazy days dozing or playing in some secluded grove. It was no wonder Adam had such a difficult time locating them.

The longer Adam observed the large animals, the more details he noticed. When he'd been with them, he had hardly looked beyond their pointed ears, slant green eyes, long tails, and those great paws with their retractable claws. Now he saw so much more. These were clearly emotional animals. They took great joy in play. They loved to ambush each other, pouncing when least expected and rolling over and over together on the ground. At such times the animals seemed to overflow with happiness. The creatures were also affectionate. Adam watched as they washed each other with their tongues. He noted how they patted one another's faces with their paws. One day Adam observed a female seize a male's forepaw between her own two and bring it up to her face so he would caress her.

Adam now realized that the faces of the big creatures were very expressive. The animals had many delicate muscles around their ears, lips, and eyelids. This made a number of facial expressions possible. Even their whiskers expressed emotion. When an animal felt uncertain, her whiskers pointed stiffly upward and forward, and when excited, her eyes opened extra wide.

Their reflexes were amazingly fast. One day one of the big animals lay totally relaxed except for its eyes, which followed a tiny flying insect. Suddenly a paw shot out and the insect was caught in a crease in the paw's pad. The animal let it go only to snatch it out of the air again and again.

Adam was impressed that these were social animals. They lived together in groups of six or eight. When one animal returned after being away, the others greeted it with high-pitched moans. At times the animals communicated by roars, but they also purred and hummed. The source of the purr was hard to locate; it seemed to emanate from the entire body.

The man also noted that one of the animals seemed dominant. The others would not meet the dominant one's eyes, but respectfully averted their own. Yet otherwise, there was no suggestion of hierarchy, and the members of the group treated each other as equals.

The animal's diet consisted of plants that were rich in protein. While they occasionally would eat avocados, they ate no other fruit. Now and then they snacked on asparagus or mushrooms, but they avidly devoured legumes, preferring beans of all sorts. They also enjoyed nuts, crushing the shells with their powerful jaws and swallowing the shell fragments with the meat. At times they binged on such foods, eating until their stomachs were distended. Then they stretched out on their sides and fell into a coma-like sleep.

The longer he watched, the more it seemed to Adam that what set these creatures apart was their capacity for play. The fun-loving character of the big creatures delighted Adam.

There were other animals that definitely didn't share Adam's delight. Several times during the months Adam observed the pride, the big creatures came across flocks of smaller, wooly animals. The wooly animals had long, mournful faces. They traveled in large, tightly knit groups that tended to huddle close together.

When the big animals found a flock of the wooly ones, they appeared eager to play with the smaller, more serious creatures. The big animals pressed their bodies close to the ground and crept nearer and nearer. Then each dashed into the flock and grasped an unwilling playmate with both front paws. The smaller animals bleated loudly and tried to escape. After a time a big animal let one of the smaller go, only to chase it down again. Now and then one of the big animals appeared to attack a runaway, slapping at it with both front paws. Later, when Adam examined animals that had been attacked, he found no sign of injury. The tawny animals had kept their blunt, powerful claws sheathed and only pretended to strike the other creature.

After a mock attack on the wooly creatures, the big animals walked away proudly, tails straight up in the air, a look of satisfaction on their faces.

These animals are powerful, Adam thought, *but they're careful not to harm other creatures.*

The blunt, retractable claws they use for digging could be dangerous. When apparently irritated or angry with another creature, one of the big animals might strike with either forepaw, but it kept its claws sheathed. An animal never struck hard enough to do serious damage, and infrequent spats quickly turned into playful wrestling matches after which the mock combatants would purr and groom each other with their rough tongues.

Despite the traits shared by all members of this animal kind, Adam noted individual differences. One female was especially affectionate. Another seemed grumpy in the morning but playful in the afternoon. Still, the man's task was to identify what was unique about the animals as a class. It was what they had in common, not how individuals might differ, that counted.

Finally Adam decided on a name. *I'll call this kind of animal "cat,"* he decided. *Surely,* Adam thought, *these fascinating, happy creatures are one of the most delightful animal kinds fashioned by the Creator.*

15

Day three thousand six hundred and eight. The next beast of the field Adam set out to name was the smaller, seemingly serious animal that the big cats enjoyed teasing. The contrast fascinated Adam. Where the cats were quick and intelligent, these animals seemed dull and, yes, stupid.

There were other contrasts. The wooly creatures were less than a quarter the big cat's size. Where the cats had large, soft paws, these animals had small, hard, split hoofs. The cats' bodies were covered with fur and their flat faces were expressive. The smaller, wooly animals had thick hair and long faces that seemed incapable of expressing emotion. While the cats preferred the company of only five or six others, the wooly creatures were herd animals with thirty or more grazing and dozing together.

Like all the animals in the garden, the wooly animals ate vegetation. The cats preferred produce rich in proteins and fats. The woolies grazed on grass and herbs. After eating steadily for four or five hours in the morning, the whole flock would find a shady spot by a stream or pond and lie down together.

One discovery Adam made utterly fascinated him. Earlier he had looked at the raids by the cats from the cats' point of view. Now that Adam was studying the wooly creatures, the cats' visits seemed more like torment than fun.

Why then, Adam wondered, *did Elohim create these two sorts of animals and let the one pester the other?*

Then Adam noted that after each raid by the cats, the wooly animals invariably moved on to another place. This seemed important, for the wooly creatures, whose flat teeth were ideal for cropping grass and herbs, grazed the same fields over and over until only bare roots were left. Even then they didn't move to pastures where the grass was thick and herbs were plentiful. The wooly animals moved to a new location only after a raid by the big cats.

Adam concluded that in creating these two kinds of animals Elohim provided them with interacting instincts, for the cats' arrival coincided with the wooly animals overgrazing of a pasture. In a sense Elohim had programmed the big cats to herd the wooly creatures that lacked the sense to move on their own.

This insight came after Adam realized that the wooly animals seemed to be much more dominated by instincts than were the big cats. The woolies were gregarious, staying close to each other. They were also followers. If one animal wandered away, although this seldom happened, the others tended to follow it. The flock preferred familiar, wide-open places. In more restricted areas where the animals were forced closer together, they became restless and appeared nervous.

After a few months with these animals, Adam was satisfied he had an appropriate name for them. Sheep. Then Adam set out in search of another animal kind to study.

16

Day fourteen thousand, five hundred. On this day Adam finally finished naming the beasts of the field. The last to be named was a tiny furry creature that scampered quickly along the ground. It had large eyes and a tail nearly as long as its body. The creature had black and white facial stripes, with five dark stripes running down its reddish-brown back and sides. It frequently sat up on its haunches to gnaw on nuts or seeds that it held in its two front paws.

The most unusual thing about this little creature was its teeth. The animal had extremely sharp front teeth designed for gnawing on objects so hard that they wore the teeth down. Adam discovered, however, that the front teeth continued to grow throughout the creature's life. In contrast, the blunt back teeth that the animal used to grind its food didn't keep growing.

What fascinated Adam most was the fact that the tiny animal had a gap between the front and back teeth. It could squeeze its cheeks together through this gap and isolate the two sets of teeth. This allowed the creature to gnaw on some inedible object with its front teeth and at the same time chew food with the back teeth. In addition, the animals' cheeks contained pouches where it stored food to be chewed and swallowed later.

How amazing Elohim was, to design into each animal kind such utterly unique features! While there were many commonalities shared by all the animal kinds, there was something truly special about each different kind that marked it unmistakably as Elohim's handiwork.

It had taken Adam some forty years to study and name the beasts of the field. Those years seemed to pass quickly, for Adam remained fascinated by the animals he studied. Again and again as Adam uncovered some oddity in an animal kind, he found himself amazed at the inventiveness of Elohim. How wonderful the Creator was. Again and again Adam was moved to praise and glorify the God of Creation.

Yet at times Adam was troubled. One day he dropped down on his hands and knees to drink from a quiet pond. As he leaned closer he saw his reflection in the water. For the first time he formulated the question that had troubled Gorel almost from the beginning.

I've been told to study the animals and name them, Adam thought. *But what about me? Elohim calls me a "man." What is man?*

What kind of animal am I?

17

Day twenty-five thousand three hundred and two.

Adam had found the birds of the air even more fascinating than the beasts of the field. Birds were such captivating creatures. Their bodies were so light and fragile. Despite the fact that all birds had two legs and a pair of wings, and that most were covered with feathers, there were so many intriguing differences between bird kinds.

Beaks were one source of wonder for Adam. Some birds' beaks were long and pointed, others were short and blunt. Yet each shape was ideally adapted to the food the bird ate. Tiny hummingbirds used their long delicate beaks to suck nectar from flowers. Several kinds of birds that wadded in shallow waters had long beaks they used to probe the bottom for food. Other birds' beaks were designed for cracking seeds, while the beaks of yet others were like powerful hammers that could penetrate the bark of trees.

Adam found bird behavior complex and at times amazing. Birds bathed. But some birds bathed in dust rather than water. Yet the bathing behavior was the same. A bird would lower its head in the water or dust, raise it, and then beat its wings. Even young birds still in their nests made this same set of motions. Adam concluded that this and most other bird behaviors were instinctive rather than learned.

Yet birds could and did learn new behaviors. Adam observed one bird eat some berries that made it sick. Birds who saw the first's reaction avoided those berries. Adam even observed one bird using a tool. This was a small bird whose beak was too blunt to reach insects that burrowed into tree bark. Adam saw members of this bird kind break thorns off cactus plants, hold the thorns in their beaks, and use them to probe crevasses in the bark for insects.

Adam found that most bird behaviors had a relatively clear purpose. But some behavior mystified him. For instance, several kinds of birds would sit on anthills. They'd spread their wings so the ants could search through their feathers. Adam even saw one bird carefully pick up an ant and bury it in its own tail feathers. Adam never was able to explain what he saw, although he supposed that the ants fed on something in the feathers that irritated the birds.

Adam had carefully observed the social behavior of the animals he named. He was fascinated to discover that birds exhibited an even greater variety of social interaction that had the animals. Many of the more social birds maintained sharply defined hierarchies. The bird or birds at the top were the first to feed, drink, or take any turn. In some flocks only the one or two birds at the top of the hierarchy were allowed to sing! In certain flocks birds landing on a tree branch lined up according to each bird's social position.

Some birds demonstrated their social position physically. The top bird was allowed to peck any bird in the flock. The next bird could peck any except the top bird, on down to the lowest bird in the order which could be pecked by any other bird in the flock, but could peck none in return. Adam was surprised how important it seemed for some bird kinds to establish and maintain these dominant/submissive roles.

Adam noted that birds often assembled in large flocks. But he was surprised that the flocks might contain birds of different kinds. When a flock did include different bird kinds, all the birds in the flock tended to feed in the same area and usually were capable of flying about the same distance.

Despite the large size of some flocks, Adam learned that most birds feel uncomfortable if other birds come too close. Fascinatingly, for some bird kinds a half an inch wasn't too close, while for other kinds having another bird within a few feet seemed unnerving. When a bird's personal space was invaded, it was likely to fly at or peck the intruder.

So many aspects of bird life mesmerized Adam. Birds communicated, but in many different ways. Some birds were unable to vocalize, but communicated by clacking their bills together. Others birds could sing dozens or even hundreds of complex variations of a basic song. Most bird species had specialized calls composed of a brief series of notes or noises. Most of these bird songs seemed to be learned. Adam found that birds exposed to the songs of other kinds often mimicked their songs as well as sang their own.

Adam was also fascinated by birds' nesting behavior. Some birds simply perched on branches at night. Others created rude, open nests of sticks and grass. Some birds made complex nests with dome-shaped roofs. One bird kind created a giant, inverted pyramid of sticks, grass, and mud, while another kind suspended its nest from trees on cables of woven grass. Some birds that nested on the ground pressed down the grass and lined the depression with their feathers. Others nested in spaces under rocks or holes burrowed in the ground. A few bird kinds built cooperatively. Individuals of one kind worked together to shape a giant dome, and then underneath individual pairs created nests with private entrances. One water bird piled up stones in the shallow part of a pond and fashioned a nest of water plants on the island it created.

Finally the man came to the last bird kind, which he later named "parrot." Parrots came in many different colors and sizes, but they had certain features in common that convinced Adam they were of a single kind.Every variety had a hooked beak, with a large upper section that fit over a smaller lower section. Their nostrils were just above the beak in a patch of bare skin, their eyes were set in the sides of their head, their legs were strong, and their toes were yoked. Most bird kinds had three toes pointing forward and one toe pointing backward. Parrots had two powerful toes pointing forward and two pointing backward. This let them grip a branch with one foot and use the other to hold food. Adam noted that parrots were particularly adept at climbing through trees, gripping branches with their beaks as well as their feet.

The beak of these birds was a wonder in itself. The large upper section of the beak was hinged in such a way that it could bring tremendous pressure. Using their beaks, some of these birds could crack the hardest nuts and most heavily armored seeds. Parrots' tongues appeared extremely sensitive. Most bird tongues were thin and narrow. Parrots' tongues were thick, almost like muscular fingers. Yet the tongue was sensitive enough to find the weak seam in a seed and flexible enough to position the seed so that the beak could shuck its shell. These birds spent much time keeping their beaks clean and sharp by chewing on hard objects, like pieces of wood.

Adam observed the most unusual use of the beak in a parrot that fed on the ground rather than in trees. This white parrot walked backward while using its upper beak to plow a furrow in the dirt that exposed the roots and bulbs it ate.

Adam noted that the parrots spent much of their time nibbling at their feathers, cleaning them and keeping them in good repair. The birds would provide this service to each other, the companion nibbling feathers a bird could not reach for itself.

Most parrots, unlike other birds, tended to seek bodily contact with companions or mates. Adam frequently saw pairs pressed together, grooming each other. But if an unfamiliar bird of the same variety tried to make contact, the bird whose space was invaded reacted with hostility or fear.

Gorel thought Adam would be happy the day he completed naming the birds of the air. Instead when Adam settled on a name for the final bird kind, he slumped to the ground and great sobs shook his body. Gorel was stunned.

Even Adam didn't understand his reaction. As Adam had studied living creatures year after year, he'd been stimulated intellectually. The animals and the birds had been fascinating, and Adam's awe of Elohim's wisdom, creativity, and power had grown. Yet at the same time Adam was becoming aware of a gnawing ache within. As long as there was work to occupy his mind, Adam held the painful emotion at bay. But when Adam realized that his work for Elohim was done and that there was no more for him to do, he was suddenly overwhelmed with a sense of utter despair.

Adam had nearly finished with his study of parrots when he came across a very large, bright red individual. Its color was so vivid that Adam exclaimed aloud, "What a pretty bird!"

Adam couldn't believe it when he heard the parrot repeat his words: "Pretty bird. Pretty bird."

Adam was thrilled, and a torrent of words poured out of his mouth. The big parrot turned its head quizzically and fixed one bright yellow eye on Adam. Then it repeated again, "Pretty bird."

When Adam realized the parrot was merely mimicking his speech, tears formed in his eyes. As wonderful as the beasts and birds were, they simply weren't suitable companions for a man. Adam lived in a beautiful, ever fascinating garden, with every physical need met. But Adam felt so alone.

And he was.

Adam was completely alone.

18

That evening Gorel sensed Elohim, hallowed be his name, approaching the garden again. As always Elohim adopted a form much like the man's but larger and more glorious. Gorel was concerned when, rather than run to greet Elohim, the man continued to slump on the ground, despondent.

This evening Elohim came to Adam's side and asked gently, "What's wrong, little one?"

Adam didn't raise his head to look at Elohim but whispered softly, "I'm alone."

Still gentle, Elohim probed. "Adam, how can you be alone? What about the creatures I've placed in Eden? You have them."

The man kept his eyes fixed on the ground. "They're all wonderful," Adam admitted. "But they're not like me. I can talk to them, but they can't respond. When I'm excited about something I can't share it with them. I've tried. They just don't understand."

Elohim waited patiently beside the dejected human. Finally Adam looked up hopefully. "Can you help me?"

"I can," Elohim said.

Immediately Adam slumped over, unconscious.

In a deep sleep, Adam was given a vision. He saw Elohim standing on a barren landscape. All around the Creator sterile earth stretched as far as the eye could see. Then as Adam watched, four streams welled up out of the earth, encompassing the barren land. Where they flowed green plants and shrubs appeared. Trees sprang up, rich with foliage, bearing brightly colored fruit. Flowers burst into being, clothing the hills and carpeting valleys and meadows, filling the air with fragrance. Living creatures appeared: livestock and birds of the air and beasts of the field. In a moment of time, a garden came into being—a garden that the man recognized as his home.

Adam's gaze returned to Elohim, and he realized the Creator was peering intently at a patch of clay. As Adam watched, Elohim knelt down and molded the moist earth. In Adam's vision, Elohim gently squeezed and shaped the clay until a human figure was formed. Then Elohim concentrated on shaping the face. When Elohim stepped back, Adam saw himself, lying lifeless on the ground.

Elohim again knelt beside the motionless form. Placing his lips on the lips of Adam's inert body, Elohim blew his own breath into the man. As the breath entered, Adam's chest began to rise and fall. A leg twitched, and an arm moved. Adam opened his eyes and gazed into the eyes of Elohim.

The Creator arose, but the human lay still, breathing deeply. Then the man's eyes closed, and he slept. When the man awoke he was in the place Adam had found himself that first day, and Elohim was gone.

Then the vision was over, and Adam was back in the present with Elohim.

"Do you understand what you saw?" Elohim asked.

"Some of it, Lord," the man answered.

"I fashioned you from the dust of the ground," Elohim explained. "Then I breathed into you the breath of life.

"Because you are fashioned from earth you are flesh, one with nature.

You are like the animals that you named in that you share biological life with them. But then I breathed my own breath into you, and you also became spirit. You and you alone in all animal creation are spirit as well as flesh. You and you alone bear my own image and likeness.

"I designed this garden to help you discover what it means to be like me. In the garden you discovered that you love beauty as I love beauty. You experienced joy in fashioning new things as I have found joy in creating. In the garden you tasted the fulfillment that comes through performing meaningful work, as I find my works satisfying. In the garden you felt compassion for the hurt bird as I have compassion for all living things. In the garden you studied and named the living creatures, entering into a reality only I know completely.

"Every experience you've had in the garden, every emotion you've felt, has helped to reveal your identity. You bear my image-likeness. No animal kind shares that identity.

"Adam, I set you the task of naming the living creatures so that you would discover this for yourself. Despite all you have in common with the animals, you are different from them. To know your true self you must look to me and not to them for your identity.

"You gave names to the animals. I gave you your name. You are Adam, man. You alone are fully a person as I am a person.

"Adam, I give you dominion over the earth, not to exploit it, but to preserve and care for it on my behalf, for the benefit of all living things."

Adam knelt before Elohim. "But, Elohim," Adam complained, "I am still alone."

"Not for long," Elohim replied. "I set you to naming the animals so you would discover your difference from them. But I had another reason as well. I wanted you to realize that you were alone. You needed to feel the depths of your loneliness to appreciate the gift I have for you now."

"What, Lord? What is it?"

"Sleep again, little one," Elohim replied, and Adam fell into a deep sleep. This time there was no vision.

As Adam slept, Elohim took a rib from his body, and from it he fashioned a woman. When Elohim finished, he brought the woman to Adam.

The first thing Adam saw when his eyes opened was the beautiful creature standing beside Elohim. Her form and face were much like Adam's own, and like Adam she was clothed with a warm radiance. All three were cloaked in light; Elohim the brightest, the two humans a reflection of him. Immediately Adam realized what Elohim had done and the nature of his wonderful gift.

"This is now bone of my bone!" Adam exclaimed. "She is flesh of my flesh. She shall be called ishah, woman, for she was taken out of ish, man." And Adam called the woman Eve.

Again Elohim asked the man, "Do you understand what I have done?"

Adam excitedly exclaimed, "You've given me woman. I'm no longer alone!"

Elohim nodded, then went on, "Yes, I've given you woman, as a companion and partner. She, like you, bears my image-likeness. She too is fully a person, with all the gifts and capacities of personhood.

"I've fashioned her from one of your ribs as a memorial. Remember that woman shares your identity completely. I didn't create her from the earth as I did you, or men might infer women are secondary and inferior beings. I fashioned her from your body to impress on you her worth and value. Adam, you are no longer alone—but only if you accept her as your equal will you avoid loneliness.

"Never forget this, Adam. Treasure Eve. Honor her as your partner, the only being suited to share your life in this world."

As Elohim spoke Adam continued to gaze in wonder at Eve, hardly hearing the Creator's words. The next moment Elohim was gone, but neither Adam nor Eve noticed his departure. Their eyes were filled with each other. Then, tentatively but joyfully, Adam reached out and took Eve's hand.

19

As Gorel watched he realized at last why Elohim, praise his name, had made him a watcher. He understood what Elohim wanted the angelic host to grasp. Elohim had taken over the planet that had been the seat of the Satan's power. He had reshaped and repopulated the planet, and then created something entirely and unexpectedly new—human beings.

How amazing, Gorel thought. *Human beings are so frail and vulnerable physically. They're far weaker than any of heaven's angels or any of Satan's demons. Yet despite their frailty, humans bear Elohim's image and thus are immeasurably precious to him.*

The angel had no idea what Elohim's plan was or what part humans were to play in the Creator's invisible war against evil. What Gorel did know, and what he must communicate to the host, was that humans are special to the Creator. Because of this, all the angels must be, and are, committed to humankind's welfare.

Gorel shuddered to think how Satan and his horde of devils would react if they discovered the importance of human beings to Elohim. Gorel had reason for concern, for more than once Gorel thought he'd detected the stench of an evil presence in the garden. A familiar stench that reminded him of his one-time colleague in Elohim's service, the spirit being now called Myrdebaal, who had rebelled against the Creator and now served the Evil One.

20

When Adam awoke, Eve was dancing in the early morning mists. She threw her arms up in the air and spun around and around, her long hair flowing over her left shoulder. Adam lay watching her, his heart filled with contentment. How wonderful Eve was!

The days since Elohim had created the woman had been the best days of Adam's life. Before Eve Adam had explored the wonderful garden Elohim fashioned for him. Adam had been awed by its beauty and captivated by the wonderful creatures that shared it with him. He had found great satisfaction in the work of caring for the garden. Arranging and rearranging the plants to create new patterns had filled a need to have some project, some meaningful work to do. But as Adam had gone about the task of naming the beasts of the field and the birds of the air, he discovered that his life was empty. He had been completely, achingly alone.

Then Elohim gave him Eve. Eve filled the emptiness in Adam's life. She had become the companion and lover he had unknowingly yearned for. Now, as Adam lay still and watched Eve dance, he was content.

That morning Adam and Eve walked hand in hand through the garden. It was her turn to choose the food they'd enjoy, and Adam expected that the first thing she'd choose would be an oblong, orange-fleshed fruit with a thin yellow-green rind. Smiling mischievously Eve led him through a meadow away from the fruit tree, then along a stream that circled the meadow. Finally she escorted him over a rise to approach the tree from behind. Adam laughed with her, delighted with the game and how much she enjoyed playing it. They sat down together under the tree's branches and ate until full, kissing away the juices that ran down each other's faces and dripped onto their bodies.

The kisses led to caresses, and the caresses to embraces. Adam gently stroked Eve's now familiar form, and she responded by delicately trailing her fingernails over his chest and stomach. When they were both fully aroused, they made love, unhurriedly at first and then urgently.

Afterward they lay close together, their bodies touching, enjoying the peace and intimacy that followed physical union. Elohim had predicted it. The two had become one. The act of love both symbolized and strengthened the bond that was becoming tighter and tighter each day that they shared life in the garden.

Adam and Eve had begun another day in Eden.

21

Day twenty-five thousand eight hundred eighty-eight. Adam was eager to share everything with Eve. At first he rushed her from place to place in the garden, showing her his crystal mosaics, his special flower arrangements, the way he integrated the colors and fragrances of living plants. He displayed all these discoveries and achievements proudly. Adam also led Eve from animal to animal, blurting out the name he'd given each and then hurrying her on to see another before Eve had a chance to enjoy the first. Finally Eve protested.

"Adam, wait. I need to go slower. I need to understand."

At first Adam felt hurt. Then he realized that Eve was right. Elohim had let him explore the garden at his own pace. There was no need to hurry Eve. They had all the time in the world.

After that Adam let Eve set the pace. There was so much for her to take in, so much for her to learn. Adam was delighted when he realized that Eve was approaching life in Eden much as he himself had. At first she'd moved slowly, enjoying each new discovery. She sat, as he had, in meadows filled with flowers, entranced by their fragrance and beauty. Eve watched the tiny yellow creatures that moved from blossom to blossom. She noticed that the tiny creatures left the field and that others arrived, and Eve followed one of them to a hive, just as Adam had.

In time Eve wanted to know the boundaries of the garden. She and Adam walked the banks of the four rivers, marveling at the complexity of the ripple patterns as the waters flowed, pausing to watch birds that waded in the shallows or swam on the surface. When Adam showed Eve how he'd constructed a map outlining the garden and used it to mark the location of the special places within it, Eve was excited. She wanted to construct a map too. With only a few suggestions from Adam, Eve created her own map of Eden, gradually entering the locations of places that were special to her.

Adam understood her need for a sense of place, so rather than teaching her his map, he watched as day by day she added features to her own. And all the time he marveled. Eve truly was flesh of his flesh and bone of his bone. As Elohim had said, the two were of one kind, male and female, each gifted with those qualities of personhood possessed by the Creator.

One day Adam and Eve came across what was left of one of the shelters Adam constructed when he first found himself in the garden. The once-supple bamboo had thickened, and the arches that had met just above the man's head now towered some fifty-five feet above the ground. The grasses that the man had woven through the stalks to make a roof were long gone. Not even shreds remained. But Eve noticed the unnatural shape of the bamboo stalks, and Adam explained what he'd done. There was no real need of shelter in Eden. But somehow Adam had taken comfort having a place set aside as his own.

Immediately Eve exclaimed, "Let's make our own shelter! Let's find a special place where we can build it. Maybe we can build it in a meadow or maybe on a hillside. And let's plant the flowers we want all around it!"

Adam was captivated by Eve's idea. Why not build a special place in the garden? A place that was just for them. Their own Eden within Eden.

All that week they walked through the garden, looking for just the right location to build their home. As they walked they passed an open area dominated by a tree with flame-colored leaves and large, delicately tinted red fruit. Adam pointed it out. "That's the only tree like it in the garden. Elohim said that we can eat the fruit of every tree in the garden except that one."

"Why?" Eve asked.

"I'm not sure," Adam replied. "But Elohim said that if we eat that tree's fruit we'll surely die."

"What does 'die' mean?" Eve inquired, puzzled.

"I'm not sure of that either," Adam said, "but Elohim told me not to eat the fruit, so I never have."

The two hurried on, eagerly scanning the landscape for just the right place to establish their home, the mysterious tree forgotten.

22

Late one afternoon, they came across the perfect spot. A crystal clear brook flowed down a gentle slope and wandered through a grassy meadow. Luxuriant fruit-bearing trees framed the broad open area, seeming to set it apart from the rest of the garden. As Adam and Eve crossed the brook, a half dozen of the large, fun-loving cats bounded toward them. The man and woman opened their arms wide, and the great beasts accepted their hugs and hugged them in return, draping great paws over their shoulders as their expressive faces showed their pleasure.

Adam fell to the ground and began rolling over with one of the great cats. A female wrapped her forelegs around Eve and fell with her, wiggling with excitement. Eve laughed delightedly and hugged the tawny-furred creature back, burying her head in the fur of its shoulder.

After greeting each animal, Adam and Eve continued up the hill, the half-dozen great cats walking companionably beside them.

What a wonderful place to be, Eve thought. *What a wonderful home. What a wonderful Creator!*

That evening, as usual, Elohim came to the garden to walk and talk with the man and the woman. They greeted him with joy and delight. "You are so good to us, Elohim!" Eve praised. "We're so happy here. Thank you. Oh, thank you!"

Elohim took each by the hand, and as they walked together, Eve excitedly shared their plan to fashion a special place in the garden.

"How big do you think the shelter should be, Lord? I want it to be large, with a dozen rooms, each formed from a different colored flower. I want one room with walls of blue flowers, those little delicate ones with a dot of white at the center of each blossom. And I want a pink room, with walls covered with those flowers that have dozens of pink blossoms on each stem. And in one room we'll have a mosaic made of crystals. That will be the room where we go to think about you, Elohim, to remember how great and good you are. Would you like that?"

Elohim smiled, and without waiting for him to reply, Eve rushed on. "And outside we'll plant all the different flowers of the garden. We'll make circles of flowers and squares of flowers, with paths in between. And we'll plant different kinds of flowers together, to fill each part of our garden with different perfumes. It will be so special. I can hardly wait!"

When Eve finally paused, Adam asked hesitantly, "Elohim, it's all right, isn't it?"

Elohim reassured him. "It's more than all right, little ones. You look ahead and plan for your future because I too look ahead and plan. The joy you feel in designing your garden home is like the joy I feel in my Creation. I'm pleased with you and with all you do, dear ones. Each emotion you feel, each use of your imagination, your every discovery and plan, helps you know me better. Remember, I made you in my likeness. We are alike in our personhood, children. Look into yourselves, and you will find reflections of me.

"How could I help but be pleased when I see myself in all you do?"

Adam and Eve were silent for a moment, not fully understanding what Elohim meant. But they felt relief. Elohim was pleased with them and with their plans to fashion a home.

For the rest of Elohim's visit, Adam and Eve talked excitedly about their ideas for the structure they intended to build and the garden they intended to fashion. Elohim listened, now and then nodding approval. It was clear that the Creator took delight them. And it was clear that they felt comfortable in his presence.

Before he left, Elohim had one last word for the couple. "Be fruitful," he told them. "Be fruitful and multiply. Fill the earth with your offspring. May the whole earth be like this garden and may every one of your descendants be as you are now."

Later, after Elohim had gone and darkness fell, Adam and Eve lay in each other's arms. "I love you, Eve," Adam said.

Snuggling closer, Eve said, "I love you too, Adam. And I love Elohim. Isn't he wonderful, Adam?"

"I saw him create me, Eve. He gave me a vision." Eve was silent, looking up into Adam's face.

"There was nothing, Eve. Just bare earth. Then Elohim came. He stooped down and began to mold the earth in his hands. As he pressed and squeezed, I could see he was making a human figure. He made its arms and legs and body and head. And then he worked carefully on the body's face. When he stepped back, I saw that what he made was me. But I wasn't alive. I was a lifeless thing made out of clay.

"Then Elohim bent over my body and put his mouth close to mine. I could see his breath as he breathed out. His breath entered my body. Then I opened my eyes. His breath was life, Eve. I was alive and I woke up. I was me!

"Everything I am Elohim gave me. And he tells us that he's made us in his own image and likeness.

"I'm learning, Eve. I'm learning what it means to be a person. And the more I learn about me, the more I learn about him.

"How good he is to us, Eve."

"I know, Adam," Eve agreed. "And the best thing he's given us is each other."

23

As the two rested in each other's arms, an invisible observer slipped away from where they lay. A moment later and a few hundred yards distant, a rushing sound marked the observer's passage from Earth's surface into a cavern hidden deep within the earth called Heart of Darkness. There the spirit being who had been observing Adam and Eve prostrated himself before his Leader, as a half dozen demons gathered around.

"What news, Myrdebaal?" rasped the Leader harshly. "What is he doing on my planet now?" The one called Myrdebaal settled back on his haunches and paused before answering.

Myrdebaal's form seemed to mock Adam's. The demon was about the same height as the human, but misshapen. His skin was like cooled lava, flinty and pitted. Claw-like toes tipped each twisted foot, and hands at the end of the creature's overlong arms featured three twisted fingers and one opposing thumb. Red eyes were set under an overhanging brow, and the jagged points of sharp teeth showed through the thin lips of his mouth. The ragged stumps of two wings hung over Myrdebaal's sloped shoulders, and a dark mist lingered around him, blurring the edges of his form and features.

Each of the others was also shrouded in darkness, and each was misshapen in some way. The deepest darkness lingered around the central figure of the Leader, Lord Satan himself.

Abruptly Satan spoke again. "I said, 'What's he doing on my planet now?' Answer me, Myrdebaal. Report!"

Myrdebaal shrugged. "I don't know what he's doing. I just know what he's done."

"Then tell us," Satan demanded irritably.

"As you know, he's reshaped the Earth. He's planted a garden where your throne stood, and he's filled the garden with peaceful, plant-eating creatures of all sorts."

At mention of the garden where his throne had once towered Satan roared in anger. "A garden! In place of my throne!"

Myrdebaal ignored the outburst and continued. "The strangest thing he's done is to fashion a creature he calls 'man.'

"He made this man-thing out of dirt. He actually molded it himself instead of just speaking it into existence. Because it's made of dirt, the man-thing is weak and powerless. If we could get at it, we could destroy it easily. But we can't get at it. He's set angels all around the place. I can't imagine why they let me through the cordon to observe the man too.

"Anyway, the Enemy seems to care for this man-thing. He gave it the run of the garden, and he visits the man-thing regularly. He even let the man-thing name the other creatures in the garden."

At this Satan exclaimed in surprise, "He actually let the man-thing name the creatures?"

Myrdebaal nodded assent.

"Then," the Leader said thoughtfully, "the man-thing can grasp something of reality and express it in words."

"Apparently so," Myrdebaal continued. "I know that it thinks. It feels. It plans. This man-thing communicates with the Enemy, and I even overheard the man-thing tell its mate that it 'loves' the Enemy."

"There are two of them?" one of the listening demons asked.

"Yes. Apparently the Enemy took some of the stuff from the first man-thing and fashioned another one. A female. I believe the Enemy expects the man-things to mate like the other animals do."

Satan pondered. "What is the Enemy up to? And what place do these man-things have in his plans?"

"There's no way to find that out," another demon growled. "He knows the future, but we have to wait for things to unfold. That's his great advantage."

"That," Myrdebaal added, "and his power."

Satan waved his hand dismissively. "Never mind that," he commanded. "The Enemy has certain advantages, true. But for some reason he's never pressed them. We can only take that as the sign of a weakness we don't yet fully understand.

"In the meantime, we've learned something from Myrdebaal's little excursion. We know that this man-thing is important to the Enemy. I suspect that the Enemy intends to use him in the war. Who knows, man may even be the Enemy's secret weapon."

"So," asked Eyrloc, who was second only to Satan, "what do we do?"

Satan smiled grimly. "We find some way to turn this man-thing against the Enemy. We find some way to use him for our benefit. And if we can't do that, we at least neutralize him as a weapon the Enemy can use against us. Come, Myrdebaal, tell us all you know about 'man.'"

Myrdebaal hesitated and then began to list. "Well, first, the man-thing is an animal, made of planetary dirt. Like any material thing, he can be destroyed. So we might try attacking through its body.

"Second, the man-thing has a first-rate mind. He examines things in his environment and reaches accurate conclusions from what he observes. He can't see into the dimensions where we and the Enemy live. But within the dimensions available to him, he thinks, he learns, he imagines, he plans. He isn't limited to what exists but has the capacity to change what is and, in a sense, to create his own reality."

Satan interrupted. "This strength can also be a weakness. If we can distort his perceptions and make him draw wrong conclusions, we may be able to make him deny the Enemy."

Myrdebaal continued. "Third, the man-thing has emotions. He feels joy and love and gratitude. He displays compassion, and he's been sensitive to his mate since Elohim gave her to him. Worst of all, he loves our Enemy, may his name be blotted out, and he trusts the Enemy."

Before Satan could interrupt again, Myrdebaal hurried on. "The man's emotions may also make him vulnerable to us. Just imagine what might happen if we led the man to love something other than the Enemy. We might be able to twist his emotions so the man-thing desires what he should hate, and hates what he should desire.

"Fourth, the man-thing trusts the Enemy and looks at him as a benefactor. He honors the Enemy as the source of everything that's good in his life. But what if we undermine that trust, so the man-thing becomes suspicious of the Enemy and his motives? Perhaps we can even make the man-thing fear rather than trust the only One who cares anything about him.

"Fifth, the Enemy gave the man-thing a mate, and the man-thing loves her. What's worse, he appreciates her and sees her as an equal partner. Perhaps we can drive a wedge between the man and his wife. If we distort their relationship, who knows what damage that may do to the Enemy's plans?

"Finally, I know the man is a moral being, although his opportunity to make moral choices is limited. The Enemy has placed him in an ideal world where everything is," and here Myrdebaal almost spat out the next word, *good*. He's placed only one restriction on the man-things. They're not to eat from one of the trees in the garden. We need to be sure these creatures see, as we've seen, the benefits of rebelling against the Enemy, and get them to eat the forbidden fruit."

When Myrdebaal finished, the other demons remained silent, pondering what he'd said. Finally Satan spoke, and in his bitter tone, each assembled demon could sense a smoldering anger.

"He's humiliated me.

"He's driven me from the stars.

"He's locked me up on this planet from which I once ruled the universe.

"He let me shape this planet to my liking, and then he took it all away from me! He smashed my planet, killed the creatures I engineered, and sent my world wandering through space. And now he's brought my planet back, refashioned it, and seeded it with new life. He's even fashioned a being with gifts that mimic our own!"

As Satan's fury grew sparks flew from his flushed face. "He's replaced us with this man-thing!" Satan shouted.

"And I won't have it!

"Hear me, host of heaven. Hear me, devils. Hear me, O Enemy of mine. I won't have it! Some way, some how, I'll thwart your plans. I'll find a way to corrupt these man-things you intend to use against me.

"I don't know how.

"But by all that is evil, I will find a way."

BOOK 3
THE DREAM

"I had a dream that made me afraid …"
(Daniel 4:5)

1

Eve stood back, hands on her hips, shaking her head. No, it would never do. It was the wrong shade of blue. Close, but definitely the wrong shade. Adam grinned adoringly. He'd seen that look many times since they'd begun creating their own Eden in Eden. He knew just what it meant when Eve wrinkled her forehead that way and slightly pursed her lips. More work for him.

Not that Adam minded. It was such a delight to please her. And of course he loved working with all the flowering plants from which they were fashioning their home. Besides, Adam knew why Eve wanted everything to be just right. Ever since Elohim had told them to be fruitful and multiply Eve had been thinking about children.

Adam knew that Eve loved each child deeply, even though none had yet been conceived. Adam loved them, too, and often thought about what it would be like when they came. He imagined a girl that would look just like Eve, with flowing hair and soft eyes. He imagined taking the boys with him to explore the special garden where they lived. They might even go across one of the rivers that bordered the garden and explore the wider world.

Eve announced her decision. "They just won't do, Adam. They're not the right shade of blue."

Still grinning, Adam agreed. "You're right, Eve. I'll take them out this afternoon. Tomorrow morning we'll go look for the right ones." Adam was rewarded with a bright smile and a kiss. Then he knelt down by the blue wall and gently dislodged the roots of the flowering vines. Even more gently he disengaged their tendrils from the tall, thin plants that served as a trellis for the vines to climb. He carefully gathered them and carried them up the gently sloping hill on which he and Eve had been constructing their home. A little beyond the top of the hill, Adam found open ground and very carefully, very tenderly, replanted the vines.

It was such a privilege to care for this garden Elohim had fashioned for them. To think that Elohim had given them dominion, making them responsible for the wellbeing of all the plants and animals in Eden. What a joy to serve the Creator doing work that Adam loved.

When each root had been planted carefully in the rich soil and every branch woven into a place where it could grow, Adam walked back toward Eve and home. As he came over the brow of the hill he saw her, seated in her favorite spot beside the clear stream that wandered down the hillside in front of their home. The fingers of Eve's left hand trailed in the water as a breeze moved strands of her blond hair to caress her cheeks. Her gaze was fixed unseeing on the border of fruit trees. She was thinking again of the future, imagining what it would be like when the children came.

How Adam loved her! Eve was Elohim's most wonderful, most precious gift.

That night Eve snuggled close to Adam and listened as his breathing slowed and deepened. Just before Adam drifted off to sleep she whispered, "Adam."

Half asleep he murmured, "Yes."

"Adam, do you think it will be soon? And will it be wonderful?"

"Yes, Eve." His voice trailed off. "Wonderful."

Eve lay quietly beside her sleeping husband. She was tired yet wide awake.

"What will it be like?" she wondered. "Our children. Our children's children. Generations on and on and on." Eve shivered with delight. "What will it be like?"

2

"Gorel." The angel heard the voice speaking within him.

"Yes, Lord," Gorel answered.

"I have a mission for you, Gorel. I want you to carry a dream to Eve.

A dream of what life can be like for her offspring a thousand generations from now."

"Yes, Lord," Gorel responded, thrilled that Elohim had called on him to serve as messenger.

"This is the dream you're to carry, Gorel. This is what it can be like for Eve's children."

3

Eve was aware of tiny, gentle hands bathing her dehydrated body. She heard musical, liquid voices, and in their tone she sensed first concern, and later a confidence that comforted her with the growing assurance that soon she would awake among the strangely loving persons who surrounded her.

At times, when consciousness seemed so close, Eve could feel the soft but buoyant bed that both supported and cooled her body. At other times she felt her head lifted. Her mouth would tingle as she sipped a foaming drink that soothed and strengthened her. And always Eve felt, with silent delight, the flow of cool moist air in constant motion gently caressing her bare body.

Then one day Eve opened her eyes and her vision was clear. She lay still, moving only her eyes at first. She was in an open room ... she supposed it was a room ... with walls covered with a profusion of flowering vines. The flowers were of every color and hue, though blues seemed to predominate. There was no ceiling. High above, the sky was fashioned of luminous, flowing waters. As she stared, Eve felt she might fall at any moment into their welcoming depths. She pulled her gaze away.

Eve glanced around the room. Her impression of openness had been no mistake. The flowering vines left window openings on every outside wall. Turning her head, Eve saw what must have been a doorway, though a very narrow one.

On the farthest wall, a picture hung, and she studied it for long minutes. The picture showed a simple scene of great beauty. A stream bubbled near a structure like the one in which she lay. Squinting, Eve made out a couple standing hand in hand, looking across the stream. Eve felt they were laughing with joyous pleasure at something on the other bank. Ah, there it was! Just across the stream, half hidden in tall grass, two great animals rolled together in play. One by one Eve picked out other, smaller animals. The smaller animals were watching the great beasts and seemed to take as much pleasure in their play as did the couple on the near shore.

The picture seemed so vital, almost living. Eve raised herself on one elbow to see it more clearly, and as she did, she heard a gasp just behind her.

"Mother! Mother! She's awake!"

Eve turned quickly, only to see the flutter of disappearing reddish hair. Suddenly exhausted from her exertion, Eve fell back and was instantly asleep.

4

When Eve awoke again, she found three figures seated on the grass that carpeted her room. She recognized the smallest as her fleeing friend. The girl's blue eyes were open wide with excitement, and she seemed to quiver like a young doe. Eve smiled at her.

"Oh see, Mother! I told you she was awake!" Now the girl could be still no longer but launched herself with a squeal of joy into the arms of the woman. Her mother laughed and returned the embrace, smiling over her daughter's shoulder at Eve.

"Welcome, woman from another world. Like Joyel, we rejoice in your healing."

"I . . ." Surprised at how her voice grated, Eve fell silent.

"Don't try to speak yet," the man said. "You've been very ill. Would you like a drink?"

Eve nodded. The woman held a wooden bowl up to her lips. Eve sipped the frosty, foam-flecked liquid and knew the full delight of the tingling liquid she'd tasted while semi-conscious.

The woman wiped Eve's lips and settled down beside her. *She must be older*, Eve thought. *She's bigger. And the girl called her mother.* But the woman's face was as fresh and unlined as her daughter's, and the form revealed under her short tunic was as lithe.

"My name is Elron," the man resumed. "This is my wife, Frondel. And our daughter, Joyel. You are our guest, for the Elder has charged us with your healing."

Joyel now clapped her hands and smiled happily at her father. "And we've done it, haven't we, Father? She's healed!"

"You've been a good nurse, Joyel. I believe her body is healed. Soon she'll regain full strength. And, I hope, will be whole.

"But come now. Our guest needs to sleep again. Let us leave her to her rest."

Three pairs of gentle hands touched Eve's arm, and then the family withdrew.

I am tired, Eve thought as she shifted on the restful bed. Her right arm brushed her hip as she turned and Eve was surprised. For the first time, she realized that Elron and his family had worn clothing. Yet they had seemed completely unaware of her nudity. They hadn't been trying to ignore it. They hadn't even looked politely away. Everything … the way they looked at her, the tone of their voices … indicated they hadn't even seen her as naked.

5

Eve recovered her strength rapidly. The next day she walked outside with Joyel, clothed in the simple garment all these people wore. Days of inactivity should have left her weak. Yet on that first walk outside Eve discovered her muscles were still supple and strong. Together Eve and Joyel walked several miles, and afterward she felt she could have gone on for many more.

Joyel was tiny. Though perfectly proportioned, she stood only some four feet tall. It had surprised Eve when she realized that Elron and Frondel were only some six inches taller than their daughter. Yet as they walked each day Eve met no one who measured as much as five feet tall. Compared to her, all these people seemed even more slight and delicate than they were.

Yet all the people were beautiful. All were well proportioned, supple, with fresh, clear complexions. They moved with quick springy steps that spoke of a constant joy of living: a joy she could hear in their happy, musical voices. Eve struggled for a word to describe them, but the closest she could come was the word Elron had used when talking of her healing. Whole. These people were whole, with a wholeness that blended inner and outer health.

While Eve was attracted to the people, she was even more impressed by the environment. One afternoon's journey with Joyel brought them to the place where she had been discovered, unconscious. There, in a broad valley, they came upon a marble altar. Lying on it was a blue-white gem set in gold.

"What a beautiful jewel," Eve exclaimed.

"Oh," Joyel explained, "that's Innocence."

"Innocence?"

"That's the jewel's name. I don't know why."

"How long has this altar been here?" Eve asked Joyel.

The girl seemed surprised. "Why, it's been here always. Ever since the Shaping."

"How long?" Eve insisted. "How long ago was that?"

Joyel shrugged. "I don't know, really. I suppose a thousand generations." And then she brightened. "You can ask the Elder. The Elder will know."

"Can you take me to this Elder?"

Joyel reached out and took her hand but shook her head. "The Elder is away now."

Eve held Joyel's hand and looked closely at her. Standing there, gazing at the girl, Eve recognized what she had sensed before but never brought into focus. *Why, these are my children's children a thousand generations from Eden!* But then she began to doubt her insight.

Still, this land was green and rich with life, like Eden. Everywhere streams of water flowed. Everywhere there was life, as flower-covered bushes and trees filled the air with fragrance and blended colorful hues that delighted the eyes with their beauty.

Eve looked up at the sky. It wasn't semi-transparent, as in Eden. It was a watery blue, with various hues weaving and flowing through it. Here too an expanse of water above the planet protected the people from the harsh emptiness of whatever lay above and beyond.

There also had been regular alternation of light and darkness—an alternation that so perfectly matched the rhythms of her own body she had noticed nothing strange. Day followed night. There were gentle dawns and quiet evenings, just as in her garden home.

This land, like Eden, was watered by mists. Here the mist filled the air each evening rather than at night. Eve recalled watching the flowers as the evening mist rose. They'd dipped toward the earth as if to welcome the moisture. Often Eve stepped outside her room and knelt on the grass as the mist rose around her, feeling herself caressed and cleansed and filled.

Suddenly Eve felt a touch of fear. This was Eden, yet not Eden. Were these truly her offspring? Or were Joyel and all these people simply fantasies, momentary creations of her imagination.

"Let's go back," Eve said finally. "Let's go back to your home. I want to speak with your father."

Sensing Eve's mood, Joyel hurried as she led Eve along a new path. This one wound up a rise and into a grove of trees. Delicate rustling leaves flashing with silver arched above them. The path led into the heart of the grove and then turned to trace the edge of a lush meadow. In the center of the meadow were a dozen of the little people, one of whom was playing a flute. This music was new to Eve, similar in some way to the music of nature. These sounds were fuller, more distinct, yet filled with a richness that made each note complex and broad and full.

"Whole," Eve exclaimed. Here even the music was whole.

But it wasn't the individual notes that made this music different. It was the flow. This was celebration music, the epitome of pure joy. Caught up in it, the little people in the glen leaped and danced and laughed, delighting in the joy the musician's flute poured forth.

Joyel began to sway rhythmically by her side, and Eve felt the music working within her too. She fought back an urge to join the dancers and, gripping Joyel's wrist, hurried her along the path and away from the celebration.

They emerged from the grove in an open field edged by a bubbling stream. In it two large animals rested on their stomachs, their legs spread wide. They were so like the fun-loving creatures of Eden, yet different. As Eve and Joyel came near one animal rolled over on its back and stretched like some great lazy cat. Joyel pulled away from Eve to scratch its furred belly. The great beast closed its eyes and expressed its pleasure with a rumbling growl. Joyel laughed and ran to catch up with Eve.

This was another thing to add to Eve's list of questions. Everywhere in the land Eve had seen animals. There were small rabbit-like animals. There were others like lambs, and several kinds of delicate, tiny deer. And then there were the great beasts like the one Joyel had just pleasured.

Why didn't I think of it before? Eve asked herself with growing unease. These animals were like but not quite the same as the animals in Eden. Why did they differ?

Joyel led Eve over a gracefully curving bridge that spanned the bright waters below. Eve examined it closely. The bridge was really a living tree: a living tree that had bowed down to form an arch over the stream. The surface they walked on was flat and slightly roughened to provide secure footing. The tree-bridge had handrails that Eve examined and found were branches growing from the living trunk.

"I've never seen anything in this land that anyone made," Eve realized, "even the picture in my room."

As they hurried on, Eve remembered. She'd returned one afternoon to find Frondel kneeling before the picture. Looking over Frondel's shoulder at the flowing scene, Eve had seen her hostess gently massaging tiny green stems. It was then she realized that the picture was formed by living blossoms growing on minute plants!

"Why, it's alive!" she'd exclaimed.

Frondel looked up at her in surprise. "Of course it's alive. What did you expect?"

After a moment of awkward silence, Eve continued, pointing to the tapestry, "So you grew this?" Frondel nodded, and Eve could sense her satisfaction and fulfillment.

"Yes," she smiled. "It's my gift."

"Your gift?" Eve asked.

Frondel smiled gravely. "Our gifts are first given to us, Eve. Then we give them to others. My gift is to nurture these tiny plants and to love them toward disciplined beauty. This is how I participate in the purpose of the One who shaped all. As with every gift, my gift brings forth a beauty that I can give to all my people."

Eve had not understood Frondel's talk of gifts. After admiring her work and gazing awhile at the living tapestry that presented its scene in such detail, Eve had walked away.

Now, remembering, Eve spoke quietly. "Joyel," she said. "That bridge back there. It's alive, isn't it?"

Eve expected her laughter. Joyel seemed to laugh at everything. Now she laughed in happiness and in surprise. "Of course it's alive. What else could it be?"

"But who made it, Joyel?"

"Made it? Oh, you mean shaped it. I suppose it was Elphendon. I know that's his gift."

Eve nodded. It was just as she had supposed. "And your house? The room where I live? Who shaped that?"

"I know that," Joyel smiled proudly. "My father shaped it. And my mother shaped the picture while you were ill."

They were almost home now. Just over the next rise was the living structure where the family that cared for Eve lived. "Joyel, one last question: What is your gift?"

"My gift? Why, I don't know. I'm not even eighty!" And with this Joyel broke away and ran on ahead. "Mother!" she called, her voice full of pleasure. "Mother! We're home."

6

That evening Eve sat outside with Elron as the refreshing mists rose from the ground to bathe the land and its inhabitants. As the cooling moisture rippled over her body, Eve could feel the doubts of the day wash away. She still had her questions. But the sense of urgency that had surged within her was gone.

"Yours is a land of great beauty and peace, Elron," Eve began.

Elron was silent for long moments, and Eve sensed his quiet satisfaction as he gazed out into the twilight. "It is a land of wholeness, friend. Beauty and peace come from wholeness."

"Elron, in spite of its beauty, it is a land that raises many questions. I must know the answers."

Her companion looked at Eve. "I had hoped the time for questions would wait until the Elder returns. The Elder will be able to answer you fully, if you'd care to wait.

Eve stood. "Yes," she said. "I believe I will wait to talk with this Elder of yours." Eve turned away and went into her room. The living mural glowed dimly with a light of its own, and for a few moments Eve enjoyed the half-visible scene. Then she turned and threw himself onto her bed. The cushioning softness took her and began to massage her muscles with its own delicate touch.

"Why, it's alive too!" Eve realized. "This bed is another shaping, another gift!" Eve sensed a wordless welcome from the living cushions; a welcome she'd not consciously recognized before but now realized had always been there when she lay down to rest.

7

What Eve did not know was that the same night she had entered this world so distant in time from her own, another had entered it too, a stranger.

The stranger had begun exploring the community while Eve was still unconscious. Soon his lean form was familiar everywhere as he poked and probed at the workings of the peaceful society. He could be seen often, squatting down to chat with various men and women, particularly as they practiced their gifts. As the days passed these conversations became more intense, and the stranger seemed increasingly disturbed. His gestures and his tone of voice might even be described as agitated.

The first incident that set the stranger on edge came on a day he paused to watch Lyndel shape her bowls. In his wanderings, the stranger chanced to enter the far side of that grove where later Eve heard the flute player's music. It was a calm morning, as every morning was calm, and the stranger had seated himself on the exposed root of one of the ancient trees. He leaned his back against its luxurious bark and closed his eyes, listening to the leaves that rustled in the breeze and to the brook that sang and bubbled nearby. Soon his alert senses picked up the sound of a woman's humming.

Ever curious, the stranger followed the sound and found Lyndel seated among a screen of bending fern-like branches. As he watched she lovingly caressed one low-hanging branch that bore some kind of heavy fruit. Approaching more closely, the stranger saw the object was not fruit at all, but a heavy, polished, wooden platter.

"Excuse me," the stranger began.

The woman turned her head gracefully and smiled a welcome. "Hello. Oh, you're one of the newcomers."

The stranger smiled back courteously. "I wonder if you could tell me what you're doing?" The stranger squatted beside her, still smiling. "By the way, I'm known as Stranger."

"Oh, excuse me!" The woman laughed, and with a quick easy motion, she sat back on her heels, wiped her hands on her tunic, and stretched out both to the stranger. "My name is Lyndel. And as for what I'm doing, why, I'm shaping bowls."

"Bowls?"

"You know," Lyndel nodded. "The bowls we eat and drink from. You must have eaten from them."

"You mean you grow your bowls?" the stranger asked.

Lyndel answered with that innocent surprise, which, over the next weeks, Stranger would find in all the little people. "Of course. How else would we shape bowls?"

The stranger was too shrewd to answer that question yet. Instead he encouraged Lyndel to explain. His courteous questions and words of appreciation drew from the little woman an explanation of shaping much like the one Eve later heard from Joyel.

The little people believed that the One who shaped them and the world gave each person a gift. The gifts enriched life in the community and were a source of great personal joy and fulfillment. When a man or woman reached maturity, his gift emerged as something deep within him responded to something in nature. Attraction grew into a calling, and from that time on, much of the individual's time was committed to his or her work of shaping.

As the stranger listened to the unsuspecting Lyndel's explanation, several strategies occurred to him. Yet he continued to express pleasure and wonder at the happy structure of Lyndel's world. And he praised the beauty of the bowls growing on the branches she tended.

The bowls were beautiful. Some were broad and almost flat, like platters. These, Lyndel explained, were for bread or fruits. She showed the complex pattern she was shaping into one of them by guiding the fern tree to lay down alternating layers of light and dark pigments. Other bowls were cup-like, and some had fluted edges for drinking. As each bowl came to maturity, it took on a polished glow that highlighted the design Lyndel had guided the tree to create.

"Are there many gifts among your people?" the stranger finally asked.

Lyndel, flushed pleased by the outsider's obvious appreciation and filled with the joy that always came as she worked with her gift, laughed happily. "Oh yes. Many. The shaping of pictures. Of bridges and paths. Of homes for newlyweds. Of beds and chairs. The shaping of grain fields and of clothing. Of flutes and trumpets. Why, there are thousands of gifts."

The stranger nodded and then asked, thoughtfully, "Lyndel, which gifts are most important?"

"Important?"

"Surely your gift is a vital one. Without your gift, people wouldn't have cups to drink from or bowls to hold their food. Your gift must be more important than, say, the shaping of a flower bed. Flowers may be beautiful, but they're hardly necessary for life."

Lyndel's forehead wrinkled in thought. "I don't understand. Are you suggesting that beauty isn't necessary to life?"

"Beauty is important, of course. But life could exist without flowers. Life couldn't exist without food and drink. So what you do, shaping bowls, is necessary. And that makes it more important."

Lyndel shook her head. "I can't imagine life without flowers. So how can you say my gift is more important?"

"Think about it, Lyndel," the stranger suggested with a friendly smile. "As you meet others these next few days, consider each one's gift. See if you can't come up with reasons some gifts are more important than others. And," the stranger added, almost as an afterthought, "though I can't quite imagine it, there might even be gifts that are more important than your own."

With these words and another smile, the stranger stood and walked away through the trees. He looked back once over his shoulder. Lyndel, her chin cupped in both hands, was frowning over his words. Stranger's smile lost its hint of friendship and turned sardonic and cruel.

8

Several days later Stranger returned to the grove. He stood in the shade of the tree where he'd rested before and listened. Yes, Lyndel was there. She was humming that same innocent and happy tune. With a look of irritation that disappeared as he approached, Stranger came to stand beside the fern tree. He waited there silently and watched Lyndel work. Though she glanced up at him, she did not pause.

Finally Stranger asked quietly, "Have you thought about our conversation?"

Lyndel smiled up at him guilelessly. "Oh yes. And I talked it over with my husband. It was a very new idea to us."

The stranger nodded. "It's important to explore new ideas. When there's only one way of thinking, there's no telling what a person may miss."

"Your idea about some gifts being more important than others was interesting, I suppose. But I think it was more troubling than interesting."

Stranger succeeded in looking surprised. "Troubling? I hoped it might prove exciting."

Lyndel shook her head. "No, it wasn't exciting. In fact, it upset me."

Stranger now looked concerned. "I'm sorry if what I said upset you. Can you tell me why?"

Lyndel nodded. "I finally figured it out, with Edron's help. You see, it wouldn't be the same." Lyndel's voice trailed off, and she seemed to struggle for words. Stranger waited patiently, encouraging her with a nod.

"Well," she began hesitantly. "Now our gifts make us happy. And they make life better for others. If someone thought his gift wasn't as good as mine, how could he feel the same joy in his? As it is we each find joy in our gift, and we find joy in the gifts of others too. So every gift is a source of joy, for the person exercising it and for others. How then can one gift be more important than another?"

Stranger nodded in apparent agreement. "That certainly is one way to look at it, Lyndel. But what if one person really is more important than others? Shouldn't part of his joy be found in understanding his significance? And in others acknowledging that he's more important?"

Lyndel dismissed the idea. "Oh, but you see, now we're each important. I'm using the gift the Shaper gave me. I am who I was intended to be, and that makes me important enough. And, since everyone else is who he or she was intended to be, why, everyone is important in the same way! Why should we trade a way of life in which everyone is important for a way in which some might be important, but others aren't? Oh no. It may be an interesting idea, that some gifts are more important than others. But it can't be true."

The stranger was far too shrewd to argue. He simply acted as if he were persuaded and took a new tack. "Lyndel, do you like to hear new ideas?"

Lyndel shook her head thoughtfully. "I don't believe I do. But it's all right if you have another idea to share."

"This is an important idea," the stranger said, going on as if Lyndel had responded enthusiastically. "In my world there are many who would see your life here as one of prisoners in a cell."

"What are 'prisoners,' and what's a 'cell'?"

The stranger explained. "A prisoner is a person who has no freedom of choice. A cell is a room in which a prisoner is kept. The cell permits the prisoner only a few choices, so that his freedom is limited."

Lyndel nodded as if she understood, so the stranger continued. "I've noticed that here in your land everything is controlled by the rhythm of the world around you. For instance, how long does it take you to shape a bowl?"

"That depends," Lyndel said quickly. "It may take only a year or two for a small bowl or a simple pattern. For a platter, or a complex pattern, like that one over there, it might take as many as ten or twelve years."

The stranger nodded. "That's what I suspected. And that's why some would say you are prisoners. You are prisoners of your environment, of the slow pace of life and growth. You have never taken control of nature, and so you are nature's slaves."

As the stranger had expected, this argument was completely beyond Lyndel. "But I'm a part of my environment," she said puzzled. "I grow with the tree and with the bowls. I don't feel like a prisoner."

"You spoke of a Shaper," Stranger went on. "Was he part of the pattern of nature? Or did he take a raw universe and impose the pattern on it?"

"He shaped all things," Lyndel affirmed, "of course."

"You call the use of your gifts 'shaping.' I suppose that means you see using your gifts as something like the activity of the Shaper himself?"

"Oh yes. Our gifts are part of his Shaping."

"But that's my point. Your shaping isn't at all like the first shaping. The Shaper determined the conditions under which you live. But you don't determine conditions. You conform to conditions that someone else has established. That, in my world, means you have surrendered control. You are prisoners without freedom, in a cell which may be beautiful but which is nevertheless a prison."

The stranger left her then. But during the next weeks he repeated this argument over and over with others in the cavern world.

One man for whom Stranger had great hopes was called Elchron. Elchron's gift was the shaping of the stones used by people to grind grain for bread. His gift was exercised by guiding the flow of waters, first to collect grains of sand and then as an abrasive current flowing around stones carefully balanced in a stream. The sand and water gradually wore away the stone, and such was Elchron's gift that over fifteen or twenty years perfectly matched upper and lower milestones were formed.

Stranger began with Elchron as he always did, by listening carefully and praising the man's skill. The stranger spoke of the difficulty of shaping stone with living waters, a task much more difficult than shaping living plants. His admiration seemed boundless, and soon he mentioned other uses to which Elchron's gift of shaping with water might be put. In particular the stranger focused on the use of water to power machines.

Stranger told the wondering Elchron how waterpower might be used to grind grain for bread. He drew diagrams to show how water might power a sawmill that could cut tree trunks into strips to replace the live bamboo which served as framework for the people's latticed homes. In all his teaching the stranger stressed the idea that power was the key to control of the environment.

"At last, Elchron, you will be like the Shaper," the stranger explained with enthusiasm. "You will take control of your world. You'll no longer just be part of nature; you will be above it, just as the Shaper is above all."

Elchron listened. And for several days the stranger was convinced that he had finally won a convert. But his hopes were crushed one late afternoon as he repeated his arguments in Elchron's home, seated at a meal with the man and his wife, Dordel. Dordel's gift was with the animals of the land, and she was always surrounded by the loving creatures. She guided them through birth, supported them in their infrequent illnesses, and when it came time for one of the animals to die, Dordel would calm and gentle it through its last hours.

"You must have seen the possibilities for animals to help humans with their work," the stranger commented to her during the meal. That was his mistake.

"Helping humans?" Dordel asked in surprise.

"Of course. For instance, animals might be harnessed to prepare ground for planting. Why, there are a hundred ways animals serve humans in my world."

The explanation shocked Dordel. "Here we serve animals," she said stiffly. "Your world must be a dark and terrible place."

The stranger should have seen his blunder. Instead he pressed on. "Aren't humans a higher creation than animals? Aren't humans more like the Shaper than they?"

"Of course," Dordel shot back.

"Then you are supposed to rule over them. So rule! Exercise your authority and take control of this world of yours. Stop being prisoners of the creation!" These words were uttered with evangelistic fervor, and again Stranger failed to note Dordel's reaction. But then the antagonism in her eyes dissolved in sudden understanding, and she laughed, reaching over to rest her hand on Elchron's knee. "Don't you see, Elchron? Why, this stranger doesn't understand 'rule'!"

Turning to Stranger, she explained sympathetically, in a tone of voice the frustrated visitor thought might better be used with some small and backward child. "You think that 'rule' means 'use' or 'control.' It's true that the Shaper trusts us to rule his world. But to him and to us, 'rule' means 'guard' or 'protect' or 'enrich.'

"We don't try to warp his creation to other ends than his, Stranger. Instead we find joy in serving all life, in bringing all living things to fulfillment in beauty. You've lost sight of beauty. And you've missed the meaning of rule. So whatever you have to say, there is nothing that we can possibly hear."

Although Stranger kept on trying to share his "new ideas" with the people, he found no one he could convince. His frustration and his agitation grew daily, and by the time the Elder was due to return, the stranger was more than ready to quit the land of peace and its infuriatingly naive people.

9

Eve awoke on the grassy carpet that served as the floor of her room in Frondel and Elron's home. She rolled over on her back and looked up through half-shut lids at the sky. It was early, and the glowing light was strengthening in the land's strange dawn. As it brightened, the light illumined layer upon layer of the flowing heavens, and it seemed to Eve that she could trace sky currents mixing and separating in luminous beauty, touching one another gently with ripples of silent joy and then flowing on, each in its own course.

How like this land, she thought. *It's simple on the surface, but underneath it flows with complex patterns and infinite variety.* Consciously she let herself be drawn into the interplay of the waters above, opening every sense as if she might not only see but also hear and touch and even smell their joyful tumbling. As the light brightened the patterns receded, and Eve felt the giddy sensation of falling, as though she were about to fly upward and be lost in the blue-green billows above her.

Eve closed her eyes and kept them shut as she sat up, envisioning her surroundings. When she opened her eyes she'd see the mural on the far wall. The living bed would be in one corner. And all would be enclosed by interwoven plants that served as walls. She breathed deeply. The air was fresh with the scent of flowers. It was subtly different from the scent of yesterday, and she knew that the flowers that grew on the bushes and trees beyond her room would have a slightly different arrangement than the day before. What a wonderful place. If only these truly were her children's children and this was their world!

As she sat there with her eyes closed, feeling more and more thankful, she felt a touch on her arm and heard Joyel's voice. "Eve, are you all right? Are you praising?"

Eve opened her eyes and turned. "I'm all right, Joyel. What do you want?"

At that moment Frondel and Elron joined them, and Elron confirmed her guess. "Come, Eve. This is the day of celebration, and the Elder will return to share it. I believe your questions will be answered. Will you join us?"

The four set off down the hill, the three little people almost running to keep up with Eve. Eve tried to slow her pace for them, but the morning's musing had lent a greater urgency to her desire to meet the Elder.

Everyone was moving toward the great valley where the jewel Innocence rested on the marble altar. As they neared the groves that rimmed the valley, the merging streams of individuals became a crowd, and Eve was amazed at the multitude. She'd seen no crowding in the land. People she had come upon had never gathered in groups larger than twenty, and she'd supposed that the land's population must be small. Yet here were lines of men and women and children streaming in from every direction.

As they neared the valley, Eve became aware that the people were singing, not loudly, but each one quietly, as if to him or her self. Where the lines converged the quiet music swelled. By the time the four reached the rim of the valley, Eve realized that a complex, swelling hymn filled the air. She could make out no words. Yet Eve recognized the sound as praise. Like everything else in this world of simple things that were in fact complex, many themes were woven through the music. Eve could hear joy, awe, and thankfulness. Wonder, confidence, security, and love were there too. Perhaps the dominant theme was love. Love as intimate companionship. Love as the comfortable assurance of belonging. Love as appreciation for acceptance.

As she listened Eve felt a hunger grow within her. She wanted to go home to Adam. She was convinced. This was the world Elohim intended for their offspring. How excited Adam would be when she shared with him this vision of a future time.

Then the foursome emerged from the trees, and Eve was stunned to see the valley packed with a great multitude. *Why,* Eve thought, *there must be hundreds and hundreds of thousands of these people.* And she'd imagined there were a few thousand at most!

The vast crowd that filled the valley was seated in orderly rows. The people sat with arms linked and eyes closed, swept up in the numinous experience. Yet there were open corridors between the packed bodies, and Frondel and Elron, trailed by Joyel, led Eve down one of these. As they passed through the crowd, Eve saw ecstatic expressions on every uplifted face, as if the shared worship brought unutterable joy.

When at last they reached the center of the valley, Eve was disappointed. Where was the Elder? Surrounding Eve was only the sea of the unlined, radiant faces of this ever-young race.

The hymn continued for over six hours without a break. Then Eve sensed a change in the music. The themes of love and worship receded, and the volume fell. Now the music spoke simply of some coming joy. And now too fragments of laughter and conversation could be heard.

Eve looked around and was surprised to see that the multitude was leaving, streaming off in every direction. Eve shifted as though to rise, but felt Elron's restraining hand on her arm. He looked over at her, and when he shook his head, her lips silently forming the question, *The Elder?* Elron nodded, and Eve settled back.

Now, in an amazingly few minutes, everyone was on the move. Within half an hour, only a few in the front row of the great congregation remained. Finally Eve spoke up. "When will the Elder join us? Are we to meet him today, or not?"

Frondel whispered to her, "Be patient, Eve. The Elder is here with us now."

Finally the last of the singing multitude swung off beyond the hills and groves enclosing the valley. It was then that a woman came to stand before Eve. When she spoke, Eve recognized a rich maturity in her voice that belied her fresh face and bright young eyes.

"I thank you for your patience. And I regret that it has taken so long for me to prepare for our conversation."

Eve rose, towering over the tiny form and blurted out in surprise, "You? You're the Elder?"

The woman nodded. "For some three hundred years I have been called Elder and have served our people. But now," and she turned to her countrymen, "I must thank you for your care of our guest. Please wait for us in the grove of celebration."

So it happened that the others slipped away and Eve sat down with the Elder of the land.

10

All through the long warm afternoon, they sat together on the grass and talked. At first the Elder, who preferred to be addressed by her name, Ellenel, gently questioned Eve. Eve held nothing back, even sharing her suspicion that this world was populated with her descendants a thousand generations after Creation. When Eve's story was told and the last of the Elder's questions answered, Ellenel responded.

"I suppose it's possible. We know of a first pair that the Shaper created and placed in a beautiful garden. We honor him as our Creator, and we honor them as our first parents. But it's hard to believe that you, Eve, are the first mother. How can you explain your presence here now, so many thousands of years later?"

"I can't explain it, Ellenel. Except that perhaps this is a gift from Elohim. You see, Adam and I haven't had our first child yet. And I've been wondering about the future, imagining what it will be like to have children and what it will be like for their children and their children's children. It would be just like Elohim to give me this gift. He's so good to us."

Ellenel was silent for a time. "Perhaps."

"But now, friend, it is almost evening. And I must ask a peculiar boon of you."

Eve was impressed by her seriousness. "What do you want?"

"Come, please," Ellenel asked, rising. "I'll tell you on the way. It's already late, and we must hurry."

As they walked rapidly, Ellenel continued. "Eve, you know that we are a peaceful people. We are committed to harming no living creature." Eve nodded agreement. "Tomorrow," Ellenel said, "the Lifewind will blow. When the Lifewind blows, the desires of every living thing flower. Our problem is that we don't know how that will affect you. Thus you will understand that my request conceals no hidden danger, but truly is for your benefit."

Eve nodded, noncommittally.

"For this reason I must ask that you accept the binding of your limbs to restrain you from harming us or yourself."

Eve was taken back by Ellenel's request. She resisted the thought of being bound. Still, she expected no physical harm from these people. And Ellenel was obviously worried.

"What is this Lifewind?" Eve asked, temporizing.

"The Lifewind," Ellenel smiled up at her, "marks the beginning and the end of our year. As the time for the Lifewind approaches, crops are planted. When they blossom and all is ready throughout the land, then the Lifewind comes. It dances among us, tossing the flowers and mixing their pollens in a great golden cloud that fills the air.

"When the Lifewind blows, all living things are moved to joyous mating. For that whole day each of us is caught up in delight, the married giving joy to each other, the children dreaming of adulthood, and the old, like myself, remembering. This is why we gather at the altar each year just before the Lifewind blows, to express our praise to the Shaper for his gift of love."

"You mean," Eve asked, "that you only know love one day each year?"

"Oh no," Ellenel answered. "We know love each day of our lives. But this particular expression of love is experienced only when the Lifewind blows. Love, and our pleasure in the company of our mates, overflows all through the year.

"Tell me, Eve. Haven't you yet learned that joy looked forward to, and joy remembered, can be as precious as the fleeting moments of actual experience?"

Eve pondered Ellenel's request. She did love these little people and respect them.

"Ellenel, I understand your concern. I can't predict how I might react to the stimulation of your Lifewind. I only know the delight of love as Adam and I enjoy it. So I will agree to your request."

Ellenel released a sigh of relief. "Thank you, Eve, for understanding. But come. We're near the place of Celebration."

The two moved into another valley. It was nearly dusk, but the sky remained bright and the air was definitely warmer than usual. There was a new scent in the air, and the breeze had quickened. The little people in the grove seemed more alive and vital than ever, and their eyes literally shone. Husbands and wives stood close to each other, exchanging open glances and gentle touches, while the unmarried and the children smiled dreamily as though sensing in the others a special blessing that would be theirs someday and that, until then, satisfied them with rich expectation.

The two moved together across the valley to a leafy bower of vines, bright with blossoms that hinted at wines pressed from purple grapes. Eve noticed that the vines were sturdy, thick with age and strength.

There a number of men and women were waiting whose gift was the shaping of the vines. Quickly one looped the strongest vines around Eve's limbs, and as the little people gently stroked the vines, Eve felt them tighten on her arms and legs. They squeezed, but not uncomfortably. She tried to move and found she could not.

Eve felt gentle hands lift up her head, and she closed her eyes. Her eyes did not open again until the night had passed, and the new day had come.

That new day was unlike any Eve had experienced. The air was golden, and as Eve's vision cleared, she saw the cause; myriads of flecks of shining yellow tossing and swirling in the dancing wind. The flowers on the vines and trees around her were fully open, their petals fluttering with excitement as they were caressed by the wind. A short distance away, Eve saw a couple walking close together. The wind tossed the woman's hair; it billowed like a shining cloud, flowing around both their shoulders as they strolled with arms linked around each other's waists. They paused to embrace and then they sank gently together into the grass and out of sight.

Then Eve became aware of her own surging emotions. The couple had seemed enraptured, and yet calm. Eve was anything but calm!

Blood pounded in her temples as her every muscle corded and tensed. The warm air suddenly felt unbearably hot and the pressure of pounding blood focused lower and lower. Eve's lungs were inflamed. Her heart pounded, pumping rushing blood through every vessel in her body.

Eve twisted in her bonds. Her body arched. Her shoulders strained, and her knees drove powerfully up toward her chest. She felt the vines bite into her flesh, but she was driven now by all-consuming desire. She cried out then for Adam.

"Adam! Adam!

"Make love to me, Adam. Make love to me now!"

11

Then Eve was awake.

She felt Adam's strong arms around her. She smelled the familiar fragrance of his body and was aroused even more. "Now, Adam," she urged. "Now!"

Eve surrendered to her passion, releasing her pent up desire. When she was finally exhausted, Eve murmured, "Oh Adam. How I've missed you. Did you miss me too?"

Adam laughed. "Miss you?"

"I've been gone so long, Adam."

"Gone?" Adam laughed again. "Why, you've been right here with me every day. And," Adam smiled, "every night."

"I haven't been gone?" Eve asked in surprise.

"I haven't had you out of my sight for more than an hour, ever. Eve," Adam said seriously, holding her tightly to him, "I couldn't live without seeing you. Even for an hour. You're so precious to me."

Convinced, Eve relaxed in his arms. "It must have all been a dream, then," Eve said wonderingly. "All a dream."

"Tell me about it in the morning," Adam smiled. "Right now I'm tired. You've worn me out, and it's still the middle of the night."

As they lay together, Eve realized she was exhausted too. In moments both of them had fallen asleep.

12

Eve slept late the next morning. The day was bright when she awoke to find Adam sitting nearby, watching her.

Eve stretched luxuriously and smiled up at her husband. "How long have you been watching me, Adam?"

"Not long, Eve. Not long enough. I love to watch you while you sleep." Adam grinned. "I love it when you wake me up in the night too."

Eve smiled in response. "Adam, that was part of my dream."

Adam laughed aloud. "Then you should dream more often."

"No," Eve said, reaching out to take his hand. "I'm serious. I had the most wonderful dream."

Adam lifted her up. "Come on. Let's pick some fruit. You can tell me about your dream while we eat."

Later, as they sat by the stream and ate the fruit they'd picked, Eve told Adam her dream. "I dreamed I was in a beautiful land filled with wonderful people. I stayed in one family's home. They thought I'd been sick, and they nurtured me back to health. At first I didn't know where I was or who the people were. Then I realized I was in a world like Eden, and that these people were our descendants.

"Adam, what a wonderful future our children have! They'll learn how to guide flowering vines to make their homes, just like we're trying to do. They'll guide tiny flowers to create beautiful pictures. Each of them will have a special gift for what they call 'shaping.' Everything they use, the bowls they eat from, the wonderful couches they sleep on—everything will be shaped from living, growing things.

"And they're so content. Husbands and wives and one or two children live together so happily. You can sense the joy in their voices. And the music! They have instruments they grow, and they make the most wonderful sounds. And Adam, they worship Elohim—they honor him as the

Shaper who made all things—and when they gather to praise him you can hear the love they feel for him. Just as we love him, Adam.

"They remember us too, Adam. They call us the first couple. They call you the First Father, and I'm the First Mother.

"Husbands and wives only make love once a year, when something called the Lifewind blows." Seeing Adam's brows raise, Eve reached out and put her hand on his arm. "I didn't like that part either, Adam. But Ellenel—she's the Elder who leads the people—Ellenel says they find satisfaction in remembering past times of love and looking forward to the next. Don't worry, Adam," she added anxiously. "We can still make love whenever we want."

Adam smiled at her. "I know. We will. But tell me more about our children's children. Are they truly happy?"

For the next few hours Eve went on about the wonderful land where their offspring would live and how happy they would be. Adam listened eagerly to each detail, as filled with wonder as Eve.

When at last Eve had told Adam everything she could remember, the two sat quietly side by side. Awed, Adam took Eve's hand in both of his. "How good Elohim is to us, Eve. Show me how our children's children praised and thanked him."

Eve closed her eyes. She could picture the worshipping multitude. As the image in her mind became more clear, Eve could almost hear the notes they were singing. Uncertainly Eve began to hum. She could hear the notes more clearly now. Then in a clear voice Eve began to sing and praise with the unseen worshippers.

As she sang, the music of the land she'd visited in her dreams seemed to swell up around the first couple. She sang more confidently, and as she sang, Adam heard thousands of voices raised in praise. Adam opened his mouth, and to his surprise found himself singing with Eve and the hidden multitude of their offspring to be. His voice, a rich baritone, blended perfectly with Eve's as the music carried their joy in the Lord up into the heavens.

There the angels of the host picked up the hymn. They too sang. For hours the music swelled, ever richer and fuller, as the voices of angels who had seen Elohim create the universe joined with Adam and Eve and with the generations of their offspring yet unborn, praising the wisdom, the grace, the goodness, and the love of Elohim.

13

"Gorel."

"Yes, Lord."

"I have a task for you. I want you to carry another dream to Eve."

"The last dream was so beautiful, Lord," Gorel blurted out.

"This dream is a warning, Gorel. It is not a beautiful dream. But Eve and Adam need to understand. What the future may hold isn't necessarily what the future does hold. The future for their offspring depends on a choice they will make. A choice they will make very soon."

"And the dream, Lord?"

"The dream is a warning to help them make the right choice. If they heed it."

"I'll take the dream to Eve, Lord."

"Here is the dream you're to carry, Gorel. Take it to Eve now, and warn my beloved children."

14

"Eve! Oh Eve!

"I'm so glad you've come back! We've been praying for hundreds of years that you'd return."

Eve peered up at the figure bending over her. It looked like … it was! Ellenel!

"But … but I just left, Ellenel. The Lifewind was blowing, and then I woke up in Adam's arms. You were a dream, Ellenel. Just a dream."

The old Elder leaned closer and gripped Eve's shoulders. "Mother Eve, it's been over three hundred and fifty years since you visited us. I'm so thankful the Shaper sent you back to us. We need you, Eve. We need you desperately."

Disoriented, Eve sat up. She gazed up at the blue-green sky-ocean high above and then at the meadow where she'd first heard the music of the land. Just beyond was the bridge shaped from a living tree that she and Joyel had crossed. Eve took a deep breath, and her lungs were filled with the unmistakable fragrance of the flowers that grew so profusely in the land of the little people. These were her offspring. Once again she was with her children's children's children.

"This isn't a dream?" Eve asked. "I thought you were a dream."

Ellenel frowned. "A dream? It may be a dream for you, Mother Eve. But for us it's all too real."

The little Elder's words stunned Eve. What had gone wrong? What had happened to the people of this happy, blessed land?

"Come," Ellenel said, taking Eve's hand to help her up. "Come, Mother Eve, and I'll tell you what's happened since you left us."

15

"Ours is a gentle land," she began. "It has remained essentially unchanged since the day it came from the hand of the Shaper. Each succeeding generation has found peace and fulfillment in the way of life he established and rejoiced in the privilege of enriching each other and the land with our gifts.

"Our memories span many generations, and each new generation senses the life-bond that links us with those who have gone before. In our entire history only one event is remembered with sorrow. That event is the loss of Innocence, the gem you saw in the valley where we gather to worship.

"From the beginning, Innocence rested on the marble altar there, a gift the Shaper gave us. The jewel represented our freedom to make choices. We have never been prisoners of his pattern. We've always been free to accept or to reject a life within the framework of his design. Any of us could destroy our way of life by removing Innocence from the altar. From that moment, the threads that weave the pattern of our lives would begin to unravel. We would be released from his way and free—or forced—to weave new patterns of our own.

"For hundreds of generations my people embraced our world and found fulfillment in the way of life the Shaper gave us. We looked at the gem that offered release from his way, and we realized that removing Innocence would bind us, not free us. So for uncounted thousands of years the jewel lay untouched on the altar in the valley. It was unguarded. Anyone might take it up. No one did. We were all too fulfilled within his pattern to even consider such an act.

"Then a few days before you joined us a stranger appeared. We took the stranger into our homes as we took you in. The stranger began to question our people. He tried to sow doubt about the loving intent of the Shaper.

"He spoke of subduing nature, of turning lower forms of life to our service. He drew plans for mighty cities, with towers that reached up to touch the sky. He explained how we could wrest what he called 'metals' from the earth and, by burning trees, mold the metals to construct his towers.

"He spoke of accomplishments not measured by personal growth and fulfillment but measured by comparing ourselves with others. Yet the greater his enthusiasm, the more horrified we became and the more sure we were of the Shaper's wisdom and love. We would not exchange the life we loved for the stranger's world where living things are enemies to be subdued and where trees and animals are grown only to be murdered.

"The stranger wouldn't listen when we tried to explain. He grew angry when we refused to take the path he urged. In time we began to run or hide when we saw him coming.

"Then one day he came upon the altar. He stood for a moment gazing at Innocence. I suppose he must have recognized it for what it was, or at least he sensed its significance. He grasped the jewel and hung it on a chain around his neck.

"The jewel seemed to make him mad. For days afterward he threshed about in the forests, screaming and uprooting plants. When he emerged he smashed our homes and destroyed the products of our gifts. During those days he began to change.

"He gradually lost his human form. His head and his neck lengthened. His shoulders narrowed and his arms pressed tight against his sides. We watched as his body gradually stretched itself taller and taller until he traveled awkwardly, weaving and undulating as he struggled for balance. A time came when he could no longer hold himself erect. He fell and clung to the earth, slithering across the grass.

"He was desperate to keep the jewel, and as he now had no neck or shoulders, he used its chain to bind the gem tightly against his forehead. Within hours, the blue gem had buried itself there. Humped ridges formed around the jewel till it peered out like another eye, flashing and cold.

"Finally the transformation was complete. The stranger's theft of Innocence had taken an awful toll. The stranger had become the Iceworm, and wherever he went he left a trail of frozen slime that withered the grass and brought death to the flowers. Everywhere he traveled in our lands, our people followed, committing their gifts to nursing back to wholeness the living things his touch destroyed. At last the Iceworm left us. He slithered off into the jumbled rocks and cliffs that rise hundreds of miles from our valley.

"With the Iceworm gone, our lives returned to normal. We again knew the joy of living within the pattern the Shaper's love designed for us. We told our children the story of the Iceworm, and when we did, we cried together for that misshapen creature who had turned aside from his destiny as a man.

"And then, too late, we learned the terrible fate to which the Iceworm had condemned us. As Stranger, he had struggled to corrupt the Shaper's pattern from within. He had urged our people to reject the Shaper's plan. And he failed. Now as the Iceworm he possessed the dead rock walls beyond the horizon, and there, unchecked, he writhed tirelessly back and forth along the cliffs. Everywhere he went he spread his trail of ice.

"Mother Eve, during the past centuries, the Iceworm has surrounded our land with glaciers. And they are growing. He is determined to choke out the life in our land with his deadly cold.

"It was too late when we discovered his plan. A pall had settled over the outer lands where Iceworm builds his ramparts of death, encircling us. Over the centuries as the glaciers have thickened and the cold pressed in on our land, plants and animals have begun to change.

"At first we sent expeditions out into the gathering cold, guided by the flashing blue light of Innocence that marks the Iceworm's location. But none of us have reached him. We were not made, Eve, to live in any world other than the one the Shaper intended.

"Finally, after many attempts, we no longer tried. Our land still supports its millions. The sky flows overhead. Trees reach up their arms to heaven and flowers bloom, and each year the Lifewind blows. But tirelessly, relentlessly, the Iceworm continues to strengthen the wall of cold. Slowly, imperceptibly, the cold is tightening a noose that will one day choke out our life.

"Oh, it will take many, many generations. But now our joy is mingled with sadness, for we know that the flow of beauty that came from the Shaper's hand will one day cease and all that speaks of love and joy in our universe will be frozen in eternal death."

16

The Elder's soft voice had grown sad as she spoke of the end of her world. For a moment now her head rested on her chest as if in resignation. Then she looked at Eve and resumed with a note of hope. "At least, we supposed there was no hope. But then we remembered you."

Here the Elder paused and fixed Eve with her bright and penetrating gaze. "I believe that your coming here the first time was planned. We lack the strength to resist this stranger. But you, with your strength and youth, fresh from the Creator's hand, may be able to conquer him and change our destiny.

"And so I beg you, Mother Eve. Come with me into the cold. Come with me to confront the Iceworm and recover our lost Innocence."

Stunned, Eve's gaze fell. She felt so inadequate. Yet surely she had been brought back to the land for a purpose. Looking compassionately at Ellenel, Eve asked simply, "How soon can we leave?"

Ellenel sighed with relief. "When we first found you, I gave instructions for supplies to be prepared," Ellenel replied. "We can leave at dawn tomorrow."

17

The next morning Eve and Ellenel stopped by the ovens. These were found in a lushly tropical area Eve hadn't visited before. The two women wound their way down into a small canyon and through a tumbled profusion of vines that were woven through thickets of tall bamboo. There the moist air was rich with the tempting fragrance of fresh bread.

When they reached the back of the canyon, they found a dozen caves from which the aroma came. Motioning Eve to follow, Ellenel led her into one of the rounded entrances. Inside, the temperature was slightly higher and the air was noticeably drier. At the back of the cave, some fifty yards from its mouth, were shelves cut into the rock. On the shelves, which were hot to the touch, stood row upon row of dark bread. "Take all you can carry," Ellenel suggested. "It's many days journey to the land of the Iceworm, and once we reach that land there will be no food that is safe to eat."

Their next stop was to pick up extra clothing and blankets. As Eve was sure would be the case, the supple tunics they would wear were woven from living plants and plucked like fruit when ripe. When Eve had arrived the second time, the Elder had spoken to a number of men and women gifted in the shaping of clothing. Together they had worked day and night to guide delicate interlaced tendrils to fashion garments and blankets some five times thicker than normal. Yet the millions of tiny air spaces between the strands that would keep them warm added almost nothing to the weight they'd carry on their journey.

As they finally set out, Eve was aware of mixed feelings. Remembering Joyel's remark about being "only eighty," Eve asked Ellenel, "Ellenel, how do you measure time? And how long do your people live?"

Hurrying along beside Eve, the Elder's trim form and flashing legs seemed to contradict the answer she gave. "I've lived nine hundred and ninety-three years, Eve. My son, born when I was a hundred thirty, is eight hundred sixty-three. My parents birthed me when my father was a hundred sixty-two, and he is still living. His father sired him at one hundred eighty-seven and lived on another seven hundred eighty-two years to reach nine hundred sixty-nine years before the Shaper welcomed him home.

"This is the pattern of our lives, Eve, and seldom is anyone visited for homegoing before at least eight centuries of preparation.

"As for how we tell time, we count years by the Lifewind. It blows each four hundredth day, bringing fertility to all things. Our crops and fruits are fertilized, and a married couple will conceive every few hundred years when the Lifewind blows. But let's not talk. We must hurry." And so they raced on, the nine-hundred-year-old woman as tireless as Eve.

They journeyed through the inner lands for some fifteen days, their path gradually winding upward. During the first week and a half, people and animals could be seen everywhere. There were no large, concentrated communities, but comfortable villages dotted the forests and meadows. At times Ellenel and Eve paused to join small groups for a meal, but they never accepted any of the invitations to stay longer. In this mild land where homes were roofless, there was no need to take shelter. The two women simply stretched out comfortably on the ground wherever night found them.

But as the days passed, Eve began to notice changes. Here and there the smooth bark of a tree was roughened; the straight branch of a bush twisted. She noted brown patches in the lush grass, and once she turned aside to examine a form of grass she'd not seen before that was choking out the normal grasses. Ellenel waited without comment as Eve knelt to examine it and then fell in behind her as they moved on. But from then on Eve watched more intently for signs of change.

By the fifteenth day the signs were everywhere. The bark on nearly all trees and bushes had become rough and scabrous. Branches knotted themselves into twisted shapes and forms. The trees, once straight and tall, now bent as if bowed down with age, while stooped bushes seemed to huddle together fearfully. New kinds of vines appeared. These wound themselves tightly about young trees as though intent on strangling them. Now too spreading weeds battled fiercely to choke out flowers. Those flowers that survived seemed to have lost their vitality. Their colors were dull and their blossoms shrunken. Even a patch of giant white lilies the two passed looked sickly, with most of their petals lifeless and brown on the ground.

The streams too had changed. In the inner lands crystal clear waters bubbled gaily over rocks and pebbles in the streambeds, and where the water paused in tiny pools, a person leaning over to look could see her reflection clearly.

Here the streams moved sluggishly. Often Eve and the Elder were forced to turn aside from some marsh where stagnant water stood motionless and the ground oozed with green slime. Soon Eve could tell whenever they approached one of these marshes for the air stank of rotting vegetation. Then they would search for higher ground and a firmer way.

Everywhere travel was becoming more difficult. By the eighteenth day the land was filled with thickets. Brambles tore at their legs as they passed. That afternoon for the first time Eve realized that Ellenel looked older. The firm flesh of her legs sagged and blue veins were bunched beneath her skin. As Ellenel stood half turned away, Eve noted that her shoulders slumped and that her skin sagged in folds that hung loosely below her chin.

The next morning when Ellenel awoke, Eve was shocked at what she saw. The Elder's once smooth face was furrowed; the dark eyebrows had turned white overnight while streaks of gray rippled through her once lustrous black locks. "You must be tired, Ellenel," Eve said, trying to cover her dismay.

"Not tired, Eve," she said with a sad smile. "I'm dying."

"Dying?"

Gravely Ellenel nodded. "Our lifespan in our own land is normally over a thousand years. But in the outer lands where the Iceworm holds sway all the Shaper's patterns are warped and twisted. Can't you see it in the trees and vines and even in the streams? Death rules here. The deeper I penetrate these lands the more rapidly I'll age until I waste away."

"But that can't be!"

"It has begun, Mother Eve. I fear it will come more rapidly now. I've tried to touch only those things that come from the inner lands. But here even the air is tainted with death. The change has begun. I fear it will not take long."

"Then why did you come?" Eve gasped, shocked and dismayed.

"I came because I will be needed. I feared you would not recognize the Iceworm when you met him. I feared and still do that only an Elder of my people will be able to take the jewel from him."

"But what good can you do if you die of old age?"

Ellenel shook her head stubbornly. "There is much that I do not understand. But I believed then and I believe now that I had to come; that without me, you would fail."

"Just as without me your world would die?"

Ellenel smiled. "You see, Eve? Compared to the death of my world, my own death is quite unimportant. I had not expected it so soon, but I am ready for my homegoing."

18

That day the ground became rockier and the air chillier. Even though the Elder wore the thick woven robe over her regular tunic, she shivered uncontrollably as they walked. She was aging noticeably every hour. Her hair was all white now except for strands around each temple that were a dirty yellow. The flesh had melted from her slender legs and arms. Now her limbs looked like grotesque sticks with lumpy knobs for knees and elbows. Her swift pace slowed to a kind of weary stagger, and Eve could hardly imagine the strength of will that forced her on.

Long before noon, afraid Ellenel would fall and break a bone, Eve halted. Ellenel's once lovely face was nearly unrecognizable. Deep furrows scarred her cheeks. Her nose had lengthened and now drooped over thin, withered lips.

Eve quickly found two long broken branches. She slipped them inside her own woven robe so that twin poles extended out the sleeves. Without damaging the garment, a simple but comfortable litter had been created. All that afternoon as they ascended higher and higher Eve dragged the little Elder behind her. Ellenel slept on the litter, her closed eyes sunk deep in her head, her dry mouth hanging open as her lungs struggled for each breath. *She won't even last the night,* Eve thought. She was aging so rapidly in these twisted lands.

That evening the cold winds brought drops of frozen rain. After midnight, flakes of snow mingled with sleet. Eve dragged Ellenel under the branches of a spruce tree and piled dead leaves over her body. Even with all this insulation, the haggard Elder shivered in the cold. Eve lay close to her, hoping the warmth of her body might preserve the dying Elder just a little longer.

The next day Ellenel weakly urged Eve to go on. The underbrush had grown thicker and more tangled as they traveled deeper into the outer lands. But about midmorning they came unexpectedly on what could only be a track formed by animals. It wound narrowly through the thickets, and although the bare ground was uneven and rocky, it looked far better for traveling than battling the underbrush. Eve hesitated only for a moment. Since the trail seemed to lead in the general direction they were traveling, she turned to move along it.

They came to a bend in the trail. Just beyond it the path widened but darkened. Eve hesitated, peering into the shadows lurking under thick foliage that cut off the light. Then suddenly there came an ear-shattering scream, so loud and so horrible it reached the Elder as she lay at the edge of death and set her frail body trembling. With that scream two giant furred animals leaped out onto the path.

The powerful animals seemed misshapen, almost clumsy. Their faces were masks of fur. Their narrow yellow eyes glared and their black snouts glistened above wrinkled lips that pulled back to reveal rows of vicious teeth, while the standing fur on their necks bristled in warning. One of the beasts stood on its hind legs, forelegs spread. The other crouched, hind legs bunched to spring, its curved fore-claws scoring the earth.

But before the beasts could spring, a cheerful, booming voice rang out. "Down, Beauty! Stay, Loveliness!"

The beasts relaxed as a sturdy human form stepped out of the shadows to stand beside the animals. The man was taller than Eve, with broad shoulders, a curly red beard, and bright blue eyes. The man grinned, and as he did his face radiated friendship. He held up his right hand, palm out, while his left rested on the head of one of the still snarling animals. "Welcome, friend! Please. Pay no attention to my pets. And be at ease; you're safe with me."

He came forward confidently, motioning his giant pets to stay back. "I am Roamer. And I welcome you to my lands."

At the sound of Roamer's voice Ellenel opened her eyes and tried to peer in his direction. Roamer glanced casually at the dying woman. "Well, I see you've brought one of the little people. I suppose it will be up to me to correct all the lies about this land you've heard from her kind. Ah well, I'm used to that."

And then, gripping Eve's hand, he said more formally, "Welcome to the Lands of Freedom. Welcome to the Lands of Truth."

19

Roamer was one of those individuals who looms larger than life. The man was bursting with vitality and enthusiasm. Beside him Eve felt overshadowed and the little people of the inner land seemed absolutely pale. Roamer took the handles of Ellenel's litter from Eve and effortlessly dragged it behind him.

The big man quickly led her to another trail through what had now become a dark forest. It was a broad trail, beaten down by many feet. It seemed that humans as well as animals lived in the outer lands or, as Roamer had named them, the Lands of Freedom.

In spite of the broad avenue along which they walked, trees still met over their heads and a musty darkness hung in the air. Yet later, when they came to an opening in the forest and the trees pulled back, the sky was hardly brighter. Still, within hours Eve found her eyes had adjusted. The shadows faded and the darkness was gone. Eve's vision seemed completely normal, the day seemed bright, and Eve began to wonder if the outer lands lacked light or if perhaps the light in the inner lands had been too intense.

Roamer was a courteous and engaging host. When Eve drew back in fear of the wolverines Beauty and Loveliness, Roamer snapped a command and sent them on ahead. Then he launched into an enthusiastic commentary on everything they passed and on the greatness of the outer lands in general. Roamer knew every tree and plant and told of each one's uses. This herb could be brewed to make a tea that reduced fever. That tree was especially valued for long-burning wood. Turpentine and pitch could be made from the needled trees ranging up the side of that broad hill. The hard wood of those broad branched trees was ideal for making furniture. Everything could be used by humans in one way or another. To Roamer the world was a rich treasure trove and there were always new secrets to be discovered as humankind moved toward complete mastery of the creation.

"But," Eve interjected later, "I thought there were no humans except in the inner lands."

Roamer roared with laughter, doubling over in amusement at her gullibility. "Excuse me, friend," he finally gasped. "I know the kind of tales they tell down there. But that anyone would believe those little wretches …" And at this he bent again to his hilarity.

"Come," he said, when he finally was under control. "Let's sit down for lunch and I'll explain. I suppose they told you that folktale about a malevolent Iceworm who's building glaciers all around to choke out their culture?" Eve nodded. Roamer sighed. "Ah well. Come. First, let's eat."

Roamer quickly gathered wood of a kind which, he explained, burned without smoke. "Don't like to choke on smoke," he explained. "Some use smokeless wood for safety. But none of the bandits of these woods dare attack me. Even if they were desperate enough, there's always Beauty and Loveliness about."

Eve had no idea what "bandits" were, but she said nothing. When the smokeless fire was burning hotly, Roamer drew a strip of raw meat from his backpack. It was wrapped in skin and caked with blackened blood. Roamer flicked the dried blood off with the blade of his knife and deftly cut the strip into one inch squares. "The loin," he commented. "The most tender meat lies near the backbone."

Eve struggled to mask her revulsion. He was going to eat animals! "Thank you," she said, "but I'll just have some bread."

Roamer seemed surprised but made no comment. As his meat sizzled over the fire on sharpened sticks, Roamer gave his version of the myth of the Iceworm. Eve couldn't understand many of his terms but was impressed by his confidence.

20

"Primitives have always struggled with questions of origins. In pre-scientific ages people naturally turned to the supernatural to explain the world around them. Myths developed—tales that attempted to give some sense of the significance of life and provide meaning to individual lives. Such myths are nothing more than desperate efforts to make reality more palatable.

"The realities are these. Our world consists of inner and outer lands surrounded by unscalable glaciers. The inner lands are stifling hot, lit with an unbearable brightness. The outer lands are as you see them, rich in variety and full of opportunity. The little people of the inner lands"—and as Roamer spoke of them as "little" the contempt in his voice made it plain he meant "insignificant"—"developed two myths to help them deal with their reality and to sustain their own dying culture.

"The first myth attempts to explain their origin and at the same time cast their traditional ways as 'right' and our ways as 'wrong.' It's the myth of the Shaper, an intelligent agent who supposedly designed the physical universe and seeded it with life. The little people appeal to this Shaper and the supposed 'pattern' he imposed to justify their ways."

At this Eve almost spoke up to tell Roamer that she knew Elohim personally and that he had shaped everything. But as she hesitated Roamer continued.

"The second myth is that of the Iceworm. You see, the glaciers are growing. At an extremely slow rate, of course, but growing. As the glaciers grow, many ecological changes take place that in turn force social change. I suppose the little people and the men and women of the outer lands evolved from common ancestors. But soon you'll see how different our races are.

"At any rate, the glaciers are growing. Our outer lands are, age after age, expanding, and the inner lands are shrinking. Wherever the influence of the colder climate is felt, changes take place in plants and animals. The imprisoning 'pattern' the little people prate about breaks down. Our kind break those patterns, too, and in the invigorating climate of freedom, we explore every possibility for human experience.

"Think for a moment. How would a decadent culture, settled in its ways and clinging fearfully to ancient values, react to those who reject their pattern and replace it with an infinite variety of patterns? Yes, just as they have! By inventing the myth of the Iceworm. The Iceworm story not only provides a reason for the approaching doom. It also allows them to hold on to the notion that they are 'good' while we are 'evil.'"

Eve nodded hesitantly. "So you think everything they told me there is untrue? It's just a story invented to support their way of life?"

Roamer grinned, "Judge for yourself. I imagine they spoke of the outer lands as a world of frozen death?" Eve nodded. "Well, come then. We'll soon be out of these forests and you can see how 'dead' this outer land is!"

21

After two hours of swift travel along the broad forest highway, Eve could see signs of civilization. With Roamer bearing the burden of the almost weightless body of the dying Elder, Ellenel no longer slowed them. Now and then Roamer glanced contemptuously toward the litter but never questioned Eve's decision to bring the little Elder along.

"A drop in temperature of even a few degrees," Roamer went, "makes many changes in a culture. It shortens the growing season, so people must supplement their grain diet with meat. In fact, many of us live on little but meat." Eve shuddered at the thought of eating animals but again said nothing.

"That drop in temperature causes many other changes. Wood must be cut to build sturdy shelters; houses must have beams to support roofs that aren't necessary in milder climates. More trees must be cut to supply firewood to warm these shelters when it rains or snows.

"The cold will also dictate that shelters have smaller rooms, for who would provide wood to heat vast open spaces? And smaller rooms? Why, such can be stacked, to make buildings several stories high. There can be many of these rooms, so people no longer must live in groups but learn to value privacy. Fireplaces that burn wood or coal can be placed in every room. But, since heat rises, the upper floors of a structure will be warmer. So it's only logical that the owner of a structure will have his family on those higher floors, while servants or employees live below. Here we have one origin of strata in society. We reflect that cause and effect when we speak of the 'upper classes.'

"And remember. We have now placed new value on material things. Wood, for instance, is used for building and is a source of heat. Thus a person who owns a forest gains control over something others need. And control of natural resources will require some agreed upon medium of exchange, for others must give the one who controls the wood something of value in exchange for it. Soon people are assigned to classes based on the wealth gained from the resources they control. Some societies stagnate as the wealthy oppress others to hold on to their position. But in other cultures, this reality is a great stimulus to invention.

"You see, each person is now forced either to control resources to earn coin with which to buy other resources or to find something for which those with coin will pay him. From this necessity has come the invention of glass for dishes and for the windows of the rich, the discovery of how to forge metals, and many other marvelous things which the people of the inner lands could never imagine.

"No," Roamer said with his infectious grin, "there's no need for myths to explain us or our world. Cause leads to effect and effect to cause in an endless, exciting chain of discovery. In these lands of ours, people are truly free: free to succeed or fail, free to be crushed by the harsh reality of life or to overcome it; free to sink down and be lost in the masses who are destined to merely survive or to rise above them and by individual effort to achieve!"

At this Eve interrupted for the first time. "Roamer, I've never heard such ideas before. But you must be wrong. In a society you describe there will be poverty and injustice. Some will be warm, and some will freeze."

Roamer raised his eyebrows. "That may be. But the opportunity is there. Opportunity and the chance to rise above circumstances and above other men make our land great."

"Or," Eve responded thoughtfully, "that 'opportunity' is what makes your land evil and the inner land good."

Roamer chuckled. "You make a value judgment, and of course that's your right. But remember. Values must be judged by how they function

in a culture. You can't take the values of the inner lands where conditions are so different and impose them on us. I prefer to call a value
'good' when it is well adapted to a culture and 'bad' when it doesn't
fit. Believe me, in the outer lands the 'patterns' the little people talk of
would never work.

"Look!" Roamer cut off any reply. "We're coming out of the forest.
Now you'll see for yourself!"

22

The land had been steadily sloping upwards, and now the forest opened
out on the brow of a great hill that fell away into an enormous valley.
The valley stretched endlessly to the left and right. It was so wide
that although the day was clear, its opposite side could hardly be seen.
And looming up from beyond that far horizon, distant and yet so vast
they hung over the valley, and even over the hilltop on which Eve and
Roamer stood, were ramparts of glaring ice.

"Look," Roamer said, pointing down into the valley and ignoring
the glacier, "civilization!"

With a great effort Eve tore her gaze away from the awesome frozen cliffs and followed Roamer's pointing finger. The valley floor gave
an impression of great activity. Eve could make out tiny things moving
at a great pace, rushing here and there. Yet she found it hard to grasp
details. So Roamer pointed out and explained feature after feature of
the plain below. As he talked the complex bustle began to take on some
kind of order.

Roamer pointed far to the left toward a bleached hill of parched
earth heaped up above a tumble of tiny buildings. "That's a mining
district," Roamer explained. "There's copper there—the iron and coal
mines are farther down the valley. Using copper, men have laid long
thin wires which can carry voices. And copper tubing carries water
from deep wells into each building.

"Over there, just to the right of the mine. See it? That moving string of wagons is pulled by a steam engine. On those wagons men carry all sorts of goods from one part of the valley to another.

"Now," Roamer went on, pointing to the end of what seemed to be tiny metal threads along which the string of wagons moved, "there is one of the cities."

The place he pointed out was covered with a pall of ominous smoke that half-hid crowded heaps of large and small buildings. "It's much more economical to produce goods in volume than to use old, hand-crafting ways. People come from all over to find work in these factory towns and so earn the money they need to live."

Eve was stunned. "They leave the land? To live there?"

Roamer nodded. "Oh yes. The coming of engines makes it possible for one man to work the fields of ten. One person can produce food for himself and for the other nine. The nine then move into towns where they can labor to mass produce goods. That way everyone can own more things. Oh, the system is a wonderful one, and I believe the outer lands are standing on the edge of amazing discoveries. Soon there'll be better healthcare, better education, people will live longer than our traditional sixty-seven years, and—"

"Sixty-seven!" Eve's shocked voice cut through Roamer's enthusiasm.

Annoyed, Roamer responded curtly, "Woman, for thousands of years the man or woman of forty was viewed as old. I'm talking of adding more than half again as many years, and after that possibly doubling the lifespan."

"But in the inner lands a girl of eighty was just a child …"

"Here life moves at a faster pace. What difference does it make if men only live into their sixties if they pack a century of experience into every year? Back there life may be long, but it's a life of empty repetition, devoid of challenge. It's senseless to compare the two."

Eve was silent. This was a far different vision of the future of her children's children than she had ever imagined. Somehow it repelled her, and yet as Roamer spoke, it did seem to offer a kind of adventure and excitement that was absent from the placid way of life of the people of the inner lands. An excitement and challenge that was absent from her life with Adam as well.

Finally Eve said, "Roamer, I'm pleased you are excited about your civilization. But our goal is to find a gem called Innocence. Can you help us find it?"

This was the first time Eve had mentioned the reason for her travel to the outer lands. Now, at the mention of Innocence, Roamer's attitude seemed to change subtly. He became a bit wary; no longer quite as expansive as before.

"I've heard tales of a gem by that name," Roamer admitted cautiously. "But in all honesty I'm afraid you've been taken in by the little people's myths. The Shaper, the Iceworm, and the jewel associated with them are simply fiction."

Eve disagreed. "I once saw the gem myself. I know it exists."

Roamer shook his head in disbelief. "Even if the jewel does exist—in some form other than in the myth, of course—what will you do if you find it?"

Eve glanced at the unconscious Ellenel. "I'll take it back to the altar in the valley where it belongs."

Roamer thought for a moment. "My dear new friend, if I can't persuade you the jewel doesn't exist…Well, I suppose I must help you. Where do you expect to find this gem?" As he asked this question, Roamer glanced beyond the valley and for the first time looked directly at the towering walls of ice.

"Exactly," Eve replied. "There, where the Iceworm is."

"I don't want to discourage you, Eve, but I've spent all my life going back and forth across these outer lands. I can guarantee you the ice walls enclosing our world cannot be scaled."

"But I must find it," Eve said.

Roamer nodded reluctantly. "I suppose if you must, you must. Come to my home. It's near here, and I'll do what I can to prepare you to pass through the valley and attack the glacier walls." Turning and calling out to Beauty and Loveliness, who emerged from the trees and took up places to his left and right, Roamer led the way along the brink of the hill overlooking the valley.

"Here we are," Roamer called out a few minutes later as he stepped beyond a bristling hedge. Roamer waited for Eve and then watched her expression as she stepped past the screen of bushes.

The buildings Eve saw were low-lying and single storied except for a central tower. This tower was round, with columns placed around it at regular intervals like some temple. Beyond the tower were manicured lawns and ponds of standing water, and just beyond those, some fifty yards from the columns, were complex wings of wooden structures, each roofed with shingles and each pitched so that its roof slanted away from the lawns and tower they enclosed. Inside the grounds many people could be seen.

"My servants," Roamer explained. "Come. They'll have our meal and rooms prepared. My servants are required to expect me every evening in each of my homes."

"Each?" Eve echoed.

"Oh yes," Roamer said lightly. "I have homes scattered all through the outer lands, for my travels take me everywhere."

At Roamer's direction Ellenel was carried to a suite of rooms of her own. The ancient woman was shivering even in her coma. Roamer ordered that a great fire be built in the fireplace of the room where Ellenel was laid. Eve hesitated, feeling she ought to stay with the dying woman. But the prospect of gaining Roamer's help to find Innocence was too urgent, and so reluctantly Eve left Ellenel in the care of Roamer's people.

Roamer led her up the stairs inside the tower to its top, where they found a magnificent meal laid out on a pair of long tables. A great haunch of meat still sizzling from the roasting pits stood between the two tables. The table on the right held meat dishes. There were pastry pies, steaming stews, casseroles, chilled pates, small crisp creatures roasted whole and great platters of cold sliced roasts. Sections of the table featured different meats. One featured steaks, another livers, tripe, and even jellies made from brains. Other sections of this table overflowed with cheeses.

The table to the left was dedicated to sea food. In the center was a great fish cooked whole, its lidless eyes staring. Around it the foods were also arranged by kinds: oysters and crabs led on to heaps of caviar, and next to that were finger-length fish fried whole in batter. There were various kinds of raw fish and squid, and of course platters of broiled fish, baked fish, fish cooked in wine sauce. Finally, to accompany the meal were meads and ales and casks of beer, with a dozen kinds of wine.

Fighting down her revulsion, Eve asked for some bread and fruit.

Roamer, sensitive to her very real pain at the thought of eating once-living creatures, led her out on to the veranda and had Eve's meal brought to her. Roamer sat with her and shared her fare, although Eve thought that twice he glanced hungrily at the dining room where the feast was spread.

After the meal, Eve and Roamer stood together on the roof, looking across the valley. The sky was inky black now, yet the dark was pierced by lurid flecks of flame that flickered from the chimneys of the factory towns below. Here and there the darkness was also dotted with yellow specks from some kind of dim artificial light. Over the valley loomed the glaciers, and though they must have been many hundreds of miles away, Eve sensed danger as she glanced toward the towering heights, as though they might topple over at any moment and crush everything beneath their monstrous weight.

"Spectacular, isn't it?" Roamer remarked, looking out on the scene. "I often stand here at night and look at it. Somehow I enjoy it more in darkness than during the day."

Eve had never known terror. Yet as she gazed at the endless ice cliffs she sensed something crawling deep in the back of her mind, and she realized might give way to terror unless she maintained firm control. Then, as they gazed, Eve and Roamer both saw a flickering icy blue light flash from the highest point of the ramparts looming over them.

"The jewel!" Eve exclaimed. "Innocence and the Iceworm are there!"

23

For some five minutes, Eve and Roamer watched the cold blue light play along the wall of the glacier. The light seemed dimmer than Eve remembered it, but it was undoubtedly the hue of the jewel she'd seen on the altar what seemed to her just days ago. Faced with this evidence, even Roamer seemed convinced.

The next morning they met again on the tower balcony. The valley looked busier than the day before and the walls of ice seemed more forbidding. But Roamer, apparently converted by last night's vision, entered enthusiastically into planning.

"You'll need new clothing, of course," Roamer was saying as he gave orders to designers to create a wardrobe for Eve. "You can't cross civilization in that simple smock," he went on in high good humor.

"The valley society must be understood as some great machine with individuals as the parts that make the whole operate. Each unit makes his or her contribution to the progress of Man. But that progress does not come through any individual part. It comes through the interaction of the whole.

Eve hardly understood a word of what he was saying. Her thoughts had turned to the little Elder who lay dying, and Eve felt an oppressive weight, as if the vast icy walls that towered so high were eager to fall on her and crush her. Completely unaware that Eve was no longer listening, Roamer went on enthusiastically.

"My point is this. In a society like that of the valley, progress comes by changes in the whole. The whole is more important than the individual. Man, not men, becomes important. In the great machine that is society, an individual man or woman is judged and valued by his function—by the way he or she fits as a part and contributes to the whole.

"Here in the woodlands above the valley, you and I can wander and let our dress and actions express individuality. But there conformity—fitting in as part of the machine—is the price of acceptance."

Roamer leaned forward and spoke persuasively, regaining Eve's attention. "I've told you something of the valley society. Individuals have a place as parts of the whole. Identity is defined by a person's function within the great machine. My friend, if you would win your way across the valley, you must become a valley person.

"You can be trained to take a role and fit into that society. In your role, performing the function of the role, you will be free to move anywhere in the valley...and across it."

"I don't understand," Eve objected. "What are you suggesting?"

"Eve," Roamer explained, "you are compassionate. You have a deep desire to help others. But in the valley, compassion is a role, not a personal quality. I think you'll be happiest if your role in the valley reflects something of who you are, but this is hardly necessary and many in helping professions such as doctor, nurse, or social worker, have no real concern for others. These professions are paid to act in caring ways whether they feel compassion or not.

"But you can't just be helpful and compassionate. You have to become a professional helper. You have to have an official role. With training, which I can see that you receive, you could learn to fill one of these professional roles. Through my influence, and I assure you I am not without influence there, you could achieve a position where you would have great honor… and freedom to move throughout the valley.

"We would in effect lay the role, the function, over your personality. You would be you, but through my training you would learn to be yourself within the context of the valley world's expectations."

"And how long would this training last?"

"How long to learn their ways and to become a part of valley society? Probably about four years. Then another three to become established in your role. Say, at best, seven years. More likely ten."

"Ten years!" Eve exclaimed in dismay.

Roamer nodded. "But, through my influence, I can guarantee you training and a role that will bring you wealth and power in valley society. With these you would have freedom to travel across the valley to the walls of ice."

Eve was horrified. Spend ten years in the valley? She could happily spend years in the inner lands. But the thought of spending even a week in what Roamer called civilization seemed a burden far too great to bear. But then she thought of Ellenel and the price the little Elder was willing to pay to preserve the inner lands. Could Eve do less for her children's children's children?

With a heavy heart, Eve agreed. "I'll do as you say, Roamer. I'll live in the valley until I can reach the Iceworm and reclaim Innocence."

"Good," Roamer said with a smile. "And since there is no use putting it off, you can begin training tomorrow."

24

The next morning before they left Eve asked about Ellenel. "Is she still living?"

"I don't know," Roamer answered indifferently. "I suppose it's possible, even though she seemed nearly dead when you arrived. Are you sure you want to see her?"

"Yes," Eve nodded. "I must. I must let her know what I plan to do. She mustn't die thinking that she's failed."

Roamer shrugged and led Eve across the lawns to the wing where Ellenel lay. Stepping into her room, Eve was assaulted by stifling heat radiating from a fiercely burning fire and from bright flickering gas lights lining the walls.

The old woman lay with her pallet drawn up close to the fire. She still shivered with cold and her teeth actually chattered. Ellenel had come out of her coma, but her glazed eyes could hardly focus.

"It looks as though she won't hear your farewell, Eve," Roamer remarked. "But never fear. We'll care for her as long as she lives.

"Now, come. Let's get out of this hothouse."

In the past two days Ellenel had aged unbelievably. Her deteriorating flesh seemed already to be undergoing the decomposition normally begun at death. But Eve crossed the room and dropped beside the pallet. She took the old woman's hands in hers and began to cry softly. Then the aged Elder stirred, and her eyes cleared. She glanced at Roamer, and then fixed her gaze on Eve.

Ellenel struggled to speak, forcing putrid breath from her decaying mouth. But no words came. There was only a whispered moan so low it could hardly be heard above the crackling of the flames. With what must have been her last strength, Ellenel lifted her head an inch or two off the pallet and looked desperately at her friend. "Sing," she managed to croak. "Sing. Worship song. Sing."

Eve was startled by the request. Then she understood. Ellenel needed comfort. Of course she wanted to hear the music of the little people one more time.

Eve closed her eyes. She could picture the worshipping multitude. As the picture in her mind became clearer, Eve could almost hear the notes they were singing. Uncertainly Eve began to hum. Her first notes were hesitant, thin, as though the room itself fought to strangle the music. But as Eve continued, she gained confidence, and the notes she sang gained strength and purity.

Within moments Eve sensed other voices joining in. Then the sound of the voices of the multitude singing back in the inner land began to fill the room. Eve didn't understand how it could be, but as voices joined in, with each note the music became more whole. Then the notes flowed together, and the tune they wove was that never-repetitious, endless song of worship and joy that only the little people whose lives flowed in harmony with the pattern knew.

As the music strengthened, changes were taking place in the room. The first thing Eve noticed was a blast of unbearable cold. The fire roared fiercely in the fireplace, but the heat she'd felt only moments before was now gone. Chilling icy cold hung like deadening crystals in the air. The cold crept out of the frozen ground and now Eve saw that the walls and ceiling of the room were thick with frost.

With the cold came looming darkness; a dark that rushed in from the glacial ice, descending as an impenetrable shadow over the valley and the ridge on which they stood.

In the crushing darkness and frozen cold, Eve now saw through the walls of Roamer's house and watched the whole valley change. The fever-ish activity there slowed. Like some great machine robbed of its power, the gears of the complex civilization ground to a halt. Within moments all below was still, wrapped in the grip of the frozen darkness.

In the room the change continued. Spun by the music, the air began to dance. A luminous radiance glowed from each molecule, and with the radiance came a cleansing heat. Suddenly Eve realized that she was comfortable in the blinding brightness! That before she had been stiff with cold and blinded by the darkness of the outer lands that moments before had seemed so pleasant.

But the most amazing changes were taking place in the other two people in the room. The music had magically recreated the climate of the inner lands in the very shadow of the glacier. In that vital atmo-sphere, the wasted form of Ellenel was transformed. Before Eve's eyes, her cheeks filled in and her dead lips flushed with life. Her hair was restored, rich in its burnished blackness. The skin on her arms and legs smoothed as the flesh returned, and when Ellenel stood up, Eve saw again the supple beauty of the young-old Elder who had set out with her. Ellenel smiled and stretched her arms high, arching her body, filled with the joy of her restored wholeness. Then her warm full voice commanded, "Look!" And she pointed to Roamer.

As the light and warmth brought by the celebration music had transformed Ellenel, it seemed to deform Roamer. Roamer did not welcome the change. He fought it. Eve sensed the furious strength of the red-haired man as he struggled. She saw fierce determination in his bulging jaw and flashing, ice blue eyes. But battle as he would, Roamer's form shimmered and wavered in the glowing light. Each time it wavered, Eve caught a glimpse of some other form beyond his human shape. As the music swelled and the light brightened, the figure of Roamer became more and more hazy and the hidden shape more solid.

Eve caught glimpses of writhing gray-brown coils that lashed in helpless fury. Rearing up, taller than the Roamer form, she saw a flattened head, slit eyes, and a broad mouth that opened and closed in furious agony to reveal a flickering, split tongue.

Now the Roamer shape had almost disappeared and a wormlike monster was revealed. It reared back, eyes glaring hatred, fury beating out in palpable waves. With the last vestige of the disguise gone, Eve saw the object of their quest. There, imprinted on the skin around the great worm's neck were the tracings of a chain. And there, driven into the skull between its two eyes and protected by bony ridges, was Innocence!

Despite the revulsion the fearsome shape aroused in Eve, she readied herself to reach for the jewel. But before she moved Ellenel spoke. "Wait! The gem can only be taken back by one of us. It is for this that I came. To meet the Iceworm in his own land and to retrieve the stolen jewel that gives him his power."

As she spoke, Ellenel never shifted her gaze from the towering, writhing, furious thing before her. "Sing!" she commanded Eve, and the music around them strengthened. Its joy and brightness laughed and tumbled and danced through the room, and as the celebration song bubbled brighter, the writhing worm became more frantic—more frantic, yet at the same time weaker. Now the ugly flattened head dipped lower, as if the neck could no longer support it. Fury burned in its eyes, but the Iceworm was helpless, imprisoned by the music that had somehow recreated the inner lands.

Ellenel approached the beast. Confident, her young-old body supple and beautiful again, she moved across the room and placed both hands on the jewel. She tugged. The worm's head jerked back as Ellenel pulled with all her strength, but the jewel could not be torn loose.

"Sing!" she again commanded, and again the celebration tempo increased. In utter helplessness, the Iceworm now lay stretched out on the floor. Ellenel placed her tiny foot on its snout, felt for a firm grip, arched her back, and pulled. Every muscle straining, Ellenel maintained pressure until the gem began to loosen. Green ichors swelled from the Iceworm's forehead as the gap between the jewel and the bony ridge where it rested widened. Then, with a suddenness that almost threw the straining Ellenel to the floor, the gem popped loose, and Ellenel, exultant, held it clutched to her breast.

With a radiant smile, Ellenel turned to Eve. "Thank you," she said simply.

"But ..." Eve began, still stunned and disbelieving.

Ellenel raised her hand. "Eve, I knew from the beginning that none of us could penetrate the outer lands and live. The cold drained us of our wholeness long before we could come near the Iceworm. Then I remembered you and I began to hope. You were so much stronger than we are. If only you would return and help me reach the Iceworm our music might hold back the cold just long enough.

"I knew that I'd begin to die when we entered the outer lands. But I prayed that I'd live long enough, that you would carry me through. When you entered the room I found the strength to lift my head and ask you to sing. And," Ellenel concluded, "you see what has happened."

"But if you'd told me ..." Eve began.

Ellenel shook her head. "No. I knew you'd never recognize the Iceworm. I knew that somehow he'd deceive you and trick you into becoming part of his civilization. I couldn't warn you because I didn't know what deceit he'd use. He's a skillful liar—a liar from the beginning. So I knew that I must come, though it would cost me my life."

"No," Eve cried, reaching out to embrace the radiant Elder. "No. I'll take you back to the inner lands."

Ellenel shook her head. "The music holds back the cold and darkness now, but only for this brief moment. No, I'll give you the gem. Take it, and hold tightly to Innocence. The Iceworm's power here in the shadow of the ice will seem unbroken. But his death now is sure."

"But what about you?" Eve asked.

"Oh," Ellenel laughed liltingly. "I'll die. But I would have died one day anyway. Now through my death, my world will live."

Ellenel held out the jewel in both hands to Eve, smiling. Eve took the blue gem, gripping it so hard it seemed to cut into her hand.

For an instant she stood there, but as the last note of music died away, the glorious light faded. Darkness and paralyzing cold rushed in. As Ellenel crumpled to the ground, a red bearded man sprang to his feet and uttered a blood curdling scream of helpless fury. Beyond the room, the activity of the valley rumbled to a start. Roamer's servants moved and spoke. But Roamer himself stood, glaring balefully at the form at his feet.

He leaned down and lifted the body, staring at what he held in his arms. The strong supple beauty of Ellenel had again fled. Her flesh was withered, and her dead eyes stared blankly out of decaying flesh.

His prize torn from him, Roamer turned and looked at Eve. With an unbelievably quick move Roamer gripped and squeezed Eve's wrist, forcing her hand open. In Eve's open palm, there was nothing but a dull black stone.

Innocence was gone!

As Roamer and Eve stared down at the worthless object, Eve heard a distant rumbling and felt a sense of impending doom. It could be only one thing. The towering walls of ice were about to fall. The rumbling grew louder and louder. Looking up in terror, Eve began to scream.

And found herself in Adam's arms, a dull black stone still clutched in her hand.

BOOK 4
THE GIFT
"Every good and perfect gift
is from above"
(James 1:17)

1

As Adam held Eve tight, her screams gradually subsided to become great, heaving sobs. At last Eve relaxed in Adam's arms, and her gasping breaths became regular and deep. "Eve?" Adam whispered. But she had fallen into a deep, exhausted sleep.

Adam held her in his arms the rest of the night, releasing her only when the morning's first light crept into the unfinished room where they lay. She slept on as Adam slipped away to choose fruit for their breakfast. When he returned, she was still sleeping, and she did not stir until well after noon. When Eve finally opened her eyes, she looked around, frightened, and then seeing Adam smiled. "I'm home," she whispered, reaching out for Adam to take her hand. With both of Adam's strong hands enfolding hers, Eve slept again.

It was several days before Eve felt able to relate the complete dream to Adam. She was still shaken by the sudden revelation of the Iceworm and by the horrible, wasting death of Ellenel. And Eve was disturbed by the transformation of the gem Innocence into the dull black stone clutched in her hand when she awoke. Most troubling of all was the uncertainty.

Again and again she asked Adam, "Did I save them, Adam? Did I save our children? Or was I too late?"

All Adam could tell her was, "I don't know, Eve. But you tried. You did your best."

When Elohim came to the garden a few days later, they asked about the dream. All he would tell them was that the dream was a warning.

"But a warning of what, Elohim?" Adam asked.

"The dream has meaning, little ones," Elohim responded. "When the time comes, remember the dream."

"When what time comes?" Adam pressed.

But Elohim simply repeated, "When the time comes, remember the dream."

Although Adam and Eve went over the dream again and again in the next months, they remained puzzled about its meaning. Certain elements of the dream were clearly significant: among them the loss of Innocence that threatened the world of their children's children's children and the ability of the Iceworm to disguise himself and to mask his evil. These were clearly keys to the meaning of the dream. But how the dream related to Adam and Eve, and the nature of the warning it conveyed, remained a mystery to the first pair. After two years passed, Adam and Eve hardly ever spoke of the dream and Eve's sleep was untroubled.

The two were nearing completion of their home and more eager than ever to have children. Now and then Eve would sit beside their stream and look for tiny flowers, imagining how she might arrange them to create a living picture like the one in Elron's home. But the darker parts of her second dream were forgotten. When she did think of the future of their offspring, Eve focused on the wonders of the pleasant and peaceful land they would inherit.

2

I would like to take credit for corrupting the Enemy's playthings. But most of the credit belongs to our great Leader. All I did was listen in as the man-thing and woman-thing talked about her dream and then report what they said to Satan. He's the one who saw the implications and developed the plan.

"Myrdebaal," he said thoughtfully one time, "do you realize how much these humans are like us?"

I was disgusted. How could Satan suggest that mere worms crawling on the surface of his planet were like spirit beings?

"Not that they come close to having our powers. But, like us, they are intelligent and they possess a sense of self. Right now they're content with who they are. But what if I appeal to their intelligence and help them become discontent?

"After all, it was when I became discontent with being the most powerful of the angels that I chose to rebel. It was when I appealed to your intelligence that you saw you were being exploited by the Enemy and choose to follow me.

"What do you suppose would happen, Myrdebaal, if the humans became discontented? Would they abandon the Enemy and come over to our side?"

Satan's ability to see opportunities and the courage to seize them are two of the traits we admire most in him. The rest of us lack originality. We're good followers. But there's no question we need someone like our Leader to direct us. Who but Satan would have imagined that these disgusting human creatures were anything like us at all?

I nodded agreement. When Satan made up his mind, he didn't care for other opinions anyway.

"Call the council together, Myrdebaal," Satan commanded. "We'll find a way to separate these creatures from the Enemy, and we'll enlist them on our side!"

3

One day Eve announced their home was finished. She and Adam gazed happily at what they'd accomplished. The outer walls of the low-lying structure at the top of the hill were of tightly woven ivy. The inner walls were formed of flowers of different colors or color combinations. A complex garden filled with brightly hewed flowers encircled their home, with the most vivid colors fading to pastels as the flowerbeds descended the gently sloping hillside. A backdrop of trees giving the impression of a single dark green curtain framed the whole.

Pleased with everything they'd done, Adam and Eve walked hand in hand among the flowers. Eve sighed with delight as the perfumes of the flowers mingled, giving each section of the garden a distinct fragrance.

"We've done it, Adam," Eve smiled.

"Yes, Eve, we've done it. We've fashioned our own Eden in Eden.

It's a wonderful place where our children can grow up and learn to love us and Elohim. Life can't be better than this, can it, Eve?"

A week later Adam and Eve set out to tour Eden and revisit its living creatures. They spent two days with their favorites, the fun-loving cats. As they walked beside one of the rivers that bordered the garden, Adam again felt curiosity about the lands beyond. "One day I'll take our boys over the river, just to see what it's like there."

"What, not the girls?" Eve objected. "I loved exploring Eden. I'm sure our girls will be just as eager to explore as the boys."

Adam smiled. He remembered the delight that Eve took in each discovery she made those first months after Elohim brought her to him. She truly was flesh of his flesh, sharing every capacity of personhood that Elohim had given to him. Of course the girls should go exploring with them. After all, they too would bear the image and likeness of the Creator just as he and Eve did.

"I'll take the girls, Eve," Adam promised. "And I'll take you. I wouldn't be whole without you."

The one dark moment in those days of re-exploring Eden came when they approached the forbidden tree. It stood where it always had in a clearing isolated from other trees. Its red leaves and rich crimson fruit were as beautiful as ever, but Eve shuddered as they passed it.

"Remember when you told me we'd die if we ate the tree's fruit? And I asked you what 'die' means?" Adam nodded solemnly.

"I know what 'die' means now," Eve said. "I watched Ellenel die. And it's horrible."

They both looked away from the tree and its forbidden fruit and hurried on. "Why would Elohim put such a terrible tree in our garden?" Eve asked.

"I don't know," Adam answered. "But he did, so he must have a reason."

Eve shook her head. "I'll never understand it. Elohim has been so good to us. Why would he put that terrible, awful thing there?"

The dark moment was soon forgotten. The pair reached a nearby meadow and was visited by a host of loveable, furry creatures eager to climb over them and be stroked.

That night they slept in the meadow, and despite Eve's earlier recollection of the little Elder's tragic death, she had no distressing dreams and awoke refreshed and happy.

When Elohim visited them a few evenings later, Adam asked about the tree bearing the forbidden fruit. "It's a gift, Adam," Elohim told him.

"But you said it's dangerous. You said the day we eat its fruit we'll surely die."

"That's true, Adam. But the tree is only dangerous if you ignore my warning. Many of my gifts are like that, Adam. All my gifts are good. But most can be misused. Believe me, I've given you this gift with only your good in mind."

Beyond that Elohim would say nothing more about the forbidden tree, and their talk turned to the wonders of the garden and this led to spontaneous expressions of Adam and Eve's gratitude. And this quickly became praise.

"How we thank you, Lord.

You are good.

Your love endures forever."

By the time Elohim left them, Adam and Eve both overflowed with joy. But as they lay down that night, Eve pondered. How could the forbidden tree that was so closely linked with death be a good gift?

4

Nearly two months later, Adam and Eve passed near the tree again. "Let's go look at it," Eve urged, remembering her earlier questions. Perhaps if they examined the tree they could discover how Elohim's gift could be good and still be associated with something as horrible as death.

For the first time, Adam and Eve hesitantly drew near the tree they'd avoided in the past. As they approached, they noticed a tantalizing fragrance in the air. The fruit smelled so good, their mouths began to water. Coming nearer, the pair could see delicate patterns traced on each red leaf on the tree's branches. How beautiful they were. And the bark was smooth, seeming to invite touch. But what most attracted

Eve was the fruit. Each tantalizing crimson orb appeared ripe and succulent, as though it were bursting with flavor.

Adam was as fascinated as Eve by the unusual tree, yet he stood back as Eve slowly circled it, carefully keeping her distance. When she reached the far side, Adam heard a startled gasp and then heard Eve exclaim, "Oh! I didn't see you!"

Hurrying around the tree Adam saw Eve face to face with one of the most beautiful of Eden's animals. This creature was nearly as tall as Eve. It stood on two legs, balancing on its long tail. The creature had no arms or wings but a beautifully complex pattern was stamped on its multicolored skin. Although its nose was flat and its lips thin, the mild, intelligent eyes in the broad face drew Adam and Eve's gaze. Both humans were surprised when the creature spoke to Eve in a deep, warm voice. They were familiar with the talking birds of Eden, but this was the first time any creature had spoken other than to mindlessly repeat the humans' own words.

"I'm sorry I startled you," the creature said to Eve.

Eve stared but said nothing.

"As Adam knows, I'm called serpent. I'm usually found here by the tree." Then, in a tone of concern, "Eve, are you feeling all right?"

Eve nodded, and then said hesitantly, "You live by this tree? The forbidden tree?"

The serpent laughed. "Oh, that. Did Elohim really tell you not to eat from any tree in the garden?"

"Not any tree," Eve corrected him. "We're allowed to eat fruit from the other trees. What Elohim said was, 'You must not eat fruit from the tree that is in the middle of the garden, and you must not touch it, or you will die.'"

"Oh, just this tree," the serpent said. "Well, I can assure you that you won't die. He's got his own reasons for telling you you'll die if you eat this fruit."

"His own reasons?"

"Of course. Don't you know the name of the tree?"

"Yes, it's called the Tree of the Knowledge of Good and Evil."

"There you are, Eve. Think about it. Elohim doesn't want you to eat because he knows that when you eat this fruit your eyes will be opened and you'll be like Elohim. You'll know good and evil."

Eve pondered the serpent's words. Elohim had told her and Adam that they were created in his image and likeness. Wouldn't Elohim want them to be even more like him by gaining this special knowledge? How could being more like Elohim be a bad thing?

The thought of being more like Elohim intrigued Eve. She was attracted to this seeming good in a way she never would have been attracted to an obvious evil.

For some reason Eve failed to remember the dream or the Iceworm's ability to fashion lies that masqueraded as truth. As Eve hesitated, the serpent gently urged, "Go ahead, Eve. Touch it."

Tentatively Eve reached out her hand and touched one of the fruit, but quickly pulled back. The touch didn't harm her, and now the fruit swung back and forth enticingly, more fragrant and desirable than ever. Still Eve hesitated. The tree was so beautiful. How could such beauty be associated with death? The fruit looked and smelled so good, and her senses seemed to confirm the serpent's words. Surely, Eve thought, it must be a good thing to gain wisdom.

Finally, deceived by the serpent and drawn by the fragrance and beauty of the fruit, Eve picked the orb she'd touched and bit into it. It was delicious! Excited she held out the piece of fruit to Adam. Adam took the fruit, gazed into Eve's eyes—and ate.

With Adam's first bite, their eyes were opened. They were both gripped by a sudden awareness that what they had done was terribly wrong. Adam threw down the fruit and turned away, but it was too late.

All around the open meadow, angels wept while demons danced and howled. Elohim had ordered his angels not to interfere when Satan entered the serpent and took over its body. The angels strained to intervene when Adam and Eve approached the tree and its forbidden fruit, but Elohim told them the humans must have the opportunity to make an informed and conscious choice. No angel could step in, for the human's choice must not be coerced or compelled in any way. It must be made freely by Adam and Eve alone.

Gorel realized now that the second dream he had carried to Eve was meant to prepare her for just this moment. But when speaking with the serpent, Eve never thought of the dream much less applied it to this temptation.

Yet the points of comparison were so clear. The dream had been about life and death, as this moment raised the issue of life and death. In the dream, an evil creature presented itself as a friend, even as Satan now cast himself. In the dream the theft of Innocence led to Ellenel's death and threatened the future of Eve's children's children's children. Now the first pair's surrender of their innocence would also result in death—in the biological and spiritual ruin of the first couple and of all their offspring.

Watching in horror as Elohim's command was violated, Gorel was aware that while Eve had been deceived, Adam was not. Adam had stood by silently as Satan and Eve talked. Why had he remained silent? Why hadn't he spoken up when Eve misquoted Elohim's command by adding a prohibition against touching to God's decree, "do not eat"? Watching Adam's eyes, Gorel was sure that Adam was aware of the serpent's deceit. Why then didn't he stop Eve? Even more puzzling, why did Adam take the fruit from Eve and bite into it? Eve had been deceived, but Adam consciously, knowingly, chose to violate Elohim's command!

For Myrdebaal the moment Adam bit into the fruit was one of utter triumph. Satan, their great Leader, had succeeded! Adam and Eve had taken Satan's path and had rebelled against Elohim. The humans were no longer a weapon Elohim could use against the demon hordes. Now Elohim would have to judge them as he had judged and expelled the fallen angels!

The thought of how frustrated Elohim must feel at this defeat filled Satan and all demons with a vicious delight. How they hated Elohim! How satisfying to defeat him. And defeat him they had!

5

For Adam and Eve the decisive act of eating did bring a kind of enlightenment. For the first time, they fully realized that the blessings they had experienced in Eden derived solely from their relationship with Elohim—a relationship they had maintained by living in harmony with his will. They had known unmixed good in the garden. Now as guilt and shame overwhelmed them, they sensed something of the nature of evil. In the past they had been and had experienced good. In the future they would come to know evil, not as an abstract concept but as an insidious force that would corrupt them and bring unimaginable suffering.

Adam and Eve would look back at their lives in Eden and realize how good it had been. They would recall the joy of innocent love and the endless delight they had taken in each other. They would remember the thrill of exploring Elohim's Creation and the satisfaction they had found in caring for the garden and its gentle creatures. They would recall the sense of accomplishment they gained in using the abilities Elohim had given them to fashion their Eden within Eden.

Most of all they would struggle to recapture something of the joy they had known on those evenings when they walked and talked with the Creator, sharing their lives with him as they were filled with gratitude and caught up in praise. The future would hold moments of joy for Adam and Eve. But such moments would be all too few and too fleeting.

Shaken, Adam and Eve now realized that their future would be far different from their past. From now on they would know evil by personal experience. They could not yet imagine what forms evil would take, but they sensed that their choice had doomed them … and had doomed generations yet unborn.

With one act of disobedience, Eve's vision of a peaceful, happy land for her children's children's children had become an impossible dream—a dream that would never be realized. At least, not until history's end.

6

For a moment after eating the crimson fruit, Adam felt dizzy and disoriented. He blinked and shook his head. What was the matter with him? Then he spit violently. The fruit that had seemed so succulent left a bitter taste in his mouth. He spat again. He needed water. He needed to wash that taste away. Instead his stomach spasmed and its contents rushed out.

Adam noticed that Eve had fallen to her knees. She was bent over, vomiting too. What had happened to them? Why did the fruit that seemed so desirable before taste acrid and harsh now? Adam dropped to his knees and continued heaving. He desperately wanted to rid his mouth of the horrible taste, but could not.

Then the serpent spoke. "Congratulations. You've broken his hold on you."

Adam, still gagging, looked up at the beautiful creature and choked out, "What do you mean, broken his hold?"

"Isn't it obvious? While you obeyed him, you belonged to him. By disobeying him, you declared your independence. You've become your own master, free to do as you want rather than bound by what he wants. That means you're liberated, as I and my followers are liberated."

The serpent's words puzzled Adam. "I've always been free. I've always done what I wanted."

"Yes, it seemed that way, didn't it? But in fact, Adam, you were in bondage to his will. He gave you freedom—but freedom within limits he set. I know there was only one limit: 'Don't eat the fruit of the one tree.' But freedom is only real when there are no limits at all. In eating the fruit, you violated his limit and you rejected him.

"Look inside yourself, Adam. Don't you feel differently about Elohim already?"

Adam did look inside. Yes, he did feel differently. Before he had loved and trusted Elohim completely. Now, even though Adam was aware of the goodness of Elohim and appreciated his many gifts, he resented the Creator and he questioned Elohim's motives. Why had Elohim placed this Tree of the Knowledge of Good and Evil in the garden? Elohim had tricked them! He'd wanted them to fail this test.

For the first time, Adam also felt fear. Elohim would surely be angry with them. What would he do to Adam and to Eve?

"I don't trust him," Adam blurted out. "And I'm afraid of him."

"Good!" the serpent exclaimed. "You were in bondage when you trusted and loved him. You did what he said without any hesitation. That's what I meant when I said you're liberated. You're now free to do what seems best to you. Free to do what you desire without paying attention to any limits he might impose."

"I see," Adam said thoughtfully. "Free. I think I'll like being free."

"Oh yes," the serpent smiled. "I think you'll like being free too. And then you can take the next step."

"The next step?"

"To join me, of course. I'm the leader of millions of spirit beings who have rebelled against the one you call Elohim. We call him the Enemy. Commit yourself to me, and I will lead humankind in a great struggle to throw off the Enemy's yoke completely."

Adam hesitated. "But, why should Eve and I join you? You say we're liberated. You say we can make our own choices, follow our own desires. If I wanted a master, I'd have far less reason to turn myself over to you than to turn myself over to Elohim. After all, he created me and he's been good to me all of my life. All I know about you is that you're his enemy and that you tricked Eve into eating the forbidden fruit.

"I also know that you've taught me what 'freedom' is. And now you want me to give up my new freedom to commit myself to you?"

The serpent was stunned by Adam's response. After Satan had engineered the angel rebellion against the Enemy, all those who rejected Elohim's rule had fallen into line and committed themselves to him. Now this pitiful human creature, a thing made of dirt, was rejecting his leadership?

Suddenly Satan realized that he had miscalculated. He had succeeded in separating the humans from the Creator. But he had assumed that rejecting Elohim meant they would have to fall in line with him. Instead the man was claiming full independence!

From now on the invisible war would no longer involve a conflict of two wills. There would be three or four or, if these human creatures multiplied as Elohim had suggested, there might be thousands or even millions of wills, each will fiercely claiming the right to go its own way. Satan had never imagined such a thing. He had no idea how the existence of millions of truly independent beings would affect the conduct of his war with Elohim.

But Satan quickly recovered from the shock. Adam had declared independence from all authority. Yet, however independent these creatures might claim to be, Satan knew they could be manipulated. Look how easily he had manipulated Eve.

Eve had misquoted Elohim's command, showing her lack of clarity about what he had actually said. Satan would see to it that humankind remained confused about the Creator and his will.

Satan had contradicted Elohim and subtly led Eve to doubt Elohim's motives. Satan would continue to attack the Creator's Word and sow suspicion of his intentions.

Satan had encouraged Eve to rely on her senses and desires as a guide to what is desirable. Satan would continue to encourage human beings to assume that what they wanted must be right, and what they desired must be good.

This basic approach was something Satan could use over and over again to manipulate these supposedly free creatures into doing what he wanted. *Yes,* Satan thought, *that's what I'll do. If they refuse to commit themselves to me, I'll manipulate them into doing what I want anyway. And all the while they'll foolishly imagine that they're free.*

All this flashed through Satan's mind in a moment, and so even though he was shocked at Adam's response, he revealed nothing. "I'm sure you are right, Adam," the serpent said, immediately. "Don't trust either Elohim or me. Trust yourself. And do whatever feels best to you.

"Let this day that you ate the forbidden fruit be forever marked as humankind's independence day."

With that the serpent began to move away from Adam and from Eve, who was still vomiting on the ground, unheeding of Adam's conversation with the serpent.

"Oh, Adam," Eve said, looking up with tears flowing down her cheeks. "Oh, Adam, what have we done?"

A moment before Adam had been taken by the notion of his new independence. Now, looking at Eve, he was shaken. The radiant glow that had clothed her from their first meeting in the garden was gone. He looked down at his own body and realized he too was fully exposed. Adam was suddenly overwhelmed by a sense of shame. Surely without his glowing cloak, Eve would see into his heart. And for all the talk of independence, Adam knew intuitively that he was now flawed and corrupt.

Then Adam saw the shock on Eve's face and realized that she felt the same shame. They weren't ashamed of their naked bodies, even though Eve tried to cover herself with her hands. After all, they had come to know each other's bodies intimately in their love play. This was deeper than that.

There was an indefinable wrongness about each of them now—a wrongness that neither could bear to have exposed. Somehow each felt unlovable and unacceptable. Each was sure that if the other knew his or her heart, rejection was inevitable. The thought that anyone might come to really know him was too painful to bear. Each felt an overpowering need for covering, not just of their bodies, but of their inner selves.

The serpent was confused by their apparent embarrassment over their nakedness. What was this all about?

It was no wonder that Satan failed to understand. Satan gloried in his corruption. He was proud of what he had become. He might disguise himself and his motives to gain some advantage, but he would never hide because of shame. There must be something essentially different about these humans for them to feel shame while fallen angels felt only an arrogant pride.

7

Adam and Eve's desperate need for covering so distracted them that they forgot all about the watching serpent. They ran to the edge of the clearing and frantically began looking for leaves large enough to cover themselves. Finally they tore leaves from a fig tree, and Eve bound them together using grape vines that Adam gathered. The leaf garments felt strange and insubstantial, but they did cover the pair's bodies. And wearing them brought momentary relief from the fear of exposure.

Satan watched the process with amusement. He gradually realized the significance of the first pair's need for covering and could hardly keep from laughing aloud. These foolish creatures clearly wanted it both ways. They wanted to be free to follow their own desires, yet at the same time, they didn't want the nature of those desires exposed. Somehow the Creator had planted within these human creatures an innate sense of right and of wrong so strong that they desperately wanted to appear right, even when they knew they were wrong!

Satan had no name for this peculiar sense. Later humans would call it "conscience" and would curse the conscience for continually accusing them.

The serpent shrugged. This peculiarity of human beings was irrelevant at the moment, although he would surely find ways to use it in the future.

It was then that the three heard Elohim moving through the garden, calling Adam and Eve. Overcome with terror Adam and Eve fled, rushing deeper into the garden in a desperate effort to hide from Elohim. Satan too began to slip away, but was stopped by a silent command from Elohim. Unable to retreat, the serpent controlled by Satan stood still.

A few moments later Elohim approached Adam and Eve, who were cowering behind a tree trunk. "Where are you?" Elohim asked.

Timidly Adam peeked out from behind the tree and replied, "I heard you in the garden and I was afraid because I was naked; so I hid."

"Who told you that you were naked?" Elohim asked. "Have you eaten from the tree that I commanded you not to eat from?"

This was Adam's opportunity to confess and throw himself on Elohim's mercy. Instead, driven by guilt and shame, Adam pointed at Eve. "The woman you put here with me—she gave me some fruit from the tree, and I ate it."

It seemed for a moment that Adam's attempt to shift responsibility had succeeded. Elohim said to the woman, "What is it that that you have done?"

Eve, as unwilling as Adam to accept responsibility for her actions, pointed to the serpent. "The serpent deceived me, and I ate."

Elohim turned to the serpent. Its involvement in Adam and Eve's tragic choice would have consequences. Elohim addressed his first words to the living creature who had served as Satan's host. The serpent and its kindred were cursed, doomed now to crawl on their bellies. Then Elohim addressed Satan, who was still in possession of the serpent's body.

"You will eat dust all the days of your life," Elohim announced. Satan's plans involving humankind would be thwarted. Every apparent victory of Satan in the invisible war would lead inevitably to Satan's ultimate defeat. Again and again Satan would succeed in manipulating humankind into taking a path that Satan chose. But no pathway would lead to the rebel angel's triumph.

Elohim spoke again. "I will put enmity between you and the

woman, and between your offspring and hers." Human beings might be deceived by Satan's wiles, but they would continue to hate and fear him. Humankind would never be fully committed to Satan's agenda as the fallen angels were. Yes, some humans would knowingly or unknowingly take Satan's side in the war. But distrust of Satan and hostility toward him would be deeply rooted in human consciousness.

"He will crush your head, and you will strike his heel." This final pronouncement sealed Satan's doom. It revealed to the rebel angel that Elohim intended to destroy him, and to destroy him through the agency of one of these creatures that Satan had misled so easily! Satan would succeed in harming his nemesis. But the victory of Eve's offspring over Satan was preordained.

As Elohim listed each of the consequences of involvement in Adam and Eve's sin, visible changes took place in the serpent. At the first condemnation, its legs withered away, and it fell to the ground, twisting and writhing. When Elohim announced that hostility would mark the relationship between Satan's followers and human beings, the creature pounded its head against the ground. As it did, the sinister shape of Satan himself could be dimly seen, blended with the shape of the thrashing serpent. Satan's tattered wings were beating futilely. His eyes blazed a fierce red and his mouth, rimmed with pointed teeth, opened and closed spasmodically.

When Elohim pronounced Satan's doom, the master demon's dark shape tore itself away from the serpent's body. Satan crouched there, glaring up at Elohim, his face a contorted mask of hatred mixed with fear. For the first time, the conviction dawned on Satan that he was doomed. Snarling defiance, the evil angel crept backward, its eyes fixed on Elohim until it reached the trees and the edge of the clearing. Then Satan turned and fled.

Shocked at Satan's reaction and at the doom pronounced by Elohim, the demons who had moments ago been dancing with delight slipped away, following their leader into the darkness.

8

Adam and Eve stood transfixed by what they had witnessed. The sight of Satan filled them with both revulsion and fear. Nothing in their sheltered life in Eden had suggested such a creature existed. Even Eve's dream vision of the Iceworm had not prepared her for this glimpse of the Evil One.

As they stood there stunned, Elohim turned to Eve and began to explain the unique consequences to womankind of her actions. "I will greatly increase your pains in childbearing; with pain you will give birth to children."

Because of Adam and Eve's sin, no Lifewind would blow once a year. Instead, each month Eve and her daughters would pass through a cycle, subject to hormones that triggered emotional and physical distress. Even more terrible, each woman who brought new life into the world would see spiritual death's impact on her child. Eve herself would stand over the dead body of one son, knowing that he had been murdered by his brother, and the pain she felt then would seem unbearable.

But Elohim continued. "Your desire will be for your husband, and he will rule over you." This too was something that Eve and her daughters would experience. In Eden Eve had loved Adam and been loved by him. But both of them had acknowledged Elohim as the source of their happiness. This was about to change.

Women would now look to men for happiness. They would desperately seek their life's meaning in relationships with the opposite sex and yearn for male approval rather than be content with the approval of Elohim. Because no one or no thing can replace Elohim in a person's life, they were doomed to disappointment.

But men would not only disappoint women. Men would exploit them. Men would take advantage of this vulnerability of women and use rather than appreciate them. In the cultures that humankind would build, women would no longer be viewed as partners but as inferiors to be used and ignored.

This was not a state that Elohim ordained. Elohim was not cursing Eve, nor was he giving men authority over women. He was explaining for her and all her daughters a particular twisting of human nature that had taken place when she and Adam sinned.

Then Elohim turned to Adam, and he explained consequences for men. "Cursed is the ground because of you; through painful toil you will eat of it all the days of your life. It will produce thorns and thistles for you, and you will eat the plants of the field. By the sweat of your brow you will eat your food, until you return to the ground, since from it you were taken; for dust you are, and to dust you will return."

Eve's daughters would seek approval and meaning in relationships with men. Adam's sons would seek meaning in their work. But no longer would work be an unmixed joy. Men's work would be challenging and difficult, for Adam's rebellion would impact all life on Earth. While women would define themselves by their relationships with men, men would define themselves by their work. Yet however much success a man achieved, he would never find fulfillment in his occupation. Man's fulfillment too could only be found in his relationship with Elohim.

Neither Adam nor Eve understood the significance of what Elohim said. Yet Elohim's words were a compassionate explanation of radical changes that would take place in the relationships they and their children were soon to experience. The most dreadful consequences had been announced long before. Then Elohim had warned Adam, "When you eat of it you will surely die." And so they did.

The day they ate, the seeds of biological death were introduced into the bodies of Adam and Eve. A time would now come for each when the body would die and return to dust.

Even more terrible, the moment they ate they died spiritually. Their sin separated them from Elohim, isolating them from his life.

The humans retained the qualities of personhood the Creator had shared with them, but the image of God was now marred and corrupted. Adam and Eve were still moral beings, concerned with right and wrong, good and evil. But their judgment was warped, and they would never be able to trust it. Their emotions were twisted too. They would love, but their love would become selfish. They would make choices, but their choices would be so driven by corrupt desires that they would yearn for and often choose evil rather than good.

The image/likeness of God had not been lost. But that image lay in ruins, rubble that testified to what had once been but what no longer was.

9

"Why did you do it?" Eve wailed after hearing the consequences of their disobedience. "How could you call that tree a gift?"

"It was a gift," Elohim responded gently. "I shared my own image and likeness with you. I made you a reflection of myself. I could make you nothing less.

"Consider this. I distinguish between right and wrong, and choose what is right and good. For you to be truly like me, I had to provide an authentic opportunity for you to distinguish between right and wrong, and to make your own choice of the good.

"The tree I planted in the garden enabled you to do just this. Without the tree, you would have been the kind of playthings that Satan and his followers assumed you were. But you are far more than playthings to me.

"I told you earlier, little ones. My gifts are good. The Tree of the Knowledge of Good and Evil was a good gift. But you misused my gift.

"It's always this way. All my gifts are good ones. But my gifts can be misused.

"That choice was—and is—up to you."

10

After a long silence, Eve asked plaintively, "Can we go home now?"

Elohim replied gently, "Eve, you have no home now. Eden is closed to you. From now on, you must live beyond the four rivers. But before you go, I have something to teach you. Come with me."

Eve reached out for Adam's hand. Gripping it tightly the two humbled humans trailed after the Creator. As they walked Adam became increasingly uncomfortable. Something was wrong. Strong, intermittent gusts of wind moaned through the trees. Each time a gust struck, branches shuddered and fruit fell to the ground. There the skin of the fruit wrinkled, and white mold formed on its surface.

A peculiar, cloying odor hung in the air near the fruit trees replacing the fragrance Adam had always associated with them. The leaves on the trees in the garden were changing too. On nearly every tree, some leaves turned brown and withered. On some trees, a few branches were completely bare of leaves, and these branches looked desiccated and dead. The bark on the trees had roughened, and on many, it was deeply scored. Adam could see vines growing in trees where no vines had been before. The vines crept up the trunks and wrapped themselves around branches, gripping them tighter and tighter in a brutal stranglehold.

The flowers that filled the garden were changing too. Here and there, a plant had withered away, leaving only a rotting brown residue. In one meadow, petals had fallen from all the yellow flowers and lay scattered and wilted. In one flowerbed, half the stalks bearing blossoms lay flat on the ground while the rest bent over listlessly. It seemed to Adam that the colors of the flowers in the garden were somehow growing dull, with none of their familiar vividness and vitality. As they passed one flowering plant, Adam noticed that long, sharp thorns had appeared on its stems. What was happening to Eden?

Strange plants were springing up too. Patches of brambles now blocked some of the broad paths that Adam and Eve had followed. Thickets of thorn bushes too dense to traverse crowded the openings to meadows where succulent grasses had grown. The grasses themselves were changing. Here swatches of stiff, sharp-edged blades had erupted and there a creeping grass was crowding out of a patch of melons. Looking closely, Adam saw that many of the melons and been broken open and that swarms of flies hovered around them.

They passed a valley that had been filled with stalks of grain. Now only half as many stood and their heads held only a few kernels where before there had been dozens. What was happening to Eden? Everywhere beauty was being replaced by ugliness and order by chaos.

Even the ground was changing. The soft, rich, and fertile earth that had nurtured Eden's vegetation and made transplanting so easy was becoming hard and unyielding. The earth beneath their feet was no longer black loam but sandy; so filled with stones, it was increasingly painful for Adam and Eve to walk. In places the surface of the ground was cracked and parched, and where the land had once supported shrubs and trees, only a few weeds survived.

Out of Adam's sight, the animals of Eden were changing too. The transformation was especially notable in the large, fun-loving cats that Adam and Eve so loved. Their blunt claws were becoming pointed and sharp, more suitable for ripping and tearing flesh than for digging. Their teeth altered shape, becoming curved and pointed, the canines longer and better suited to pierce and hold living prey. Their friendly faces were taking on a merciless cast and their tails lashed back and forth as they picked up the scent of creatures that now aroused their hunger.

Other animals and birds were changing too. The claws on eagles and hawks grew sharp, and their beaks curved cruelly. With these changes, each predatory creature became more alert, peering around intently and for the first time sensing an appetite for living flesh. Everywhere the animals that still fed on plant life shifted uneasily, as if realizing that they had now become the hunted, potential victims of pitiless foes.

Adam did not see these changes in the animals of Eden, but as the three walked on together, he and Eve drew closer to each other, sensing but not understanding a growing hostility that emanated from this place that had been so welcoming. When a sudden roar shattered the quiet, Eve shuddered and gripped Adam's arm. Appalled by the changes taking place in Eden, Adam looked down at Eve and angrily accused her. "Look what you've done," he hissed. "Just look what you've done!"

Too frightened by what was happening around them to respond, Eve hung her head and continued to cling to Adam's arm.

Finally Elohim paused and motioned Adam and Eve to come up beside him. "Look," he told them.

There in a now weed-filled pasture was a flock of the wooly animals. They were clearly disturbed, huddling fearfully in the middle of the open field.

"Adam, go quietly and bring two of these animals to me."

As Adam approached the animals milled anxiously. He stopped, waiting for them to quiet. Then, crouching, he slowly and cautiously moved toward them again. Several of the animals watched him, and as he crept closer more and more heads turned. Adam stopped again. In a moment these creatures would panic and flee. Adam dropped to the ground and waited.

When the flock quieted, he crawled on, his body pressed to the ground, pausing whenever one of the animals glanced his way. He was still ten yards from the nearest animal when the flock bolted. Adam sprang to his feet and dashed after them. He dove, and his hands closed on two of the creatures. As they struggled and kicked, the hooves of one struck Adam in the ribs, drawing blood. Despite the pain, Adam held on to the two animals. Gripping one under each arm, he carried them to Elohim.

While Adam had been pursuing the creatures, Elohim had piled a dozen large stones in a heap. He was standing by these stones when Adam handed the first of the animals to him.

Eve never forgot what happened next or the horror she felt. As Elohim held the first of the frightened animals, blood suddenly spurted from its throat and gushed over the stones and onto the ground. Then Elohim took the other, and it died the same way. Elohim stripped the pelts from the two bodies and fashioned clothing for Adam and for Eve.

"Put them on," he said.

When Adam and Eve were dressed in the skins of the two animals, Elohim took their dead bodies and laid them on the heap of stones. As Elohim stretched out his hand over the bodies, fire erupted from the stones and completely consumed them.

Elohim turned and looked intently at Adam and Eve. Eve was crying, heartbroken at the gory deaths of the two animals. "Look at me, Eve, Adam," Elohim said. "Never forget what you've seen.

"If Satan had his way, I would destroy you now. I would be right to do so. But I love you, and I will open a way for you to return to me. Until that way has been opened, whenever you or your children approach me, you must bring the blood of an innocent animal. Until that way is open, their blood will cover your sins as their skins now cover your bodies. Never forget. Teach your children.

"Now you must go."

Elohim pointed toward the east, and with bowed heads, Adam and Eve set out in that direction. As they walked, they became aware that animals of every kind were streaming past, fleeing Eden with them. Ignoring each other in their flight, great and small predators bounded along beside the harmless creatures that would later be their victims. Overhead flocks of birds filled the air, fleeing Eden too. A sense of urgency gripped the first pair and their pace increased, but the fleeing creatures left the hurrying Adam and Eve far behind.

11

Late that afternoon the humans reached the river that marked Eden's eastern boundary. The once briskly flowing stream was now choked with sand bars and almost dry. Adam and Eve crossed over and climbed the steep bank on the far side. At the top they looked back. A bright figure stood astride the path where they had crossed, a flaming sword in its hand. Terrified, Adam and Eve hurried on, never realizing that Elohim had placed the cherubim there not only to keep them out of the ruined garden but also to keep Satan from closing forever the way to the Tree of Life.

Satan was at his expansive best, relaxed and apparently without a care. No one would have guessed that earlier that day one of his greatest triumphs had been spoiled by the unpredictable humans and by the Creator's revelation that he intended to destroy the rebel angel.

"Did you see?" Satan chortled. "Those humans are so gullible. 'Independence.' Hah!"

Baz, one of the Thrones on the council, laughed. "They're on their own now. Out of the Enemy's camp they're at our mercy."

Chashmagoz spoke up enthusiastically. "Yes, and did you notice what happened when they were following Elohim, may his name be forever cursed? There was a tasty surge of pain when the man-thing hurled some words at the woman-thing."

"What words were those?" Eyrloc asked.

"Call Myrdebaal," Satan ordered. "He was to stay close and watch. Let's find out what he overheard."

I rather like being considered our expert on humans. Ever since I was first assigned to watch the man-thing in the garden, whenever questions come up about humans, our Leader and the council turn to me. It's quite an honor. Of course, I always hold something back. This time I only held back a little.

"Myrdebaal," Satan began, "sit down."

I relished it! To be seated with our Leader and members of the council!

"Chashmagoz tells me he sensed a delicious rush of pain from the woman-thing. Tell us what happened."

"Chashmagoz is right. The man-thing and woman-thing were following the Enemy. As they walked the man-thing was filled with anger when the woman-thing touched him. He hissed at her, 'Look what you've done.' That's when pain radiated from the woman-thing."

"He didn't strike her?"

"No. He just spoke words. 'Look what you've done.' And 'Just look what you've done.' I wasn't close to her, but I could definitely taste pain."

Chashmagoz peered at me suspiciously. "You didn't suck up some for yourself?"

"I would have," I told them, "but it was so sudden I wasn't ready. It wasn't a strong pain. But it definitely was pain. It wasn't like the pain felt by our creatures before the Enemy destroyed them. It had a different flavor. But it was tasty."

What a fool! Of course I'd greedily sucked up nearly all the pain, leaving just a bit to tantalize any of our kind who might be near enough to notice it. In fact the pain the woman-thing had felt was almost overpowering. And it was nourishing. I felt stronger after eating it than I've felt in ages.

"What you're saying, Myrdebaal," Satan said, "is that these creatures feel a sort of mental pain? That they can suffer without their bodies being damaged?"

How perceptive our Leader is. Even I hadn't thought of that. "Yes, O Exalted One. The man-thing never touched her. He just hurled words at her."

"Now," Satan continued, "this is fascinating. The creatures we fed on before the Enemy interfered had to die to satisfy our cravings. If all we have to do is get these humans to make each other miserable, why, they may produce an unending supply of anguish for us to feed on!

"And it shouldn't be hard to make them miserable. Now that I've isolated them from the Enemy and convinced them to cling to their independence, there's no way they can resist us."

The prospect of tormenting the humans and their offspring excited the council. It excited me as well. After all, at that time I was the only one who knew how strong the inner pain they felt could be. So I joined the others, and we praised Satan for his wisdom and his accomplishment in preparing the humans to become a food source for our kind. After all, it was and is politically correct to praise our Leader. It's safer too. Underneath Satan is a most unpredictable being.

"Myrdebaal," Satan directed, "keep observing these creatures. I want you to develop a list of every painful thought and emotion they have. We'll set some of our better minds to work on ways to make life as miserable for them as possible."

I bent my head respectfully. But I didn't leave, and no one on the council ordered me out. They were becoming used to my presence. It was almost as though I belonged, although I knew I didn't.

"Now," Satan said, "what's this about Elohim killing two animals and making coverings for the humans?"

Merigox, an authority, reported, "I saw it, but from a distance. Elohim, may his name be forgotten, opened their throats and blood poured out. The animals were dead in moments."

"It was a quick death, then?"

"Yes, very quick."

"Did you sense any pain?"

"None at all. There was just a quick pass and the blood flowed."

"We can conclude the Enemy didn't do it to feed on the creatures' suffering?"

Eyrloc shook his head in puzzlement. "But why else would he kill one of his creatures? What's in it for him?"

Except for the scraping of claws and the uncomfortable shifting of wing stubs, it was quiet in the council room. No one could imagine a practical reason for killing the two animals. Finally Satan spoke. "It must have something to do with using the skins to make a covering for the humans."

"Why do they need coverings anyway?" Merigox asked.

Satan grinned. "It's a very human thing, Merigox," he said. "I saw it after the humans ate the fruit. They felt guilt and they felt shame—two emotions that are unknown among us. The humans knew they had done wrong and deserved to be punished. That's guilt. And neither of them wanted the other to discover how disobeying Elohim had corrupted him or her inside. That's shame. They tried to hide both by covering themselves with leaves.

"Since Elohim replaced the leaves with animal skins, I suspect that the skins have something to do with covering guilt and shame."

"But," Baz objected, "what can animal skins have to do with covering human guilt and shame?"

"I have no idea," Satan replied. "But if there is a link we need to find it. And we need to make sure that the humans do not find it!

"We need to put our best minds to work on how to confuse humans about Elohim and his motives. And we need to come up with a purely selfish reason for his killing of animals.

"Baz, you and Chashmagoz line up recruits to work on this. I want a preliminary report from your team in ten days."

12

Some ten days later the report was submitted. It identified several strategies that could be used to corrupt any knowledge of Elohim the first humans might pass on to their offspring. It even included drafts of possible stories we might someday introduce to imbed our corruptions in human cultures. While preliminary, the report seemed promising. If the humans adopt the view of the gods we intend to promote, they'll loose touch with Elohim forever!

The first recommendation seemed obvious. As the humans multiplied, we would need to introduce stories that distorted the facts about man's origin and the motives for creating him. For instance, suppose that the gods—it was better not to focus on the fact that there was really only the One—felt they had to work too hard. One of them, call him Marduk, responds by creating humans to do the work. We could shape a legend that would surely put humans in their place

When Marduk hears the words of the gods,

His heart prompts him to fashion artful works.

Opening his mouth, he addresses Ea

To impart the plan he had conceived in his heart.

"Blood I will mass and cause bones to be,

I will establish a savage, 'man' shall be his name.

Verily, savage-man I will create.

He shall be charged with the service of the gods,

That they might be at ease

Or invent a story that would convince humans that rather than being created in Elohim's image, they were fashioned from the substance of a condemned deity. For instance,

It was Kingu who contrived the uprising,

And made Tiamat rebel, and joined battle.

They bound him, holding him before Ea.

They imposed on him his guilt and severed his blood vessels.

Out of the blood, they fashioned mankind.

He imposed upon it the service of the gods—

The report also recommended inventing tales that confused or covered the link between sacrifice and sin. "Suppose," one demon suggested, "that we say the gods were irritated because humans are noisy and determined to destroy them. Later they change their minds because they've had to go without sacrifice. It should be easy to confuse the reason for sacrifice. Just present something like this":

I poured out a libation on the top of the mountain,

Seven and seven cult vessels I set up.

Upon these pot-stands I heaped cane, cedar wood, and myrtle.

The gods smelled the savor,

The gods smelled the sweet savor,

The gods crowded around like flies about the sacrifice.

The report was preliminary, but it showed something of our genius for distorting the truth. The substitution of a sacrifice of cane and cedar wood and myrtle for the sacrifice of animals was a nice touch. There's so much we don't know about Elohim's plans for these humans. And we can't imagine the reason for his killing those animals. But if the Enemy insists on it, we want to eliminate it. The more we confuse this issue the better. Whatever Elohim's reasons for killing animals, we'll be able to deceive the humans about it.

What was utterly puzzling to us was the fact that Elohim had not simply executed the humans when they rebelled. He had said that if they disobeyed him they would die. Yet the humans are still alive. Elohim even clothed them before sending them out of Eden!

It made all of us wonder. Are the humans going to get away with their sin? That would hardly be right or just as Elohim makes such a fuss about justice. Is it possible he's abandoned justice for the sake of these miserable creatures?

No. That just couldn't be. Or could it?

13

After they crossed the river, Adam and Eve trudged on eastward. Eden and the home they'd lavished such care on lay behind. Neither spoke of it, but each knew they could never go back—even if they could get past the angel with the fiery sword. Eden was no longer Eden. They had seen the once-beautiful garden they'd explored together deteriorate before their eyes. Even the birds and animals had fled the disintegrating refuge.

But this land beyond the rivers was far from Edenic. There the vegetation had been lush with flowers everywhere. There fruit trees had been everywhere, and patches of grain with heads full of kernels were always just over the next hill. There were trees here, too, and now and then a few flowers. But as Adam and Eve trudged on, no fragrance of ripening fruit evoked hunger and no golden stalks of grain waved invitingly. Adam and Eve were still too stunned to notice, but all too soon hunger would drive them to realize what the loss of Eden implied.

As the light faded, Adam began to look around for a place to sleep. Only then did he notice how different this land beyond the rivers was from Eden. There was grass, but unlike the soft, lush grasses of Eden, this grass provided only a scanty covering for the hard ground. It could never serve as a cushion on which they could rest. Finally, just before full dark, they came upon a cluster of pine trees. Fallen needles lay thick underneath the trees. Adam scraped needles together to make a bed slightly softer than the ground.

That night Adam didn't reach out to cuddle Eve as they fell asleep. Instead he lay a distance away from her. Eve turned her back to Adam and lay there stiffly. For the first time each wondered what the other thought and how the other felt. Earlier they had sensed these things intuitively. Now they felt uncomfortable and uncertain with each other. Finally each fell asleep, separated by an uncomfortable distance and by an appalling awareness of isolation.

By midnight, the air took on a distinct chill. When the mists that watered the earth rose, Eve woke up shivering. Why was it so cold? It had never gotten this cold in Eden. She hunched her shoulders and drew her legs up, but she couldn't warm herself. Finally, hesitantly, she moved closer to Adam. She pressed her back against him, and in his sleep Adam wrapped himself around her as he had so many nights.

As their bodies warmed each other, Eve fell asleep, tears in her eyes. Once they had cuddled close for the sheer delight of feeling each other near. Now only the cold drove them together. Would Adam ever love her again as he had before? Eve felt so unlovable, so unacceptable. How could he care for her now?

14

The next morning Eve awoke alone. She was warm again, but she felt a surge of panic. Where was her husband? Had Adam left her?

Eve scrambled out from under the trees where they'd slept and peered around. She couldn't see Adam anywhere! He had abandoned her! She was alone.

Eve slumped to the ground in tears. Her body heaved with silent sobs. Of course he'd left her. He must hate her. How had she ever let the serpent deceive her? Why had she eaten that cursed fruit? She was a fool. She didn't deserve Adam or his love.

Nearby Myrdebaal quivered with delight. He'd done nothing to harm Eve and here she was in the grip of the most delicious anguish he'd ever tasted! What caused it? How could he and his kind get her to feel such pain again? And again and again!

Eve's eyes were so filled with tears that she didn't see Adam approach. His hands were empty, and he looked grim and unhappy. But when Adam saw Eve weeping, his face took on a look of concern and he ran to her. Dropping down on his knees beside her, Adam took Eve in his arms and asked urgently, "Eve. What's wrong? Are you all right?"

With a wail Eve threw her arms around Adam and pressed her face into his shoulder.

"Oh Adam, I thought you'd left me. Never leave me, Adam. I couldn't live without you."

Adam said nothing but hugged her closer and kissed her hair.

"I'm sorry, Adam. I didn't mean to do it. I know it was all my fault. But don't leave me, please."

Finally Adam spoke. "I didn't leave you, Eve. I was just looking for something we could eat. I won't leave you. I promise."

Even as Adam spoke, he knew what he should have said. Eve actually thought she was to blame for their expulsion from Eden. Adam knew better. He was to blame. The serpent hadn't deceived him. Adam could have stopped Eve by speaking up. Instead Adam had waited, for some reason even he did not understand, consciously exposing Eve to danger. But this was something that Adam simply could not admit. He was too ashamed.

So, rather than say the words that could have relieved Eve of the terrible burden she carried, Adam simply reassured her. "I won't leave you, Eve," he whispered again.

And Adam wouldn't leave her. He did love her. But he knew he didn't love her enough to admit that the responsibility was his. Deep down Adam too was afraid—afraid that if Eve ever learned what he had done she would no longer love him.

Watching, Myrdebaal was puzzled. Outwardly the two seemed to be reconciling. But inwardly pain radiated from both the humans. The flavor of their pain differed slightly but there was no doubt that each was suffering.

How wonderful, Myrdebaal thought. *We don't have to do anything to cause these humans pain. They cause their own pain!*

Neither Myrdebaal nor the two humans understood that what Adam and Eve were experiencing was one of the effects of spiritual death. Their sin had driven a wedge between the husband and wife as well as between them and Elohim; a wedge that blocked the intimacy that had been theirs in Eden. Each was now aware of his or her own flaws. Each felt so unacceptable that it was nearly impossible to be honest with the other. From now on each deceit, each half-truth, would drive fresh wedges to rob them of that complete and total acceptance that made intimacy possible.

"It's all right, Eve," Adam was saying. "I'll never leave you. I do love you."

Eve's sobs slowly subsided, but she continued to hold Adam tightly. "I love you too, Adam," she whispered. "Thank you for loving me."

Adam tenderly wiped Eve's tears away with his hand. "Eve," he said. "Eve, we have to look for food."

Eve looked up in surprise.

"I couldn't find any fruit trees here. Or any grain. There are a few berries we can eat now. But we need to find food."

Eve followed Adam as he led her to berry bushes growing beside a dry streambed. She didn't look back at the place they'd spent their first night away from Eden. But she wouldn't forget that night either, or how terrible it had felt lying there so close and yet so far from her husband.

15

They found only a few berries on scattered bushes. These were red and when plucked each tiny berry was hollow. After an hour of searching through brambles filled with sharp thorns, each had only been sble to find and eat a few dozen ripe berries, and each had scratches on arms and legs.

"This won't do," Adam finally said. "There aren't enough of these berries. We have to find more food."

Again Eve followed as Adam set out toward a nearby hill. The land between them and the hill was dark and rocky with a few sparse patches of grass. Eve picked her way carefully. The stones hurt her bare feet.

"Hurry up, Eve," Adam shouted back at her. Eve, with her eyes on the ground, hadn't realized how far ahead Adam had gotten. She tried to run, but a sharp pain in the ball of her left food made her stop. She lifted her foot and saw blood oozing from a wound left by a sharp stone.

"Hurry up, Eve!"

Eve hobbled on as fast as she could, afraid she might lose sight of Adam. But then Adam reached the top of the hill. He seemed to slump as he looked at the landscape around them. A few minutes later Eve joined him. She dropped to the ground and gripped her painful foot in both hands. Even sitting she could see as much of the landscape as Adam could.

Behind them the ground gradually sloped downward. In the distance she could see a shimmer of water and realized it must be the river that had marked the easternmost border of Eden. The sight made her realize she was thirsty, and she longed for a drink from Eden's cool, crystal waters. Yet a depressing haze lay over the once-delightful garden beyond the river, and Eve could make out nothing familiar. There was no hint of the vibrant green vegetation that had filled the garden the day before. The only color she could see was an occasional flash of red near the river, and Eve shivered at the thought of the spirit being with the fiery sword who stood guard there.

To the right a flat, arid land stretched as far as she and Adam could see. It was the dreariest sight Eve could imagine—a lifeless, tedious expanse. Heat radiating from the dry surface of the empty land made the air shimmer. Clearly the mists that watered Eden never rose to water that monotonous land. Just as clearly they could not expect to find food there.

To the left the landscape looked more promising. The pair could see a series of gradually descending hills. The hills seemed to be little but rock and sand, but where they dipped, Adam and Eve could glimpse valleys where strips of green hinted at the presence of larger bushes and trees.

Ahead the land sloped upward. This land featured thicker vegetation, and here and there flashes of color suggested flowers. As the land rose, the pair could even make out what seemed to be forests. But above the band of trees they could see ridges as rocky and barren as the desert to their right.

After studying the vista, Eve asked, "Which way shall be go, Adam? Where will we find food?"

"I don't know," Adam answered irritably.

"It looks like there are trees to the left," Eve suggested. "Maybe they're fruit trees."

"Yes, and maybe they're not," Adam muttered. "I just don't know."

"There are flowers on the hills ahead of us. Maybe it's like Eden that way. We always had plenty of food in Eden."

"Eve," Adam said harshly, "Eden's gone. There's no place like Eden out here beyond the rivers."

"I know," Eve whispered. And again tears welled up in her eyes.

Adam saw the tears but looked away. "We've got to find food. I think our chances are better if we go left, down that way."

Eve nodded and stretched out her hand. Adam grasped it and pulled her to her feet. This time he kept hold of her hand as they walked northward toward the sloping hills. They had taken only a few steps when Adam realized that Eve was limping.

"What's wrong?"

"It's my foot. I hurt it."

"How?" he asked, and then demanded, "Let me see it."

Eve sat down, and Adam knelt beside her. Looking at her left foot, he saw an angry red puncture wound and noted that the rest of her foot was bruised. Adam sat her foot down carefully but couldn't disguise a look of disgust.

"I'm sorry, Adam," Eve said.

"It's not your fault, Eve," Adam said. "Your feet are badly bruised. It must hurt you to walk."

Eve nodded. "They hurt. But I'm trying to keep up."

"My feet hurt too, Eve," Adam said. "But my feet aren't as bruised as yours. We'll just have to go slower. Maybe if you lean on me it won't be so bad."

Eve smiled. It was almost worth the pain to have Adam be so kind and solicitous. "I'll try, Adam," Eve said. They set out again with Adam's arm around Eve taking some of the pressure off her left foot. Their pace, though still slow, picked up.

After an hour, the stones disappeared and the ground was softer. But the first valley with its prospect of fruit seemed as far away as ever. It was growing warmer, too. Eve reached up, felt her brow, and was surprised to find it was wet with perspiration. She looked at Adam and saw that sweat was running down his face. The light seemed no brighter than it had been in Eden, but the temperature was already much higher. She remembered the cold of the previous night and wondered. Would it be like this everywhere outside the garden?

16

As it grew hotter and the sweat ran down his body, Adam became irritable. The animal skin chafed where it looped over his right shoulder, and he itched wherever it touched his body. His feet too were now bruised, and it was painful for him to walk. His mouth was dry; his throat parched. And he was getting hungrier and hungrier. He became almost desperate to reach the trees and water, but he had to go slow because of Eve.

The more he focused on his discomfort the more irritable he became. All right, so he'd disobeyed and eaten from the forbidden tree. It was wrong, but was it really so terrible? Elohim cast them out into this for just one bite of fruit?

As Adam's mood darkened, he felt more and more Elohim's victim.

Surely Elohim hadn't needed to throw them out of the garden. Adam had been sorry for what he'd done. Why couldn't Elohim just let it go? Tell him, "Well, don't let it happen again," and then let things be as they were before.

What Adam chose not to remember was that he had eaten deliberately, and that afterward he'd been frightened and ashamed, not sorry. Oh, he was sorry when he began to experience the consequences of his choice. But he had not felt that godly sorrow that leads to repentance—to an overwhelming realization that his disobedience was an affront to the Creator who loved him. What Adam had felt was fear and his first instinct had been to shift blame to Eve, and even to blame Elohim for giving her to him. What Adam felt was resentment rather than repentance, and this reaction revealed something of how serious his sin had been. Unknown to Adam, this initial expression of hostility toward Elohim was a foretaste of an alienation from the Creator that would dominate his own life and the lives of his offspring.

"Adam," Eve begged, "can we rest a minute?"

Adam hadn't realized it, but as his resentment had grown he'd increased their pace. Eve, struggling to keep up despite her painful feet, was nearly exhausted.

"No!" Adam barked.

"But Adam, my feet hurt. And I'm so thirsty and tired."

Adam slowed his pace slightly. He was growing tired too. And he was growing thirstier and hungrier. But those trees were still hours away.

"All right, all right," Adam muttered. "We'll rest."

As Eve dropped to the ground and began to massage her painful feet, Adam remained standing, gazing at the tree line far ahead. *It's hot*, he thought. *It never got this hot in Eden. And it was cold last night. It never got cold in Eden either. I'm hot and I'm thirsty and I'm hungry. I want to go back. I want to go back home.*

"Adam," Eve said hesitantly. "I'm all right now. I can go on."

Adam looked down at her. They had to go on. They couldn't go back. Adam reached down and helped Eve up. She clung to him and then took his hand and smiled. For a moment she looked like the Eve of Eden, and Adam remembered that imperious shake of the head as with hands on hips she told him, "This just won't do." He remembered how eager he'd been to please her and how he had agreed, "You're right. It won't do."

Now as Adam looked into her eyes he realized that the Eve he'd known was gone. This Eve depended on him. She was looking to him, expecting him to take care of her. It was more than Adam could bear, for Adam knew he was helpless in this land beyond the rivers. For the first time since they'd fled Eden, Adam was truly afraid. Afraid for himself, and afraid for Eve.

Five hours later, they were close enough to recognize some of the trees ahead of them. With excitement Adam realized that three of the trees bore figs and at least one of the smaller trees carried another familiar fruit. Despite their painful bruises, Adam and Eve ran. But before they reached the trees Adam stopped suddenly. Something was wrong. Adam could see figs growing on the branches. But rather than the rich brown of the figs he'd picked in Eden, this fruit was a light green color. And the other fruit tree bore only a few tiny round balls, miniatures of the ripe red orbs with which they were familiar.

When the two reached the trees and picked some of the figs, they found them not only green but hard and inedible. Adam and Eve looked at each other, stunned. The trees in Eden had always borne ripe fruit as well as fruit in other stages in development. There were no ripe figs on these trees in this land beyond the rivers. Adam and Eve had walked for most of a day to find food. And there was no food here.

Thirstily the couple drank from the tiny stream that ran through the valley. Then they spent the last hours of daylight searching the valley for something to eat. They found half a dozen stalks of grain and shared the two handfuls of kernels they bore. But the food only seemed to make the pair hungrier.

When it grew dark, Adam found a little hollow, and they lay down together on the hard ground. As the air cooled, they huddled close to each other for warmth, so hungry now that sleep refused to come. At midnight a mist rose from the ground chilling them further. Eve began to shiver uncontrollably. Adam held her tight but he was chilled too. Finally, when the mists subsided and the air cleared, they drifted closer to sleep.

Until Adam was jolted awake by the distant roar of a hungry animal. The roar was answered by another, and for several minutes two or more big cats filled the air with terrifying screams. Adam listened as Eve slept on. He held his wife tightly and thought, *What have I done? Oh what have I done!*

17

Adam was awakened by a gnawing pain in his stomach. His body ached from the night spent on the unyielding ground, and he awkwardly removed the arm that lay over Eve's shoulders. Today they had to find food.

First though, Adam needed to drink. He rose stiffly and walked to the nearby creek. He knelt down there, resting both hands on the bank and bent his head to the water. It was cool and fresh. Adam drank deeply and then settled back on his haunches. It was then he noticed the tracks just to his right.

Deeply imprinted in the soft mud were the paw prints of one of the big cats along with prints of smaller animals. Adam looked around fearfully. He hadn't witnessed the transformation of the fun-lovers of Eden, but he had heard them roaring during the night. Whatever they were now, they were no longer the animals he had romped with in Eden.

Adam looked around hurriedly. He saw a dead tree nearby and tried to break off a short but sturdy branch. He strained, and finally it snapped. Adam found a large stone near the stream and used it to break off the half-dozen smaller shoots attached to the branch. He gripped the wood and swung. It felt solid and reasonably heavy. Equipped with this club Adam felt safer. Then suddenly he thought of Eve, still asleep in the hollow. What if the animals had found her while he was at the stream!

Adam was unaware of the fact that all through the night angels had surrounded the place where they slept. The snarling of the big cats was an expression of their frustration. Hunger had driven them to the sleeping couple, but the angels had kept them away.

Panicked by the realization that Eve was alone and that the big animals might be near, Adam ran back to the hollow. There she was, still asleep. Adam looked around anxiously but saw no sign of any animals. He lay down his club and gently shook his wife.

"Eve. Eve. It's time to get up."

Eve turned over and groaned. Her whole body hurt, especially her back. Gingerly she rose to her hands and knees and looked up at Adam. Her heart sank as she remembered that she and Adam now lived in a painful new reality.

Adam helped Eve up and waited as she twisted and turned, trying to relieve the pain in her back. "Come get a drink, Eve. Then we have to look for food."

Adam stood guard at the stream as Eve knelt down and drank. She saw the animal tracks but made no comment. Adam said nothing about his fears, but the alert way he peered along the bank, and the way he held the club, made it clear to Eve that Adam thought they were in danger. When Eve finished drinking, Adam led his wife along the little creek, moving downstream.

They walked for most of an hour, often fighting through thickets that grew near the stream. Nowhere did they see fruit nor did they find berries or grain. Adam pushed on, breaking a path for Eve, but hunger was making Eve weak. She was determined to keep up, but finally could go on no longer.

"Adam," she called. "I've got to rest. I feel so weak."

Adam was frustrated. Eve was slowing him down. But he couldn't leave her and go on ahead with dangerous animals possibly nearby. Yet they had to find food. Probably they should abandon this creek and push on over the hills to another valley. But how many hours would that take? With the day growing hotter, could Eve make it with no food or water?

Frustration grew into resentment and resentment turned into anger. Why was he burdened with a woman who couldn't keep up? Why was she so weak? She was slowing him down, making it harder for them to survive. It wasn't fair. None of it was fair.

"Not now," Adam barked. "You're holding me back as it is. Just keep up."

Eve found herself crying silent tears. She was trying so hard. She'd pushed herself to keep up. Even though she felt sick as the hunger and the weakness grew, she hadn't complained. She hadn't even asked to rest until she'd become dizzy and felt she was about to faint. Why didn't Adam understand how hard she was trying?

Still Eve said nothing. Sick and faint, she forced herself to keep moving.

"Hurry up," Adam said angrily. "We've got to find food."

18

For Myrdebaal the morning provided a continuing revelation. When Adam had been hurt by the hooves of one of the creatures Elohim killed in Eden, there had been a flash of physical pain, but that was brief and unsatisfying. Even the pain of the puncture wound in Eve's foot had provided the demon with no more than a tasty morsel, and afterward the pair had more or less ignored the discomfort of their bruised feet. But the emotional pain both felt was intense and delicious. Fascinatingly, the humans seemed to provoke each other's suffering!

Now, for instance, Adam was radiating an emotional pain that to Myrdebaal tasted like a medley of guilt and anger. Eve was radiating suffering that tasted of self-pity and rejection. It was clear from the humans' behavior that neither one understood what was happening inside the other. Each was so wrapped up in his or her own emotions that neither could identify or sympathize with the other. Most excitingly, neither seemed willing to share what he or she was feeling. Bottled up inside, their emotional aguish became more and more intense and satisfying.

Myrdebaal, feasting ecstatically on this suffering, nevertheless made a mental note to explain this peculiarity of the humans to Satan and the council. If his kind could keep the humans from sharing their feelings, keep the painful emotions bottled up, let the emotions fester, they'd feast indeed! The humans would become more and more miserable, to the benefit of Satan's followers.

What a prospect! Myrdebaal shivered with delight. Satan's demons might at times resort to causing the humans physical pain. But Myrdebaal realized that the emotional anguish on which he'd been feeding could support the horde's passion for pain for ages and ages.

Back at the Heart of Darkness, where Satan met with his council, the Leader was struggling with a dilemma. What course should he choose for dealing with these humans?

On the one hand, Elohim had predicted that a seed of the woman would one day cause his downfall. It might be wisest to destroy the human pair now, before they could have any offspring. On the other hand, Satan had easily detached the human's from their allegiance to Elohim. In the process Satan's scout, Myrdebaal, had discovered that he and his followers could feed on human suffering.

If Satan let the first couple live and reproduce, there was a good chance he could thwart Elohim's plans simply by manipulating the humans. And, should they multiply, he and his followers would have a constant source of delight through the ages. Letting the humans live would be a gamble, of course. But Satan had to admit that life had been dull from the time Nemesis struck Earth until he had engineered Eve and Adam's disobedience.

Finally Satan decided. He would not kill the humans. Yet. He'd let them reproduce. He'd learn more about how they could be maneuvered to thwart any plans of the Enemy. In the meantime, he and his followers would feel—and enjoy!—their pain.

19

Adam's angry tone when he told Eve, "Hurry up," was almost more than Eve could bear. She stumbled on, blinded now by tears. How could Adam be so cruel? What had happened to the man she'd thought loved her completely? Eve tripped and fell. She tried to get up, but she felt too weak and too discouraged.

When Adam looked back and saw her crumpled on the ground, his anger and frustration evaporated. He ran back to Eve and knelt beside her.

"Eve. Eve. Are you all right?"

The alarm in Adam's voice reached something deep inside Eve. *He does care*, she thought. Looking up through her tears, she smiled at her husband. "I fell. I'm sorry, Adam. I just feel so weak."

Adam put his arms around her. "Of course you do. You need something to eat."

"Thank you, Adam," Eve murmured.

"I'm sorry, Eve. It's my fault. I've pushed you too hard. I'll try to do better, darling."

Adam's contrition relieved Eve's fears. Adam did love her. It was just this terrible land beyond the rivers and the fact they were both so hungry. "I can get up now, Adam," Eve said and tried to get to her feet. But dizziness took her and she slumped back.

"Wait a moment, Eve. Get your strength back. It's all right."

Eve leaned gratefully against her husband, hearing his heart beat, sensing the return of his love for her. How terrible the emotional ups and downs they had both been feeling! Would it ever be as it had been in Eden where each loved the other all the time? Where no anxiety or anger or guilt or frustration interrupted the free flow of their love for each other? Eve had no idea of what might lie ahead, but at the moment, resting against Adam's chest, she felt secure and at peace. *How I need him*, she thought. *How I need his love.*

Adam's love for Eve had returned. But even as Eve rested in his arms, his thoughts returned to their precarious situation. What should they do next? Where might they find food? Would they be able to cross another stretch of barren land to reach the next valley?

Adam thought briefly of Elohim, silently begging him to provide food for Eve. It was just a passing thought, an involuntary prayer, but it was the only thought of dependence of the Creator Adam had had since they'd left Eden. What had happened at the Tree of the Knowledge of Good and Evil had changed Adam far more than he understood. Without consciously thinking about it, he had assumed that he must depend on himself now and that he could build a new life for himself and for Eve without Elohim's aid.

This was not a conscious decision. Instead it represented Adam's new orientation to life, and was yet another impact of sin on his personality. Adam knew intellectually that Elohim still loved him and loved Eve. But since being expelled from Eden, both of them had acted as if Elohim had no active role to play in their lives. It seemed to them that they were on their own and that this was the way it should be.

The prayer that flitted through Adam's mind faded from his consciousness immediately. But Elohim had heard.

"I can get up now," Eve said.

Adam helped her up and for a long moment held her close. "Eve," he said gently, "we need to find food soon. When we do, we'll leave this valley and go to the next one. Maybe the fruit there will be ripe."

"All right, Adam," Eve answered, "whatever you say."

The rest restored Eve somewhat, and she followed close behind as Adam led the way downstream. Then the stream turned sharply left, and as they came around a bend, they found a stand of grain and next to it a melon patch. They ran excitedly to the grain and began to rub the heads between their hands, separating the kernels. The kernels were plump, and they tasted like the grain of Eden, rich and earthy. When they'd each eaten several handfuls and had drunk again from the creek, they broke open one of the melons and scooped out the sweet flesh with their fingers. Finally full, they stretched out under a nearby tree.

Adam awoke first. He could feel that the day was heating up. How far was it over the sloping hills to the next valley? Could they make it before nightfall? Or should they stay here where there was food?

As Adam was pondering what to do, he heard the snarl of one of the great cats coming from up stream. "Wake up, Eve," Adam said urgently. "We've got to leave."

"Why?" Eve asked sleepily.

"It's the animals. They're following us."

"But," Eve objected, "they're our friends."

Adam shook his head. "I'm afraid they're not friends any longer." Again the snarl came, and now Eve too sensed hunger and hostility.

"You're right, Adam. We have to leave."

Quickly the two pulled off more heads of grain and wrapped them in leaves. Each drank as much as he or she could from the creek. Eve took a melon, and Adam picked up his club. "Let's go this way," he said and led them up the hill out of the little valley. When they reached the rim, Adam saw another range of low hills. Beyond it, tree tops indicated there was another valley. Without looking back, the two set off, unaware for the moment of the increasing heat of the day.

After just two hours, the mouth of each was dry and the pair yearned for water. They stopped to eat the melon and then, restored by its juices, hurried on. In another three hours, they approached the new valley and saw through a gap what seemed to be broader lands beyond a stream. Adam and Eve looked at each other and smiled. The vista looked more like Eden than any they'd seen since being exiled from their home.

When they reached the gap, they paused. Below them lay a small lake fed by a bubbling stream. The lake lay in the center of a valley that was dotted with fruit trees. Beyond the lake, they could see stalks of standing grain.

"Oh Adam," Eve said delightedly. "Maybe we can stay here. Maybe we can make this our home."

Adam nodded, smiling. This place felt like home. Hand in hand, they walked into the valley. Even though the day was hot, it was cooler in the valley. The fruit on some of the trees was ripe, and the fruit on others was ripening. Perhaps they could settle down here. Perhaps the stress they'd felt since leaving Eden would be relieved here and they might again experience the peace that had nurtured them and their love.

That evening they again ate some of their favorite fruit. They walked hand in hand around the placid little lake and picked more heads of grain. They drank cool water from the stream, and when Eve found a leafy bower where the grasses were soft and thick, they felt that they truly were home.

That night Adam and Eve made love again. They lay relaxed in each other's arms, the sense of intimacy that they'd lost restored completely.

"Let's not let anything drive us apart again," Eve whispered.

"Nothing will, Eve," Adam assured her. "Nothing will ever change my love for you."

20

This restored harmony was more than Myrdebaal could bear. Where had all that delightful emotional anguish gone? And where had the sick, cloying contentment come from? Something had to be done!

When Adam and Eve fell asleep, Myrdebaal returned to the Heart of Darkness and asked for an interview with Satan. The Leader was eager to hear the demon's report and didn't wait to summon the council. Myrdebaal reported the events of that day and what he had learned about the humans. Myrdebaal even released a large portion of the anguish he'd eaten, so Satan could savor the tastes of guilt and anger and self-pity and rejection.

Satan was delighted. Surely his decision to let the man-thing and woman-thing live was the right one.

"But, great Leader," Myrdebaal went on, "now they've found a valley where they feel safe. All those delicious emotions are gone. All I can taste now is a contentment that sickens me."

"What are you suggesting, Myrdebaal?" Satan asked

"Master, if you could somehow get them out of the valley …? Make life difficult for them again?"

Satan laughed. "Get them out of the valley? I can do better than that. After all, I'm the ruler of this world.

"Go bring Persifor to me."

Myrdebaal was dismissed when he returned with Persifor. Satan conferred in private with this Demon of Destruction, and when Persifor left Heart of Darkness, Myrdebaal noted a malevolent grin on his distorted face.

Satan followed Persifor out and motioned for Myrdebaal. "Stay here a while. Return to the valley in the morning, just before they awake. Then come and tell me what happens."

As Myrdebaal turned to leave, Satan called out to him. "And, Myrdebaal, bring me my share of their anguish."

That night Persifor visited the valley. He passed through it like a raging wind and left it in ruins. Trees fell into the stream, stirring up the bottom, so that by morning it ran thick with mud. Branches torn from tree trunks were scattered everywhere. Every fruit was stripped from the remaining trees and blown away or thrown violently against the ground and crushed. A hole opened in the bottom of the lake, and the water disappeared, leaving acres of reeking mud. The wind flattened the standing grain and blew away every head, the kernels with the chaff. There was nothing for the humans to eat in the entire valley.

Persifor had done his work silently, so silently that neither Adam nor Eve had been aroused. That morning Eve awoke and sat up. She looked around but could not believe what she saw. Eve shook Adam sharply. "Adam!" she cried, horrified. "Adam. Wake up. Look at our valley."

Adam sat up, rubbing his eyes.

"What's the matter, Eve?"

"Look!" she shouted. "Look!"

Adam's heart sank as he saw the destruction all around. What had become of their peaceful valley? While Eve felt horror and revulsion, Adam's first emotion was an overwhelming sense of despair. He'd tried so hard to take care of Eve. And just when he felt they were safe, this!

"Why?" Adam shouted, looking upward. "Why did you do this to us? Wasn't losing Eden enough?"

Nearby Myrdebaal doubled over in glee. He loved the taste of Eve's horror, and he loved the flavor of Adam's despair and anger. The joke was that Adam was angry at Elohim when the destruction had been caused by the demon Persifor.

These humans, Myrdebaal thought, *they're so much fun. When something goes wrong they blame the Enemy. And if something seems to go right they take the credit themselves. And we're ignored, left to enjoy the spoils!*

Myrdebaal left, hurrying to report to Satan. Back at the Heart of Darkness, Satan had several of his best minds debrief Myrdebaal and develop another preliminary report, this time on additional strategies his minions might adopt to keep the humans in a state of emotional anguish. Working from Myrdebaal's account, the committee of demons presented their working paper to the Leader.

Their first proposal was to cause "natural disasters" such as droughts, floods, hurricanes, tornados, plagues, which the humans would blame on Elohim.

The demons would delight to suggest to the humans that such events were Elohim's punishment rather than due to natural causes or demons' deviltry.

To ensure this interpretation, the committee recommended that in the future demons avoid causing such disasters shortly after some sin of the humans. Rather, disasters should be caused when the humans were feeling especially thankful or had performed some notable act of obedience. Humans should feel that Elohim was being unfair in punishing them.

Another recommendation was that disasters should be caused when the humans felt secure. Infrequent disasters wisely timed might keep them in a state of uncertainty and doubt, undermining trust in Elohim.

An important insight was expressed in the recommendation that demons encourage misunderstandings between the humans. Adam had felt a need to act quickly and resented the fact that Eve slowed him down. Eve felt hurt by Adam's failure to understand that she was doing the best she could. It was important to make sure neither truly understood the other.

There was much potential here. It should be easy to encourage tension between task-oriented males and relationship-oriented females. And misunderstandings could be nurtured. It would be easy to whisper to each that the other is insensitive. Demons might suggest to each the other really understands his or her feelings, but doesn't care. This should create resentment, hostility, and anger—all of which we find delicious!

Above all humans should be prevented from honestly expressing their feelings to each other. When humans truly understood each other's perspectives and emotions, resentment and hostility are reduced. They may even be replaced by those "positive" emotions, which we find revolting. If Adam and Eve were a valid example, the more closely linked emotionally humans are, the more intense the suffering misunderstanding and resentment cause. This "love" Elohim and the humans speak of seems to make humans especially vulnerable.

Myrdebaal missed the final surprise Persifor had arranged for the humans back in the devastated valley. As the discouraged pair left the place they had hoped would become their home, they came upon the remains of a small animal, torn apart by some predator. Blood spattered the grass around the tattered corpse, and a bit of fur fluttered in the breeze. Looking closely Adam and Eve could see the expression on the little creature's face, its dark eyes staring sightlessly and its mouth closed tight as if fighting not to scream.

Eve turned away and buried her face in Adam's shoulder. She unknowingly echoed Adam's earlier cry: "Why has he done this to us, Adam? Why does he hate us so?"

The darkness that encompassed Satan and his demons had begun to settle over the humans too. Distrust of the one being who loved them unconditionally, the one being who could and would help, was growing.

21

During the next few weeks, each day fell into a grim pattern. Every evening Adam and Eve searched for some sheltered place where they could rest. Each night was cold, and although Adam and Eve huddled close together for warmth, their sleep was restless and fitful. Each morning, they awoke more tired than the morning before and searched for something, anything, they might eat. Some mornings they found a few berries, some stalks of grain, or a familiar vegetable to gnaw on. Other mornings they found nothing edible and had to set out with stomachs aching for food.

The land too seemed patterned. The barren hills were cut by streams about a day's walk apart. Each stream wandered through a deep or shallow valley where trees and grasses grew. Day after day, Adam and Eve traversed the barren landscapes hoping that the next valley might provide plenty of food and a place to settle, at least for a short time. But each day's walk left them disappointed and more exhausted than they had been the day before.

Once they found a date palm and gorged on the ripe fruit. But that was more than their systems could handle. The next day they were too sick to travel. When the illness passed, they wrapped several pounds of dates in leaves to bring with them but ate them sparingly and always with other foods they gathered.

Another valley held a good-sized stand of barley. The day they discovered it, they ate all they could hold and the next morning made packets to carry the rest of the grain with them. Despite such infrequent finds, they never seemed to have enough to eat. Both Adam and Eve were steadily growing weaker.

As they trudged over the barren landscape during the day, neither had energy for talk. When they reached the next valley in the late afternoon or evening, they felt overwhelmed with disappointment. It was all they could do after drinking from the stream to search briefly for food and a place to sleep. All too often, it was too late to find any food before nightfall, and they went to bed hungry as well as exhausted. They huddled together at night but neither seemed to have anything to say to the other.

Now and then Adam would whisper, "I love you, Eve."

Eve would nod her head in acknowledgement or mutter, "I love you too." Beyond this and the few necessary words they spoke the next morning as they searched a valley food, they simply didn't talk.

This silence bothered Myrdebaal, who still tracked Adam and Eve. Neither of the two experienced an intense pain of the sort that demons love to feed on. Their emotions seemed to have shut down as all their energy was devoted to the struggle to survive.

Gorel, who was still assigned to watch Adam and Eve, was disturbed for another reason. He knew that these humans were important to Elohim, blessed be his name. He had seen the guardian angels that were sent to protect the pair from the great cats. But he had also had orders from on high to stand aside when the destroying demon Persifor devastated the valley the two humans loved.

As Gorel watched the condition of Adam and Eve deteriorate day after day and sensed their underlying despair, Gorel felt a growing compassion for them. Adam had displayed such special qualities in Eden. And Gorel had been moved by the love the two felt for each other, even though as an angel he could not experience such love himself. Gorel knew that Elohim cared for these humans. But if Elohim cared, why did he let them go on day after day without hope?

22

More than two months passed before Adam and Eve reached the brow of one of the barren hills and saw an unexpected vista. Rather than a narrow valley below them, there was a broad plain, stretching out to the horizon. The pair could make out lakes and forests and great stretches of grassy meadow. Here and there they could even see animals grazing—animals they had known in Eden. It seemed almost as though the valley lay there, calling to them.

Eve burst into tears and clutched Adam's arm. "O Adam! It's so beautiful. I thought we would never find anything like this again."

Adam was close to tears too. Could it be that their harsh journey was over and they could settle down at last? He put his arm around Eve's waist and simply hugged her as they gazed at the great plain before them.

Finally they began to walk toward it, wanting to run but too weak to do so. It took them over an hour to reach the edge of the plain where a thin cover of grass grew. As they walked farther, the grasses thickened and became more like the green carpet they had known in Eden. But they soon realized that this was no Eden.

The edges of many of the blades of grass were serrated. When they tried to walk through a patch of this saw grass, Eve cried out. Looking down she saw bloody scratches on her ankles and calves. Nor could they reach the water in the first stream they came to because of brambles growing along its banks. Later when Adam knelt to feel the soil in a bare patch underneath a tree, he found earth that was dark but much too hard to dig into with his fingers.

Yet these drawbacks seemed as nothing to Adam and Eve. The string of barren hills lay behind them, and an obviously fertile plain lay ahead. Even though it was getting too late to search for food that night, the land gave every promise that they would find something to eat the next morning. For the first time in weeks, when Adam and Eve lay down to sleep that night, they talked about their future.

"Adam, do you think we can stay here?"

"I think we can, Eve. Did you see the lakes and all the trees? And there's grass everywhere. We're sure to find food. We can build a shelter near the food, maybe make this plain our home."

"I want to stay here, Adam. I'm so exhausted. I was just about ready to give up and die."

"I know, Eve. I felt the same way."

"You did?" Eve asked, surprised. "I didn't know you were ready to give up."

"Well, I was. I was so tired all the time. I was afraid you wouldn't be able to keep on."

"I don't know how I did."

"I'm so proud of you Eve. You didn't even complain."

Eve laughed. "I was too tired to complain. If I hadn't been so done in, I'd have complained all the time."

The conversation was a brief one. Somehow each felt more fatigued now they'd reached the plain than they had before, as their relief on finding a place they might stay resulted in a mental let down, and the exhaustion they'd held back by sheer force of will took over. That night they slept so soundly that they were unaware of the night's chill or of the mists that drenched them after midnight. They slept so soundly that even the growing daylight failed to rouse them, and it was afternoon when Eve and then Adam awoke.

The two spent the rest of the day exploring the edges of the plain. Adam had been right. There was food there. They found two trees filled with ripe fruit and noted others where fruit was ripening. They found a small plot containing stalks of grain that Adam thought would soon mature. There were wild berries and melons. They even located several plants with edible roots. The water in the stream was pure and cold, and near it was a shallow cave that reached back into a hillside.

During the next week, Adam and Eve ate and rested. They gathered grasses and made a nest inside the cave, having discovered that it protected them from the drenching night mists. With rest and plentiful food, they again began to enjoy each other's company. For the first time since being expelled from Eden, it was fun to explore together. They held hands as they surveyed the nearby area, laughed and kissed, and the fifth night they made love.

Afterward as they cuddled, Eve sighed and said, "I've missed feeling close."

Adam squeezed her hand. "I know. Me too." Warm and contented, the two fell asleep in each other's arms.

23

Three months later, Adam announced, "Eve. We've got to move."

Shocked, Eve objected. "But why? I like it here."

"I like it here too, Eve. But haven't you noticed? We're running out of food. We've eaten all the grain and berries here. We've pulled up most of the vegetables. The fruit that was ripe when we got here is falling off the tree and rotting. And the fruit on the other trees isn't ripe yet. We've got to move to a place that has food."

Eve felt a crushing disappointment. She'd filled the cave where they slept and made love with fragrant leaves and had transplanted several flowering bushes outside its entrance. The cave was far from the house of flowers they'd built together in Eden, but to Eve it felt like home. And Eve was sensing a greater and greater need for a home. Still, Adam was right, and so reluctantly she set off with her husband to look for another place to settle.

They found an ideal location a full day's walk farther into the plain. There seemed to be plenty of food nearby. There were trees bearing a different kind of fruit. There was another plot of grain, and again melons and several familiar vegetables grew nearby. This time they set up house in a stand of bamboo near a lake. As Adam had when he first became conscious in Eden, they bent young bamboo shoots to form the framework of a house and then wove in branches to enclose it. Eve loved her little bamboo hut and again spent time adding special touches to make it seem like a home.

The two were happy there for a few more months. Then Adam again announced, "Eve, we've got to move." This time Eve had noticed that their food supply was almost exhausted and had been dreading the announcement. But she knew Adam was right. They would have to move on.

"Adam?" Eve asked when they had located a third place to settle. "Will it always be like this? I want a place we can stay. I want a home."

Adam didn't answer.

"Adam," Eve insisted. "Really, will it always be like this?"

"I've thought about it, Eve. And I'm afraid it will. Wherever we go, we'll eat all the food sooner or later. It's even worse than that. In this place we have no ripe grain. There are grain stalks here, but the heads haven't even formed. It will be months before the grain ripens, and before that happens, we'll have eaten all the other food and have to move on. And some of the vegetables we like to eat are just sprouts here.

"What happens if we have to move on and find there are no trees with ripe fruit and no mature grain or vegetables? I don't like to keep moving either, and I think it's dangerous. But I don't know what else to do."

After a time Eve said hesitantly, "Maybe we'd better ask Elohim to show us what to do."

Neither Adam nor Eve had mentioned Elohim for many months. Eve had thought about him, even though it was painful to remember how she'd been deceived by Satan and betrayed him. Adam had pushed away every thought of Elohim.

On the one hand, he was burdened with a sense of guilt and shame, and on the other, he was still angry at Elohim for expelling them from the garden. Since it was too painful for Adam to deal with these feelings, he repressed each thought of the Creator as soon as it occurred. But the more Adam had refused to think of Elohim, the more distressed he had felt.

While the two traveled in the barren lands, Adam had been too exhausted to think about anything other than survival. But since they'd been living on the plain, thoughts of Elohim had been a nagging presence, as if the Creator were inside Adam's head reminding Adam of all they had shared.

"Adam," Eve persisted, "let's ask Elohim for help. He said he'd make a way for us to return to him when he sent us out of the garden. I know Elohim still cares for us."

Still Adam didn't answer. He knew that Eve was right. Elohim still cared. But how could he ask Elohim for anything? It was all right for Eve to think of appealing to Elohim. The serpent had deceived Eve.

But Adam had sinned willfully. He'd forfeited any right he'd had to approach Elohim for a favor.

"I can't, Eve," Adam finally admitted. "I have no right to ask Elohim for anything."

"But, Adam," Eve said, "we have to have help. And besides, it isn't about our right to appeal to Elohim. It's about him and his love. I know we sinned, but he still loves us."

Adam shook his head. "You appeal to Elohim, Eve. I can't. I just can't."

Neither spoke about Elohim again, but each night before they slept, Eve tried to picture their Creator and appealed to him for help. There seemed to be no answer, but Eve persisted. She remembered how kind Elohim had been when he walked with them evenings in Eden and how he'd listened as they shared their plans for their own Eden in Eden. Sometimes Eve thought about how Elohim had clothed them after they sinned, although she still felt upset whenever she pictured the deaths of the sheep.

Some months later, the sixth time Adam and Eve were forced to relocate, they couldn't find a suitable area. They walked deeper and deeper into the plain but either there were no food stuffs or what there was wasn't ripe. Each time before they set out, they'd prepared packages of food to take with them. Now that food was almost gone.

As they became more and more anxious, Adam and Eve fell back on silence, as if refusal to acknowledge their fears would change their situation. One evening as the couple ate the tiny ration of food they now allowed themselves, Eve said, "Adam. I've been praying to Elohim every night."

Adam glanced at her and then looked down toward the ground.

"Adam, please pray with me. We have to have his help. We can't go on alone."

"You can pray, Eve. I can't. I don't deserve his help."

"Please, Adam," Eve begged. "Please appeal to him with me."

Adam shook his head. "No," he said. "You appeal to him. You deserve his help. I don't."

Eve began to weep quietly. In torment, Adam cried out, "I can't. I just can't."

Myrdebaal was delighted. At last these humans were feeling anguish again. How tasty! Myrdebaal considered sucking up the agony and keeping it all for himself, rather than share it with Satan. But suddenly the radiating pain stopped. And then Myrdebaal himself began to feel pain! Something like a searing heat was scorching his body.

Peering around for the source, Myrdebaal saw two shining figures advancing toward Adam and Eve. These were powerful angels indeed, so powerful that their approach drove the demon back and away from the humans. By the time the two shining figures reached Adam and Eve, Myrdebaal had turned and fled.

24

Adam and Eve were stunned at the sight of the bright lights. Awed and frightened, they clung to each other as the lights approached and they made out the shining figures. At first they thought Elohim was approaching, but he had never allowed them to see him except with his essential being cloaked. Some of his brightness had shone through, but not as much as radiated from these beings.

"Eve," the first of the two said, "we are messengers from Elohim. He has heard your prayers and sent us to help you."

"Adam," the second said, "you are correct. You are not worthy to appeal to Elohim. But he has chosen to love you anyway. Remember when he covered your sin with the blood of slain animals? He clothed you in their skins as a reminder of that covering.

"Trust Elohim, Adam. Look to him and away from your past sins and failures. Elohim has forgiven you and has sent us to help you."

Adam and Eve were almost blinded by the brightness of the two messenger angels and covered their eyes with both hands. "Look at us," the first messenger commanded, and as the couple opened their eyes, the splendor faded and the two angels standing before them looked like ordinary men.

The first angel continued, "Elohim waited to send us until you both understood that you cannot survive in this land beyond Eden by constantly moving from place to place in search of food. Especially as you will soon have children. You need to settle down in one place, grow the food you need, and provide shelter and clothing for your offspring. To do this, you need skills you never developed in Eden. Elohim has sent us to teach you those skills.

"So pick the place you want your home to be. We will teach you how to survive in this land beyond the rivers of Eden.

"Choose well. In the morning we will return and your training will begin." With that the two messengers vanished, leaving Adam and Eve staring at the spot where they'd been standing.

"He answered my prayer, Adam," Eve exclaimed. "He really answered my prayer!"

Adam nodded. "And Adam, did you hear what he said about you? Elohim doesn't answer prayers because we deserve what we ask for. He answers prayers because he loves us. He's forgiven you, Adam. You don't have to be afraid to talk to him."

It was too much for Adam to grasp. He'd been held too long in the grip of his guilt and shame to grasp the significance of the messenger's words. But Adam would remember. Adam would think about the messenger's words. And in time Adam would find peace.

For now, though, Adam chose to be practical. "Eve," he asked, "where would you like our home to be? Our real home, where we can raise our children?"

"What about by the lake where we built the bamboo shelter? I liked that place."

"I liked it too," Adam said. "In the morning, when the Shining Ones return, we'll tell them we want to live by the lake. We want that to be our home."

Eve smiled. "Yes, when the Shining Ones return."

24

When Adam and Eve awoke the next morning, they found themselves on the banks of the stream that flowed into the lake they'd chosen for their permanent home. The two angels had transported the humans there while they slept. Adam and Eve drank from the stream. Eve offered the messengers some of their remaining food. One of the two men smiled and shook his head.

"Thank you, but no. Don't be deceived by our appearance. We look like you at this moment, but we are spirit beings, with no need to eat or to drink. We wear this guise because our natural state is too glorious for you to bear.

"But don't be afraid. Elohim has sent us to serve you, to prepare you for your life here in the land beyond the rivers."

"We're not afraid," Adam said boldly, although he was terrified by these Shining Ones.

"Good," the first messenger said, smiling. "Then sit down with us and eat, and I will explain our mission."

Adam and Eve did as the messenger said, and the four sat together on the bank of the flowing stream. The ground was soft and the grasses lush. A pleasant breeze blew in from the lake. Since they'd camped there months earlier more fruit had ripened. It hung, invitingly, from nearby branches. Across the stream, flowers bloomed, and the air was fragrant with their scent. Eve was aware of the whisper of the flowing waters. It seemed to her they were almost back in Eden.

"Don't suppose for a moment that you are back in Eden," the first messenger began gravely, as though he had read Eve's thoughts. "This is the land beyond the rivers. In Eden food was always present. The animals were your friends. The climate was always mild. You found pleasant work to do that you enjoyed. There was never any doubt of your survival. Elohim graciously provided everything you needed.

"Here food plants and fruits mature only once or twice a year. You must gather food when it's available and store it against the months when nothing is ripe. Here no animals are your friends. Predators like the big cats you once thought of as fun-lovers are a danger to you and your children. Elohim has planted a fear of you in their hearts, but if they become hungry enough, they will stalk you and try to kill you. Here temperatures are sometimes mild, but much of the year is either uncomfortably hot or dangerously cold. You will have to provide warm clothing to wear during the times of cold.

"In Eden you enjoyed your work. Here work will be painful toil. You will have a constant struggle to provide food and clothing for your family, for the land itself has been corrupted by your sin and will actively resist you. Weeds will try to choke out the crops you plant. The land will produce thorns and thistles. Drought and blight, birds and insects, will rob you of your harvests.

"To survive in this land beyond the rivers, you must master many skills. If we had not been sent to teach you these skills, you would surely die.

"But Elohim did send us. We are here to teach you. For the next months, you must watch and listen carefully. Your survival depends on mastering what we will show you."

"Adam," the other angel explained, "I will teach you what you and your sons must learn. Eve, my companion will show you what you and your daughters must learn."

25

The appearance of the two powerful spirit beings had driven Myrdebaal back. The power they radiated was too great, and so, fearful of Satan's reaction to what might be viewed as his failure, Myrdebaal reluctantly returned to the Heart of Darkness.

Fortunately Satan seemed more concerned than angry. He sent several demons of higher rank to check out Myrdebaal's report. Even they had been unable to draw near enough to observe the humans. Like Myrdebaal, they had felt a searing heat, and the splendor of the two angels had forced them to draw back.

Satan listened thoughtfully as they related what happened when they tried to reach the humans. It was clear to him that Elohim had sent two of the mighty angels who ranked just below himself to visit Adam and Eve. There was no way for any of his demons to get close enough to observe what they were doing. Even Satan was not powerful enough to confront both of these angels at the same time.

Satan told Myrdebaal to return and watch at a distance, but to let him know as soon as the two angels were gone.

26

For months the first messenger ranged the area with Adam, showing him the resources of the land and how to use them. The first day they walked some twenty miles to a stony area on one of the hills that bordered the plain. By the time they arrived, it was nearly dark. "We'll sleep here tonight," the messenger announced.

"But," Adam objected, "Eve …"

"Eve will be all right," the angel told him. "My companion will keep her safe. You both have much to learn and little time."

Adam hadn't been concerned for Eve's safety while he was with her. But this was the first time he'd been separated from her. Eve had experienced life without Adam in her dreams, but for Adam, she'd been by his side from the day Elohim created her.

The thought of a night without her next to him made Adam uncomfortable. But this was something Adam couldn't bring himself to share with the angel. Obediently, he lay down and finally fell asleep.

The next morning, the messenger led Adam to a section of the hillside where fine grained rock was exposed. "This is flint," the messenger explained. "From this rock you can fashion all sorts of tools."

The angel selected a round chunk of flint, and then hunted for a large piece of harder stone. As Adam watched the angel struck the flint with the stone in such a way that pieces of flint flaked away. As the angel carefully chipped flakes from first one side of the rock and then the opposite side, a tool began to take shape.

The finished tool was rounded at the top. Two sides slanted sharply forming a jagged cutting edge at the bottom. The messenger placed the rounded end in Adam's palm. "Grip it," the angel said.

Adam's hand fitted comfortably over the rounded end. He hefted its weight and looked expectantly at the messenger.

"This is a hand ax," the messenger said. "You can use the sharp edge to cut, chop, scrape, or to dig up roots. It is one of the basic tools you'll need to survive."

Adam looked at the tool in wonder and felt the cutting edge. "Now," the angel instructed, "you make a hand ax."

Adam found another round flint rock and tried to fashion it as the angel had. Shaping the flint was more difficult than Adam had thought. At first Adam ruined several pieces of flint by striking too hard and flaking off too much. But after several hours, during which his hands developed painful blisters, Adam became more adept. Finally he produced a serviceable hand ax, although the edge was more ragged than the one produced by the messenger.

"Now make another," the messenger angel demanded. Adam's hands were now bruised and bleeding, but obediently he selected another stone and began to work. He was still chipping on this third hand ax when night fell.

Adam was tired and his hands hurt. Being forced to sleep apart from Eve felt unnatural, and he tossed and turned for several hours before sleep came.

The next morning Adam finished the third hand ax and was told to make another. His hands hurt constantly, but despite the pain, Adam was becoming more skillful. He finished the fourth ax in just six hours. When it was done he looked expectantly at the angel. "It's a day's journey to the lake," the angel commented. "What do you want to do?"

Adam looked at his swollen hands, thought for a moment, and picked out yet another round rock and set to work. This time as he labored the angel picked through the flakes that had been removed in working on the hand axes.

"Don't discard the flakes of flint, Adam," the angel instructed. The angel then showed Adam how, by further careful chipping, flat, rectangular pieces could be transformed into knives and scrapers. He showed how longer, rounded chips could be trimmed to punch holes in hides or serve as boring tools. And he selected thin, sharp pieces of flint that could be inserted in split sticks to fashion hand sickles for cutting grain.

When Adam finished his fifth hand ax, the angel seemed satisfied. "You and your children will become more adept in the years ahead. You'll find ways to shape this kind of rock to serve many different purposes.

"Now, let's return to your Eve and to my companion."

27

While Adam was learning to fashion tools from flint, the other angel taught Eve to build fires, grind grain, bake bread, and make pottery.

"Grain will be the staple food for you and your family. I'll teach you how to use the grain to make bread. My companion will teach Adam to prepare fields where grain can be planted. When the grain is harvested, you'll need to store it for seed for the next planting and for food until the next crop is ripe. You must have storage pots in which to keep the grain dry and safe from rodents. To make the pots and to bake your bread, you must have fire."

The angel had Eve collect bits of dry grass and small twigs. He placed them on a circle of bare earth near the stream. He then produced two hand-sized rocks. "These are firestones," he explained. "Strike them together close to the dried grass."

As Eve struck the stones, sparks fell in the dry grass. The angel blew on them gently and the grass began to smolder. When it burst into tiny flames, he added twigs, and when they began to burn, he added larger sticks.

Eve was fascinated by the fire. She reached out tentatively to touch it and quickly pulled back her finger. "It's hot!" she exclaimed.

"Yes," the messenger agreed. "Fire is hot. Fire is a vital tool, but it is dangerous too. Build your fires on bare ground to keep the fire from spreading."

Next the angel led Eve around the lake and taught her how to recognize clay that could be used to make pottery ovens and vessels. He taught her to mix the clay with just the right amounts of sand. He showed her how to roll long, thick ropes of this mixture. He placed a long rope of clay on the dry ground, forming a circle. He then laid another rope of clay on top of it. He repeated this process, laying ropes of clay on top of one another. With each new rope or two, he carefully smoothed the clay inside and outside of this structure. When the clay walls were about two feet high, he selected slightly shorter ropes of clay, fashioning a beehive-shaped roof with a small hole at the top. Finally the angel cut a semicircular opening at the base of the beehive and had Eve build a fire inside. All that day, Eve kept the fire burning, and by the next morning when the oven cooled, the clay was no longer soft but hard as stone.

The next day the angel had Eve mix more of the sand and clay. This time he began by looping a rope of clay in a tight, flat spiral to serve as the base of a pot. He then had Eve add strips of clay to the base, smoothing the sides as she added to them.

Using this technique, Eve shaped four pots of different shapes. Eve then gathered a large amount of wood. The angel directed her to pile this wood around the pots, being careful not to damage the soft clay. Eve then used the firestones to set the wood alight.

Again she spent the day keeping the fire burning. The next morning, two of the pots had cracked and were useless. But the other two had fired perfectly and could be used to hold water or grain.

The third day the messenger brought Eve two stones. One stone was flat, with an indented center area. The other stone was rounded on the top, but nearly flat on the bottom. "This is a hand mill," the messenger explained. "You use it, Eve, to grind grain."

The angel taught her how to grip the rounded stone, extend her arms, and rock back and forth, pushing and pulling it over the lower, flat stone. He dropped a few kernels of grain on the surface of the lower stone. As Eve dragged the round stone back and forth, the grain broke down into a coarse powder. The messenger added more kernels, and as Eve continued to work, the pile of flour grew.

At first Eve thought this new toy was fun to play with. But long before the angel was satisfied with the amount of flour, Eve's lower back began to hurt. By the time she had ground enough grain, her shoulders and arms had added their protest. This making of flour wasn't fun at all. It wasn't even work. It was toil!

But there was no time for Eve to rest. The angel had Eve build a fire inside the beehive oven. As it heated, he showed her how to mix the flour with water and to form flat loaves of bread. He then slapped each loaf on the rounded exterior of the hot oven. When one side of each flat loaf was cooked, the messenger peeled it off the oven's surface and then slapped the uncooked side back on the oven.

Eve was entranced by the aroma of the baking bread. It smelled so good! When the loaves were done, she held one of them up to her nose and breathed in deeply. She tasted the bread. It was good! *Adam will love this*, Eve thought. *I can't wait to show him.*

By the time Adam and the first messenger returned, Eve had removed the pots from the ashes of the fire she'd built around them, had ground more grain into flour, and had baked a dozen more loaves of flat bread.

Adam and Eve were both excited by the skills they'd been taught. Each enthusiastically showed the other things they had made. Yet each accomplishment had been realized at the expense of significant pain. Elohim had warned Adam that one consequence of his sin was that human beings would survive only at the cost of "painful toil." The first pair was beginning to realize that this distressing prediction had been only too accurate.

If the first couple assumed that these early lessons were all that the messenger angels had been sent to teach them, they were wrong. During the next months, Adam and Eve each had many skills to learn.

The first messenger showed Adam how to fashion hoes and sickles and hand plows. Adam learned how to clear land for crops by the careful use of fire. He learned to fell trees by cutting a wide strip of bark from around the trunk so the tree would die, and then use controlled fires around the base of the trunk to burn away the wood until the dead tree could be pushed or pulled over.

Adam learned how to prepare the ground for planting and how to use sticks to poke holes in the ground in which to drop seeds. He learned to scratch shallow furrows in the earth with a wooden hand plow and to plant fields by scattering grain. He watched in dismay as birds stole many of the kernels of grain he scattered and experienced frustration as rabbits and other animals ate young plants as they appeared.

The angel showed Adam the location of groups of animals and told him which might someday be domesticated. Adam learned to tell when it was time to harvest olives and how to press out oil that bread could be dipped in and that could be burned in crude lamps.

Eve too had many more things to learn. She learned how to dry fruit to be eaten long after its season had passed. She was told what she must do to prepare and cure hides to clothe her husband and children and how to sew hides tightly together to hold liquids. She learned to milk goats and make yogurt.

The angel taught her how to draw fibers from cotton and from wool and how to weave them into cloth. She learned which growing plants were good to eat and how to prepare them for food. The angel showed her other plants that had healing properties and could serve as medicines.

Finally, after being with Adam and Eve for over a year, the angels gave the first couple one last gift.

"It will take you years to prepare the ground and secure your food supply." The second angel held up several dozen bars of what looked like pressed figs. "Take these cakes. One meal will give you strength and energy for forty days. While these cakes last, prepare. Do what you must to do to guarantee your food supply. Clear land, make a supply of pots, build a shelter of clay bricks, dry berries and fruit. Plant, harvest, and store grain.

"Even in this fallen world where weeds and thorns abound, Elohim has provided all that you need for a good life. Your part is to accept his gifts and to endure the toil that's necessary to utilize them.

"Now he has one additional gift for you. The LORD Elohim refashioned this world in six days. On the seventh day he rested. In honor of his work, he grants you each seventh day on which you too can rest. Do not be afraid to rest the seventh day. He will see that you lose nothing by honoring it. The day of rest will restore and refresh you. Freed from toil this one day in seven, you will find joy in your love for each other and in his love for you. Remember the seventh day. And set it aside as holy.

"We came here at Elohim's direction to bless you. Now we leave you with his blessing."

With these words, the two messengers dropped the forms that they had worn while with the humans. Adam and Eve were momentarily blinded by the brilliant light that masked the spirit beings' true forms. When their sight returned, the angels were gone.

28

Seven days later Adam and Eve awoke exhausted. They had taken the angels' warning to heart. Adam had thrown himself into clearing land for planting. Eve had used all the nearby firewood and spent a day searching farther and then carrying loads of wood home. The other days she dug clay and shaped it by hand into bricks that could be used to build their home. The food bars from the angels gave them energy, but the work was difficult and their bodies ached.

"It's the seventh day," Eve reminded Adam, who was about to get up and return to work. She reached out and grasped his arm. "Come back. Lie here with me."

"The seventh day," Adam repeated gratefully. "We can rest."

The two spent the morning dozing in each other's arms. Then they slipped into the pleasantly warm waters of the stream. For a time they lay in the shallows as the water soothed tired muscles. Then Eve playfully splashed water on Adam.

Soon they were laughing joyfully, each splashing the other. Finally Adam caught Eve, wrapped his arms around her, and fell with her into the stream. They came up sputtering and laughing, and Eve broke away and fled to the shore. This time when Adam caught her, they lay together in the grass, kissing, and soon found themselves making love.

Afterward they lay close, relaxing in the warm air. Then they made love again, gently and languidly. Afterward they napped again. When they awoke, it was late in the afternoon. Eve felt such peace. The day of rest really had restored them. Eve felt rested physically. But more important, she again felt close to Adam.

During the six days, they had worked from dawn to dusk, each on separate tasks. When night came, they were too tired to do more than touch each other's hand or share a brief kiss before they slept. The seventh day had given them time for each other, time each required but that Eve needed desperately.

Then Adam sat up suddenly. He'd heard movement in the brush nearby. He gripped one of his hand axes and cautiously got to his knees. There, gazing quietly, he saw a young sheep, one of the animals that

Elohim had killed to clothe him and Eve. Cautiously he approached the unwary animal and caught it up in his arms.

"Remember what Elohim told us in the garden," he asked Eve, "about how we were to approach him."

Eve nodded slowly, remembering the revulsion she'd felt as blood spurted from the creature in Elohim's hands. "I remember," she said, shuddering slightly.

"Eve, it's time we came to Elohim to thank him. I know now that he loves us in spite of what we did in Eden. He let us live. He sent his angels to teach us how to survive in these lands beyond the river. And he's given us this day to rest and to love each other. Now it's time to show that we love him too."

Reluctantly Eve nodded agreement.

Binding the lamb, Adam collected stones and piled them up to form an altar. Eve brought wood and piled it on the altar. Adam then picked up the living animal, carried it to the altar, and using a flint knife cut its throat. Eve closed her eyes, unable to look as the blood splattered the stones and the ground around the altar.

Adam then laid the body of the lamb on the firewood and set it ablaze. Quickly the wood caught, and soon the body was surrounded by the flames.

As the body of the lamb burned, Adam lifted his arms to heaven and spoke. "O Elohim, we come to you this seventh day in the way you have told us to come. We come to thank you, Elohim, for sparing our lives, and for the good gifts you have given us. Accept our praise, O LORD Elohim. Accept our worship. And one day, please, bring us home to you."

Adam and Eve stood hand in hand gazing into the fire as it consumed their offering. As it burned down to embers, Eve looked up at Adam. "I don't understand it, Adam," she said. "I don't know why he told us to kill an innocent animal when we approach him. But Adam, I know its right."

"I know, Eve," Adam said. "I don't understand it either. But I can feel it. He's accepted us. He's forgiven us. He loves us.

"I know it's the right thing to do, the only thing to do."

"We'll have to teach this to our children, Adam," Eve said as they turned away from the altar. "We have so much to teach them."

BOOK 5
EVE'S DAUGHTERS, ADAM'S SONS

"Death reigned from the time of Adam"
(Romans 5:14)

1

Eve was pregnant at last. Five exhausting years had passed since the Shining Ones had taught them skills they needed to survive in these lands beyond the river. Working from dawn to dusk, Adam had cleared fields where barley and wheat could grow.

When he wasn't at work in the fields, Adam searched the nearby area for other resources. He found beehives and collected honey. He located a stand of olive trees and fashioned a rude press that produced oil for their bread and fuel for their clay lamps. Several times Adam returned to the distant hills to fashion more flint tools. He took Eve with him on the overnight trips, afraid to leave her alone despite the fact that they'd seen no sign of dangerous animals.

During these years Eve fashioned and air-dried clay bricks and helped Adam built a simple two-room house. She fired pots for storing the harvest, dried figs, tended their vegetable garden, and prepared the two meals they ate each day. The work was exhausting, but each felt an urgency to prepare for an uncertain future. Each was also driven by the hope that soon they would have children to provide for.

The constant labor placed a strain on their relationship. Adam was too tired after a day's toil to talk with Eve much less to make love. Eve felt more and more isolated. She yearned for the leisurely days in Eden where they'd had time and energy for each other, where they'd spent hours talking and exploring and making love.

Often Eve found herself uncertain about their relationship, wondering if Adam was upset with her. Whenever she asked, Adam was reassuring. Of course he loved her. No, he wasn't upset with her or angry. He was proud of her, proud of the things she was accomplishing. Apparently Adam wasn't affected in the same way she was by their lack of time for each other. He simply assumed everything was all right in their relationship and channeled his energies into his work.

The seventh day of rest that Elohim established kept them going. For Adam and Eve, the seventh day was a time to recuperate physically. More important it was a time to refresh their love for each other. As they relaxed in the grasses by the stream, Eve was able to share with an attentive Adam. Often they dreamed together of what it would be like when the children came. On those seventh days, there was also time for fun—time to splash each other in the water, to play tag, to laugh, and to share intimacy.

During these years of preparation, Adam and Eve were unaware of the guardian angels Elohim set around them to fend off demonic attacks. Shortly after the Shining Ones left, Satan had again launched Persifor against them. This time the Demon of Destruction was met by a team of angels who formed a barrier Persifor could not penetrate.

Satan sent other demons to probe the barrier, but none intent on harming Adam or Eve could get through. Surprisingly, Myrdebaal was allowed to come close enough to observe and to taste the first pair's exhaustion. Best of all for Myrdebaal was the pain felt by Eve when she had doubts about Adam's love. At such times a persistent ache radiated from her. Even though the pain was dull rather than intense, Myrdebaal relished its distinctive flavor.

This was additional evidence that it was unnecessary for demons to actively promote human suffering. The humans were perfectly capable of causing their own pain. Eve's longing for reassurance from Adam, a consequence of the fall, was self-imposed pain. But it was pain made worse by Adam's insensitivity to her needs as work consumed his thoughts and his time.

While other angels guarded Adam and Eve, Gorel continued to serve as a watcher. He too felt the first pair's exhaustion and was aware of their emotions. Gorel found himself identifying strongly with the humans. Unlike Myrdebaal, Gorel was distressed by the humans' pain and found delight in their moments of joy.

But neither Adam nor Eve, nor Myrdebaal nor Gorel, were prepared for the complications that were to be introduced when the longed-for children were born.

2

"She's beautiful!" Adam exclaimed, gazing at his infant daughter.

Eve looked up, happiness shining in her eyes. "That's only the thousandth time you've said that Adam," she teased.

Hatipha, their firstborn, was beautiful. She had dark hair like her father. The dimple in her chin was a mirror image of Adam's, but her eyes and mouth were pure Eve.

By age three, her personality was taking shape. Hatipha would sit beside her mother as Eve worked at shaping pottery storage jars. The little girl's legs would spread wide, her eyes squinting in concentration as she struggled to create miniature jars of her own. The ropes of clay that she rolled had to be exactly right, each the same diameter. The inner and outer walls of her tiny pots had to be perfectly smooth. The fact that her small muscle coordination hadn't developed enough to make perfection possible was a source of intense irritation. Hatipha's jar would bulge on one side. She'd try futilely to straighten it, and when the frustration was more than she could stand, she'd explode and pound the uncooperative clay with her fists.

"Sweetheart," Eve would say, "that was a fine jar. You didn't have to do that."

Sometimes she'd tell Hatipha, "It's all right, honey. When you're older, you'll be able to make jars just like mine."

Well-meant remarks like these upset Hatipha even more. She'd break into tears and stomp away, muttering, "Hate jars! Hate clay!" Or she'd sit there with a fierce look on her little face and insist, "Not older. Now!"

When Hatipha did get older, she took great pleasure in making perfectly shaped jars. On the days they were making pottery, Hatipha insisted that she be the one to look for just the right quality clay and that she be allowed to add the sand until the mixture was just the right texture. She worked as intently as she had as a child but now with great skill, and pots and jars quickly took perfect shape under her strong, talented hands. She'd gather and stack the wood needed to fire the pottery, too, and tend the fires herself.

By then Hatipha was critically inspecting Eve's jars and was quick to point out deficiencies in her mother's work. By the time Hatipha was an adult, she had taken over each step in the production of any pottery objects the family needed.

"I can do it better," she insisted. "Let me do it." Even though Eve enjoyed working the clay, she let Hatipha have her way. It was easier than arguing with her firstborn, for whatever else might be said about Hatipha, she was stubborn. She wouldn't give up until she got her way.

Often when Eve felt irritated at Hatipha's bossiness, she mentally listed her daughter's many good qualities. Hatipha was certainly responsible. Any job Hatipha was asked to do, she attacked willingly and with gusto. Her skill at organizing and her seemingly endless energy guaranteed that the job would not only be done right but be done more efficiently than Eve or any of the other children could do it. Hatipha would see through the most demanding tasks whatever the cost. And, if Hatipha seemed overly critical of her mother or a sibling, she didn't sit on the sideline nit-picking. She jumped right in and set an example for them all. Yet for her, there was only one right way to do things—Hatipha's way. And in fact, Hatipha's way usually was best.

Hatipha was also eager to learn. As a young child, she constantly pestered her parents for information. Why did Eve make a tea of this plant when Adam was tired? Or of that plant when his nose ran and he sneezed? What was this other plant good for? Why did they mix sand with the clay to make the pottery? What would happen if they used clay without sand? Or if you mixed in twice as much sand? Hatipha questioned, probed, experimented, and had a gift for solving any practical problem that came up in running the household. Hatipha was so efficient that sometimes Eve felt unnecessary, as though her oldest daughter had taken over their home.

If Hatipha was critical of her mother, it was very different with her father. Adam never experienced his daughter's competitiveness and doted on her even as she idolized him. As a toddler, Hatipha had loved it when he played with her hair, curling it around his finger and telling her how much he loved her. She was never so happy as on the seventh day when Adam had time to play with her, crawling on his knees as she rode on his back screaming with pretend fright as he tried to buck her off. Or when after romping, he lay back in the grass and she could lie close to his big body and feel warm and safe.

On those days, she wanted all his time and all his attention. When she was put down to nap and Adam and Eve slipped away for some private time, Hatipha fought sleep, filled with jealousy and anger. She wanted her father for herself, and the rivalry between Hatipha and her mother probably began in those earliest years.

Oh, Hatipha and Eve loved each other. Dearly. And each could list admirable qualities in the other. But underneath the love a fierce competition raged.

This competition probably influenced Hatipha's indifference to spiritual realities. Before Hatipha could talk, Eve told her stories about Elohim and the wonderful garden he had created for her mother and father. The stories of a perfect place where fruit grew on every tree and stands of grain could be found in every valley seemed unreal. In the world Hatipha knew, her mother and father labored to near exhaustion six days a week. Stories of the Shining Ones made no sense. There was no need for such miraculous teachers. Her parents were the ones who taught her and they knew everything, especially her father.

It wasn't that Hatipha didn't believe her mother. She certainly believed her father, who told her the most wonderful stories about spending time with the animals and giving them their names. But while she believed the stories, they somehow just weren't real to her.

When her father sacrificed a lamb to Elohim, she was fascinated by the flowing blood. But while Adam and Eve were deeply moved at such times, both humble and thankful, Hatipha felt nothing but curiosity. What made the blood flow like that? What would happen if another animal's throat was cut? Would it bleed too? She even wondered, half ashamed, what would happen if Eve's throat were cut. Not that she wanted that to happen, of course.

So while Adam and Eve, deeply aware of their flaws and failures, praised and worshipped Elohim who had created and forgiven them, their oldest daughter stood by, a spectator who sensed no need to involve herself in what was happening between Elohim and her parents.

3

Hatipha was eight years old when Adam and Eve's second child, Abihal, was born. At first Hatipha was fascinated by the tiny bit of flesh that was her sister. She felt the baby's fine hair, blond like that of Eve. Hatipha held out her little finger and let the baby grasp it. When Abihal squeezed her finger, Hatipha noted how weak the grip was. It enhanced Hatipha's awareness of her own superiority. Abihal was so weak, and she, Hatipha, was so strong.

Hatipha could have responded to Abihal's frailty in one of two ways. She might have felt contempt for her infant sister. If she had, Hatipha would probably have ignored or teased her sister unmercifully as Abihal grew up. But what happened was that Hatipha felt an overwhelming rush of love for the helpless infant and, from the first, appointed herself Abihal's protector.

Hatipha took every opportunity she could to care for infant Abihal and resented the times her sister had Eve's attention. As Abihal grew older, she was always in Hatipha's company. Hatipha took it as her personal mission not only to care for her sister but to teach Abihal everything she would need to know.

To Eve, Hatipha's obvious love for Abihal was an answer to prayer. During her pregnancy with Abihal, Eve had been anxious about Hatipha's reaction to the baby. Hatipha had such a critical spirit and had developed a rivalry with her mother that all too often expressed itself in open hostility. Eve had prayed daily that Elohim would protect the new baby from her sister—a necessity that hurt Eve deeply as she remembered the harmony she'd experienced in the dream of what might have been for her children's children's children.

"What have we done?" Eve often wondered anxiously as she observed her eldest and recognized a darkness in Hatipha's character that left Eve near despair.

There was no use speaking with Adam about her concerns. While Eve clearly saw the flaws in their daughter's character, Adam saw only the baby girl whom he had played with every seventh day, who had grown up to show such talent and ability. To Adam, Hatipha could do no wrong.

Whenever Eve tried to share her distress, Adam either ignored her or responded by reciting a list their daughter's many positive qualities and accomplishments. In fact it irritated Adam when Eve seemed to run down their daughter. Busy in the fields all day, Adam never had a chance to witness the friction between mother and daughter, and Hatipha, who yearned for her father's approval above all, was careful not to reveal the hostility that was so obvious when she and Eve were alone. It was no wonder that Eve, who knew her daughter only too well, was worried as time for her delivery drew near.

Eve was relieved to see Hatipha's intense love for her little sister. It also seemed such a blessing. With Hatipha caring for Abihal, Eve could concentrate on her many roles as Adam's wife and co-provider for their family. Eve never realized that Hatipha's love for Abihal was actually depriving Abihal of an intimate relationship with her mother. It was also depriving Abihal of the godly influence that Eve might have been in Abihal's development.

4

While Adam and Eve were unaware of the implications of Hatipha's co-option of her younger sister, Myrdebaal was watching with malicious intent. He'd studied Hatipha all of her life and was well aware not only of her strengths but of her weaknesses. The observant demon was increasingly fascinated by the complexity of these humans as revealed not only in Adam and Eve but now in their first two offspring.

Myrdebaal had noted the intensity of three-year-old Hatipha as she struggled to shape jars from clay. It was clear she was a perfectionist. As she grew older, Myrdebaal saw that her perfectionism had become intense competitiveness that often found expression as a critical spirit. Driven to do everything just right herself, Hatipha had no sympathy for those who failed to live up to her own high standards.

In Hatipha's case, this was her mother. Somehow Eve could never meet Hatipha's expectations—a situation exacerbated by Hatipha's competition for Adam's attention. The resulting conflict between Eve and Hatipha, although it generally lay beneath the surface, was painful for both—an inner distress Myrdebaal found both fascinating and flavorful.

Hatipha's ability to plan and organize was undoubtedly a strength, but this too had drawbacks. Her love for order and her skill in laying out tasks efficiently led Hatipha to conclude that her way was the right way, always. She transformed her procedures into inflexible rules that she tried to impose on others in the family. She became impatient with anyone who violated her rules or who seemed disorganized.

The result was further isolation from them and an emotional barrier between her and anyone unwilling to accept her leadership. Myrdebaal realized that this kind of barrier makes it almost impossible for a free expression of feelings, with the consequence that painful emotions are bottled up inside where they can never be resolved. These repressed feelings provided some of the most delicious pain a demon could wish for.

Hatipha's skill in setting goals and efficiently accomplishing tasks had another downside. In focusing on the details of life, Hatipha tended to lose sight of larger issues. Because she concentrated so much on accomplishing tasks in this world, the spiritual universe of which her parents were aware seemed to Hatipha unreal and irrelevant. The seventh day wasn't viewed as a day for rest and relationships but as an opportunity to compete for her father's attention. For Hatipha, the stories of Elohim and the Shining Ones were interesting but irrelevant tales with no link to real life, and the sacrifices that moved Adam and Eve to repentance and worship seemed meaningless ritual.

This especially was a source of wonder and amusement to Myrdebaal, who knew the spiritual universe to be the ultimate reality. Hatipha, who so clearly revealed many of the flaws in fallen human nature, was ignoring the one source of relief from the grip of spiritual death on her life.

The image of the Creator was still visible in Hatipha's many strengths. But the corruption of that image was just as clearly revealed in the distortions by those strengths of her character. For instance, Hatipha did love her sister. But the love was flawed, and unbeknownst to Hatipha, she was using her sister in her struggle to replace Eve in Adam's estimation.

Later, when two of her brothers had grown up, Hatipha would admire the one who was most like her and set her mind to marry him, never realizing that she was dooming both of them to a life of constant bickering and conflict. When two highly motivated individuals who are each used to being right marry, they often find themselves driven to be acknowledged as the one who is always correct.

5

Gorel had also been observing Hatipha. He had been shaken by Adam and Eve's rebellion against Elohim. As the years passed, the angel was even more shaken by what he saw in the character of Hatipha.

She had not sinned in the same way Adam and Eve had. She violated no command of Elohim, for the Lord had given no new commands to humankind. But the flaws Gorel saw were proof that something terrible had happened within human beings. The problem was not sin as a violation of the known will of God. The problem was spiritual death and its impact on human personality.

Gorel had no idea how Elohim could bring the dead to life. But he was sure that nothing less than an inward resurrection could bring members of the human race back into harmony with the Lord.

6

Abihal's birth was an easy one. Eve felt the labor pains begin just as the first glow of morning's light began to diffuse through the curtain of water vapor that sheltered Earth from the sun's most harmful rays. A few hours later, her second daughter entered the world, silent and smiling, as if assured of her welcome. At age eight, Hatipha was old enough to help and so was present at the miracle of birth. She watched, wide-eyed, as Eve strained and then, wondrously, her sister appeared.

Hatipha's passionate attachment to her baby sister began the first time Abihal gripped one of Hatipha's fingers in her tiny fist and looked up, wide eyed, at her big sister. From that moment, Hatipha became Abihal's second mother, with an influence on the littler girl greater than either Adam or Eve. While Hatipha yearned for Adam's approval, Hatipha was the one Abihal sought to please. Abihal adopted Hatipha as her mentor and never questioned anything her older sister said or did.

As the years passed, Myrdebaal was surprised at the differences between the two girls. At three Hatipha had displayed the drive and perfectionism that were so dominant in her character. At three Abihal was indifferent to work of any kind, preferring to sit beside her mother and sister as they worked and play with a straw doll Adam had made for her.

While Hatipha aggressively criticized others and demanded things be done her way, Abihal was uncomfortable with conflict of any kind. When either Hatipha or Eve made unkind remarks to the other, tears appeared in Abihal's eyes. Those tears and Abihal's need for harmony moved Hatipha enough to keep her sharp tongue under better control.

Eve was always grateful to Abihal but mistakenly took the little girl's reaction as support for her mother. Hatipha knew better. Hatipha understood that Abihal simply couldn't stand conflict and would always try to make peace, simply because she had a deep need for harmony. Still, Eve appreciated Abihal's intervention and gratefully welcomed her growing role as a buffer between herself and Hatipha. Family life seemed much more harmonious when Abihal was there.

As Abihal grew older, she developed greater skill as a peacemaker. Whenever she heard loud voices, indicating an escalating disagreement, Abihal would rush to the scene to smooth things over. Whether the dispute was between her father and mother, between Hatipha and Eve, or involved other brothers and sisters, Abihal was eager to mediate.

While Abihal's efforts were usually successful, they were often misplaced. Too many disagreements over issues that needed to be discussed and resolved were set aside when Abihal intervened. Some of these festered under the surface, driving hidden wedges between family members. But Abihal could never see that at times a shouted argument is a necessary step toward resolution.

Later, when Cain was nearly grown, he and Hatipha seemed always on the verge of coming to blows. Each was strong willed. Each was a perfectionist. And each identified strongly with Adam and competed for his approval. The fact that Adam had a soft spot for his eldest daughter and that he almost never praised Cain made the competition between the two even more intense. These two might never have married except for Abihal; for as Cain was growing up, Abihal kept his rivalry with Hatipha under some semblance of control. After Hatipha and Cain married, Abihal wasn't there to mediate, and their competition for dominance became more and more destructive.

Abihal had a gift for seeing each person's side in an argument, and for helping each better understand the other's point of view. This made a great contribution to maintaining harmony in Adam's family. But Abihal was largely blind to Hatipha's flaws and was intensely loyal to the sister who was almost a mother to her. In any mediation Abihal sought a resolution that protected her big sister's feelings and prerogatives. Abihal was so skillful a mediator that in most cases she was able to protect her sister without seeming to take sides and without offending the other party.

What Abihal appreciated most about Hatipha was that she could talk to her big sister about anything. And Hatipha, who was so critical and demanding of others, seemed to accept Abihal as she was, without trying to change her. If Hatipha had viewed Eve and the other members of her family with the same tolerance, the lives of all of them would have been happier.

But Hatipha's tolerance came at a price. What she derived from her relationship with Abihal was her younger sister's complete and unquestioning acknowledgement of her leadership. The admiration that shone in Abihal's eyes reinforced Hatipha's view of herself as a person who was always right and never, ever wrong.

While the close tie between the two girls seemed to meet basic needs of each, it tended to exclude other family members from a closer relationship with either. If Abihal had shared with Eve or her other sisters as freely as she did with Hatipha, she might have gained vital perspective and avoided the one choice that would have such tragic consequences for much of the human race.

One of the fascinating things about Abihal was that, except when she intervened to mediate some dispute, she was almost invisible in the family. Adam, Eve, Hatipha, and the brothers who were born after Abihal, all had strong opinions. The parents understood this. They realized that they needed to give their children an opportunity to express their views about important, and even unimportant, family decisions. So while the opinions of the others were solicited, no one asked Abihal what she thought or felt.

Abihal seemed comfortable with this situation. She never appeared to notice and made no effort to speak up. She simply listened and went along with whatever decisions the others made. Yet Abihal's treatment was essentially unfair. In her old age, after a lifetime of being disregarded, Abihal at last demanded the attention and influence she'd been denied when younger. It was then that the contact Satan's followers made with her at Myrdebaal's instigation bore its destructive fruit.

But during her growing up and her childbearing years, Abihal remained a sweet, loving, and essentially passive person. She was as beautiful as her sister Hatipha, but in a different way. Hatipha was dark, with shining black hair, an oval face, full lips, and a straight, strong nose. Hatipha was nearly as tall as her father, stronger and yet as supple as her mother.

Abihal was blond, almost petite. Her nose turned up slightly and her blue eyes looked innocently out of a pixyish face. Although small and apparently delicate, Abihal, like Eve's other daughters and Adam's other sons, was strong and healthy.

These early generations following humankind's creation were unique. Without the passage of millenniums to introduce the errors in the genetic code that are responsible for most human illnesses, glowing good health and extremely long lives were common in the earliest generations. During her eight hundred and sixty-six years of life, Abihal would give birth to seventy-nine children, and those offspring would be as healthy and attractive as Abihal and her two husbands.

7

Abihal, like Hatipha, heard her parents speak often of Eden and Elohim. She listened to Adam's stories of the Shining Ones Elohim sent to help him. The two girls were also present at the frequent sacrifices. Abihal regularly stood back beside Hatipha as Adam offered lambs to Elohim and watched as their parents stood before the altar praising and thanking the Creator. Adam often explained the significance of the sacrifice to his children.

"After your mother and I disobeyed Elohim and ate fruit from the forbidden tree, Elohim searched for us. We tried to hide because we were ashamed and afraid. We knew we had done wrong and deserved to be punished.

"We tried to pass the blame. I blamed your mother. She blamed the serpent that a terrible being named Satan controlled. But we each knew what we did was wrong, and that no one had forced us to disobey the Creator. We were each responsible for the choice we made.

"It was then that Elohim sent us out of the garden where we had been so happy. He told us that our choice had raised a barrier between us and him and that there was nothing we could do to change the consequences of that choice. We both knew he was right. We knew that we were different inside.

"Our choice had changed us. Elohim called that change 'spiritual death,' as much of what was good in us was now corrupted by evil. Ever since that first disobedience, we've both made choices that we never would have made in Eden. Those choices have hurt you as well as brought us pain and suffering.

"We begged Elohim to forgive us and to let us stay in the garden. He told us he couldn't let us stay. We had to leave and go out into the world where we could survive only by painful toil. But Elohim did forgive us. And he promised that some day he would make a way for us and for our children's children's children to come home to him.

"As a symbol of forgiveness, Elohim killed two sheep and made clothing for us. He explained that as the lamb's skins covered our body, their blood would cover our sins until the one who would make it possible for us to return to him appeared.

"Elohim also told us to offer the same animals as sacrifices whenever we wanted to approach him. Their blood would cover our sins until he could take the sins completely away.

"That's why we offer these sacrifices. Offering the sacrifice shows Elohim that we welcome his forgiveness and that we are eager to return to him. Remember this, because you will sacrifice too. You can talk to

Elohim at any time. But whenever you want to approach to worship him, you must bring a sacrifice."

Later, when Abihal questioned Hatipha about her view of the sacrifice and the stories their parents told, Hatipha assured her little sister that the stories were probably true.

But Hatipha added, "What I don't understand is why the stories are important. What difference does it make if we worship Elohim or not? We still have to work for everything we have. I do believe that Elohim sent Mom and Dad out of Eden. I guess I even believe their stories about Shining Ones, though I've never seen them. But I think Elohim just ignores us now. Whether we have enough food depends on how hard we work, not on what Elohim gives us."

Abihal accepted her sister's view of Elohim's irrelevance. But she was fascinated by her parents' accounts of the Shining Ones. Abihal wished she could see a Shining One and often expressed her desire to Hatipha. When that happened, Hatipha smiled indulgently and made no comment.

But Abihal's repeated comments gave Myrdebaal an idea.

8

Myrdebaal had studied Abihal as closely as he had her sister and their parents. Again the demon had been surprised. This human was so different from the others. Like them, she was intelligent, emotional, and had the capacity to make decisions. Yet her personality was distinctly her own.

Relationships were especially important to Abihal. She'd forged an intimate bond with her sister and seemed to feel close to her parents and other siblings. But relationships were so important to Abihal that they affected her judgment. Her refusal to back off and let Hatipha and Cain fight it out when they differed contributed to the disastrous choice they made to wed. Later, without Abihal there to mediate, the two engaged in a constant struggle for dominance during their marriage.

Similarly, Abihal intervened constantly in support of her sister.

Although Abihal's skills at negotiation led to seemingly acceptable compromises, her intervention kept Hatipha from receiving the feedback from others that might have tempered Hatipha's arrogant notion of her own superiority.

Thus while Abihal was appreciated by her parents for keeping peace in the family, Myrdebaal realized that Abihal's desire for peace at any price could have long-term negative effects.

While Abihal could see both sides in any conflict, her passion for peace at any price often kept her from confronting when one person was obviously out of line. Whatever the dispute was about, Abihal chose to work toward a quick resolution even when she realized the resolution was only temporary or superficial.

One thing that all the family members appreciated about Abihal was that she never repeated any sensitive information she had about them. Yet even this admirable trait had its downside. While Abihal never gossiped, she developed the habit of keeping her own counsel, a habit that kept her from checking her ideas with others. Abihal shared only with Hatipha, and as Abihal grew older, she often chose to withhold significant thoughts from her older sister.

One day when Myrdebaal overheard two family members commenting favorably on this trait of Abihal's, Myrdebaal had a sudden insight that led him to make an unauthorized journey to the Heart of Darkness to offer a suggestion to Satan.

It was most unusual for any demon to independently come up with a truly creative scheme. Swelling with more than a little pride, Myrdebaal begged an audience with the chief fallen angel.

As Myrdebaal explained his idea, Satan sat back with eyes closed. But soon the shreds of his mighty wings began to quiver. Then his mouth twitched, and Myrdebaal sensed the Leader was struggling to hold back an evil smile. When Myrdebaal finished his presentation, Satan asked, "And what benefit do you see to us if we play this trick on your human?"

Myrdebaal was ready with his answer. "O Great One, we introduce a competitor for the human's allegiance, and we further distort humanity's view of Elohim, may his very name be forgotten. I can imagine that a time will come when the deities we introduce will be worshipped by the humans as if they were Elohim himself."

Satan nodded. "Exactly!" Then he added, thoughtfully, "I don't know what it is about you, Myrdebaal. Of all my followers, you're the only one with imagination. Perhaps you've been studying these humans so long that you've begun to think as they do.

"Whatever it is, you are becoming more and more useful to me."

At this unexpected praise, Myrdebaal fell to the ebony floor and spread out what remained of his wings in some approximation of humility. He thought, *Of course I'm useful. And I expect to be rewarded.*

But when Myrdebaal spoke, it was to shower compliments on Satan.

"It is my greatest pleasure to serve you, Master. That is the only reward I expect."

Satan laughed. "Well said, little demon. You lie almost as well as I do. Well, get out. I need to put your plan into action."

9

A week later Abihal was working alone in one of the nearby forests. She'd piled her sled high with firewood and was about to slip the harness over her shoulders and set off for home when she saw a flickering light through the trees. Fascinated, she set the rope down and moved cautiously toward the light. As she approached, she saw that the light shone from a figure that was moving toward her. Immediately she thought of the Shining Ones in her parents' stories, whom she'd longed to meet.

Her heart pounded with excitement as she moved closer to the figure that now was waiting for her with arms outstretched. Then she was standing just a few feet away. Slowly she reached out her arms to accept the apparition's embrace. But before they touched, the figure backed one step away.

"Do not touch me, Daughter of Eve. I am a Shining One, come to tell you that you have been chosen."

"Chosen?" Abihal asked, thrilled to be so near the mythic figures.

"Chosen," the figure echoed. "You have been chosen as a vessel to contain knowledge of the truth and to reveal it to humanity at the proper time. Until then you must keep what I am about to tell you a secret."

Overwhelmed and exhilarated, Abihal exclaimed, "Oh, I will. I'll keep it a secret."

For a moment, the light from the figure flickered, as if about to go out. But the light soon steadied. In fact the demon Baziya was having trouble maintaining his disguise as an angel of light. It took so much concentrated effort to maintain the light-field around him that he could hardly speak his lines and keep up even the dimmest glow. If Abihal had ever seen one of the true Shining Ones, or had compared her parents' description with that of the being who stood before her, she could never have been taken in.

"The truth is," Baziya continued, "Elohim no longer cares about human beings. He has withdrawn to a far away place and has no knowledge of what happens here on Earth. But we Shining Ones could not desert you. We remained here and took up the burden of watching over you.

"All we desire in return is that you honor us, praying to us rather than to Elohim. In return, we will grant you your desires and guide you all the days of your lives.

"As a sign of our good faith, I will grant you one desire. Think carefully. What do you most want in this world? Tell me, and it shall be yours."

Abihal didn't hesitate for a moment. "O Shining One, what I want most is a baby brother or sister."

It had been a gamble for Satan to have Baziya offer to grant Abihal's wish. But Myrdebaal had reported that Abihal had been asking her parents for a sibling for some time. And Myrdebaal had overheard Eve telling Adam that she was pregnant.

Again the light surrounding Baziya flickered as the demon felt a flood of relief. Regaining control, Baziya told Abihal, "I grant your desire. Your parents will have another child. Soon."

"Oh thank you, thank you!" Abihal exclaimed.

"This proof of our power and of our concern for you must be kept a secret for now. Tell no one that you saw me. Tell no one what I promised. When my promise has been kept, you will store up the fact of our existence in your heart until the proper time comes."

"I will, Shining One."

"You must also think of me whenever your parents and family offer sacrifices to Elohim. Replace him in your mind with an image of myself and silently address all praise to me and to my kind."

Abihal nodded agreement. "But what are you called? Is Shining One your name?"

"No, Abihal," the visitor replied. "In fact, there are many like me. In time we will reveal our names to humankind. For now, simply think of us and worship us as the Others.

"The time will come, Abihal, when you will introduce us Others to human beings. You will teach everyone that Elohim has deserted his creation. You will teach them that the Others are the powers who now control all that happens.

"If you teach them well, we will answer their prayers. We will guarantee them plentiful harvests. We will make their women fertile. But we will do these things only if they abandon Elohim and worship the Others.

"Now I must go. Keep my secret. Hold it in your heart until the proper time."

10

The whole family noticed a difference in Abihal when she returned. When they asked her why she seemed so happy, Abihal simply smiled and said, "It's a secret."

Watching, Myrdebaal thought, *I knew it! I knew she'd never tell the others.*

If only she had. Under her parents' questioning, the obvious differences between the true Shining Ones who had taught them survival skills and the imposter who had spoken with Abihal would have become clear. But Abihal kept the secret. Whenever the family approached Elohim with a sacrifice, in her heart Abihal honored the Others.

When centuries had passed and Abihal was old, she would travel from place to place calling on the people to worship the Others rather than Elohim. And miraculous signs would support her teaching that the Creator God had abandoned humankind and that the Others now controlled events on Earth. It was the Others who were to be worshipped and sacrificed to. It was the Others whose anger had to be placated and whose favor should be sought by humankind.

Gorel was shaken by the fact that Elohim had allowed Baziya to approach Abihal. Why had Elohim lowered the hedge he placed around the first couple and their children? Why had he allowed the demon to trick her? Where were her guardian angels when she needed them most?

The only answer Gorel received was from one of the true Shining Ones with whom Gorel shared his concerns.

"The visit from Baziya was an opportunity for Abihal to make a personal commitment to Elohim. Her parents have faith in Elohim and have taught their children about him. But each individual must have a personal trust in our Lord. There must be a point in time when their commitment teeters in the balance and a choice is made.

"This was the moment for Abihal to commit to the truth she had been taught or to reject it in favor of a lie. Abihal chose the lie."

Gorel was still troubled. "But, didn't Elohim know the choice Abihal would make?"

The Shining One nodded agreement. "Yes. Elohim stands outside of time. He knows everything that has happened, that is happening now, and that will happen until the end. But that does not make Abihal's choice any less real or make her any less accountable.

"Elohim does not manipulate humans to force one choice rather than another. He gives them freedom to make their own choices, and creates opportunities for them to make the right choice. What a human does with the opportunity is up to him or to her."

Gorel was beginning to understand Elohim's wisdom. Yet he feared that Abihal's choice would have a disastrous effect on human history. Her choice of evil, however well-meant, would open a floodgate through which unimaginable evils would rush. Yet in that process, Elohim would reveal to angels, to demons, and to humankind what evil is and why he must not simply punish wrongdoing but must ultimately put an end to evil itself.

11

Cain's birth was difficult. Eve went into labor in the evening. It was twelve hours later that Cain finally appeared. It seemed to Eve that he had fought to remain in the comfort of the womb, and Eve was exhausted after the birth.

Her struggle with the delivery was too much for Adam to witness. Leaving his two daughters to help with the childbirth, Adam walked to the far bank of the pond, built a fire, and sat by it all night. As he listened to Eve's cries and gasps, he shuddered. Was this what Elohim had meant when he'd warned that "with pain you will give birth to children?"

Overwhelmed by the thought that his disobedience might be the reason for Eve's suffering, Adam struggled all night with a growing awareness of his guilt. What might it have been like for his wife and companion if they had not sinned and their children had been born in Eden? And what might the children have been like?

When Eve finally delivered her first son and the girls washed the baby, Adam entered the room where his wife lay. She was holding Cain close, and the baby's eyes were closed as he nestled close to his mother, calmed by her warmth. It had been a difficult delivery for the baby as well as for Eve.

Later that day, when Cain was awake, Adam held his son and examined him. Cain had a full head of dark hair at birth. His face was ruddy, his eyes already seemed penetrating, and his mouth was wide though his lips were narrow. Cain's physique suggested he would grow up to be extremely strong. Already, on the first day of Cain's life, Adam had seen the infant place both hands beneath his chest and push himself up to his knees. Adam nodded approvingly. He would certainly welcome another worker in the fields. With three women already in the family, he needed sons.

The first four years of Cain's life were spent with the women. They watched him as they did their work. And Cain needed watching. He was curious and adventuresome, boldly toddling into the stream that flowed near their home the first time he saw it. Even though he was in over his head before any of the women could react, he seemed completely unafraid of the water. As he grew older, he continued to love the water, swimming in the lake, fashioning crude rafts, or lying in the shallows as the water lapped against his body.

Watching over young Cain wasn't an easy task. He was fiercely independent and determined to have his own way. Abihal laughingly insisted that Cain had invented the word "no" at age two and intended to use it at least once every minute. Hatipha found the balky child infuriating, but at the same time, she admired his assertive approach to life.

Aware that one day she would have to marry one of her brothers, she found herself speculating on what life with Cain would be like. She recognized him as a kindred spirit—one who would make his mark in this world. Hatipha began to sense that together they might do great things. One thing Hatipha could not stomach was mediocrity. Certainly the curious, intense child she watched over his first four years would never be mediocre.

When Cain was five, he went into the fields to work with Adam.

The years in this land beyond the river had changed Adam. In Eden he'd been a free spirit, fascinated by everything he saw, eager to discover more. Adam had delighted in the beauty of the garden, had been thrilled to study and then to name the birds and animals. He had found opportunity after opportunity to use his imagination and to be creative, transplanting flowering plants to reflect his own notions of what was picturesque or charming.

When Elohim had fashioned Eve, the two of them had undertaken unhurried adventures together, delightedly sharing everything they saw and did. In those days, Adam was laid back and spontaneous, always ready to drop what he was doing and go off with Eve to find something new.

This land beyond Eden had changed Adam radically. Here he felt the constant burden of responsibility for his family's well-being. He had to clear fields for planting. He had to make trips to the rocky hillside for flint to fashion into axes and knives. Here Adam had to constantly fight weeds that tried to strangle the crops he planted. He had to harvest grain and vegetables, pick figs, press olives for oil. And for years he had to do most of this alone.

Under these pressures, Adam had changed from the loving and fun companion he had been in Eden into a serious and even dour individual who concentrated almost entirely on his work. So it was no great surprise when Cain joined him in the fields that Adam was a hard taskmaster. Adam would explain a task several times if necessary. But he then expected Cain to do the job and to do it well.

For Cain the transition from his life of freedom with his mother and sisters to a life of endless toil with his father was a shock. Every time he began to wander off, Adam caught him and brought him back to work. Adam did this kindly, but firmly, and soon Cain learned there was no avoiding work. Adam gave Cain tasks that he was capable of doing. But every task in the fields was toil, a difficult, constant struggle with a nature that itself had been corrupted by Adam's earlier sin.

In time Cain began to take pride in doing his work and doing it well. He and his father made a good team, and as they worked together, Cain came to admire his father's competency. Cain determined to not only be like him, but to be even better. After a few years, work became competition to Cain and he thrived. By the time Cain was twenty, he could work as hard and as long as his father with even greater efficiency.

With Cain helping, the men provided plenty of food for Adam's growing family. They added rooms to the house, until finally it took the form of an open square with each room's doorway facing the inner courtyard. This courtyard became the social center for the family. The women brought their hand mills outside so they could chat as they ground grain into flour. They cooked together on a large beehive oven. And the entire clan gathered for the day's two meals, dipping their fingers or warm bread into large platters full of cooked vegetables.

The one great disappointment to Cain was that Adam never remarked on his work. Cain always worked hard. Cain stayed with every task until it was completed. And Cain's work was never shoddy. Often Cain observed Adam looking over at him as he worked, but Adam never said a thing except to now and then suggest something that Cain might do better or comment on some technique that Cain might improve.

Yet it was Cain who discovered how to give their flint tools sharper edges. One day Cain was looking at a dull knife and casually picked up a blunt stick whose end had been hardened in fire. He rested the end against the knife near the dull edge and pressed down. Cain was surprised to see a tiny piece of flint flake off. He examined the blade and realized it was sharper. Still experimenting, Cain pressed down on the blade at other points and discovered that he could sharpen the whole blade by removing many tiny flakes.

This method of pressure-sharpening flint tools was a major discovery. Yet when Cain showed it to Adam, his father simply nodded his head, picked up another stick, and tried the technique himself. When he realized that it worked, he told Cain, "Let's get to work and sharpen all these tools."

12

Adam's attitude deeply pained Cain, but rather than express resentment, Cain determined to work harder to earn his father's approval. Adam, of course, was unaware of Cain's feelings. He never wanted to hurt his son and in fact was proud of him.

But for Adam doing a job well was its own reward. No one had praised him as he worked day and night to provide for Eve and later for the girls. Fulfilling one's responsibilities was a duty, and to Adam no one should expect praise for doing his or her duty.

Yet at the same time that Adam withheld praise from Cain, he was quick to express delight in his daughter Hatipha. He glowed when she presented him with some morsel she'd reserved for him at dinner. He always declared how good the morsel was and what a good cook Hatipha was. When Hatipha mentioned a new pottery vessel she'd finished, Adam always wanted to see it, however tired he was from the day's work, and Adam praised Hatipha's skill in creating the vessel.

The special bond between Adam and his firstborn daughter was recognized by everyone. Eve also noticed Adam's apparent indifference to Cain, but whenever she brought up the subject, Adam ignored her counsel.

"Couldn't you just tell Cain you appreciate his hard work?" Eve suggested.

"Cain knows I appreciate him," Adam replied.

"But he works so hard."

"Of course he does. That's what men do. We don't need anyone to tell us we're doing our duty."

"Please, Adam. Just a word or two from you would mean so much to your son. He looks up to you so much."

Then Adam would fall silent, and after a while Eve would change the subject.

Adam wasn't sure why it was so hard for him to praise Cain for his work. Adam recognized Cain's good qualities and realized that he should encourage the boy. But somehow the right words never came.

Sometimes Adam looked over as Cain worked beside him and thought, *He really is a good worker*. Sometimes Adam thought, *I really am proud of that boy*. But Adam never expressed those thoughts to Cain, and although Adam did love Cain, he never told Cain, I love you.

Cain was as silent as his father. At times Cain would watch Adam as they worked together and think, *I do love him*. Or think, *I want him to be proud of me*. Yet those thoughts were just as hard for Cain to express as praise was for Adam. So the two worked on side by side, Adam silently proud of his son and Cain silently yearning for some sign of approval.

13

The fact that Hatipha was showered with praise by Adam should have bothered Cain more than it appeared to. Whenever he was aware of jealous feelings, Cain reminded himself that Hatipha deserved the praise and, because she was a woman, needed it more than he did.

In fact, Cain admired Hatipha. She had all those qualities that were important to him, for Cain was very much like her. Both Hatipha and Cain were intent on doing things right. Both committed themselves to accomplish what they set out to do. Both set great store by success and were willing to go to any lengths to do well. Both set goals and organized tasks into the necessary steps to reach them.

Although Cain often felt unappreciated, he did not fall into the trap of doubting himself. Cain recognized his strengths and whenever disputes arose was sure that he was right.

Sometimes he and Hatipha were set a joint task, and it was at those times that their arguments grew heated. If they were to set out together to find a better source of firewood after fuel in a nearby grove of trees was depleted, Hatipha was set on going south while Cain was set on going north. When they reached a promising grove, Cain insisted that he mark any brush or trees to be cut down while Hatipha argued against each tree he selected. Typically they were still arguing when they reached home pulling their sled filled with wood.

Cain would think, *She's so infuriating.*

And Hatipha would think, *He's so stubborn.*

Then Abihal would appear and everything would be smoothed over so the family could have peace. While deep down both Hatipha and Cain admired each other, they apparently couldn't help competing for leadership in any shared task. Finally Abihal went to her mother and her father and suggested gently that things would be quieter if the two were given different tasks.

Abihal was right. Things were quieter. But every so often arguments would still erupt if Cain or Hatipha heard the other talking about a task he or she had to do. Neither could help volunteering advice when the other was obviously making a mistake.

That being the case, Adam was more than a little surprised when Cain approached him and said he wanted Hatipha as his wife. At the time, Cain was nearing forty and Hatipha was some eighteen years older. Of course, in those days of lengthened lives the eighteen-year difference was irrelevant. And, obviously, the only person any of Eve's daughters or Adam's sons could marry was a sibling.

Adam talked the request over with Eve, and Eve went to Hatipha. "I've thought about it," her daughter replied. "Cain's a hard worker. Together we'd make a good team. I'm good at everything women need to do, and he's good at what men need to do. Besides, who else would I marry?"

In this, Hatipha ignored Cain's younger brother Abel. Abel was definitely too irresponsible to be considered.

So it was decided. Cain and Hatipha would wed and would have a family of their own. In time, as their family grew, they would move some miles away and establish their own settlement. In the meantime, they would remain with Adam and Eve and the other children.

14

Adam and Eve realized that the decision to wed was one of the most significant that their children or their children's children would ever make. So they insisted that their union be initiated with a solemn ceremony, during which Adam would offer sacrifices to Elohim and each parent would speak publicly to the bride and groom, Eve to Hatipha and Adam to Cain.

When the appointed day arrived, the family gathered at the altar just beyond their home. Adam killed a sheep, sprinkled its blood on the ground and the altar, and then burned the body. As was now customary, he saved the hide to use for clothing and to fashion into rope. But this hide would be special. Hatipha had decided to fashion two vests from it, one for her and one for Cain. They would wear these on special occasions as reminders of their union.

As the sacrifice burned and Adam offered prayers to Elohim for the young couple, Hatipha listened impatiently, while Cain thought of nothing but his bride. Abihal consciously substituted the Others whenever Adam mentioned Elohim's name. Young Livi struggled to suppress her excitement, biting her lip and jumping up and down despite stern looks from Eve. Of the children only Abel truly entered into worship.

After the sacrifice, Eve spoke to her daughter and the rest of the family.

"Elohim created us male and female. He created us in his own image and likeness, and gave us to each other. Hatipha, you have chosen Cain to be your husband. I know that life here, far from Eden, is difficult. There will be times when you and Cain will disagree, times when you hurt each other deeply.

"Remember that we are no longer as we were in Eden. The image and likeness of Elohim has been scarred by the choice your father and I made. None of us are innocent. We all do and say things we don't really intend. So be kind to each other. Be ready to forgive every hurt, and remember that your partner is not the only one to blame for your distress. You are responsible too."

Then it was time for Adam to speak to Cain. For perhaps the first time, Adam expressed appreciation to his eldest son.

"Cain, you are a strong and skillful man. I know you will provide for your wife and family. One of the difficult lessons that I have had to learn is that we men need to provide for our wives' emotional as well as material needs. We need to let them know that we love them. We need to listen to their concerns and not be so wrapped up in our work that we have no time for family. Elohim gave us the seventh day for rest and to spend with our spouses. Use this time wisely.

"Cain, when you move away from your mother and me, you will be the one to offer sacrifices to Elohim. You do not know him in the way your mother and I know him, for we met with him face to face. But I tell you now that Elohim loves each of you deeply. You must honor and trust him completely, for he is the only one who can bring any person home to be with him one day.

"Continue to ask Elohim for help with your work and your relationships. Bring him the sacrifice that he has ordained, a lamb or a sheep. And pour out the blood of the sacrifices on the altar before you burn it. This sacrifice is a reminder that we all fall short of Elohim's glory and that despite our failures, Elohim loves us and will cover our sins until the day comes when he will take our sins away completely.

"Be a good husband. Be a good provider. Be a good father. And always be a worshipper of Elohim, whose name be praised, both now and forever more."

As Gorel watched this ceremony, his heart was filled with praise for Elohim. Truly Adam and Eve were still his children, still committed to their Creator. They had sinned and were flawed creatures, but they and their offspring were redeemable. Gorel no longer doubted that one day, in the distant future when history came to an end, those humans who worshiped Elohim would be welcomed into glory and a final home far more wonderful than Eden had ever been.

16

Born just five years after Cain, Abel didn't take after either of his parents or any of his siblings. Each member of Adam's family had a different impression of Abel. To Eve, Abel was a delight, a friendly, fun individual who was easy for her to talk with. To Adam, Abel was amusing but undisciplined. Adam saw Abel as too much a talker and too little a worker.

Able's eldest sister was convinced that he was an absentminded dreamer. He was likeable enough, Hatipha thought, but just about useless when it came to contributing anything tangible to the family's welfare. Abihal, despite her gentle acceptance of all the family members, saw him as something of a threat. Her role in the family had always been that of peacemaker. But Abel could read people and often diffused potentially tense situations with humor, something that made Abihal feel useless.

The person in the family who was most critical of Abel was his brother, Cain. Although Abel was a truly genuine individual, he wasn't a hard worker. Cain saw willingness to work hard as the most important quality a man could have. Cain was convinced that much of Abel's good-humored talk was just a slick attempt to get out of doing his share. Even so, it was difficult to stay angry with Abel. He was fun to be around, even for Cain.

Like Cain, Abel spent the first four years of his life with the women. While it was hard for them to keep track of the mischievous little boy, it was even harder for them not to laugh at his antics. At two, Abel toddled into the store room and before anyone had missed him was sitting on the floor, digging both hands into one of the grain storage jars, scattering kernels all over the room. When Eve tracked him down, she motioned to the girls to come quickly and share the look of sheer delight on Abel's little face.

At two-and-a-half, Abel realized that the womenfolk became upset and anxious when they didn't know where he was. For weeks he made a game of watching for the right moment to slip away to find a hiding place. The women would drop what they were doing and search frantically for Abel while the little boy held both hands over his mouth to keep from laughing out loud. After a while the game lost all its appeal to his mother. Some strong words supported by gentle spankings finally convinced Abel the game was no longer fun.

At three, Abel was speaking in complete sentences and discovered he had a gift for mimicry. His impressions of family members kept everyone laughing, even the person being imitated. The only one who really disliked Abel's parodies was Hatipha, for he was able to reproduce her sharp tone and critical words all too accurately.

At three-and-a-half, Abel discovered the power of a loving touch. Each day he was sure to stroke each of the women's hair several times, murmuring, "Pretty. Pretty." Or he would pat one of their faces and say with utter sincerity, "I love you." There was nothing any of the women could do but hug the little darling and murmur, "I love you too." Even Adam responded to Abel's professions of love and would pick up the little boy, hug him, then toss him high in the air and catch him. Only Cain failed to welcome Abel's affection. Cain would hold him away and say bluntly, "You're a big boy, Abel. Big boys don't act like that."

At four, Abel began to notice if any of the women seemed tired or unhappy. He would rest a chubby arm on her shoulder and say with concern, "Are you all right? It's all right. Abel will help you." And Abel would insist on helping, refusing to take no for an answer. This sensitivity to the womenfolk endeared him to them, for Adam and Cain tended to be too wrapped up in their work to be sensitive to women's feelings or needs.

These early years not only shaped family members' perception of Abel, but they also shaped the boy himself. He loved being the center of attention and tended to be despondent when he was ignored. Throughout his life, Abel strove to be funny and entertaining in order to be noticed. The hardworking Cain, to whom little attention was paid by the others, was convinced that Abel was self-centered and spoiled. He often compared himself to his brother and took comfort in the fact that he was different, with far more important contributions to make to the family.

At five, Abel went out to work in the fields with the men. There the social skills that he depended on failed him for the first time. Adam and Cain were totally focused on getting work done. They had no time for frivolous talk and were immune to the little tricks that had endeared him to the women.

Just as Adam had carefully selected tasks the young Cain could accomplish and had carefully explained each step, Adam set out to train Abel. Cain had quickly taken to his work and seemed driven to excel. It seemed to Adam that Abel could hardly care less for any kind of work. Instead of hoeing, young Abel would gaze off into the distance, daydreaming. If Abel was set a task that took him out of sight, he was likely to lie down for a nap or to slip off to explore.

This behavior frustrated his father, but Cain took a perverse pleasure in it. Abel's actions put Cain in a good light. Now Adam and all the rest would realize what a good son Cain was, and Cain might receive the recognition he deserved.

But despite Abel's irritating traits, Adam couldn't help loving the boy, and though he tried to be stern, Adam wasn't able to be as strict with Abel as he had been with Cain. Adam's leniency understandably irritated Cain. It wasn't fair of Adam to have been so firm with Cain and so indulgent in his treatment of Abel. But Cain said nothing. He committed himself to being the good son. In the end, he would earn Adam's approval by being reliable and hard working.

Adam realized that Abel wasn't the worker that Cain was. But it was essential that everyone contribute to the family's welfare. Adam would simply have to find some work that Abel was suited to do. During the next years, he tried Abel at tool-making, field clearing, wood gathering, and a variety of other tasks. Abel cheerfully set out to do whatever Adam asked, but before long, he invariably drifted off into daydreams or wandered away exploring. Abel could be counted on to help when the whole family gathered to bring in the grain harvest or worked at picking figs or olives. But there seemed to be nothing that Abel could do by himself.

Finally Adam decided to challenge Abel to domesticate sheep. The family needed the animals for sacrifice and for their wool. The placid creatures ran wild on the great plain but often were difficult to locate when needed. Adam realized that if his son could build and maintain a flock of these valuable animals, he would be making a significant contribution to the growing family.

Able was delighted with the assignment. He could trample through the woods and meadows searching for sheep. He could go at his own pace with no one there to pressure him to work harder at some boring task. And perhaps not surprisingly, Abel discovered he had a gift for working with the sociable animals.

In the wild sheep were found in smaller flocks of fifteen to twenty animals. When Abel located one of these flocks, he'd observe it closely to identify the leader. He'd stay near the flock until they became used to him and then find a way to get a rope on the leader. Gradually, slowly, he would lead the flock to a large meadow he'd enclosed with a barrier of brambles. After Abel captured three of these flocks, he decided to take a different approach. He would spend time with the animals he'd assembled, and he would build his flock from the lambs the ewes produced. Abel reasoned that if the sheep knew him from infancy, they would probably follow him wherever he led them.

Time proved that Abel was right, and he happily took on the role of family sheepherder. Because there were no predators on the plain at that time, Abel often led his sheep to good pasture and left them to spend a day with the family. For Abel it was the best possible situation. He had freedom to explore the woods and meadows and streams with plenty of spare time to return home to visit the womenfolk as they worked.

Adam was pleased that he'd found an occupation for Abel that suited his nature, and he frequently commended Abel for the skill he'd shown in domesticating the sheep. Adam's reaction to Abel both puzzled and frustrated Cain, who still saw his brother as a lazy idler, for Cain looked down on sheepherding as little more than an excuse to avoid an honest day's work.

The fact that Abel was gone at least half of the time looking after his sheep suited the other family members. Abel was likeable and generally fun to be around, but he needed to be taken in relatively small doses. Abel's need to be the center of attention tended to turn his mother and sisters into little more than an audience. When he didn't receive the notice he craved, Abel revealed himself to be both spoiled and impatient, and he tended to turn his humor against family members. Abel always seemed sorry after one of these incidents and apologized. But the words came so easily that more than one sibling doubted his sincerity.

In fact Abel was sincere. He was very aware of his weaknesses. When the family gathered for one of Adam's sacrifices, Abel bowed his head and wordlessly acknowledge his flaws to the Lord.

"Oh Elohim," Abel prayed. "I'm not as hard a worker as Cain or Hatipha. I've been angry with Cain for not giving me credit for what I've done with my sheep. I shouldn't be, because he works so hard and I haven't given him enough credit either. When I was imitating sister Livi last week, I went too far and hurt her feelings. I saw the pain in her eyes and didn't even say I was sorry. Inside I know what I should do, but too many times I do the opposite.

"O Elohim, I fail so often. I don't deserve your forgiveness. But I know you do forgive. I praise you for that, because I need to be forgiven."

Only Abel among the brothers and sisters truly understood the teachings of their parents, felt shame or guilt, and trusted Elohim completely.

After the sacrifice was completed and the family gathered to share a meal, Abel always seemed completely himself, laughing and joking, taking the role of entertainer. No one suspected the painfully realistic way in which Abel assessed himself or the depth of his trust in Elohim.

18

Myrdebaal found Abel the most disgusting of the humans. All this ridiculous good humor! While Myrdebaal could sense pain as Abel examined himself during the sacrifice, what Myrdebaal couldn't understand was how the pain so quickly vaporized and was gone. His confusion was understandable. One thing demons have no capacity to grasp is forgiveness and the release from guilt that forgiveness provides.

Other than that, however, the demonic insight into fallen human beings was impressive. Myrdebaal had sent regular reports on his observations of Adam and Eve's children to headquarters and Satan kept a team of demons at work developing strategies for manipulating humans. He intended to develop a manual to guide his followers when attempting to thwart any plan Elohim might try to put into effect. At the same time, the strategy manual could be used to maximize human suffering. Satan realized that the further humans stray from Elohim's path, the more pain they cause themselves and others.

Of course, Satan himself had demonstrated the effectiveness of the basic strategies demons would continue to use against humans. They would sow confusion about what Elohim had said and encourage misunderstanding. They would undermine confidence in his word and challenge its reliability. They would persuade humans to trust their senses and rely on their reason, and promote the notion anything desirable must by definition be good. Then, after humans choose to sin, we demons suggest that they blame Elohim for giving them the opportunity to make a choice in the first place.

The latest plans for controlling humans included specific strategies linked to personality characteristics. Satan's followers were to recognize that each human being is an individual with distinctive strengths and weaknesses. When seeking to co-opt any human, they are to take time to analyze both strengths and weaknesses. Then individual humans can be attacked at the point of their strengths rather than their weaknesses.

The reason for this is a human's awareness of a weakness tends to make him or her cautious. But awareness of a strength tends to make a person act carelessly and rashly. For instance, Baziya used Abihal's pride at keeping secrets to gain her promise not to reveal his nonsense about the Others. Working from Myrdebaal's reports, other demons created a list of specific tactics field demons might use.

- Use a human's need to do things perfectly to nurture criticism of himself or herself and others.

- Use a person's leadership ability to undermine the initiative of others.

- Use a person's intelligence to convince him or her that he is always right, so that he fails to consider options or others' opinions.

- Use a person's sensitivity to others' needs to make him or her vulnerable to making decisions on feelings with not enough thought.

- Use person's loyalty to friends to cloud his or her moral judgment.

- Use a person's eagerness to make peace to keep him or her from taking a stand when that is appropriate.

- Use a person's willingness to accept others to convince him or her that tolerance is more important than truth or righteousness.

- Use a person's capacity to be entertaining to encourage him or her to demand the spotlight and become spoiled or egotistical.

Ah, Myrdebaal thought as he considered these and other tactics, *What fun we'll have with these humans.*

19

Back in the human settlement in the land beyond the rivers, Abihal took a step she'd been thinking of for some time. Perhaps if she had better understood Abel she wouldn't have approached Adam about marriage to his younger son. But Cain and Hatipha had been married for two years, and Hatipha was already pregnant. Abihal was eager to have a child of her own and Abel was the only adult male available, although two other girls had been born to Eve.

Besides, Abel was appealing to her. Abihal enjoyed being with Abel. He was amusing, friendly, and most important of all, Abihal knew he avoided conflict. When a situation began to get tense, Abel would use humor to diffuse it, or if that failed, he would simply walk away. Abihal was sure that life with Abel would remain peaceful, and Abihal had to have peace. It seemed to her that this likeable brother would be a perfect match.

Able hadn't thought seriously about marriage before Adam talked with him about wedding Abihal. He enjoyed his life as it was. He had his sheep to care for. He had a rather comfortable role as a younger brother whom almost everyone liked. No, he wasn't looking for more responsibility just then. Besides, there were already two younger sisters in the family. Abel assumed that many other children would be born to Adam and Eve. Thus there was no hurry. Abel knew he would marry someday. But why now?

Yet as the father and son talked and as Adam told Abel about his conversation with his daughter, Abel warmed to the idea. It would be good to be a husband. There was much about Abihal that Abel appreciated. Also Abel remembered that Elohim had told his parents to be fruitful and multiply. If this pleased Elohim, perhaps he should marry and produce children who would worship the Creator.

Later that evening, Abel and Abihal talked. While neither had the same kind of passionate commitment to the other that marked Adam and Eve's relationship, they did share a mutual respect and honest liking. It was only when Abel spoke of his religious motivation to produce children who would know, love, and worship Elohim that Abihal grew silent and withdrawn. Abel, who commonly chattered on without paying a great deal of attention when he was entertaining, failed to notice. But there were two watchers who did notice. And each of them was deeply concerned.

When Baziya had approached Abihal disguised as an angel of light, Gorel had begged his superiors to be allowed to intervene. His request was passed from one rank of angels to the next, all the way to Elohim himself. And Gorel's request was denied. The reason given, Abihal must have an opportunity to make the right choice, seemed unsatisfactory. What chance did a mere human have against a demon?

In fact Abihal had sufficient information about both Elohim and the Shining Ones to see through Baziya's disguise. For reasons of her own, Abihal didn't want to expose the masquerade. Her subsequent repudiation of Elohim and adoption of the Others did not demonstrate the power of demons. What it demonstrated was the reality of the spiritual death that had been transmitted to Adam's offspring.

Abihal did not become alienated from Elohim because she chose to worship the Others. She chose to worship the Others because she was already alienated. She was alienated because in her spiritual blindness she failed to recognize and accept Elohim's transforming forgiveness, powerfully symbolized in the many sacrifices she had witnessed.

Abihal's choice had been made years before, and although Gorel remained troubled by it, he accepted the wisdom of the Almighty.

But now there was another issue. Abel, who was a true worshipper of Elohim, was about to wed the unbeliever. How could such a marriage ever be blessed? How could Abel be protected from the pernicious influence of this devotee of demons?

On the opposite side of the struggle, Myrdebaal was just as concerned as Gorel, and for a similar reason. What if Abel converted Abihal to the truth and to the worship of Elohim?

Before Abihal had discussed the possibility of marrying Abel with her parents, she had gone into the forest where she could be alone and called out to the counterfeit Shining One. Filled with hope, she had asked if the proper time had come to reveal the secret she'd been told in order to enlist Abel in her coming crusade. Myrdebaal was relieved to note she had prayed aloud. At that time listening in on thoughts was beyond those of his kind. Myrdebaal hurriedly reported the request to his superiors who passed it up the ranks to Satan. To Myrdebaal's surprise Satan himself came to hear what Abihal was saying.

Satan, who could not stand outside of time and see the end from the beginning as Elohim did, pondered for a time. Finally he decided that he could not risk exposing his plot to corrupt human religion just yet. He needed a much larger population to influence.

Finally, in near desperation, Abihal asked for a sign. "You promised to provide signs to authenticate my message. Give me a sign now. If I am to tell Abel my secret, cause the tree before me to fall to the left. If I am not to tell Abel my secret, cause the tree before me to fall to the right."

Satan smiled. This was an easy sign to provide. The great fallen angel himself approached the chosen tree and, with an effortless shove, caused it to fall—to the right.

Ignoring Abihal's awed thanksgiving, Satan returned to Heart of Darkness, leaving Myrdebaal to continue watching. It seemed unlikely that either human would convert the other. What a fascinating game Satan intended to play with the couple's children! He'd assign the most competent of his demons to Abihal's offspring and do everything possible to ensure that they too turned their backs on Elohim when the all-powerful Enemy gave the children opportunities to trust him.

Elohim would play fair and refuse to manipulate the humans. He would give them authentic opportunities to make their own choices.

Satan, on the other hand, would play as unfairly as he could. He would try every shameful trick he could conceive to keep the humans from committing themselves to Elohim. But even Satan realized that in the end each human would make his or her own choice. The choice might be made consciously and deliberately. Or the choice might be made hastily, almost unintentionally. But there would be a choice, for or against. Each human would make it—and would be responsible for the consequences.

Thus despite their uneasiness about the implications of the marriage of Abel and Abihal, Gorel and Myrdebaal each stood back and watched to see how the marriage would affect the partners and their offspring. What neither realized was that the marriage would be all too brief.

Abihal and Abel were married two weeks later. Abel provided two animals from his flocks to sacrifice to Elohim, one for himself and one for Abihal. As Adam officiated, Abel's heart was filled with praise and love for Elohim. But Abihal consciously replaced Elohim's name with the name of the Others, and her heart knew only uncertainty and doubt.

20

It was the seventh day. Adam's family was relaxing by the lake, the adults lounging on the soft grass. Abel and Abihal lay on one side of Adam and Eve, Cain and Hatipha some distance away on the other. The distance between the adults clearly marked the uneasy relationship that now existed between the three couples.

The grandchildren were splashing in the water, watched over by Abi, Eve's youngest. Cain's two boys, both dark complexioned and sturdy, were loudly engaged in a water fight that quickly turned into a wrestling match with each boy fiercely determined to win. This time as they fought, each was struggling to hold the other's head underwater. Livi rushed to break up the contest before one of the two drowned.

Little Dathan, Abel's son, was sitting in the shallows, happily slapping at the water with both hands, laughing in delight as the drops splashed his face and body. Cain's boys, their fight broken up by Abi, looked at Dathan then glanced at each other. Together they began to move slowly through the water toward Dathan. Then they attacked with a sudden rush and began to bombard him with a cascade of water. Dathan, surprised and frightened, burst into tears and tried to cover his face.

Abihal leapt up and dashed into the water to rescue her son. She roughly pushed Cain's two sons aside and snatched up the little boy. Cradling Dathan protectively in her arms, she returned to the adults, soothing reassuringly, "Mommy won't let the bad boys hurt Dathan."

That was too much for Hatipha. "Bad boys?" she snorted. "Abihal, you're so overprotective. Let Dathan grow up, why don't you? My boys weren't hurting your precious Dathan."

Abihal stared at Hatipha. "Your boys are wicked. They're mean. They're always fighting with each other, and they torment Dathan. Instead of picking at me, you ought to discipline them!"

Cain and Abel looked over at each other and thought, *Women!* Abel wanted to support his wife. Dathan had been frightened. But it was just water. If Abihal hadn't jumped in Dathan probably would have gotten over it. Dathan might even have splashed Cain's boys back. True, Cain's boys were always fighting and their teasing of Dathan often seemed malicious. And Dathan was several years younger. But Abel was sure that having Mommy intervene every time there was a spat wouldn't help his son grow up to be a strong individual.

Eve tried to calm the two women. "Hatipha, Dathan is Abihal's first child. Of course she's protective. Your boys are too rough. But Abihal, maybe you are just a bit overprotective."

Rather than calm the women, Eve's remark made the situation worse. Hatipha and Abihal each felt Eve was taking sides against them. But before the situation could deteriorate further, Abel jumped up.

"Abihal, let's take Dathan for a walk. Maybe find some of those berries he likes so much."

As the three walked off along the lakeshore, Hatipha laughed sarcastically. "Oh, that woman! Always trying to keep peace until it's her precious little boy."

It seemed to Adam that too many of their seventh days were ruined by family arguments. He and Eve had talked about it but were at a loss about what to do. Finally Adam decided to have a talk with Cain.

The next day as Adam and Cain were weeding at one end of a field and Cain's boys were working at the other, Adam brought up the subject. "Cain," Adam began bluntly, "I want you to do a better job controlling your boys."

It wasn't a diplomatic way to begin, and as Adam went on, Cain became defensive and hostile. "Those boys of yours are nasty. They're mean to each other and to Dathan."

Struggling to control himself Cain said mildly, "They're just boys, Father. They work hard and they play hard too."

The two men worked on side by side as Adam pondered what to say next. Finally he went on. "No. It's more than that, Cain. They have a mean streak. They need to be controlled."

"They're not mean. They're just intense. They each want to be the best. What's wrong with that?"

"Cain, it's your fault. Your fault and Hatipha's. You need to discipline them. Make them stop trying to hurt each other. Stop trying to hurt Dathan."

At this Cain stood up and stared at Adam. "That's it, isn't it? Dathan! My boys could beat each other senseless for all you care. It's when they tease that cry baby of Abel's that you get upset."

Adam stood up too. "No, that's not true."

"Yes, it is! You've always favored Abel. I've worked hard for you while he was wandering off in the woods. You let him get away with it and now you're favoring his son over mine. It's not fair!"

Adam was so surprised at Cain's outburst that he could think of nothing thing to say. He bent over and went back to work, saying, "Let's finish this row, son."

Adam wanted to defend himself. He wanted to explain that Abel was, well, different. But Cain's accusation had struck home. However much he told himself that Abel was different from Cain and that he loved the two equally, Adam had to acknowledge that he favored his younger son. But this wasn't something Adam could admit to the angry Cain.

Cain was taken aback by the strength of the resentment and anger he felt. He'd always loved and admired Adam. He'd worked hard to gain Adam's approval. But Cain could count on one hand the compliments he remembered getting from his father. Cain had always known Abel was the favorite, something that made him try harder to earn his father's approval. But that Adam favored Abel's son over his own two boys was almost more than Cain could bear.

As they worked silently side by side, Cain felt utterly helpless. What more could he have done? He'd mastered everything his father taught him. He'd been a totally dutiful son, doing whatever Adam asked, pushing himself to finish the jobs assigned no matter how exhausted he felt. Doing everything just right, striving for perfection. But did Adam appreciate him? Did he ever say, "Good job"? No, all Adam did was worry about finding something that lazy Abel was capable of doing. And then Adam had praised Abel when Abel proved capable of herding sheep. Herding sheep! As if that was a difficult task.

21

Myrdebaal had sensed the increasing tension in the family with enthusiasm. Not only was there friction between the family of Cain and that of Abel, there was tension between each man and wife.

There was open warfare between Hatipha and Cain as each struggled to dominate the other. When Cain insisted his wife make more pottery storage jars, Hatipha was just as insistent that she needed to take a three-hour journey to check out the ripeness of figs. If Hatipha wanted Cain to dig out some of the blue clay she used to make pots, Cain simply had to finish weeding the vegetable garden. When the two finally dragged their sledge to the clay deposit, Cain and Hatipha fought over whether the best clay lay on this bank or the other.

Neither understood what lay behind their constant bickering. Cain, who had channeled all his energy into pleasing his father, was unwilling to surrender his identity again, this time to his wife. And Hatipha, who was driven by a deep need for her husband's approval, mistook agreement with her demands for acceptance and appreciation. Trapped by needs and emotions, which neither understood, the battles between the two continued to escalate, as did their pain and their alienation from each other.

The tension within the home affected their two boys, who followed their parents' example and adopted fighting as the way to deal with every difference. Adam had been right. The boys were quickly becoming cruel and vicious, even as their parents had begun to lash out at each other not just to win, but to hurt.

The situation in Abel's family was hardly better. Abihal kept the secret of the Others locked up inside and drew away every time Abel spoke of Elohim. Abel's trust in Elohim was deep, and he often thought about the love the Creator had shown to his parents. Somehow Abel felt sure that Elohim loved him as well, and as he cared for his flocks, Abel found many things for which to praise the Creator. It seemed to Abel that he could see and hear and taste and touch the Creator and that Elohim was always present with him.

But when Abel tried to share this with Abihal, she drew back. As hard as he tried, Abel could not seem to reach her. As the months and then years passed, the two had less and less to talk about. When Dathan was born, Abihal focused all her attention on the child, and Abel felt even more isolated. Worse, it seemed to Abel that Abihal was trying to protect their son from him. When Abel came too near, Abihal would draw the little boy to her and put her arms around him protectively. Nothing was said, but the body language was more than clear.

Thus while the misery in Cain and Hatipha's home was marked by shouting and argument, the misery in Abel and Abihal's was shrouded in a painful silence.

22

Both angel and demon observers were well aware of what was happening to the humans. The pain that radiated from the two households was unmistakable and increasingly intense. To Myrdebaal these emotions were delicacies. He fed on them greedily. Yet as the humans' anguish increased, he began to worry. Dare he try to keep all this delicious agony for himself? Finally Myrdebaal decided that he had to invite Satan to experience it for himself. What was happening in the human camp was too significant not to report.

When Satan showed up with Eyrloc and Kasiyah, the four evil spirits hovered over the humans' home, bathing delightedly in the various aromas of the pain that saturated the air and penetrated the very structures where the humans lived. This was more than Satan had hoped for, and the fallen angel silently congratulated himself on deciding to let the humans survive.

After soaking up enough anguish to satisfy them for the moment, the four demons moved off to consult. "Myrdebaal, you say you've sensed these flavors of pain since the young humans have coupled?"

"Yes, Mighty One. Originally there were spurts of anguish now and then. Now there's a film of torment over everything, with frequent, intense spikes of agony."

"How do you explain this, Myrdebaal?" Baz asked.

"Well, it seems that the more intimate a human relationship, the greater the potential for pain. This thing they call marriage, where a man and a woman live together, is most promising from our point of view. At first there are mild spikes of pain as one or the other says something that hurts the spouse. Sometimes the hurtful thing is said intentionally, but usually these hurts are rooted in misunderstanding.

"As these spikes are repeated, a thin film of pain spreads over everything. As more and more spikes occur, the film thickens. The thicker the film, the more frequent and intense the spikes of pain become. In time, both spouses are living in a state of agony that they try to disguise by hostile shouts or by a demoralized silence.

"I really can't take credit for any of this. The humans have done it to themselves."

Satan chortled as he savored the situation.

These humans. They cut themselves off from Elohim and delight in their "freedom." And all they get by refusing to commit themselves and their ways to him is misery. And how we delight in misery!

The situation that delighted Satan caused Gorel great distress. He could sense the film of suffering as well as the demons could, and each time the intensity of the humans' anguish spiked, Gorel felt sick. What were these humans doing to themselves? When would it end?

23

About the same time, Adam and Eve were speaking quietly. "Oh Adam, they're so unhappy. What can we do?"

Adam shook his head in discouragement. "I don't know, Eve. I know they're miserable. But I don't understand any of them, and I don't know how to fix their relationships."

Tears began to flow down Eve's cheeks. "Adam, I remember how happy our children's children were in my dream of the future. There was none of this arguing or misunderstanding. They truly loved each other. Everyone was happy being himself or herself. They were delighted with their gifts and the way their work served Elohim and the community. I don't know why it can't be like this for Cain and Hatipha and for Abel and Abihal."

"I'm afraid it's as Elohim said," Adam suggested despondently. "We died when we ate the fruit, and our children were born just as twisted and warped inside as we.

"Maybe they can't be happy, ever. Maybe they'll suffer all their lives."

"I can't believe that," Eve said. "We love each other. We don't hurt each other."

"But Eve, we do. Remember how upset with you I've been? Remember how I've failed so many times to think of your feelings?"

Eve reached out and took his hand. "I know, Adam. I've hurt you, too. But we don't live like that all the time. We forgive each other as Elohim has forgiven us."

"And they don't?"

"No, they don't," Eve answered. "I think it's because they haven't really understood Elohim and his ways, because they haven't asked him to help them when they can't help themselves."

"Then maybe we'd better have them appeal to Elohim," Adam suggested.

"Yes! Adam, you've sacrificed for us and our family. Now Cain and Abel have families of their own. It's time for them to bring their own sacrifices and appeal to Elohim for themselves and their families!"

On the next seventh day, Adam and Eve called their children and grandchildren together. "I know you've been unhappy," Adam began.

"You've each been hurt and you've each hurt your spouse and children. When your mother and I left the garden, we said and did things that hurt each other too. We didn't mean them. We love each other. But somehow words that hurt were there in our hearts and came out of our mouths.

"We realize this was one consequence of disobeying Elohim. It was one of the things that happened because the image of himself that Elohim shared with us became distorted when we sinned. The image wasn't gone. But it was damaged. So the very best we can do on our own isn't good enough. We have to have help from Elohim, and we have to live with each other according to his ways.

"Cain, Abel, you each have your own household now. You need to bring your own offering to Elohim and appeal to him to help you and your family. You need to rely on him to show you his way to live with each other and give you the wisdom and love to do it."

Adam's proposal seemed good to both Cain and Abel. While Adam was still the head of the family, by suggesting they present their own offering to Elohim, Adam for the first time was acknowledging his sons as adults with their own rights and responsibilities. The two men immediately agreed. Adam decreed that they would take another day off from work and set the time of the sacrifices for noon the next day.

That afternoon Abel visited his flocks and selected two perfect males for the sacrifices. Cain went out into his fields and carefully selected the very best of the vegetables and melons he'd worked so hard to cultivate. Carrying the crops home, Cain was excited at the prospect of the sacrifice. He would give Elohim the best he had. His hard labor had never earned the approval of Adam. But at least he would earn the approval of Elohim, his father's God.

Early in the morning, each brother collected stones to construct his altar and gathered wood to burn on it. Abel brought both of the lambs he'd selected, offering one of them to Cain. Cain shook his head. "I have my own sacrifice," Cain said smugly.

When the time for the sacrifice arrived, Abel brought his lamb to the altar. Lifting it up before Elohim, Abel cut the innocent beast's throat. He sprinkled the blood on the ground and on the altar and laid the body on the wood. Before Abel could strike a fire, flames came up from the altar and consumed the sacrifice.

Able fell to his knees and thanked Elohim for accepting his offering. He begged the Creator to heal his relationship with Abihal and to deepen the love he felt for her and that he was sure she felt for him. When the fire on his altar finally flickered out, Abel stepped back to stand with his wife, who was holding Dathan in her arms.

Then Cain stepped forward. He had asked to offer his sacrifice last so that his words of supplication would be the last words, the words his father and his family would remember with pride. But there was a gasp from Adam and Eve as Cain laid the vegetables he had grown on the altar.

"Son," Adam whispered, "where is your lamb?"

"I have no lamb," Cain said proudly. "I offer Elohim the very best of the produce I've grown."

"But the blood," Adam said more loudly. "Elohim told us to bring a lamb, a reminder to us that he covers our sin."

Cain paid no attention to his father. He laid the vegetables on the altar and raised both arms toward the heavens. "Oh Elohim," Cain cried, "I bring you from my harvest, the product of my labor. May it please you, for I honor you this day with the very best my fields have produced."

But no fire sprang from the altar to burn Cain's offering. Upset, Cain angrily struck firestones together. Although bright sparks fell on the kindling, the wood did not ignite. "Go get me a brand from the cook fire," Cain said harshly to Hatipha. This time she did as he said without argument and hurried back with a brightly burning branch. Cain took the torch and held it to the wood on his altar. The wood refused to burn.

Cain found himself becoming more and more angry. Why wouldn't the wood burn!

Then Cain heard a voice. He looked around. No one had moved. Apparently he was the only one who could hear it. "Why are you angry?" the voice said. "If you do what is right, will you not be accepted? But if you do not do what is right, sin is crouching at your door; it desires to have you, but you must master it."

It was the voice of Elohim! And Elohim had rejected his offering!

Devastated, Cain turned and ran. He ran farther and farther until he was exhausted. Finally he fell to the ground and lay there, howling uncontrollably. No matter what he did, it wasn't good enough. His faithful labor wasn't good enough for his father, Adam. And now the best of the produce he'd raised wasn't good enough for Elohim.

What did Elohim want? Did he want Cain to go crawling to Abel to beg for a lamb, just because Elohim had decreed a blood offering? Well, Elohim would just have to take what Cain offered. For Cain would never, ever accept a lamb from his brother's hands.

24

Early the next day Cain scratched at Abel's doorway. His brother looked out, saw Cain, and reached out to grip his arm consolingly. Cain shook off Abel's arm but then grasped his hand.

"Brother," Cain said, "come walk with me."

As they walked, Abel's obvious concern infuriated Cain. Who was Abel to feel sorry for him? Abel was the idler, the timewaster, the useless one, too lazy to work. Abel was the one who had stolen Adam's love from Cain. Abel was the one Elohim accepted, while Cain was rejected, Cain, who had always been the good son.

Satan had remained in the area to feast on the suffering emanating from the humans. Now he sensed Cain's growing anguish and rage. Drawn by the scent, Satan slipped into the field where the two were walking. As Cain's rage escalated to a maddened fury, Satan sensed an opening.

Over a century before he'd taken over the body of the serpent to tempt Eve. Now he became aware that all the barriers within Cain were down. In the grip of anger, Cain was defenseless against the evil angel's invasion. With a dimensional twist, Satan slid sidewise into Cain's body. Satan felt the rage surge through Cain's every nerve and neuron. Satan did not control Cain, but he was so excited by the sensation that he fed some of his own energy into the human.

At that moment Cain exploded. He bent down and snatched up a heavy rock, lifted it over his head, and with all his strength, Cain brought the rock down on Abel's head, crushing his brother's skull. Without uttering a sound, Abel crumpled to the ground. Cain, still in the grip of his fury, knelt beside the body and pounded and pounded his brother's head into a featureless mass of pulp.

His chest heaving, Cain stood back and looked down triumphantly at his brother. As Cain stood gasping for breath, Satan slipped out of his body. How satisfying that had been. To feel the hurt and anger from within was a far more intense experience than feeding on the emotions that radiated into the air.

Fascinating! Satan had never imagined that it would be possible to actually enter into a human being, to crawl along its nervous system, to share every sensation from within. Satan had not caused Cain to kill his brother. Satan was quite certain that Cain had planned the murder before he invited Abel out into the fields. But that burst of energy Satan had fed into Cain's nervous system had certainly strengthened Cain's resolve and precipitated the strike.

This was something that Satan would have to set his minions to explore. He had known that demons could manipulate external circumstances. But to actually slip inside—what fantastic potential for evil this offered!

25

As Gorel hovered, immobilized, over the mutilated body of Abel, he heard singing. A band of angels was approaching, chanting a hymn of praise. The angels gathered around Abel's body and, as Gorel watched, Abel's spirit emerged from the corpse. The angel chorus sang louder as Abel stretched out both arms to them. The angels surrounded Abel's spirit, lifted him up, and the hymn took on a note of triumph as they bore Abel away.

26

The blind fury that gripped Cain gradually subsided. His panting breaths slowed. He had done it, just as he planned! Abel, whose very existence had been a constant reminder of his failure to gain Adam's approval, was dead. His tormentor was no more!

Cain looked at the bloody rock he held in both hands, and suddenly the exhilarating sense of triumph was gone, leaving Cain feeling stunned and empty. Cain was vaguely aware that he should feel guilt or at least remorse. Instead he simply felt drained.

It had been Abel's own fault. If Abel had been willing to work, as Cain had worked, Adam would have seen how superior Cain was. But Abel had to be different. Abel had to get Adam's attention by being lazy. It had worked out just as Abel planned. Abel got all Adam's attention, and there was no thought for him, for Cain. And all this time Cain had been the good one. *Well*, Cain thought, *no more attention for you, brother*.

Cain hadn't considered what he'd do after he killed Abel. Now he looked at his brother's body and realized he had to dispose of it. Let everyone think Abel had gone off to be with his sheep. After a few weeks, they'd begin to worry. Then they'd look for him. Cain would search hardest of all, making sure everyone saw how worried he was about his brother. But Abel would never be found. Adam would come to depend on Cain, and Cain would finally get the credit and the attention he deserved.

Dropping to his knees, Cain began to dig, using the rock with which he'd smashed his brother's skull as a shovel. It was hard work. A few inches under the surface the soil became hard and unyielding. Frantically Cain pounded with the rock to pulverize a little dirt, then scooped it out with his hands. He'd never finish before Adam came out to the fields to begin the morning's work!

An hour later Cain had only been able to create a hollow eighteen or twenty inches deep. He'd never finish in time! Finally Cain rolled Abel's body into the shallow grave. He'd have to pile brush and branches over the body and finish digging the permanent hiding place that night. And he'd have to make sure he and Adam worked in another part of their fields that day.

When Cain finished covering the body, he stood up. He felt totally drained. But when he looked down at himself, Cain realized he wasn't just crusted with grime. He was splattered with his brother's blood.

He'd have to get to the lake, wash off, and get back to the fields in time to intercept Adam.

As Cain ran, he felt fear building. What if Adam was curious about the pile of brush that hadn't been there the day before? Cain would lose everything! Adam would never forgive him. And Eve. His mother would be crushed. Cain knew Abel deserved what he'd gotten. But if the others knew Cain had killed his brother, what would they do to Cain?

Reaching the lakeshore, Cain splashed out waist deep and began to scrub himself furiously. He had to get all the dirt and blood off! He ducked under water and frantically scoured his face. Had he gotten everything? He could see that his arms and legs were clean now and only a few dull brownish spots remained on his clothes. But he couldn't see his face or neck. He kept on rubbing, feeling the terror grow.

He couldn't stay in the water any longer! He had to run back to the fields, find Adam, and keep him away from his brother's temporary grave.

27

That morning Adam awoke just before dawn. Adam hadn't slept well. He'd been shocked at Cain's affront to Elohim, rejecting the one way the Creator had told the humans to approach him and offering produce from his fields instead. Where had Adam gone wrong? All of Cain's life, he'd seen his father bring lambs to the altar and offer their blood. What had possessed Cain to bring vegetables and melons? No wonder Elohim had rejected the offering.

He'd have to go to Cain and explain again. Cain would have to ask Abel for the extra lamb Abel had brought the day before, expecting Cain to sacrifice it. Adam worried about Cain's reaction. Cain was proud and he resented his brother Abel. Would Cain be willing to accept the lamb and do the right thing by offering the innocent animal to Elohim?

Why did life have to be so hard? It wasn't just the painful toil that weighed on him here in the land beyond the rivers. It was the burden of the failings of his children and his own failings as well.

Adam admitted to himself that he hadn't been wise in the way he raised Cain. He should have been more encouraging, should have praised his son more. But Cain had seemed so responsible, so self-sufficient. He was such a hard worker. He seemed to thrive on challenge, on working as hard as Adam. The two had labored side by side all of Cain's life. Didn't Cain sense the pride Adam had in his son? Didn't he know that Adam took great delight in the way the two of them shared the challenge of providing for the family?

Discouraged by his own failings and concerned about how Cain might react when Adam urged him to offer the lamb that Elohim had decreed, Adam couldn't bring himself to get out of bed. He lingered for over an hour beyond his usual time for rising. Even then, he puttered around the house before heading out to the fields. As Adam walked toward the field he and Cain were weeding, he saw Cain coming up from the lake, his clothing dripping and body glistening with water.

Adam waved, but when the paths of the two men converged, neither spoke. Finally Cain broke the silence. "Father, let's go to the olive orchard today. We'll need to check the olive press soon, anyway."

Adam walked on toward the fields. Then he nodded agreement. "All right, Cain. Let's go to the olive orchard."

On the way Adam brought up the sacrifice and urged Cain to honor Elohim by sacrificing a lamb. Cain remained silent while his father talked, his heart pounding. When Adam finally asked Cain if he would get a lamb for the sacrifice, Cain seemed to agree. "All right, Father. The next time I talk with Abel, I'll ask him for a lamb."

Adam was pleased with the outcome of their talk. Cain was secretly amused. The next time Cain spoke with Abel would be—never!

28

Five days later as the family was eating together, Abihal finally expressed concern about Abel. Abel was often gone with his sheep for a week or more. But Abel had always told her when he was leaving and when she might expect him back. It wasn't like Abel to simply disappear. Abihal had been a little worried when she woke up that morning and found Abel gone. Each day she'd become more anxious. Now, she told them, she was certain something must have happened to her husband.

Adam wasn't concerned, however. He was still feeling elated over the success of his talk with Cain, and he felt that he and Cain had been closer during the succeeding days. Cain didn't seem as serious or driven as he had been; somehow he seemed more relaxed. But Adam was surprised when Cain spoke up in support of Abihal.

"I think Abihal's right. It's not like my brother. I know he's unreliable, but to leave Abihal and Dathan without a goodbye? I don't think he'd do such a thing.

"Besides," Cain added, glancing at his father, "I want to get that lamb from Abel so I can offer Elohim the right sacrifice."

Urged by both Abihal and Cain, the whole family decided to search for Abel. They set out in pairs to visit the different pastures where Abel often left his sheep. If the flock had left one of the areas recently there'd be tracks they could follow, and surely they'd find Abel with his sheep.

When Cain's two sons found the flock where Abel had last left it and saw that the grass in the meadow had been eaten down to the roots, all agreed that something must have happened to Abel. Adam and Eve offered fervent prayers to Elohim to help them locate their lost son. Abihal appealed to the Others. Cain, satisfied that the murder would never be found out and pleased with the way things had been going since Abel's disappearance, pretended to pray. But inside he laughed at the others. Elohim. There was nothing Elohim could do now. Elohim might be the giver of life, but he, Cain, was the taker!

Thus Cain was shocked when his father roused him and his family early one morning with the news that Elohim wanted the whole clan to gather in one of the fields. What could this be about? When everyone had assembled, Adam led off. Cain's heart began to sink as he realized they were approaching the field where he had buried Abel. When Adam approached the grave site and stopped there, a cold sweat stood out on Cain's forehead. Then they all felt the presence of Elohim and all heard his voice address Cain.

"Cain. Where is your brother Abel?"

Cain was barely able to choke out the lie. "I don't know. Am I my brother's keeper?"

Elohim's voice sounded like thunder as the blood pounded in Cain's ears. "What have you done? Listen! Your brother's blood cries out to me from the ground."

As Elohim's spoke, the earth covering Abel's body began to shake. Dirt and pebbles danced. Cain watched in horror as earth flew up into the air and showered down in heaps around the grave. In moments, Abel's dead body was exposed. Then the showers of earth ceased and the family gazed at the undecayed corpse, the crushed head covered in still fresh blood.

Abihal covered her eyes and turned away, wrapping her cloak around Dathan's head. Eve screamed and would have dropped down to embrace the corpse if Adam, a look of loathing on his face as he stared at Cain, had not held her back. Then Elohim spoke to Cain again.

"Now you are under a curse and driven from the ground, which opened its mouth to receive your brother's blood from your hand. When you work the ground, it will no longer yield its crops for you. You will be a restless wanderer on the earth."

At this Cain fell to his knees. "My punishment is more than I can bear. Today you are driving me from the land, and I will be hidden from your presence; I will be a restless wanderer on the earth, and whoever finds me will kill me."

As Cain responded, Adam and Eve drew several steps away from their son. Then Abi, Abihal, and Dathan stepped back to stand beside them. Finally Cain's two sons stepped back as well to stand close to their grandparents. Only Hatipha continued to stand by Cain, a blank and vacant look on her face.

"Not so," Elohim went on. "If anyone kills Cain, he will suffer vengeance seven times over."

There would no escape in death for Cain. Cain was doomed to live with the knowledge of what he had done and what that terrible crime had cost him. Then the Lord put a mark on Cain, so no one who came across him would kill him. The mark seared into Cain's forehead would become a legend. Throughout Cain's long life, the mark would cause strangers to draw back from him in horror. It would not be until centuries after Cain's death that some of his descendants adopted the mark of Cain as a source of clan identity and pride.

Each member of the family felt Elohim's presence withdraw. Adam looked down at Cain, still on his knees beside Abel's body. "Go!" Adam said. "Get out of my sight."

Then Adam turned and, supporting a stumbling Eve, began to walk away. Abihal looked one last time at the body of her husband and followed her parents, leading Dathan by the hand. She had been anxious when she didn't know where Abel was, but now that she knew he was dead she felt a sense of relief. It was better this way. Now Abel's trust in Elohim could never corrupt her son.

Cain's two sons still stood looking uncertainly after their grandparents and then back at their father and mother. Adam stopped and turned back. He motioned to his two grandsons to follow him and held out his arms to them. Still uncertain, they took one hesitant step after another. Then, breaking into a run, the two boys rushed into their grandfather's arms. Cain was left by the grave, alone except for Hatipha.

His wife grunted as she helped Cain up. Her once powerful husband seemed to have no strength left. She led Cain away from the grave to a grove of nearby trees and left him there. Then Hatipha followed the others back to their home.

Without a word to anyone, Hatipha went into the rooms that had been her family's quarters. She gathered up extra clothing. She poured as much grain into a cloak as it would hold. She picked up two firestones, and then stood looking around. She gazed for a moment at her hand mill, but shook her head. The stones were too heavy for them to carry, and she knew that the journey would be long. Finally she stepped out the door and set off to join Cain.

Hatipha never looked back. She didn't see the eyes peering at her from the other doorways. Nor did she see her two sons, each with an arm around their grandfather Adam, watching as she disappeared into the woods.

29

Satan was seated in the council room at Heart of Darkness, again in the best of spirits. "I've done it," he boasted. "This time I've defeated him for good!

The demons on the council rustled what was left of their wings and clicked their claws in appreciation. Not that any of them understood what Satan was so proud of.

"You remember," the great fallen angel went on, "when he cursed the serpent in the garden Elohim, that pitiful excuse of a deity, predicted Eve's seed would bring about my doom? You do remember. He said that I would bruise her offspring's heel and that he would crush my head. Well," Satan chortled, "he got it all wrong!

"Don't you see? I slipped into Cain's body, and I crushed Abel's head! And I wasn't harmed at all."

Finally the other council members realized why Satan was in such good spirits. Satan was right. Elohim had made a mistake. Their Enemy wasn't all powerful after all. Not only had Satan been the one to crush the seed of the woman, he'd disqualified Cain from serving as Elohim's weapon against him. Cain had been exiled from the presence of Elohim and from fellowship with those who worshipped him.

"Bravo, Satan!" Baz cried, and the others joined in. "Bravo!"

"Of course," Myrdebaal mocked in a whisper, "that doesn't mean Eve can't have another son."

Satan's ears were too good. "What's that!" he shouted. "Who said that?"

Meekly Myrdebaal spoke up. "Sir, I only said that Eve might have another son."

"So she might," Satan agreed. But the leader was too happy over his recent triumph and over the discovery that demons could actually invade human personalities to let Myrdebaal's comment dampen his mood. "If she does have another son, Myrdebaal my boy, I'll just come up with some new scheme and defeat Elohim again.

"What my recent victory tells us, my friends, is that he isn't all-powerful, and that we can win. We can win! Think about that and pass the word of my victory to all my followers. Let everyone hear, and let everyone realize that we can win."

30

In the next weeks, Eve wept every tear that she had for Abel. At last she understood the mysterious words Elohim had spoken to her in Eden. "I will greatly increase your pain in childbearing," he had said. Surely there was no pain greater than Eve experienced when she saw her son, his features a bloody pulp, and realized that her firstborn son, Cain, had murdered him.

Eve remembered the joy she'd had in her boys when they were young. They were so special, so inquisitive, so happy. But as she'd watched them mature, she had noticed disturbing traits in each. She'd worried about them then. She had felt Cain's pain as he struggled unsuccessfully to win Adam's approval. She had agonized over Abel's seeming inability to find his place in their little community. The weaknesses of each of her sons disturbed her, and Eve had spent many an hour praying for each of them, all the while feeling the pain of a parent who wants desperately to help but doesn't know how.

Yet that pain was nothing to the anguish she felt now. She and Adam had brought flawed beings into the world, persons who lacked that vitalizing spiritual dimension that brought every other gift of personhood into harmony. It was all because of her and Adam's corruption by that first sin. It was their own flawed nature that was passed on to their children. Because of her and Adam, every child born into the world would be born with that terrible flaw. Childbirth, despite its offer of hope for the future, did doom mothers to pain.

Still, Eve continued to hope. As she pondered the significance of Abel's murder and Cain's exile, she remembered something else that Elohim had said in the garden. One of her offspring would bring about the crushing defeat of the Tempter and make a way for her and her children to return home to Elohim.

When Cain had been born, she thought he was the promised one. She had told Adam that morning, "With the help of the Lord, I have brought forth the man!" She had been wrong. Cain wasn't the promised deliverer. Neither was Abel, whose body now lay alone and cold in the ground. But they could have other children. Perhaps she'd bear another son, and this son would be the promised one.

So, even though her heart was heavy and she often wept for her lost sons, Eve encouraged Adam to make love to her. Two months later she realized she was pregnant again. Eve had no concept then of the many sons and daughters she would bear during her long life. Neither she nor Satan imagined that many thousands of years would pass before the promised seed came, nor that billions of men and women would be born, live out their lives, and die as the invisible war continued.

31

The child was heavy now in Eve's belly, and her back ached with the strain of carrying it. Yet as the delivery grew nearer, Eve felt a growing excitement. She had struggled to make sense of the murder of her son Abel by his brother. Finally she had come to see it as definitive proof that Elohim's way was good and that rejecting it led only to pain and suffering.

Life had been good as long as she and Adam lived in harmony with Elohim's will. Once they declared their independence, everything had gone wrong. At first she'd viewed her and Adam's suffering as punishment, as personal revenge taken by the angry deity for daring to disobey him. Later she realized this view was completely wrong. Elohim loved them. What he felt was compassion, not outrage; grief rather than hostility.

Even though Eve knew nothing of the angelic protection Elohim provided, she remembered the Shining Ones he had sent to teach the skills she and Adam needed to survive. No, Elohim wasn't their enemy. They were the enemy. Every hurt they had suffered, they'd inflicted on themselves. Their history proved that their act of disobedience in Eden had been far more significant than they had imagined. The suffering she'd experienced, the real and imagined hurts inflicted by Adam, the flaws in their children's character, the murder of Abel by Cain—all these were evidence they were in the grip of that spiritual death of which Elohim had warned them.

But now with Abel's murder, there surely was sufficient evidence of the terrible consequences of insisting on living independent lives. Now that the true nature of their sin had been demonstrated, Eve was sure the promised deliverer was about to be born. The son in her womb, so eager to enter the world, would crush the evil one who had deceived her. Her son would open the way for a complete return to Elohim, humankind's true home.

But when the day came for Eve to deliver her sixth child, she brought forth a girl. Eve had been so sure, and so wrong. It seemed that death must continue to reign, and for days after the birth, Eve was gripped by despair over what the future must hold for her, her children, and her children's children. For as long as death reigned, humankind was doomed to commit evil acts and to experience their awful consequences.

32

Cain and Hatipha had run from their parents and their own two sons. Strangely, while Cain felt no guilt over the murder, he did feel shame. He couldn't bear the thought of being seen by those who knew what he'd done.

The two fled into a vast region of flat lands that stretched in every direction for over two thousand miles. While hardly Eden, these lands were inviting, with great stretches of meadow interspersed with lakes and forests. Many different food plants grew wild there, well-watered by the mists that rose from the ground each night. While the flatlands themselves lacked outcroppings of flint, this essential resource could be found in bordering ranges of hills, as could the ores of many metals. And beyond the hills lay more lands, a few arid desert, but most rich and fertile. These vast areas constituted the single continent that held ninety-eight percent of the planet's land mass. In Adam's time this entire continent, which thousands of years later would be called Pangaea, was available to hold the rapidly expanding human population.

Cain and Hatipha were not thinking about the distant future or about distant lands. They were simply fugitives, hoping to find a place far from the accusing eyes of their family where they could settle. They fled for a little over a month until finally, exhausted, they decided to put down roots in a broad clearing surrounded on all sides by thick forest. Cain examined the ground and found it fertile, and the surrounding forests made them feel secure. They were well hidden from anyone who might pursue them.

While Cain set out to prepare the ground, Hatipha searched for fruits and vegetables to eat and for grain they could use for seed. Each night they slept in a simple shelter Cain constructed by leaning branches against the trunk of a fallen tree. It was a simple life with barely enough to meet their most basic needs. Often Hatipha thought of the conveniences she'd become used to—the sturdy mud brick house, the oven where she'd cooked the bread made from flour that she'd crushed on her grindstones, the extra clothing she'd made from wool as well as sheep skins, the clay pots she'd fashioned for storing grain and water. She had none of these amenities now and yet she felt strangely happy.

The revelation of the murder Cain had committed had changed her husband. Cain seemed subdued now. He worked just as hard or harder at his farming, but the old competition between husband and wife had ended. Cain no longer resisted Hatipha's suggestions but accepted them passively. With rivalry no longer an issue, Hatipha found her hostility toward Cain gradually fading away. Now she felt sympathy for Cain and also a growing affection. He had been wrong to kill his brother, but surely he had been wronged as well. If only Adam had expressed appreciation for all Cain's hard work, Hatipha was sure that the murder would never have taken place. If only Elohim had accepted the sacrifice of the best of Cain's crops, Cain would never have been driven to attack his brother.

As her love for Cain grew, Hatipha showered her husband with affection, comforting him as well as she could. It wasn't surprising that near the end of their third month at the clearing Hatipha realized she was pregnant.

Cain failed to share his wife's delight. Something terrible was happening in his fields. The grain Cain planted failed to sprout, and when Cain dug out a few of the kernels, he discovered they were rotting in the ground. Cain had also planted a few vegetables, and despite his best efforts, these were being choked out by weeds. No matter how hard Cain labored, the land simply refused to produce crops.

Finally Cain faced the reality he dreaded to confront. Elohim had told him, "When you work the ground, it will no longer yield its crops for you." But Cain was a farmer. He loved the land and had no greater satisfaction in life than watching growing plants mature and produce a harvest. In spite of the Creator's words, Cain had been sure he could work the land. Now it was clear that he would never farm again. He truly was doomed to be a "restless wanderer on the earth."

It was this sentence that had struck fear into Cain's heart when the murder was discovered and Elohim's sentence pronounced. Cain's first response identified the one element of that sentence he could not tolerate, and he'd blurted out, "My punishment is more than I can bear. Today you are driving me from the land..."

Throughout the span of Cain's long life he tried again and again to farm. But each effort produced only fresh failure, and Cain was forced to wander on, gathering foods that grew wild, never able to settle in one place. During those hundreds of years, he and Hatipha produced eighty-nine children, the first of whom he named Enoch.

Cain and Hatipha lived to see their great great great grandchildren number in the thousands and establish dozens of settlements on the great plains. While Cain could not farm, he passed on his knowledge of agriculture to his offspring. During the last years of his life, Cain lived with Enoch in the settlement-city Cain had established for this son he'd come to regard as his firstborn.

During their years together, Hatipha told and retold the story of the murder of Abel. In the minds of Cain's offspring the killing became a heroic deed, a blow stuck for freedom from an oppressive family and a corrupt religion. In this, Hatipha played an important part in preparing the way for the preaching of her sister Abihal and the coming triumph of the Others.

33

Eve finally got over the disappointment that her sixth child was a girl. She and Adam would have more children. Surely she would soon produce the man child who was to be their deliverer. But for the next ninety years, each of Eve's children was a daughter. Then, at last, she was sure she was pregnant with a boy. Surely no girl would kick as powerfully and regularly in the womb. This child must be male.

After Cain fled, Myrdebaal continued to observe the first couple. Satan assigned other demons to follow Cain. With each new generation, more and more demons were added to the ranks of observers. This excited the demon hordes, for every human life produced its share of pain and suffering, and there was great competition to be assigned a human. Satan made the assignments and demanded his share of each human's pain to feed on. Other members of the council bartered their support for shares of their own, and it wasn't uncommon for a demon assigned a human to end up with less than thirty percent of its suffering.

Even though the multiplication of the humans delighted most of Satan's followers, the Leader felt a gnawing unease. He could not forget the prediction made by Elohim that one of Eve's offspring would crush him. When Myrdebaal reported that Eve was sure she was about to bear a son, Satan faced the old dilemma. Should he destroy the humans and remove forever the risk of Elohim's prediction coming true? Or should he rely on his ability to thwart Elohim's plans by manipulating the humans? His initial decision had been to let the humans multiply so he and his followers could feed on their suffering. Certainly that decision had provided great delight for him and for them. But now Satan questioned his earlier decision. Now Eve was pregnant with a son and was sure this child would be the one to crush Satan and deliver humankind.

Satan determined to raise the issue with his council. It was out of character for the mighty fallen angel to seek advice, but in this case it wouldn't hurt to hear what others thought. It also wouldn't hurt to recall Myrdebaal and have him sit in on the discussion. After all, Myrdebaal had shown unusual insight, while nearly all other demons simply awaited Satan's orders.

When the council gathered at Heart of Darkness, Satan posed the issue to be debated. "Should we destroy the humans now, or let them live on?" Satan reminded the dark figures ranged around him of Elohim's prophecy and of how he had eliminated Cain and Abel as possible deliverers. "But now," Satan went on, "Eve is about to have another son. Our safest course may be to simply eliminate all humans."

This suggestion brought shrieks of protest from the assembled demons. The combined misery of the humans fed their hungers. If humankind multiplied at its present rate, the prospects for demons were exhilarating. *It is only to be expected*, Satan thought. *These demons think only of themselves, not about me.* Finally Satan shouted them down and said scathingly, "Don't you know anything? Don't you realize that if I'm crushed, you're doomed? Who do you think can take my place? Who do you think protects you from Elohim's wrath?"

At Satan's outburst, the assembled demons fell silent. They hadn't thought of that at all.

"Don't suppose that if humankind is destroyed we'll have nothing to feed on. Elohim destroyed the creatures we evolved to feed us, but then he created humans. If we destroy the humans, either we or he will invent some new creature that we can adapt to our purposes. It's not as if destroying the humans will end our war with Elohim."

Then Myrdebaal spoke up. "Great One," he asked, "do we have to destroy all the humans?"

At that every red-rimmed eye turned to the junior demon. "Didn't Elohim say that it was Eve's seed that would do the crushing? Why not just destroy Eve before she can give birth to another son?"

Satan was stunned. Why hadn't he thought of that? Of course! Abel was dead, and Cain was an outcast. If his demons killed Eve before she could give birth, there'd be no son left to fulfill the prophecy! Hoping that no one had noticed his shock, Satan hurriedly announced, "Just what I was about to say, Myrdebaal. As long as we kill Eve and her unborn son, the prophecy can't come true."

Satan wasted no time. He immediately organized a strike force of his most destructive demons. They would hit the settlement where Adam and Eve lived with their children and grandchildren and level it to the ground. The first attack would be led by Persifor, the Demon of Destruction, who would unleash a tornado. He would be followed by Pazuzu who would scorch the earth with fire from the heavens. To ensure that no one survived, a team of seven demons known collectively as the Udugs would pummel the area with great rocks.

In one lightning attack, Satan would purge the earth of Adam and Eve, her unborn son, and of the children and grandchildren who still lived with them! It was unfortunate that his servant Abihal and her children would also die in the attack. But like every human who attaches himself or herself to the Evil One, Abihal was expendable.

The attack force was enthusiastic about the mission. The humans would experience raw terror as disaster followed disaster, and the demons would feed greedily on their dying agonies. Thousands of other demons determined to accompany Satan's warriors in hopes of snatching some morsel of human misery. They would all fly to Adam's settlement and at the last possible moment slip across the boundary between their own dimension and spacetime to strike the humans.

Near midnight the attackers assembled. Launching themselves, they sped like dark shadows toward the lakeside homes, grinning mouths filled with ragged teeth, eyes flashing red in expectation. But as the demon strike force neared its target, they saw that a curtain of light stretched between them and their intended victims. Their way was blocked by a force of angels.

Enraged by the opposition, the most powerful of the demons, supported by the accompanying horde, charged directly ahead, intending to force an opening through which Persifor, Pazuzu, and the Udugs could pass. As the great demon army focused its energy, the forms of the lead demons darkened perceptibly, their bodies hardening as their temperature dropped to that of deep space, just three degrees above absolute zero. But the angels focused their energies, too, and as they did the forms of the front rank of angels blazed brighter and brighter, their temperatures rising to match the heat at the heart of the hottest star.

The two forces collided in a violent cataclysm of thundering noise, roiling black clouds punctuated by continual flashes of lightning. The jolt seemed to shake the entire unseen universe, and the mass of struggling spirit beings became tangled together in utter chaos just a short distance from the human settlement. Only one thing was clear. The demons had been halted short of their target.

As the struggle continued, individual demons and angels dropped out of the raging battle, totally drained of energy. Then, slowly, gradually, the dark forces were driven back. Screaming in rage, Satan urged his underlings on, but it was no use. In this first pitched battle of the invisible war, Satan's forces were losing. As more and more demons weakened and were forced to abandon the struggle, the curtain of light marking the angel forces expanded until finally the last of Satan's minions withdrew.

Eve, unaware of the spiritual battle that raged nearby, was about to deliver. With one last deep breath and an urgent push, the first couple's third son was born. It was a boy at last! Exhausted but filled with quiet delight, Eve named this son Seth, "granted," for Eve thought, *Elohim has granted my prayers and given me the promised seed*. But again Eve was mistaken, as Satan had been. The promised seed was to be a distant descendant of the first woman, not a child of her body.

34

After the defeat of his forces, Satan retreated to Heart of Darkness. There he reached one important conclusion. He must avoid major confrontations with the Enemy's army. Rather than attempt to win by force, Satan must win by stealth and deceit. His demons could not overwhelm Elohim's angels. But demons could deceive and confuse humankind and keep individuals from committing themselves to the Enemy. So Satan set his demons to work drawing up fresh strategies for the corruption of mankind. Myrdebaal nodded agreement as he reviewed the plans.

- Make no direct mass attacks on humans who are protected by angels.

- Remember that Cain killed Abel, who was committed to Elohim. We don't need to attack humans ourselves. We can get other humans to exterminate those we want out of the way.

- Glorify war and convince the humans killing is heroic. One day we may want to call war holy and use it to promote our cause. Also, war seems an ideal way to magnify suffering.

A major element in the plan was to replace the worship of Elohim with the worship of demons. Abihal had been easily deceived and moved to worship the Others rather than Elohim. The demons would use

Abihal to spread the counterfeit religion. Various aspects of this part of the plan quickly won Satan's approval.

- Don't deny the existence of the Creator. Suggest that he no longer is interested in human beings.

- Convince people that their sins made the Creator angry and that if he returned he would punish them.

- Present the Others as deities who currently control what happens on earth and to human beings.

- Keep the focus of religion on material benefits to be gained and punishment to be avoided in this life. Minimize the importance of what might happen after death.

- Emphasize sacrifice as a means of bribing, placating, or gaining a favor from the Others. Sever any link in humans' minds between sacrifice and sin.

- Emphasize fear of the Others. Never let a human feel that he or she can trust a deity completely.

- Persuade the humans that their well-being depends completely on correctly performing essentially meaningless rituals and keeping meaningless taboos established by the Others.

- Separate religion from morality. Portray the Others as disinterested in how their worshipers treat each other. The Others are not morally superior but are simply more powerful than humans.

- Encourage fear of the Others by portraying them as unpredictable, not governed by morality or affection in their relationships with humans.

In the millenniums to follow, these elements would be interwoven into nearly all the religions initiated by demons and adopted by human beings.

35

As the years passed, Adam and Eve had many more sons and daughters. Their children married and had children, and these children wed and had more children. Each time the population of the original settlement neared a hundred, Adam sent fifty or more out onto the vast plain to establish a new community. Before Adam's death at age 930, settlements had been established far beyond the original plain, interspersed with settlements established by Cain and Hatipha's descendants. Yet despite the first couple's consistent efforts to communicate knowledge of Elohim, few of their descendants and nearly none of Cain's shared that personal relationship with Elohim that meant so much to Adam, to Eve, and to Abel.

After Adam and Eve died, Satan decided it was time to unleash Abihal. No one then living could contradict Satan's messenger and testify to the true nature of Elohim. Once again the demon Basiya was sent to Abihal in the guise of a Shining One. Abihal was an old woman now and tired, but the visit of the Shining One revitalized her. As the decades and centuries following the first visit of the counterfeit angel passed, Abihal had remained devoted to The Others. Now at last her time had come. She was still the chosen one. She was now to openly promote worship of the Others to all mankind.

Gorel and the other angels who watched over the human population were concerned. Why hadn't Elohim commanded them to block Basiya? Why had Elohim permitted him to send Abihal on her mission to corrupt the true faith? Again the answer came. Humankind had the truth, passed on from Adam and Eve to each succeeding generation. Now as before, men and women must have the chance to choose between the truth and the lie.

Yet as the angels observed the success that accompanied Abihal's preaching, they became more and more upset. Abihal was a true believer, a powerful and persuasive speaker, and her words were backed up by demonic miracles. Yet Elohim held the angels back, not permitting them to intervene. Elohim would not manipulate humans or bribe them with material blessings. Each individual must distinguish between truth and lie and make his or her own free choice.

36

As Abihal approached the settlement, she saw that a crowd had assembled. Her son Abdon had arrived first, announcing her coming. These days news generated excited anticipation, and everyone in the settlement had gathered to hear what Abihal had to say.

At one time realization of her fame had thrilled Abihal. Now she was too weary to care what strangers thought of her—too exhausted to care about their adulation. All that counted was her message. She sensed that soon she would pass over to the Others; this might be the last time she would rally a settlement to join the hundreds of others that had already pledged allegiance to her gods.

Yet as she trudged toward the cluster of huts sheltered by great shade trees, Abihal felt her energy return. She'd given the same speech hundreds of times now, yet each time it seemed fresh and new. Each time as she looked into the eyes of those who had not yet heard, she was filled with a sense of urgency, felt power surge through her, giving her strength she knew she didn't possess. She could feel it now, building within her.

Abihal passed through the crowd of some hundred people, walking steadily toward Abdon who stood by the low stand he always carried with him. When she reached his side, Abdon dropped to his knees before her, head bowed in respect, waiting for her to motion to him to rise. When she did he turned to the waiting people and introduced her. "This is my mother, Abihal, daughter of Adam and Eve, high priestess of the Others, the gods of this world."

Then Abdon stood back, and Abihal stepped up on the low stand where she could be seen by all. She began to speak, her gentle voice barely audible as the people crowded closer to hear. She had learned years ago to speak softly, that people who strained to hear were more receptive to her message than those she loudly harangued.

"I am Abihal," she began, "the daughter of Adam and Eve, our first parents. Adam and Eve were without parents. They were fashioned directly by El, the Creator of all, who placed them in a beautiful garden. There my parents angered El by eating fruit El intended to keep for himself, a magical fruit that was the source of his wisdom. El was furious when my parents ate the fruit and became wise. El drove them out of the garden, and because he was jealous of the wisdom they had gained, El left his creation for a far off realm, never to return.

"My parents were alone, abandoned. Despite their wisdom, they were unable to make their way in the world. But El had also created many lesser gods and goddesses. When the angry and jealous El deserted my parents the lesser gods remained with them. It was two of these lesser gods who taught Adam and Eve the skills needed to survive in this world. It was one of these lesser gods, whom I call the Others, who came to me when I was young. He commissioned me as messenger of the Others.

"For centuries the Others watched and waited to see how humankind would fare in this world. Just a hundred years ago, moved by concern, the Others chose to reveal themselves through me. They knew that humans are like sheep without a shepherd. And so the Others determined to come to humankind's aid.

"I tell you the truth. The Others control all that happens on this earth. If you will honor and worship the Others, you will prosper. Your crops will be abundant. Your wives will be fertile. Your days on earth will be filled with joy. You will appeal to the Others for aid, and they will help you.

"I tell you the truth. The Others control all that happens on this earth. If you will not honor and worship the Others, you will be cursed. Your crops will suffer blight. Your wives will miscarry. Your days on earth will be filled with suffering and misery. You will cry out to the Others for aid, but they will turn their faces away from you.

"I tell you the truth. This day the Others give you one opportunity to abandon El, the Creator God who has abandoned you, and to worship the Others, who control all that happens on this earth. Pray only to the Others, honor only the Others, sacrifice only to the Others, and they will bless you.

"Choose the Others, and they will assign one of themselves to be your own special deity, a god who will watch over you and yours. Reject the Others, remain faithful to the Creator who has abandoned you, and you will be alone in the world, without supernatural aid, helpless when drought or blight or sickness strike.

"As proof that I speak the truth, I now call on the Others to give you a sign of their power and a warning of what awaits if you reject them."

At this Abihal pointed dramatically to a nearby grain field. "Watch," she cried in a surprisingly loud voice. "Watch what happens when I raise my arms." She raised both arms, and at that moment, a terrible wind struck the field of grain, whipping the stalks, tearing off heads ready for harvest, twisting and shredding the remaining straw.

The people cried out in awe and terror, but Abihal shouted above the clamor. "Shall I lower my arms?"

Now the people were begging Abihal to stop the destruction of their grain fields. But again she shouted, "Will you worship the Others?" At this nearly all the people fell to their knees, pledging their allegiance to the obviously powerful gods Abihal represented.

Abihal lowered her arms and the winds stopped. She pointed to the grain fields. Most of the grain was still standing, but in the broad strip where the demon who attended Abihal on her mission had directed the winds, only stubble remained.

With the demonstration over and most of the people in the small community thoroughly converted to the worship of the Others, Abihal and Abdon trudged out of town. Within a day or two, other children of Abihal would come to this settlement to instruct the people in the worship and service of the Others, the demons who claimed to be the gods of this world.

Adam and Eve were gone, their testimony to Elohim silenced. The Day of the Others had arrived, and with it a new stage in the invisible war between good and evil began.

BOOK 2: THE DAY OF THE OTHERS

It was far too large for a newborn. Its head was covered with coarse black hair, and its body was red and blotchy. On each hand there were six perfectly formed fingers. The baby peered down at her with cruel, intelligent eyes, and when it smiled she saw two rows of tiny teeth.

So this was how the god had answered my prayers, *Myrfel thought. This child he had given her was to be the instrument of her revenge.*

The second book in the Invisible War series, *The Day of the Others* chronicles the in-between years of the Creation account and the Flood. When Tubal Cain discovers metal working, human society begins to change, creating new opportunities for the ranks of demons who masquerade as humankind's gods to prey on humanity's growing depravity.

Through the stories of Tubal Cain, Enoch, and other fascinating characters, *The Day of the Others* describes the societal advances that lead to the evolution of a unique civilization marked by material progress and spiritual decline. But when demons mate with human women and produce giants known as Nephilim, angels intervene, and the whole world rushes toward a cataclysmic judgment that will change the face of the planet.

BOOK 3: THE BLIND PROPHET

Not even the haruspex, familiar with the dark forces, saw the towering, misshapen creature that reached into the body cavity and stirred the entrails with a long, claw-like finger.

Then the shadow withdrew, and the shaken haruspex looked again at the exposed entrails. The liver was twisted so that its tip pointed directly West.

"The gods have spoken, Great King," the haruspex said to the Commander. "You are to go West. You are to attack and to destroy Jerusalem."

Zaki is God's chosen witness to the Invisible War between angels and demons. But Zaki, embittered by the events surrounding the Babylonian invasion that took away his sight and his beloved parents, does not intend to do God any favors.

The Blind Prophet is the third novel in Dr. Larry Richard's Invisible War series that chronicles the titanic struggle between good and evil from Creation to history's end. The reader will follow Zaki, God's chosen prophet, as he experiences despair, soul-eating bitterness, and his ascension to the heights of peace when God reveals his truth and love for the Jewish nation. *The Blind Prophet* offers an imaginative and engrossing story that runs parallel to the biblical books of Daniel and Ezekiel. This book offers the reader insight to the volatile spiritual battle raging during the time period of the Babylonian exile and the remnant's return to Jerusalem.

The Blind Prophet is now available in bookstores everywhere.

BOOK 4: THE 69TH WEEK

According to the Blind Prophet, the end of the Invisible War is drawing near. The demon Myrdebaal, assigned by Satan to search the Scriptures for clues as to how the war between the Dark Lord and the Creator will end, has found evidence that the Creator's plan hinges on the appearance of a Messiah.

As the predicted date of the Messiah's appearance draws near, demons infest the Holy Land, searching for possible candidates.

In Nazareth the two sons of a master builder working on the city of Sepphoris are arguing. The one, Simeon, is intent on going to Jerusalem to reclaim a heritage abandoned by their father; Yakov. The other, Shm'ul, to staying. Neither has any idea that their friend and neighbor, Yeshua, is anything other than an ordinary Jew of Galilee, working beside them as a builder to support his widowed mother and siblings.

But years later that neighbor begins to preach and perform miracles. Simeon, now a rabbi and confidant of the High Priest, is sent to investigate.

When Satan discovers that no demon is able to attack this Yeshua, he determines to manipulate the Jewish leaders into killing Yeshua before the decisive 70th week begins. When Simeon is humiliated in an honor contest with Yeshua, his hostility provides Myrdebaal with the opportunity he and Shaitan have been seeking!

But Satan has missed one vital clause in the prophecy. A clause that will turn his final victory into total, crushing defeat.

BOOK 5: POSSESSED

Maggie Crowder is desperate. She's convinced her son is demon possessed. But the North Carolina Department of Social Services has threatened to take Colin away if she stops current medical treatment. Then a stranger thrusts an open newspaper into her hands, and she sees an article about an attorney named Ken Black.

Black manipulates the media, making her desperate effort to get help for her son into a national sensation. But the publicity draws unwanted crowds as devotees of wicca and the occult as well as evangelical Christians pour into Raleigh. Black finds himself urged by an unknown woman who can tell the future to ask for a spirit guide to aid him. When he hesitates Black becomes the target of what appear to be attempts on his life.

As the case is being heard mysterious pentagrams associated with Black Magick appear on the courthouse wall and sidewalks. The tension builds as a hostile judge with his own agenda presides over testimony that first challenges and then supports the possibility that demons might possess human beings.

As the story unfolds the truth about demon possession and exorcism gradually becomes more clear, finally exploding in a totally unexpected courtroom confrontation between the spiritual forces of good and evil.

If you've ever wondered about demon possession or oppression in our time, or the role of angels in believers' lives, you won't want to miss this fifth of the six novels in Dr. Larry Richards' Invisible War Chronicles.

BOOK 6: THE THIRD TEMPLE

On January 27, 1984, 15-year-old Ari went on a raid intending to destroy the Mosque on Dome of the Rock so the Third Temple of Biblical Prophecy could be built there. As an adult Ari, a Ph.D. in Archaeology, discovered the true site of original temple, where the temple Jesus knew also stood.

The Third Temple, the last of the six books in Dr. Larry Richards' Invisible War Chronicles, tells the exciting story of what lies ahead for Jerusalem, the Middle East, and the world.

In spite of intense Arab opposition the Third Temple is built, only to be hijacked by the First Counsel of the European Union and the American President, who are revealed to be the AntiChrist and the Beast of the book of Revelation. Ari and the beautiful Israeli reporter who broke the story of the true temple site flee to Canada. But the reach of the AntiChrist is worldwide, and despite devastating plagues and famines that kill a third of Earth's population, the AntiChrist's control tightens.

Then angels intervene. The demons who have waged an invisible war against humanity become visible, viscously attacking humans as they sense their end is near.

Carrying the story beyond the Second Coming of Christ *The Third Temple* explores unnoticed prophecies concerning the fate of Satan and the demons who follow him, and the blessed future awaiting the Jewish people as well as Christ's church.